Burden of Proof

Center Point
Large Print

Also by DiAnn Mills and available from Center Point Large Print:

Deadlock
Deadly Encounter
Deep Extraction
Double Cross
High Treason

This Large Print Book carries the Seal of Approval of N.A.V.H.

BURDEN
of
PROOF

DiAnn Mills

CENTER POINT LARGE PRINT
THORNDIKE, MAINE

This Center Point Large Print edition
is published in the year 2018 by arrangement with
Tyndale House Publishers, Inc.

The text of this Large Print edition is unabridged.
In other aspects, this book may vary
from the original edition.
Printed in the United States of America
on permanent paper.
Set in 16-point Times New Roman type.

ISBN: 978-1-64358-021-0

Library of Congress Cataloging-in-Publication Data

Names: Mills, DiAnn, author.
Title: Burden of proof / DiAnn Mills.
Description: Center Point Large Print edition. | Thorndike, Maine :
    Center Point Large Print, 2018.
Identifiers: LCCN 2018040850 | ISBN 9781643580210
    (hardcover : alk. paper)
Subjects: LCSH: United States. Federal Bureau of Investigation—
    Officials and employees—Fiction. | Government investigators—
    Fiction. | Murder—Investigation—Fiction. | Large type books.
Classification: LCC PS3613.I567 B87 2018b | DDC 813/.6—dc23
LC record available at https://lccn.loc.gov/2018040850

Dedication:
Kirk and Edie Melson. Love our friendship!

Acknowledgments

The following people helped me during the writing and researching process of *Burden of Proof*.

Many thanks, family and friends, for your patience, encouragement, and willingness to assist me in creating this story.

Todd Allen—Your critiques strengthened my story. I appreciate your diligence to the craft and our sessions of brainstorming.

Jason and April Barrett—Love you, Isabella, and Lucas!

Shauna Dunlap—I treasure our friendship and your expertise with FBI procedure.

Karl Harroff—Your expertise with weaponry is a plus to my books. Thanks for always answering my questions.

Ruth Leuthold and Jennifer Mackey Degler— Thank you for naming Romeo the bull.

Edie Melson—Thank you for helping me brainstorm the ending.

Dean Mills—You are my best cheerleader! Lots of love for supporting me.

Alycia Morales—Thanks for your insight to my story.

1

Eerie feelings are rarely something to ignore, and hostage negotiator Special Agent April Ramos feared her arrival at a critical scene might be too late. She raced up the apartment building's six flights of stairs to the rooftop patio, urgency beating into each step. Houston police had phoned the FBI for assistance when a family-related dispute, resulting from a job layoff, drove a man onto a rooftop ledge threatening suicide at any minute.

April stopped in front of the door leading to the distressed man. She didn't want to startle him. SWAT had given her his name and visual confirmation of his location. She'd persuade him to embrace life and seek help instead of giving up. Determination poured into her body. He wouldn't jump on her watch.

She knocked and pushed the door slightly open. "Benson, my name is April. I'd like to talk to you. Can I join you?"

"We can talk fine this way." His voice shook with out-of-control emotions.

"Sure, if that's what you want. I understand you're upset. I would be too if my company downsized and I no longer had a job." She dug deep for his emotional label. Anger? Regret?

Shame? "Would you like something? A bottle of water?"

"I want my life back."

Poor man. "We can work through this. Let's talk face-to-face."

"Just you there?"

"Only me."

"Okay."

Relief offered a swirl of hope. She entered the rooftop area to a faintly lit living space and garden designed for residents to relax. Benson teetered on a four-foot ledge, his feet dangling over a busy Houston street below. He turned to her in the shadows, and the sight of him shook her. Snow-white hair and medium build—an uncanny resemblance to Simon, her partner.

Focus on helping this man.

"Hi, Benson." She approached him slowly, her shoes noiseless on the turfed rooftop. Most people didn't want to end their lives but needed a reason to live.

His hands hung loosely at his sides. "I'm warning you—this is a waste of time."

"Making a new friend is never a waste." Within five feet of his position, she stopped. "Please, let's talk." She gestured to the chairs. "Those look very comfortable."

"Appreciate you coming all the way up here, but no thanks." Despite the cool November air, sweat beaded on his forehead and dripped down the side of his face. She longed to see his eyes and make the emotional connection of one human to another.

"Okay, we'll talk this way." She spoke silent confidence into her mind.

"Make it fast. I have things to do." He leaned slightly down. "Do the cops think their flashing red lights will change my mind?"

"Ignore them. You and I can be friends, Benson."

He waved his hand as though discounting her. "You have no idea what I'm thinking or what's happened. Go away."

"You're right. I'm clueless about your problems, but I want to hear your story. I'm your friend and I'm not leaving you."

A minute ticked by. He faced the night, motionless. Where was he? Had her friend approach been too pushy? "Tell me about yourself. Where did you work?"

"Developmental Energy Solutions."

"The one housed downtown?" She'd heard on the news of massive layoffs due to Chapter 11.

"The same."

She needed to provide him with an opportunity to open up. "What were your responsibilities?"

"I'm an energy engineer. Oversaw a team that analyzed environmental concerns in new building construction."

Finally, a few more words. "Sounds impressive. I've read about the company's research on green building. How long were you with them?" ,

"Twenty-four years." He spat the words. "Eleven months short of retirement."

"Why not join me over here"—*away from that ledge*—"and we can talk about what happened today?" She raised her hand for him to take it, but he ignored her.

"I'm fine right where I'm at."

Please, life has more to offer than pain. "Benson, I hate it when big business is unfair to its employees."

"Right. No warning. Went to work, and first thing, my boss called me to his office. Gave me my notice. A security guard escorted me to my desk. I was given a cardboard box and ten minutes to pack my stuff. Twenty-four years reduced to a box." Benson trembled, his face rigid.

"I'd be angry too. It's very difficult for me to imagine what you're going through."

"I wanted to kill all of them. The security guard wouldn't let me say good-bye to my team. Check emails. Nothing. Later I learned many of my friends were also let go."

"How awful. The owners are extremely insensitive. There's no regard for the people who work hard for them. No wonder you're upset."

He rubbed his face. "How am I going to pay my bills? Child support? College tuition?"

"I have a friend who can help you find a steady job with benefits."

"I won't take charity."

She kept her hand extended, longing for him to grasp his tomorrows. "This is a work program. They'll help you find a job that matches your skill set. We—"

"It's my responsibility to take care of my family. If I can't, there's no reason to live. All I have is life insurance. No medical. Nothing." Hopelessness threaded his words into a tapestry of anxiety.

"You have experience and knowledge that's in high demand."

"Are you lying to me?" His tone rose into mounting hysteria. He whipped his head her way. "I despise liars."

"I wouldn't deceive you. It's a program for those who've lost their jobs and want to work. Come down and we'll talk about it."

His shoulders slumped. "Impossible."

"We could sit on the ledge together." Bold move, but if putting her life in danger saved his, she'd do it.

"Up here with me? Sure."

She held her breath while he scooted down on the ledge. This meant progress, but the trauma wasn't over until he walked off the rooftop.

He pointed to a spot about ten feet from him. "There's a good place for you."

She still couldn't see his eyes, even with a light mounted to the building above them. She smiled as though they were sharing light conversation.

"Halfway?" Without waiting for his permission, she seated herself nearer than he'd requested. If she inched closer, she could touch him. He clasped his hands in his lap, and for the next few minutes he looked out at the flickering city lights.

He turned to her. "You're not very big."

"You're not the first to say that."

"Where are you from?"

"My parents were born in the Philippines. I met the world here in Houston. Tell me about your family."

For the next hour, she coaxed Benson into reliving treasured memories about his family, his hobbies, a dog from his boyhood days. Yet he refused to relinquish his position on the ledge. Flashing lights from HPD below awaited the outcome.

"In the last three seconds, he sank the ball and won the game," Benson said.

April laughed. "Shortest guy, second string, and your son proves he's a powerhouse," she said.

"Got accepted into A&M." His face saddened. "My life insurance ensures graduation. See why I have to lay a path for my kids?"

Don't go there, Benson. "There are many ways you can keep your son in college without sacrificing yourself. Tell me about your daughter."

"She's tiny, like you. Long blonde hair. Fifteen. A real beauty. Makes good grades. Looks like her mom when I first met her." Benson talked for another forty-five minutes about his daughter and ex-wife. He appeared happy and relaxed.

"I'm hungry," she said. "Want to grab something to eat?"

"We could do that," he said slowly.

"What do you like?" A surge of satisfaction coursed through her. She'd learned a lot about Benson, and she believed he had a solid future ahead of him. "For me, this time of morning, it's eggs, bacon, hot biscuits and honey. Or pancakes?"

"My stomach's growling."

"And coffee," she said. Her hand moved within an inch of his fingertips.

"Houston has great coffeehouses," he said. "My wife and I used to explore different cafés. Then she decided being married to me no longer had any meaning."

"I've been hurt in relationships, and it's not fun. Ready to join me?" she said. "My treat."

"No need. I have money." He reached into his pant pocket. "Can't believe I don't have my wallet."

"It's okay. You can buy the next time."

"This must be my sign." His voice sank low. "Child support due today. Our paychecks are delayed due to bankruptcy proceedings."

"Benson, I'll help you sort out finances. I'm your friend, and we'll take this one step at a time."

He placed his hands on each side of him,

gripping the ledge. "You're paid to talk to me. You're no friend. I don't even know you."

"You've shared with me about your family. You love them, want the best for them. You are a survivor—I believe in you."

He gave her a sideways glance. "Did my ex call the cops when I told her what happened?"

"Yes. She was very concerned about you."

"Right. That's why she reminded me of my financial obligations tonight."

April sensed she was losing him. She grappled for words. "After breakfast, we'll put together a plan."

"I had one before you arrived."

"But we've talked through a new one."

"It's over." He flung himself over the ledge.

"Benson!"

2

It was 4:30 Friday morning, an hour after Benson jumped, and April was battling depression. The walls of her cubicle seemed to close in, strangling her with instant replays of the tragedy. Fresh. Raw. Unbearable in every sense of the word. In the six years she'd worked hostage negotiation, she'd lost only two people, including Benson.

"Need to talk?" Special Agent Simon Neilson stood at the opening of her cubicle, his prematurely white hair another reminder of how she'd failed Benson.

"I'll be okay."

"Sure you will, on down the road. I'm talking about right now."

She forced a thin smile. "Time is a healer, and experience limits future mistakes." She swallowed a lump in her throat. Simon had drilled those words into her over the years, but it didn't make the situation any easier to bear. "I'm trying to follow your advice."

"Rules are there to guide us, give us perspective when the world around us goes awry."

"I know. I keep thinking about how I could have done things differently." She took a few seconds to compose herself. "Any word on Benson's family?"

"We've notified his ex-wife. They have two teenage children."

"He told me about them. Loved them." Abhorrently unfair, and the searing through April's stomach proved it. "I want to visit the family."

"We can go together. How many times this morning have you heard this wasn't your fault?"

"Didn't count." She'd been trained in defusing volatile people. Her success rate had been outstanding until a few hours ago. The victim who'd died hit her perfectionism way too hard.

"April, I know you've heard this before. He had a choice."

"*Choice* is a complicated word."

"You're not God."

"Trust me, I'd make sure life around here operated differently." She grabbed a few seconds for positive self-talk, but guilt tossed ugly accusations. "I thought I'd gained his confidence."

"You were on the rooftop for nearly three hours. You did all you could do to talk him down." Simon shook his head and sighed. "I worry about you, April. Sometimes I think you care too much."

"It's who I am." Compassion for others was etched in her DNA. "I'd rather be guilty of reaching out to someone hurting than stand by and do nothing."

"I hope it doesn't get you killed."

"If it does, my parents will gladly confirm they were right about my career preference." They would be ecstatic if she used her doctorate as a university professor.

"Your goal is not to prove them right but to show them a woman who is fulfilled in her career. Go home and get some rest. How about dinner with me and the wife tonight?"

A diversion or salve for her conscience? "Only if you two come to my home for dinner."

He moaned. "The last time I couldn't move for twenty-four hours. Chicken adobo?"

"Of course." She struggled with her turmoil and resolved to mask her defeatist attitude. "Thanks. Simon Neilson therapy always makes me feel better."

As she gathered up her purse to head home, her facade fell flat. She'd followed the rule book and still failed.

3

April's stomach rumbled, and her fridge at home looked like she'd hung a Vacancy sign on it. Donuts were the last thing she needed after the earlier emotional trauma, as though filling her body with sugar and grease might reduce the overwhelming guilt, but her car still swung into the busy parking lot of a popular donut shop a few blocks from her home.

How sad she also looked for something sweet to soothe the ache of loneliness. The idea of calling someone special, sharing her miserable past hours, and doing the same for him tugged on her heartstrings. Maybe her future held the possibility, but right now no one stood backstage, waving.

A slight chill blew in from the north, and she grabbed her FBI jacket from the backseat, slipping it over her blouse. Inside the shop, she took a place in line behind four other customers.

What drove a man to give up on himself and life? Benson had invited her onto the roof with him . . . so she could watch him commit suicide? For a while, she believed she'd gained his trust. Then an absent wallet destroyed his confidence and hers.

A young woman behind her scolded a crying baby. "I told you to hush. All this way, you've whined and screamed. I'm hungry, so deal with it. Should have left you alongside the road."

The insensitive words irritated April, especially on the heels of the earlier incident. Loving mothers treated their children with tenderness, not like they were liabilities. They protected them from a world that was often harsh. April turned to the young woman who held the crying baby in pink pajamas. Tears stained the child's cheeks, and mucus flowed over her lips.

"Are you a real FBI agent?" The mother looked to be in her early twenties, long ponytail, taller than average.

"Yes."

The young woman shoved the baby into April's arms. "Take her for a few minutes, please. I need to breathe."

April attempted to return the baby, but the mother stepped back. "She's making me crazy."

"I see you're upset. We can talk." April patted the baby's back, but the child only cried louder.

"I'm done with her." The young woman rushed toward the entrance and disappeared into a mass of parked vehicles.

"Hey—" What just happened? April held the baby close to comfort her and detected a dirty diaper. She was shivering, too. Shrugging off her jacket, April stepped out of line to wrap the baby—who wailed louder than before.

The mother might have gone to her car for a diaper bag.

Seven minutes ticked by. April pushed through the entrance of the shop into the cold air, cradling the crying baby girl. At least the jacket kept her warm. April scanned the parking lot and walked to the rear. The young woman had disappeared.

"Well, little one, looks like it's just you and me," she whispered and walked toward the front of the shop with the intention of calling Child Protective Services. "Wish I knew how to ease your tears."

A man jogged her way. "Stop! You have my daughter."

What had she been hit with now? April sized him up for a potential struggle. Trim build. Wore a brown leather jacket and a cap pulled down over his forehead. And a distinct frown.

"Why did you kidnap my daughter?" Despite the cool air, sweat beaded his brow. Before April could respond, the baby whirled to him with open arms. "Isabella, Daddy's here for you." He attempted to take the baby, but April stepped back.

"You can't take this child. A woman gave her to me, and I'm sure she'll return in just a minute." He was close enough to inflict harm.

His face reddened. "Just give me my daughter, and we'll be going." He grabbed April's arm.

She kicked him in the shin, and he winced but didn't release his hold. She held the baby tighter and kept her away from the man's grasp. "Stand down. I'm FBI." April couldn't protect Benson, but she could keep this child from potential harm. The baby's tears settled into a sob.

He looked at the jacket and released her arm as though he'd been burned. "This is yours?"

"Yes. I'm Agent April Ramos. This baby is under my care until I find her legal guardian."

"I'm Isabella's father." He reached into his pocket. "She was kidnapped last night, and I followed the car here. My driver's license—"

"Only proves your name."

"I'm asking you for the last time to give me my daughter."

"Or you'll do what?" She made eye contact.

He rubbed his hand over a stubbly chin. He trembled. "What if she were your daughter? How would you react?"

"I certainly wouldn't accost an FBI agent."

He hesitated. "I need help with a serious situation."

The moment the words were uttered, April's instincts kicked in. "Is this about the woman who left me with the baby?"

He glanced around the parking lot as though he planned to grab the baby and bolt. "Can we talk? The diaper bag is in my truck, and Isabella needs to be changed. I smell her."

Fat chance of that happening. "Why don't you get the bag, and I'll change her inside the donut shop while you tell me your problem."

He shook his head and opened the inside of his

jacket just enough for her to see a Beretta. He closed his jacket, covering the weapon. Her Glock was tucked in her shoulder bag. "Don't reach for your gun," he whispered. "I don't want to hurt you."

"Sir, it's difficult for me to be sympathetic when you've pulled a gun on a federal officer. What about endangering your daughter?"

A muscle twitched below his eye, and he patted the gun inside his jacket. "Follow me to my truck, and I'll explain."

"No."

"You have no choice."

She always had a choice, but not when an innocent child was placed in danger. She'd fight for this baby when the only risks were her own. He gestured for her to take the lead and pointed to a 2018 green Chevy pickup, extended cab. He slid her shoulder bag down her arm and placed it in his opposite hand. There went her Glock and phone. All she needed was an opportunity to seize control. They passed a woman with two small children. No point calling out to them when the man beside her had a gun.

They neared the truck, and out of habit, she memorized the plates. He clicked a key fob. "Open the rear driver's-side door," he said. "A diaper bag's inside with everything you need to change Isabella. And a clean sweatshirt and pants." He looked into the baby's face, and his facade saddened. "Sweetie, I know it's cold, but that diaper has to come off." The baby jabbered some unintelligible language.

April obeyed him, and he backed up six feet, eliminating the opportunity for hand-to-hand combat. She laid the baby with her head nearly touching the car seat midway across. Her diaper-changing skills were at ground zero, but she managed and used a wet wipe to wash the baby's face. "She is beautiful."

"Thank you." His voice shook. Maybe he was second-guessing his actions.

She needed him to trust her. "I'm ready to hear your explanation."

"Not yet. Put Isabella in the car seat." He kept his distance.

No one was in sight to even question the crime taking place. Once the baby was secure, he pressed the barrel of the gun against her back.

She sighed. Was he reading her mind or had she left all logic at the office with Benson's suicide? "Let's talk about what's bothering you and get this straightened out."

"Open the driver's door and scoot over to the other side. Don't try a thing, or I'll use the gun."

She obeyed and crawled over the console. As soon as her feet hit the floorboard on the passenger side, he was seated and locked the doors. No way to kick him with the console . . .

"Don't forget the seat belt," he said.

"Sir, your actions will have serious conse-quences."

His brown eyes bored hard into her face. "I'm a desperate man."

This must be a domestic or custody dispute. The baby no longer cried, a blessing since April questioned what kind of insanity she'd met for the second time today. Images of the early morning death slammed into her brain. In truth, the memory would never leave her.

"Do you live alone?" her abductor said.

"Yes."

"Address?"

She gave him one.

He typed into his phone. "That belongs to the FBI." He pulled the Beretta from his jacket and aimed it at her. "This is a life-and-death matter. I hate pulling you into my circumstances. But I have no choice when my daughter is threatened."

Definitely a troubled man. She'd gain the upper hand at her home. With that reassurance, she gave him the correct address.

"We'll talk there." He typed into his phone and placed the truck in reverse.

✯ ✯ ✯

While Jason drove to Agent Ramos's home through heavy traffic, he worried the cops were on his tail. Emotion for what he'd experienced over the last several hours threatened to break loose. He'd shed nearly as many tears as when Lily died. Now Russell . . . And he'd almost lost his baby girl. Jason stared at Isabella through the rearview mirror. "Daddy is so sorry for what you went through." She'd been the victim of his worst nightmare: an abduction.

"Are you ready to talk?" the agent said.

"Not yet." The tiny woman beside him probably had hand-to-hand combat skills beyond his imagination. He'd done his best to avoid a flying fist or foot. At least he had her purse, most likely containing a cell phone and a weapon. A huge risk. But her influence in law enforcement could right a terrible wrong. Several of them. "I'm thinking through how to present my story."

She nodded. "Okay."

"I'm Jason, and you've met my daughter, Isabella."

April nodded. "I'm glad I was there. Would you like for me to call Isabella's mother and let her know her daughter's safe?"

"Isabella's mother died a year ago, giving birth to our daughter." He'd disappointed Lily too. She'd kissed Isabella at two hours old, just before saying good-bye to them forever. What had he just done? "Nabbing a federal agent was an impulsive decision. Not my normal way of handling a problem."

"I won't deny you're in a lot of trouble. Let's talk this out."

He swallowed hard. "No amount of talk can fix the tragedy affecting my life."

"Then I need to hear what you have to say."

After two more turns, he pulled into a driveway in front of a cottage-style home. A risky plan formed, one of justice and a way to solve a murder.

4

Jason told April to carry Isabella into her home while he shouldered the diaper bag and April's purse. Holding a gun on an FBI agent who had his daughter in her arms marked his degradation, so he replaced it inside his jacket.

In her kitchen, with the door locked behind them, he requested warm water to make Isabella a bottle. "Filtered, if you have it."

April blinked as though his request sounded odd. "Yes, of course. Are you ready to tell your story?"

Isabella whimpered for him to take her. But he couldn't. Relief and fear about the future slapped against him like pounding waves. But he refused to give in to the despair. "There's a bottle in the diaper bag and a can of formula. Four scoops for eight ounces of warm water. She likes it with the chill off."

"A little hard for me to prepare a bottle and balance her at the same time."

"Move to the table and I'll do it."

April complied, and he went through the familiar motions of knowing just when the water was warm enough. He walked to the table, and Isabella grabbed it. His baby girl was so hungry. He sat across from them—his daughter and the FBI agent. Shrugging off his jacket, he draped it over a chair and laid his weapon on the table. He breathed a prayer for focus . . . and strength.

"Go ahead," she said, her voice soft, even kind.

"What I'm about to say sounds crazy, but I swear it's the truth." He drew in a deep breath. "I've been falsely accused of murdering my best friend."

Her lack of emotion indicated people regularly admitted the bizarre. "I'm listening, Jason. If I can help, I will."

"Okay." He forged ahead. "I live near Sweet Briar in Tyler County. Own Snyder Construction."

"Your name is Snyder?"

"Yes. Last night my project manager called a meeting after hours. Said it was an emergency, and Russell never exaggerates. We've known each other for years, like brothers. In the home construction business, problems range from upset customers to tempers flaring among the crew. When I got there, I didn't hear the familiar sound of country-western music bursting from the sides of his truck. I knew whatever he wanted to discuss had to be serious. We waved when we got out of our trucks, but he looked pale." He studied April. Still no response to his story. "Do you need all these details?"

"The more you tell me, the more I'm able to understand the problem."

He nodded. "It was spitting a chilly rain. We went inside the office, and I reset the alarm.

Flipped on a light. I suggested Russell take a seat, but he said he couldn't. I watched him pace and waited for him to talk. Like you did for me."

Isabella finished her bottle. Poor thing must not have eaten since last night. He clenched his fist at how the kidnapper had neglected his daughter's needs. He reached into her bag for a jar of organic toddler vegetables and beef and a spoon. He popped the lid off the jar with one hand. "Could you microwave this for me?" he said. "Put it in a glass bowl for about twenty seconds. Not plastic."

April blinked. If she denied his request, then what? But she carried Isabella to a cabinet and followed his directions. She bounced his daughter until the microwave chimed. He stood until she returned to the table.

"Where was Isabella when she was abducted?"

"With my parents. Normally she's with me, but she needed to sleep." Isabella folded her little hands and he quickly prayed. April touched the bowl before inserting the spoon. When Isabella opened her mouth and took a bite, he continued. "I told Russell whatever was wrong, we'd figure it out. My concern was his wife."

"Why?"

"She's fragile and sometimes he has to take care of her."

"Physically or emotionally?"

"Emotionally. Tough childhood. Russell said

his family had been threatened by our county sheriff, Willis Lennox, and he needed my help. We had a powerful enemy."

"The sheriff?"

Jason nodded. "Willis is also related to Russell—his sister is Russell's wife." Isabella widened her mouth for April to fill it. Had he made a serious mistake in forcing a federal officer to hear him out? Was he no better than the woman who kidnapped Isabella?

God, I keep asking this, but I need Your help.

"You're saying the county sheriff, Russell's brother-in-law, threatened his own family?"

"I know it sounds ridiculous. Willis believes I helped his wife and son escape his abuse. He could have thought Russell knew too."

"Did you help Willis's family leave him?" April said.

"Whether I did or didn't doesn't matter."

"I understand. You have no reason to trust me. Go on." She had the placate-the-hostile tactic down solid.

"Russell wanted me to fix the situation. Before I could answer, someone fired through the side window." The visceral images jarred him. "I realized Russell had been hit in his left shoulder. He jerked and staggered. I reached for him, but a second shot came through the window and got him in the chest. I helped him to the floor." Blood spurting from Russell's chest . . . Searching for a pulse with bloody fingers . . . Vacant eyes that signaled death.

Again, as in the moment of knowing his best friend was dead, grief sank its claws into Jason's heart, and his stomach burned raw.

"I'm sorry, Jason," she said.

He'd stared at the man who'd always been there for him. "Russell was the best man at my wedding. Comforted me when my wife died. The sad part is his death and my wife's are one year apart."

Her gaze flew to his. "Yesterday was Isabella's birthday?"

"Yeah. We celebrated it last Sunday."

"Take a deep breath, Jason. No need to rush. What happened next?"

Her words strengthened his resolve. "I called 911, and something akin to fury came over me. I grabbed a company baseball bat and walked out onto the sidewalk leading around the back of the office. There's a huge parking area in front of the warehouse. A light's mounted on the building's roof. No signs of anyone. No sounds but insects. I called my parents. Told them about the shooting, said I'd be delayed."

"You could have been shot too," she said.

"My mind didn't go there. It seemed paralyzed. I went back inside and put the bat back into the closet with the crews' baseball equipment. Shortly afterward, two deputies arrived. They'd been in the area when the call came in. One of them is another good friend. We all went to high school together, played football, fished, hunted. I explained the shooting, showed him the broken window. We talked about me calling Carrie, Russell's wife."

"Did you?"

"Yes. She took the shooting hard, but I didn't tell her he was gone. This is a part I don't understand, but she asked if I'd shot him."

"Why did she ask that?"

"According to Carrie, Russell claimed he and I argued earlier in the day, some nonsense about not giving the crew the day off after Thanksgiving, which we've always done." He wiped Isabella's mouth. "We hadn't argued. She hung up on me. The ambulance arrived. I called her back and left a message that I'd meet her at Tyler County Hospital in Woodville."

"So you left the deputies?"

He shook his head. "Willis wanted to take my statement at his office, so I drove there, and the other deputy followed me while my friend searched for evidence. When I parked my truck, Willis came from the office and jerked me out, clamped on cuffs, and charged me with murder. He said Russell had phoned him asking for help at the construction office, said I'd threatened him. I'm telling you, Russell didn't make a call while we were there."

"What was the other deputy's role?"

"Willis sent him back to the crime scene."

"Did you contact anyone?"

"I reminded him of my right to make a call, but Willis refused. I sat in a cell for the next seven hours trying to put pieces together while grieving for Russell. Then around 5 a.m., Willis released me. Claimed there'd been a mistake. Told me to get Isabella and go home."

"Had Willis made another arrest?"

"No. I drove to my parents' house. Tried calling them but no answer. I found my parents tied to chairs on opposite sides of the garage. I freed them and learned Isabella had been kidnapped by a masked woman." He took a breath. "A beat-up Honda that had been at the curb was gone. I took off after the signal and followed the car to Houston."

"What signal?" April moistened her lips. "How did you know Isabella was inside the donut shop?"

Jason pointed to an anklet, shaped like a heart pendant, on Isabella's right foot. "It's a tracker. I had it designed to protect my daughter after receiving a threat in my mailbox."

April examined the anklet. "Was this before or after you helped Willis's wife and son leave him?"

"After. I assumed the threat was from Willis."

"In what way was he abusive to his wife?" she said. "I'm looking for a bigger picture of him."

"He used his fists on her and their eight-year-old son."

She cringed. "I'll need more information about that later. If Willis released you, there are no murder charges."

"Well, not exactly. On the road here, I found out Willis changed his story. Supposedly I overpowered him and escaped jail. Now I'm wanted for assaulting an officer and murder. Add abducting a federal officer. What I can't figure out is why he arranged to have Isabella kidnapped."

"Are you sure the two incidents are related?"

Jason rubbed his face. "I think so."

"Does the sheriff know about the tracker?"

"The only ones who are aware are my parents, Russell, and maybe Carrie. The anklet requires a key to remove, and the device is monitored on my phone. My only thought is Willis planned the nabbing to get even about his missing wife and son." Could he have handled any of this differently? Made better choices? "I wouldn't put it past him to bargain with Isabella in exchange for the whereabouts of his family. But why frame me for murder?"

She nodded slowly. "If I had my phone, I could search for an update."

"I'll check." He entered his password and navigated to a local Houston news site. There it was, and he read. " 'From Sweet Briar, Jason Snyder, wanted for murder, assaulting a county sheriff, and kidnapping, is still at large. He's driving a green Chevy pickup truck and is considered armed and extremely dangerous. Snyder has his twelve-month-old daughter with him. The child's grandparents, who are also guardians, reported Snyder abducted his daughter from their home. If you see Jason Snyder, call local authorities at once. Do not attempt to approach him.' " He glanced up as the reporter gave Jason's license plate number. "The blatant lies here make me furious. Now kidnapping a federal officer will get me shot on sight."

"What do you want from me?"

"Help me prove I'm innocent of killing Russell Edwards."

April inhaled deeply. "Your story is . . . unusual. I can definitely call my supervisor to have him look into the reported crimes."

Jason shook his head. She could very well set him up for an arrest. "Won't work. I need you to go with me to Sweet Briar. Help me find the evidence to prove my innocence."

"I'm sorry, but my work has me here in Houston."

Jason stared into her dark-brown eyes. "For now, you have no choice." He waved his weapon in front of her face. "Since I'm pointing a gun at you."

Clinging to Isabella, she stared across the table.

"Your actions will get you killed, Jason. Why should your daughter lose her mother and father?"

Truth flowed through her words, and for a moment he reconsidered his plan. Guilt pelted him. He'd made the right decision to find Isabella, tuck her away someplace safe, and search for what he needed to right the wrongs.

5

April studied Jason, looking for signs of deceit in his body language. All appearances indicated he told the truth. Could he be so delusional he believed his own lies? His wife's death might have sent him into irrational waters. And he might have pulled the trigger on his friend. *Complicated* didn't touch the way his story swung.

One trait she saw in Jason—he cared for his daughter. April would use it.

"I'm on your side," she said. "But what about Isabella? She's already been traumatized. How will you keep her safe?"

"I'll take her where she'll be well cared for and protected."

"Like last night? Do you even have an idea of who abducted her, other than Willis may have planned it? I want to help you, but not this way." She looked at Isabella. "If this beautiful baby were mine, I'd move heaven and earth to give her the best life has to offer."

"No one loves her more than I do. No one."

Confusion coiled around April's mind. She heard the caring in his voice, saw it in his actions. "The best thing you can do for your daughter is to turn yourself in. I'll make sure my report says you approached me for the sake of Isabella."

"Impossible."

The moment the word left his mouth, she recalled Benson saying it with the same desperation. Was Jason suicidal? Her heart sped. She couldn't let that happen again, wouldn't. "I want what's best for you and Isabella."

"What makes you think they'd believe me over an elected law official? I'm a documented fugitive."

"What if Isabella were hit in cross fire?"

"I wouldn't let a situation put her in danger. I'd surrender first."

"What about the deputies who arrived on the scene? Won't they vouch for your innocence?"

"Kevin, my friend, has proof of my innocence. He took photos of the crime scene and recorded the findings on his phone. He was writing a report when I left to give Willis my statement. That's where you come in."

"He doesn't need me to hold his hand while he talks to the FBI."

"Kevin isn't the problem. Willis is. I need to find out who killed my best friend and why Willis is trying to frame me for his murder. He threatened his brother-in-law, and I'm aware of other underhanded dealings. I need you to talk to Kevin, persuade him to tell you what he knows. And hope Willis doesn't take revenge on Kevin."

She heard the pleading in his voice. Was it a ploy to gain her sympathies? "Why me?"

"I see compassion in you that reminds me of someone else. I think Kevin would feel better if he had support in bringing in evidence."

The Kevin person might be able to persuade Jason to see his foolishness. "No one is above the law," she said. "The guilty person can't hide forever."

"Some are clever enough to avoid justice." He shook his head. "You don't know what goes on in my part of the state."

"You're right, I have no clue. But I can arrange—"

"I'm not a crazed killer on a rampage."

"I believe you."

"Do you? Before I learned about Isabella being snatched, I wanted a good lawyer to make the false charges go away. I will find justice."

"I'd feel the same way. Is there anyone here in Houston who can help? A criminal defense attorney? I know a few who have outstanding reputations."

"Not yet, but thanks. Time for us to get going. I'll give you ten minutes to pack."

"I'd like to discuss this first."

"When we're on the road."

She'd find a way to overpower him. His story was too bizarre to be true.

6

April stuffed an extra set of clothes into her weekender. Once the FBI realized she was missing, they'd track her cell phone. Although Jason had her device and her Glock, the tracking ability would still be enabled.

She'd get them back.

What were the odds of a negotiator being held hostage? The phrase *fight, flee, or freeze* marched through her thoughts. She chose to freeze and hope Jason came to his senses. Her nightstand contained a gun, but he stood in front of it with Isabella, and she refused to risk the child's life.

April longed for solid intel.

The image of County Sheriff Willis Lennox looked a bit Hollywood stereotypical: a corrupt public servant out to bully the people. Highly unlikely.

Jason held Isabella, giving the impression of the doting father, while his gun was tucked inside his jacket. He stood far enough away from her that she couldn't secure the advantage. Kind words and kisses could be a disguise. What kind of father killed a man and escaped jail? If he was innocent, why not proceed according to the law?

While she added a toothbrush and toiletries to her packing, Jason asked if she had a little extra money. "Stopping at an ATM is out of the question."

ATM security cameras were positioned to not only image him but to also capture the license plates of his truck. If she lied, he'd simply look through her wallet. "I have around two hundred dollars."

"Once I'm a free man again, I'll pay you back."

"Reimbursement is the least of my worries."

"Maybe for you, but I pay my debts."

Peculiar fugitive. He'd pay his debt to society.

"Is there a reason why you're not calling your deputy friend?"

The lines fanning around his brown eyes aged him. "I have a loose plan. Can't call him from my phone since it can be traced, but I still need to take possession of the report and photos." Through a strained voice, he continued. "I'd rather you make the exchange and take Kevin's statement." He slipped the diaper bag over his shoulder with April's bag. "Right now, what's important is to get on the road."

"Jason, I see how much you love your daughter. You've risked your life to protect her."

"Do you ever say anything that doesn't sound like a textbook response?"

"I'm trying to be your friend. Let me help you." She'd said the same thing to Benson. *Learn from your mistakes.*

"April, how does evil affect you?"

An odd question. *How is he wanting me to*

respond? "Evil challenges me to end it so others can live free from fear."

"Then keep your eyes and ears open because you're in for a ride." His phone rang, and he yanked it from his jean pocket. "This should be an eye-opener. I'll put the call on speaker so you can hear how the law is handled in my neck of the woods." He set Isabella on the bed and selected Speaker. "Hey, Willis."

April concentrated on the phone call.

"We can put an end to this," Willis said.

"How? Are you dropping charges?"

"It's up to you. As it stands, you murdered Russell Edwards. He called me about twenty minutes before you killed him asking for help."

"Russell and I were friends—he was Lily's brother, my brother-in-law."

"Nix the family card. Your wife's dead. Now he is too, and you're going to pay."

"Two bullets came through the office window."

"There's no broken window to prove that, and the bullet lodged in Russell's body."

"The first bullet is in the wall opposite the window. Kevin put it in his report and took photos."

"Nothing has come across my desk with those facts. Someone tampered with the security cam too. You're not so smart after all."

"You rigged it."

Willis chuckled. "This can go away. You know what I want. Make it easy on yourself."

"Blackmail, murder, and kidnapping will get you life."

"There's no way this will end without spilt blood. Everything you have will vanish. Just a matter of time. Wouldn't you like to have Isabella returned?"

"Where is she?"

Did Jason want Willis to think he hadn't found Isabella?

"Tell me what I want to know," Willis said, "and we'll make a swap."

"I don't have a guarantee."

"Neither do you have Isabella. Tell me what I need, and I'll locate your daughter."

"You arranged for her kidnapping?"

"I said I'd locate her."

"I'll find her on my own."

"Think about it, and I'll get back with you later." Willis hung up.

April released a breath held from an attempt to analyze the conversation. "Can I see the caller ID?"

Jason handed her the phone: Willis Lennox.

"I assume the man was the same Willis who's county sheriff?"

"The same."

Could Jason have staged the conversation? Did he think she'd believe him without confirming the man's voice on the other end of the phone?

7

"I'm on your side," April said to Jason.

He shook his head. "I'd like to believe you. But I think you're concerned about Isabella, the one thing we have in common."

April had met delusional killers before, and she knew how to gain their confidence. She could befriend him, make him think she sided with his claims. Enlist all her active listening skills.

She didn't believe in his innocence . . . but something didn't seem quite right, and she had yet to detect a lie indicator in this wild story. And the phone call from the so-called Willis caused her to ponder Jason's claims. If he'd let her search for intel on his charges, she might be able to leave a message for the FBI.

"You lead the way out." He pulled April's phone from her bag and tossed it with his onto her bed. There went the ability to be tracked. He pointed to Isabella. "Would you take her?"

She bit back the bitter taste of another opportunity to gain control of Jason. Her every plan seemed to put Isabella at risk, and April wouldn't put the baby in harm's way. She gathered up Isabella.

"I'll lock the door and set the alarm."

"How kind." A fugitive concerned about protecting a hostage's home?

"I detect a bit of sarcasm."

More like disbelief. Jason thought he could get away with breaking one law after another. Couldn't he see the danger for Isabella?

Her phone rang. "I should answer that."

"No time."

"The FBI office is expecting me to report in."

Jason snatched the phone from her bed and read the caller ID. "It's Simon."

"He's my partner."

A moment later, Simon left a message.

"Would you press in your security number?" He held out her phone, and she entered her code. The message was important to her too.

He tapped Voice Mail and Speaker. "April," Simon said. "I'll be at your place in about twenty minutes. I'm concerned you're taking this morning too hard. So let's talk about it a little, and then you can sleep before our 2 p.m. debrief. I know how hard you took the suicide. We've learned Benson had a history of depression. I'll say it one more time—you did your best. Anyway, knowing you keep nothing but healthy stuff at your place, I'm bringing bagels and cream cheese. Seriously, I'd like to have the paperwork completed by end of day so we can enjoy our weekend. We're looking forward to dinner tonight."

Jason bounced the phone in the palm of his hand. "What suicide?"

She wasn't in the mood to go into detail. "I tried to talk a man down from jumping. He'd lost his job earlier in the day. Saw no other way but ending his life."

"Hey, I'm sorry. I hear the sadness in your voice. Now you're thrown into the middle of this."

"I'm working through it." Both cases.

He nodded. "Let's go. No time to waste."

Outside, she noted the license plates on Jason's truck were different from the report out of Sweet Briar. "Your plates don't match the crime report."

"I stole them. Add that to the list."

Her training told her not to irritate the distraught person. Engage him in pleasant conversation. With luck, the owner had reported the plates missing to the authorities. She tossed her weekender into the back of the double cab while balancing Isabella and glanced at the car seat. "Top-of-the-line brand?"

He gave a half smile. "It's a Chicco. Reviews and research say it's the best."

Jason asked her to secure Isabella into place and click the safety harness. He exercised the same precautions as before, omitting another chance for her to apprehend him. She closed the truck door.

"Open my door and slide over. You know the drill." He kept his distance while she obliged. "Don't forget to buckle up."

Jason roared the engine to life. She stole a look behind her through the truck's passenger-side window, but he wasted no time backing onto the street. Maybe Simon had underestimated his arrival, and even now he was approaching her street.

"He'll soon find out you're not at home, and within a matter of time, news will break that an FBI agent is missing." He tapped his fingers on the steering wheel. "Will the donut shop have us on their security cameras?"

"Yes, if anyone looks. My car's there too."

"Right. And people witnessed us leaving together." He paused for a moment. "The woman who kidnapped Isabella is also on the security footage, right?"

"Yes, she is."

"My knowledge of how investigations work and the procedure stuff is limited to TV shows. Do you have Simon's number memorized?"

"Yes. Why?"

"I'm thinking on down the road you may need to let him know you're okay."

Really? She was a hostage held by a wanted man. "Our phones are inside my house."

"After we leave the city, we'll pick up a couple of burners."

A flicker of hope reignited. Buying a phone from a store and activating it would leave a trail for the FBI to follow.

She waited a few minutes to begin a conversation aimed at getting answers to her questions and garnering his trust. "Why do you think the woman shoved Isabella into my arms?"

"Did you ask?"

April explained the woman's comments to Isabella. "I turned to talk to her, to see if I could be of help. She said the baby was making her crazy. Before I could ask another question, she left the shop. I thought she'd gone after a diaper bag, but obviously not. Then you showed up."

"Here's my take. She'd either had enough and didn't know how to care for a baby, or she spotted me pulling into the parking lot. If she recognized me, she got scared and saw an FBI agent to hand off my child. You were convenient."

"Are you sure you didn't recognize the woman?"

"I was following the tracker, not her. Never got close enough to read the license plate number. When I drove up to the donut shop, I saw a car matching what I'd seen at my parents' and rushed inside."

She pushed away her own feelings about a baby caught up in the middle of a critical situation. Isabella needed to be in a foster home, but April knew better than to bring up the subject. "I'm glad I took Isabella."

"I'm hoping it was divine intervention for my daughter and me."

April grappled for an idea of how to deal with

a killer who loved his daughter above all things. How did she find the right gauge to sort out the facts? "Are we taking Isabella to your parents?" When he kept his attention on the road, she lowered her voice. "You don't have to answer. I'm concerned about her too."

He lifted his chin, appearing to contemplate giving her an answer. "Yes. I hope to convince them to take a vacation."

Jason flipped on the AM 740 radio station from Tyler County. An update indicated an ongoing search for him. No mention of a female FBI agent as hostage. "An AMBER Alert has been issued for twelve-month-old Isabella Hope Snyder. Last seen by her grandparents at 8:00 Thursday night in Sweet Briar, Texas. Authorities believe her father, Jason Snyder, facing murder charges, took her as a hostage after he escaped custody. The baby is dressed in pink pajamas." The reporter went on to play Sheriff Willis Lennox's report. " 'We'll do everything we can to bring in this killer.' "

"Even I understand Willis means dead or alive."

She heard the same implication. "If you surrender to the FBI, the truth will surface."

"Not happening," he said.

Until she witnessed the evidence clearing him from his charges, she needed to stay on the task of befriending him. "Have you told me everything?"

"Not sure. . . . The shooter might not have been very skilled because it took two shots to kill Russell: the first shot broke the window, and the second hit its target. Willis is a crack shot, so as much as I'd like to think he pulled the trigger, it might not have been him. But I bet he's still responsible. If not, I have no clue what's going on. The question is who killed Russell and why." He hesitated. "It bothers me that Willis is claiming the window isn't broken. If he was telling the truth, someone replaced it."

Did he expect her to believe him? Had an innocent man been set up?

Whoa, April. You won't know if he's lying until you learn the facts. She shoved aside her doubt to concentrate on her job. Most fugitives believed they weren't guilty, while some justified their behavior.

"When Isabella is safe, do you want to talk to your deputy friend?"

"That's the plan." Jason stared into the rearview mirror. "Hey, pretty girl."

Isabella babbled.

"She's my reason to go on living," he said. "I will not have her growing up thinking her father killed a man."

8

April stared out at the surprisingly blue sky with meringue-like clouds. The area had been hard hit with high winds and rain earlier in the week, but the current absence of gray clouds held promise. She could use a positive sign.

She'd given up talking to Jason for the present, as he appeared to be preoccupied and nonresponsive to her attempts at light conversation. They'd been on the road close to an hour.

He took side roads and highways toward Sweet Briar. License readers set along the road to image his truck meant little until law enforcement realized he'd switched plates. He thought his bases were covered, but agents were trained to locate him through a variety of technology. Cell phone and computer records, interviews with family and friends, and behavior analyses were just starters. She'd rather Jason surrendered.

The countryside hosted goats, horses, and cows among some dormant fields, depending on the owner's prerogative. A peaceful life.

The farther they drove toward the Big Thicket of East Texas, the denser the woods. She peered into the trees and saw only blackness. A bit of a metaphor for the way she felt with Jason in these bizarre circumstances.

She stole a look at the man. Lack of sleep creased his features, and that meant he'd make a mistake . . . and give her an opportunity to gain control without endangering Isabella.

They passed a Pentecostal church on the left and a Chevron station on the right.

A Confederate flag waved in front of a log cabin on cement blocks.

A billboard—*hoghunttoday.com*.

Gorgeous homes sprang up alongside deserted mobile dwellings. The next field held an oil rig. From all the recent rain, most residences had natural water hazards as part of their landscaping. He turned onto 105 toward Sour Lake, then north toward Sweet Briar. Who named a town Sour Lake?

Jason peered into the rearview mirror. "Isabella, are you okay back there?"

A mix of unidentifiable sounds met April's ears.

"Watch my girl," he said. When April swung to the backseat, he caught his daughter's attention in the mirror. "Daddy loves you."

The little girl touched her heart.

"I want more love," he said.

This time Isabella tapped her fingers together to indicate "more" and touched her heart.

"You taught her sign language?"

"Yep. She's saying a few words. Her vocabulary consists of *no*, *Da*, *eat*, and *Fuff*. The latter's our dog, Fluffy, a boxer. My wife named the overly friendly beast."

"Protective?"

"Are you kidding? All he does is bark."

"Has Isabella taken any steps?"

"She's been standing in her crib since she was nine months old. Been expecting her to take off at any time. I thought for sure she'd walk at her birthday party. But no, she's saving it for another special occasion."

"Who keeps her while you work?"

"No one. She's gone with me to the office and on the job site since the beginning. She rides in a harness on my back and wears a miniature hard hat. My job is to check in with the foreman and ensure they are following specs, but I don't ever put her in danger. If a situation looks unsafe, I hand her off to Russell. Guess I won't be doing that anymore." He paused. "Russell and his wife gave her a T-shirt that says, 'Snyder Construction Official Mascot.'"

Who was Jason Snyder? He'd opened up to her about Isabella, personal things about his and his daughter's life. Did this mean she was earning his trust, and he'd let down his defenses so she could right this mess?

Jason blinked to clear the grit in his eyes. His reflexes were working at half speed. He must keep his eyes on the road and avoid law enforcement until he could figure out who'd fired two shots into the construction office's window. He'd taken a different stretch of road to possibly throw off law enforcement and give him time to deliver Isabella to his parents. The shooting replayed in his mind—how Russell jerked when the first bullet hit his arm. Then the second into his chest. Impossible to eliminate the memory.

When he tried to give his mind a reprieve from Russell, thoughts about Isabella's kidnapping flooded in. He gripped the steering wheel until his knuckles turned white. He wanted to strangle the woman who'd taken his daughter. God help him, but he wanted her to feel the same paralyzing fear.

When Lily died, Jason believed the hardest task ahead of him was being the best father and providing for Isabella's care. But he'd failed Lily and their little daughter and subjected Isabella to a dangerous situation. He'd breathe easier when Mom and Dad had her. But were they really safe since they'd also been victims? For certain, his parents must take a vacation until the false charges were lifted. But he'd have to face the consequences of his own actions. The future looked like a mass of gray clouds.

He was counting on God to clear his name, but Jason would work his part too by taking responsibility to expose the truth. Forcing the agent beside him on this venture hit the top of the dumbest things he'd ever done. She couldn't be trusted any more than she trusted him.

"What's your area of the FBI?" he said.

"Collateral duty as a negotiator. I work public corruption."

What irony. "I should have figured out the negotiation part."

"Jason, how can I make you see this isn't the right way to seek justice for Russell?"

"I'm the one with the most to lose, and the odds are against me." Her priority was to talk him into surrendering. Everything she said had an ulterior motive.

But maybe, if he could convince her to believe in his innocence, she'd help him sift through the illegal activities in Sweet Briar and find the evidence to release him from being held responsible for Russell's death.

Tough house to build but not impossible.

Isabella whimpered. He glanced at the time and realized she needed a bottle and a diaper change. He pulled off the road to a farmer's lane and turned off the engine. "Can you mix up a bottle and change her?"

"Sure. Four scoops per eight ounces of water?" April unsnapped her seat belt.

"Yes. Bottled water is on the floorboard behind my seat. Not warm, but it will have to do. Only one left. Climb out the same way you got in. Don't run off."

She looked around at nothing but pastures and woods. "I'd hate for you to shoot me."

"I'd laugh if not for my miserable situation."

"You need sleep."

"I will once I figure out what to do with you while it's happening." He exited the truck, stepped back, and she scooted out from his side.

Again she changed Isabella on a towel-covered rear bench seat. Nasty job, but someone had to do it. April used hand sanitizer and mixed the bottle. "I have a question. Or rather, confirmation" Isabella latched on to it before April could shake it thoroughly.

"Go ahead."

"When Sheriff Lennox said he could make this go away, he meant your telling him how to find his wife and son?"

"You heard right."

"Help me to understand, Jason. You're saying Sheriff Willis Lennox charged you with murder, arranged for Isabella's kidnapping, and now says he can make it go away if you give him what he wants?"

"Exactly. Doesn't that fall under the jurisdiction of public corruption?"

"It does." She placed Isabella into her car seat.

He wondered if someone could have picked up his trail. Or had he temporarily left them scrambling?

"The truth is the only thing guaranteed to exonerate you."

"Time to get back on the road."

April climbed into the truck. "And even if you comply with his demands, it doesn't answer the question of who killed Russell."

"I have no answer."

"It's a critical piece of your problem. The way I see it, you won't give him what he wants, so he's out for vengeance and breaking the law in the process. And so are you."

"Right. Wish I'd talked more with Carrie, Russell's wife. See if I could have found out why Russell told her we'd argued. But when Willis unlocked the cell, he suggested I leave her alone."

"You mentioned she was emotionally fragile."

"Carrie battles depression and takes medication. It's gotten worse in the last year since Lily passed. The two were really close." A burst of pain spread over his skull. Lights flashed across his vision . . . the onset of a migraine.

"Is this the first time Willis has bent the law?"

"Not by a long shot." Jason grimaced. "Bad pun. None of this is anything to joke about."

"Why hasn't anyone reported him?"

"Maybe they have."

"We should take your story to the FBI now."

"No," Jason said, more than a little irritated with her insistence the FBI could make everything right. His trust in law enforcement had hit rock bottom. "Truth means a lot to me. I don't have

59

validation of Willis's latest dealings yet. But I will." An invisible drill found its place behind his right eye, brought on by stress and no sleep. No surprise there. His meds were in the glove box, but if he took them, his body would require a two-hour nap to chase the headache away. He needed water and something in his stomach before downing the Imitrex. "We have to make a stop. My parents may have information about the woman who took Isabella. Time to purchase burner phones."

9

The hum of truck tires normally lulled Jason. The rhythmic sound relaxed him and allowed his mind to wander. Under more pleasant circumstances, he'd turn off the radio and mentally construct his latest building project, adding special touches to personalize the owner's home or remodeling concept. One of those inspirational moments moved him to design a playhouse for Isabella that mirrored their farmhouse. Once she started walking, he'd construct it.

But the migraine had zapped creativity from his brain. His thoughts wavered between keeping Isabella protected from Willis and eliminating the false charges. What were the next logical steps, and how could he overcome the overwhelming odds stacked against him like a sapling in the middle of a tornado? The faint whine of tires interfered with his thinking, or perhaps the stress and headache botched his thought process.

He drove over the Trinity River, sometimes referred to as Dallas's sewer pipe. Low-lying areas around the river were filled with murky marshes and swamps, home to water moccasins.

"Are there many snakes out here?" April said.

"Yes, and gators. I don't recommend tromping through there. Gators believe in eating trespassers."

"Very funny. I'll be fine as long as I have my gun." She eyed him. "You're pale. Jason, are you ill?"

"I'm okay."

He neared State Highway 287 in Kountze, where a Brookshire's grocery carried what he needed to help eliminate the headache and move his threadbare plan into action. Although Sweet Briar lay twenty miles down the road, without getting something to eat and relief for his migraine, he'd get shot or killed by one of Willis's men before getting there.

Jason turned into Brookshire's parking lot, his head aflame. He scanned the parking lot for police cars. None in sight.

He reached under his seat and pulled out a nondescript ball cap, different from the one he'd worn in Houston. From his glove box, he grabbed a pair of sunglasses. His shirttail hit the left side of his jeans where he'd tucked April's gun. Shrugging off his jacket, he spotted a dirty cap in the backseat. He reached for it and slapped it against his knee. "This isn't much, but I'd like for you to wear it. I've got to pick up a few things here, and I need your cooperation. A migraine has hit me hard, and we need phones. You want me to turn myself in, and I will when I have the name and evidence of who murdered Russell."

She stared at him with those huge brown eyes,

a look of intelligence and beauty. But he needed to remember her negotiation skills meant she'd lie to accomplish her goals.

"I hope you find the proof. But what if you don't?" she said.

"Not a consideration. And when I have it, you'll receive all the credit and probably a promotion for believing in an innocent man." He pressed his lips together.

April blinked. "Thanks for thinking of me, but how can you investigate a murder by yourself?"

"I have truth on my side and the expertise of an FBI agent."

"What if I refuse?"

He swallowed hard. "I have the gun, remember?"

"Right. For a moment, I forgot. What's my job in the grocery?" she said.

"Pose with me as a happy family." He counted to three, taking deep breaths to manage the head pain.

"You're not wearing a wedding ring."

His shoulders lifted and fell. "I put it away for Isabella."

"All right. Let's go."

He unlocked the door and they emerged from his truck, like they'd done previously. "There's a clean towel beside her car seat. We'll need it to protect Isabella from the cart's germ-infested child seat."

She peered at him curiously as he backed away

from her. Would she scream for help? He wanted to think Isabella had her priority. For him, his daughter took front and center.

A twist of pain seared his head. Isabella hadn't been safe since he found her.

Am I risking my daughter's life to save my own skin? God, I need help.

They walked inside Brookshire's and straight to the aisle containing hair supplies, where he could purchase color to shampoo in, something to cover his light-brown hair . . . Red. Those looking for him might be temporarily deluded. He snatched it and moved to purchase a case of water and snacks for them and Isabella. Specifically, dry saltines for him. He also picked up four phones and hoped he'd selected good ones. After grabbing bottles of Tylenol and Aleve to alternate every two hours for the head pain in case the Imitrex didn't kick in soon enough, they stepped into a checkout line.

Two police officers moved in behind them. Jason forced his insides to stop shaking. Isabella giggled at the officers. He sneaked a look at his daughter, who usually shied away from strangers.

"Hey, cutie," one officer said, "are you talking yet?"

"Small vocabulary." Jason touched Isabella's head. "And the word *no*."

"She's beautiful," the officer said. "I'm sure you're proud of her."

Jason smiled at April. "We are."

"She looks like her daddy except for her mouth and chin."

He froze. *April, please don't give us away.*

"I'm glad she got something from her mother." April leaned over Isabella and kissed the tip of her nose.

Would she yank his daughter from the cart and alert the officers? Would a firefight ensue?

"Doubt those blonde curls last long with your dark hair," the officer said.

What if Isabella were hurt? He'd never forgive himself. Time to surrender—

"I agree. They'll darken as she grows older," she said. "We'll enjoy them while we can."

April had made her choice.

Jason paid cash for his purchases, and they made their way to his truck. "I appreciate your help back there."

"I keep my word."

"You won't regret it."

"I did this for Isabella. If she hadn't been with us, I'd've initiated a takedown."

"No doubt." The truck chirped as he hit the button on the key fob to unlock the door. "When you get inside, would you hand me the prescription bottle in the glove box?" When she retrieved the bottle, he continued. "Put it in the drink holder." He tore into the package of saltine crackers and quickly chewed a handful. Twisting off the lid of the Imitrex, he swallowed two with water. His stomach churned.

"The dosage says one tablet."

"Not when a migraine is a jackhammer." He turned into the drive-through of a McDonald's about a mile down the road. "Breakfast?" he said to April. It was about 9:20. "Not sure when we'll have a chance to grab something to eat. We're about twenty miles from home. But I can't face what's ahead without giving the meds time to work."

"Bacon, egg, and cheese biscuit and a large black coffee. My brain craves caffeine this morning."

He ordered apple juice for Isabella. "Would you open a bottle of water and dilute it for Isabella? She's probably hungry. There's a finger-food meal in her diaper bag."

"I'll take care of it." She studied him. "You look horrible. How long before the Imitrex manages the pain?"

"Hard to say." He didn't order anything for himself. While waiting in the drive-through, he scanned the area for law enforcement.

Soon they received their order and were on the road again. Within five minutes, he found a run-down, one-story motel called the Texas Horseshoe, apparently named because of its shape. No sign of security cams outside. Jason drove over rough ground to the back of the motel.

"What are we doing?" she said.

"I need to shake this headache. Can't think clearly, so we're taking a detour. Back here no one can see my truck from the road." Slapping on the baseball cap and sunglasses, he turned to her. "Well, it's not the Ritz," he said.

"Or a Motel 6."

He offered a weak smile and switched off the engine. "Same routine. Are you refusing?"

She shook her head. What was she thinking? Planning?

The three of them exited the truck, and Isabella willingly went to April.

The desk clerk looked like he'd seen his best years during the Depression. A smile buried deep in his wrinkles when Isabella attempted to get her daddy to hold her. Jason paid cash for the room, and the manager gave him a key. No security cams were in sight.

They walked to their room.

"Are you going to sleep?" she said.

"Haven't figured it out yet. This whole thing feels strange, like a nightmare that goes on and on. When Lily lay sick, she said, 'The darkest moments of our lives are intended for God to use in a mighty way.' It's hard for me to see anything positive coming out of this except for a killer to be locked up."

"If Lily were here, what might she say about the risks you're taking? And the danger for Isabella?"

"I'm putting my daughter in my parents' hands."

"What if the kidnapper returns?"

"My parents know how to use firearms. Besides, the woman who kidnapped Isabella would be a fool to show her face near my folks."

"You're sure?"

He had doubts, lots of them. "Lily believed in fighting for truth. I'm doing this for our daughter." He gasped and stopped. If he passed out, she'd gain control, and he'd be locked up.

"You're not the kind of man who watches things happen and sits idly by," April said.

"I could have gone to the FBI a long time ago about Willis. But like a coward, I ignored him while he destroyed innocent lives. Never again. My daughter will have a legacy she can be proud of."

Inside the room, he pressed the remote for a ten-year-old TV sitting precariously on a flimsy table, and it brought the latest news. "Update on the Jason Snyder fugitive case. We can now confirm Snyder has his baby daughter with him. County Sheriff Willis Lennox reports Snyder will kill his baby daughter if pursued. It's rumored he has also abducted FBI Special Agent April Ramos, a hostage negotiator from the Houston office who has been reported missing. Snyder is armed and considered dangerous."

"Media will need to do a 180 on me," he said. "Right now I have to get some sleep."

"And you want my cooperation again?"

"You won't like it, and I'm sorry."

She held out her wrists in a gesture of understanding.

10

April held her breath while Jason vomited in the small motel bathroom. Thank goodness the room had a window. Even with it open, the stench nearly overpowered her, combined with the musty, moldy smell of the room's age and previous occupants.

Twice he'd made a quick trip to the porcelain bowl, dragging her with him. She struggled to hold Isabella and keep her balance. Jason finished his retching and swished his mouth with water. No moans or swearing. Only apologies.

She attributed part of his sickness to the auburn hair color fumes. He'd insisted upon shampooing it in before resting. During the application, he'd tied her to the bathroom doorknob. Both times he questioned the tightness of the rope and apologized.

"Do the headaches happen often?" she said.

"Not since Lily died. Hey, I'm really sorry about this. I thought coloring my hair was important, to give me a little edge from being recognized, but it didn't help my stomach or head."

"Just feel better." Maybe he blamed himself for his friend's death, and the guilt triggered physical symptoms. A characteristic April could use in her negotiations. Back at Brookshire's, she really wanted to reach out to the officers for help, but the gun in Jason's waistband and the varying emotions of the past several hours stopped her. Yet in the decision to protect him, she'd made progress in building trust. The scary part came when she admitted feeling something more than compassion for him.

"What settles your stomach and gets rid of the pain?" she said.

"Sleep and the Imitrex to work. I've probably flushed them down the toilet, but I can't take any more for a while. After a nap, I'll alternate the over-the-counter meds." He took deep breaths. "Thanks for putting up with my . . . health issues. I think I can sleep now."

"No problem."

He righted himself from the sink and gripped it. Even sick and matching the pallor of the toilet, he had a ruggedness about him. If they'd met on a blind date at a coffeehouse, she'd have found him appealing, possibly attractive. Glancing at the time, she calculated her captivity had lasted longer than her last date. She'd officially lost her mind.

"Puking my guts out slows down my plans."

She jostled Isabella, who wanted her daddy to take her. "Are you feeling any better?"

"Will be. I'll fix her a bottle, and she might sleep beside me."

"Let me do the honors."

He lifted his wrist, tied to hers. "We'll manage it together."

They moved to the lumpy bed and cardboard nightstand that reminded her of crack houses in Houston. She mixed formula with bottled water, and he shook it. Seemed like Isabella drank a lot of formula, but April had no experience.

He laid her purse on top of the TV. "I'm leaving the news on for both of us. And it might help fill in the time while I sleep."

"I need a nap too," she said. "No sleep last night."

"Everything okay? Are you sick?"

A kidnapper who displayed sympathy. "Like you, I'm tired."

"If you need to talk about the suicide, I have a good ear."

Again she wondered, Who was this man? "Uh, thanks."

He placed a pillow on the opposite side of the bed so Isabella wouldn't topple off. The news caught both their attention.

"A truck matching the description of Jason Snyder's was seen northeast of Cleveland on Interstate 69. Security cameras caught Snyder, his daughter, and FBI Special Agent April Ramos entering and exiting a grocery store in Kountze. Authorities are following what they believe is Snyder's path back to his home in Sweet Briar. Snyder is a hunter and may be heading into the thick woods and marshes in the area. Do not approach this man. Report any suspicious activity to local law enforcement." The reporter gave a recap of Russell Edwards's murder, complete with pics of Jason and Russell.

Jason rubbed his forehead. "I've got to be careful. Rethink my strategy." He took Isabella and stretched out on the faded bedspread, forcing April onto a chair beside him.

She fought the tug at her eyelids, telling herself she must form her own plan. But soon they were all asleep.

★ ★ ★

Jason woke to quiet. His head hurt, but the pain was manageable, and his stomach didn't churn. He moved slowly to take a glimpse of Isabella. He turned to April slumped in a chair beside him. Both slept, peaceful and untroubled. April, the negotiator, who'd lost a man in the early hours of the morning and now was tied to a man wanted for murder. Her dark hair lay across her face, and he wondered if under different circumstances they might have been friends. For certain, he'd always be grateful for her saving Isabella from the kidnapper.

He needed Tylenol, yet that meant waking April. Time to get moving too. The migraine had set him back almost two hours. He craved information like Isabella longed for a bottle every three hours and twenty-two minutes or less. Before waking Isabella and April, he wanted a few minutes' conversation with his dad.

Slowly he eased up, forcing his mind to focus and will away the pain. April opened her eyes but said nothing. Her gaze flew to Isabella, curled up next to him. She stirred, and he patted her back.

Sitting on the bed in the motel room, with one of the new burner phones in working order and on speaker, he looked up at April studying him. If only she believed him, he wouldn't have had to tie her wrist to his with a rope from his truck.

"Can my phone be traced when I call my dad?" he said.

She nodded.

"Don't have much choice, and I'd like for you to hear the conversation. I'll toss it in the trash when we leave." After he pressed the familiar numbers, Dad picked up on the second ring.

"This is Jason."

"Are you all right?"

"Working on it. I have Isabella, and she's fine. The woman who nabbed her escaped."

"What about the FBI agent?"

"She's here with me, listening to our call. Do you have a minute to answer a couple of questions? I'll make it fast."

"Go for it."

"Tell me about the woman who took Isabella."

Dad snorted. "About 9 p.m. the doorbell rang,

74

and your mother answered it. A person dressed in black and wearing a stocking mask shoved your mom inside. Waved a .22 in our faces. I figured her for a man because of a husky voice until I saw the red nails, chipped and broken. Don't know why I remembered that. She should have worn gloves. Wanted to know where to find Isabella. We refused to tell her. I thought she might shoot us. She took our phones. I asked her who put her up to this, and she said, 'None of your business.' She ordered us into the garage. Tied us up."

Jason trembled with fury. Normally he handled life with patience, but not when it came to his daughter and parents. "This could be part of a plan to nail me with a murder rap, but why involve Isabella? Willis has me in enough trouble without nabbing her."

Except forcing Jason to talk by snatching Isabella sounded like Willis.

"Son, how have you made Willis mad? Did he shoot Russell?"

Jason had already dragged his parents into this swamp. When Willis wanted something, he made sure he wrapped his hands around it. No matter who was hurt in the process. "It's hard for me to believe he'd arrange for his brother-in-law to be killed and leave his sister a widow." Anger tightened its grip, and he pushed it away. "Willis has excellent marksmanship. He couldn't have been the shooter unless the two shots were intended to throw off the investigation."

"Think about his actions as a deputy and sheriff," Dad said. "He's capable of anything. How many times have you and I talked about reporting him?"

"While he played the role of head deacon? Sang solos at church?" Jason needed to stop asking questions and find answers. "I'm trying to figure out how to proceed."

"I heard Willis tell his men, 'Don't kill Jason. I want him to stand trial for Russell's murder.' "

"He won't kill me and risk an investigation from another source. My guess is the order was for your benefit so you'd tell him where to find me." Jason believed Willis wanted him alive, but vengeance walked the line of hate.

"Son, you've gone quiet on me."

"Sorry. We can expose him, and you've wanted to pursue it for a long time. I've been a coward. I'm finished ignoring Willis. He declared war with his lies, and I'm ready."

"We can locate a reputable lawyer to get a conviction and give him a permanent home behind bars. Sweet Briar needs a sheriff who honors the law. I'm going to do a little legwork and talk to Kevin."

"No, Dad. Find me a lawyer. Prayer would help too. I'll handle the rest. Do you have time to check on the construction crew? They're working on a house near the post office. The foreman can handle everything."

"Edwardo?"

"Yes. He's a good man." Jason paused to clear his head. "The men need to be reassured of their paychecks."

"Will do, and I'll get the neighbor kid to feed and water your cattle and dog. I'd bring Fluffy here, but with your mom's allergies—"

"He'll be fine. The least of my worries right now. Glad you have the foresight to take care of my place. Make the arrangements until this is settled." He winced at the pain in his head. "Also, I need a huge favor. For Isabella's and your sake, I'd like for you and Mom to take a vacation beginning today."

"No, Son. I'm not a runner. We will help you fight this battle."

"All right, Dad." Jason ended the call and closed his eyes.

11

April startled, a pounding at the door causing her to jerk on the rope tying her to Jason.

"Open the door, Jason. This is Sheriff Willis Lennox."

Jason bolted from the bed, pulling her with him, seemingly alert. He grabbed her weapon from atop the TV, sticking it in his waistband.

"Jason, I know you're in there with Isabella and the FBI agent. I'm alone—let's talk this out. Get you a clean slate. You know how to unravel the charges against you."

The voice sounded like the man who'd called Jason earlier. The sheriff had made unusual claims earlier and now. Distrust marched across her mind, and she questioned the integrity of Sheriff Willis Lennox.

Jason untied her. Her moment of rectifying a criminal's behavior had arrived. But whom should she believe? She moved to the window facing the outside. She slipped her fingers behind the threadbare drape and peeked through. A man built like a linebacker dressed in a sheriff's uniform had his right hand wrapped around his holstered gun. No one appeared to be with him, and no other cars were in the motel's parking lot. She turned to Jason and whispered, "I don't see anyone else."

A thought squeezed into her brain. "How did he learn you were here?"

"He has eyes and ears everywhere."

"Now, Jason." Willis pounded on the door.

Jason motioned for April to take Isabella, and she lifted the baby from the bed. April darted to a corner away from the door.

"How do I know you're not going to blow my head off?" Jason said.

"If I had backup, this door would have been knocked off its hinges. You'd be dead, and I wouldn't have my information."

"What information?"

"Use your head. Tell me where Billie and Zack are hiding, and I'll make this go away."

April clutched Isabella to her chest. Had Jason spoken the truth? "Sheriff Lennox, this is Special Agent April Ramos. If you open fire, you risk shooting a baby," she said. "There's a better way to resolve this."

A sardonic laugh met her.

Jason wrestled with opening the motel door and facing the consequences outside. Someone might get hurt, maybe killed, and as much as he detested Willis, he didn't want him dead. Confronting him had merit, especially when April had already heard enough from Willis to possibly have the FBI investigate him. Jason needed questions answered too. But Isabella and April needed to be out of harm's way. If his life ended in the next few minutes, Mom and Dad would raise his daughter with Christian values, just as they'd done with him.

He nodded at April to show he was in control. "Take Isabella into the bathroom. Stay with her." Holding his daughter tugged at his heart. It could be the last time if Willis put a bullet in him, but her safety depended on the next few moments.

"Jason," she whispered, "I'll put Isabella in the bathroom, but if I'm not here with you, I can't help."

He peered into her eyes. No hostility or deception. "You're taking care of my most treasured possession. That's all I ask. Both of you get into the bathtub."

"All right." As she made her way to the bathroom, April gave him a troubled look, one he couldn't read. Neither did he have time to ask.

A dull ache persisted at the top of his skull, and the smell of hair color still clung to the air. He couldn't do this without divine help, and he hoped he was making the right decision. "Willis, I'm ready to talk."

"You and I have unfinished business. Let's start by getting the law off your tail."

"How, since half the state's looking for me?"

"I'll make it happen. Even thought about you surrendering to me down at the church after we come to an agreement. I'll admit to a mistake. The drama looks good for both of us."

"Who killed Russell?"

"Not me. But I know who did."

"Who?"

"You tell me where my wife and son are and maybe we can work something out."

"Where's the evidence showing I had nothing to do with Russell's death?"

"Depends if I get what I came for. A deal works two ways. I'm giving you thirty seconds to open this door before I blow off the lock. Think about never seeing your daughter again and her facing the shame of having a murderer for a father."

"If I'm in jail, you'll be no better off than you are now."

"I'll go after your family until I get mine back. I still win."

Willis had him cornered. "Leave your gun on the ground outside."

"I'm betting you have one too."

"I'm not getting involved in a shoot-out." He glanced toward the bathroom and prayed a bullet wouldn't sail through the wall and hurt Isabella or April. "We're grown men, Willis."

"I can't leave my weapon here—what happens if someone walks by?"

"Then put it in your patrol car."

"Your thirty seconds are ticking away. I can have backup here in less than ten minutes."

Jason swung open the door. Willis's gun hung at his side, and Jason refused to lose sight of it. "Keep your hands away from your weapon."

The sheriff's right hand inched toward it. "You know I always get what I want. Carrie swore out a statement. Nothing looks good for you."

Jason pulled his Beretta. "Get any closer to your gun, and you won't have any fingers left. Hands in the air. Now."

Willis obliged and grinned, showing all his capped teeth. He tipped his hat and stepped inside the small room. A bag of peanuts stuck out from his shirt pocket. "Thanks for the invite. Glad you came to your senses." He eyed him through narrow gray slits, with the same arrogance that had pushed their high school football team to number one three years in a row. The same arrogance used to bully folks into doing what he demanded.

Jason closed the door. "I'm listening."

"When I'm ready." He peered around. "Where's Isabella? Poor thing has a loser for a daddy. But I give you credit for finding her. And where's the FBI agent?"

"I locked her and Isabella in the bathroom."

"Where's her gun?"

"I have it."

"You know I have clout in this county. What I say goes. Two weeks ago, I made you a fair offer with a warning. Only one thing is on my mind— how to find Billie and Zack."

"Which warning are you talking about? The note in my mailbox about keeping my eyes on Isabella? Or the talk we had at my office where I give you information about Billie, about which I have no clue, and you'll stop trying to ruin my reputation?"

"You stuck your nose into my business."

"And you killed your brother-in-law to scare me into telling you their whereabouts. Had my parents held at gunpoint and my daughter kidnapped. Low move, even for you."

His brows narrowed. "I told you I had nothing to do with Russell's death. But we can work this out and go on with our lives."

"If Billie wants to contact you, she knows how."

"I'll find 'em." He growled his words like a predator. "The thing is I'm not a patient man. I want my wife and son back home."

"Why? To black Billie's eyes and break Zack's other arm? Invest in a punching bag."

"Nobody takes what's mine and gets away with it. Trust me, every minute you delay gives the law time to find you."

"And I'm telling you I have no idea where they are."

"Sitting in jail has a way of loosening a man's tongue." He paused as if silence might change Jason's mind. "If I can track you down, others will too. They might not be as generous. This is your last chance to go free and keep your family alive."

Jason thought of Isabella. All the things he wanted to do with her and for her—all the things Lily had written down in her journal, the important life-changing events for his daughter. "Willis, whether I'm sitting in jail or walking free, I can't tell you what I don't know."

"I'll sweeten the deal with cash," Willis said. "How does $15,000 sound?"

Giving in to Willis switched on a green light for him to continue bullying folks like he'd done for years. But Jason loved his daughter more than life, and truth right alongside her.

"Is this a cash deal?" Jason said.

"The money's in my trunk."

As if Jason might consider the offer. He pointed to the bed. "Have a seat in my office, and we'll write this up. You'll drop the charges. Call off your dogs. Right?"

"Sure. It'll take me all of five minutes."

"One question here, Willis—why was Russell killed?"

"He made the mistake of marrying my sister."

12

April strained to hear the conversation, but all she heard were the sounds of a scuffle. The springs on the bed squeaked. Still nothing from Jason or Willis. What was going on? She practiced the art of controlling her temper. Hostage negotiation required it. In turn, she expected every member of law enforcement to abide by the regulations in place to protect the innocent and ensure justice reigned. She'd witnessed distorted interpretations in the past, designed to reshape facts for selfish motives, but County Sheriff Willis Lennox's methods went against every procedure manual she'd read.

Everything Jason claimed manifested itself in a crooked sheriff. Jason's story held credibility. April thought she might burst with fury, tossing her negotiation skills, as well as her patience and understanding, down the toilet. In the cramped bathtub behind a moldy shower curtain, she patted Isabella's back and told herself to calm down. The baby girl caused a surge of protectiveness to swell in April's heart. Something had changed within her. She'd taken a new stand in this inconceivable situation.

"April, I could use a little help." Jason's breathless voice moved her into action.

She crawled out of the tub with Isabella and opened the bathroom door. Willis lay on the bed facedown and cuffed. "How did you get the upper hand?"

"I don't know." He sighed. "Not sure if it was desperation or a God thing. Or both."

She looked at the beefy man, his sunglasses resting on his receding hairline. "You must be Sheriff Willis Lennox." She pasted on a smile and joined Jason. "I'd shake your hand, but I see you're indisposed. That was quite an interesting conversation between you and Jason, one the FBI will value. Glad I heard every word." Too bad Jason had taken her cell phone—she'd have recorded the whole thing. Another fact slammed against her mind. "You intended to kill all of us."

He snorted. "Your testimony against mine, and you two look real cozy holed up in a motel room." He nodded at the messy bed.

Willis was the worst spineless coward she'd ever met. "How do you justify helping a man by breaking the law? Really? He gives you what you want, and you exonerate him for a murder he claims he didn't commit?"

Willis ignored her and twisted his head at Jason. "Do we have a deal? You're running out of time."

"I don't advise this," April said. "He's breaking one law after another. You have rights."

"I have no choice."

April shook her head. "He'll find a way to kill you."

Jason touched her arm and mouthed, "I'm not making a deal."

April heard engine sounds and looked out the window. "Two patrol cars are driving in."

"On time too," Willis said. "No way out of this, Jason. You and your lady friend are dead. Isabella might get hit too."

Jason grabbed him by the throat. April tugged at his shoulder one-handedly and nearly dropped Isabella in an effort to pull him off Willis. "Jason, he wins if you do this. You'll never be able to prove his crimes."

But he couldn't seem to stop.

She gripped harder. "You're a good man. This isn't you."

He shook off his hold on Willis and clenched his fists before stepping back. "What do you suggest?" he said to April.

"Let me call the FBI. I heard every word and will do everything in my power to help you and put this jerk away."

"Call the FBI," Willis said. "You can use my phone."

"I suggest you keep your mouth shut," April said to Willis. No wonder Jason lost his temper.

Jason appeared to regain control. He took another step back. "I promise you'll face murder charges even if I die trying."

"And you will. My people are in places you'd never think to look."

Jason turned to her. "I need for you to get Isabella away from here." He kissed his daughter and leaned into April's ear. "Please make sure the FBI learns the truth."

"I will." For a moment, her heart took a dive. She willed away a strange attraction that had her spellbound . . . and confused.

"Delay things outside for as long as you can," he whispered. "Then take Isabella to Vicki and Ted Snyder in Sweet Briar. Talk them into leaving town."

He trusted her with his daughter, his reason for breathing. She grabbed the diaper bag. He tucked her Glock inside. He still had his Beretta.

He opened the door wide enough for the deputies to hear. "Hold your fire. This is Jason Snyder. I'm releasing FBI Agent Ramos and my daughter so Willis and I can talk." He moved aside for April to leave, and she walked into the afternoon sunlight to see that two deputies had their weapons drawn.

She shivered. Jason could very well sacrifice his life for Isabella . . . and her. How would she handle two deaths in one day? "Stand down," she said. "None of you wants to shoot an innocent baby and a federal officer."

The deputies holstered their guns. One walked her way. "ID please." His name tag read *Kevin*

Viner. Jason's friend. She dug through her purse while balancing Isabella on her hip. He examined her ID and returned it. "What's the situation inside?" he said.

"As Mr. Snyder said, Sheriff Lennox and Jason are talking."

"Is Jason surrendering?"

"It appears so," she said. "Sheriff Lennox knows him well."

"Are you taking Isabella to his folks?" Deputy Viner said.

None of his business. "I'll see to the welfare of the baby when Sheriff Lennox and Jason are finished discussing their terms. While we're waiting, I need a phone to contact Houston FBI."

"We have this handled without involving the FBI." Deputy Viner had the impassive expression working for him.

"Are you refusing a federal officer the use of a phone?" April held her ground, realizing that if Jason succeeded in getting away, she'd technically be an accomplice. Yet nothing she'd heard from or about Sheriff Lennox had given her cause to believe he was interested in upholding the law. Not only had he threatened Jason and her but an innocent child. What made him think the law didn't affect him? Never had she chosen to believe a fugitive over law enforcement.

The rules girl had burned the playbook.

Deputy Viner handed her his phone. "My

concern was not denying you the phone but letting you know we have this case handled without FBI involvement."

She pressed in Simon's number and walked away from the deputies. "This is April."

"Where are you? Are you okay?"

"I'm fine. I have Isabella Snyder."

"You persuaded Snyder to give himself and his daughter up?"

"No. He's talking to Sheriff Lennox. I'm with two deputies from Sweet Briar. I've just witnessed the epitome of lawlessness. I'd like for you to do a—"

"Sheriff, everything all right in there?" Deputy Viner shouted.

April needed to intervene. "Simon, I've got to go. Temperatures are hot. Talk to you soon."

Had Jason been given enough time to escape?

April moved behind the deputy's car to protect Isabella from possible gunfire. Jason was armed. Would he return fire to the one man who supposedly had the evidence to exonerate him?

"Give Sheriff Lennox time to negotiate," she shouted but didn't approach them.

A text sounded in the burner phone Jason had given her.

Car seat left 4 u

The deputies ignored her. Deputy Viner repeated his question to Sheriff Lennox. When silence met their ears, the deputies rushed the door. An engine roared to life. Jason's truck sped around the rear of the motel and onto the highway.

He'd dodged the deputies by escaping through the bathroom window.

April hugged Isabella close to her. In her catharsis, she realized Jason trusted her. "Your daddy is a brave man," she whispered. "I'm ready to help him find the proof of his innocence."

13

The deputies and Willis raced after Jason in patrol cars, leaving April holding Isabella with no visible means of transportation. True to his text, Jason had deposited the car seat outside the rear window of the motel room where he'd made his escape.

When April explained her FBI status to the desk clerk, he handed her the keys to his Camry, and she promised she'd have his car returned by the following morning.

The dear man even installed the car seat.

April drove north toward Sweet Briar, passing more sections of the Big Thicket within the boundaries of the state park.

She processed the events of the past several hours in chronological order, replaying conversations and determining where to look first for evidence to show who'd killed Russell Edwards. How beneficial it would have been if she'd been able to record Willis's and Jason's conversation. When time allowed, she'd document all the details floating through her mind. Occasionally she glanced at Isabella in the rearview mirror, chatting with the sweet baby the way Jason had. The news radio shared no reports of him being apprehended. Neither had he called.

Time to contact Simon.

Once she had her partner on the line, she quickly explained what happened when Willis arrived at the motel. "I want everything you can find on Sheriff Willis Lennox, unsolved crimes in Sweet Briar, cell phone records, Snyder Construction, and any information about Billie and Zack Lennox. Everything. Send me the crime scene report for Russell Edwards's murder. I'm looking for documentation of two bullets smashing through a window, broken glass inside or outside. The bullet caliber used to kill Edwards and the autopsy report when it's completed. Don't forget backgrounds on all his deputies. I'm calling you from a burner, and you can text or call me on this number."

"Where did you get the phone?"

"Jason bought it for me."

"Are you pretending to be on his side?"

An alarm sounded in her brain. Her job skills required her to walk a tightrope of the rational, which she'd totally abandoned. "I believe he was set up for murder, and that person arranged for his daughter to be kidnapped."

"You came to this conclusion in a matter of a few hours?"

"Willis Lennox threatened to kill Isabella along with Jason and me. Last time I checked, that's illegal, even for law enforcement personnel. Willis stated he'd drop the charges if Jason agreed to tell him how to find his wife and child—Billie and Zack. From what Jason's told me, Willis may have abused them. I'm convinced Jason didn't shoot anyone."

"Hold it. You believe he's innocent, and the sheriff is out to get him?"

A nudging in her spirit pushed her forward. "Yes."

"What if both men are wrong? What if both men are right, and they're acting upon what they allege as valid information?"

"My allegiance is to truth, but Willis made this personal."

Simon's tone softened. "I'm concerned about you being caught in the middle. Think about what happened prior to this."

"I'm fine. I'm taking Isabella to her grand-parents." She explained how she'd obtained the Camry. "When I get there, hopefully making sure the elder Snyders take off on a trip, I'll call or text where I'll be staying. Would you arrange a car for me and for this one to be returned?"

"Sure. Leave the keys on the rear driver's side tire, and agents will do the same with the replace-ment vehicle."

"Thanks. Who's on the ground in Sweet Briar working this case?"

"This isn't an FBI case."

"It is when a federal officer is threatened. And don't forget about the reported kidnapping."

"Granted, but you can handle those aspects from here in Houston."

"Fine. I'll file my report online ASAP. When I'm back in the office, I'll walk you through what I know." She started to end the call, then remembered. "Two things I'd like to have before then— number one, I want to see the local hospital records for Billie or Zack Lennox. Number two, Sheriff Lennox's original charges against Jason and any release paperwork."

She'd do her own digging into Carrie Edwards. She simply needed access to the Internet.

"I'll spin a few cycles and get back to you."

"Thanks. Talk to you soon." She disconnected, Simon's questions replaying in her head. *What if both men are wrong? What if both men are right, and they're acting upon what they allege as valid information?"*

Her stomach twisted. The idea of facing another failure—

She dismissed even a hint of it. She'd heard Willis's every word.

In the small, single-stoplight town of Sweet Briar, she glanced on both sides of Main Street at two antique stores, a flower shop, a barbershop next door to the Cut 'N' Curl beauty salon, a sign indicating a church to the right, and a small restaurant called Sweet Briar's Home Style Cooking. She parked the car outside the diner and entered with Isabella. Surely someone could

95

give her directions to Vicki and Ted Snyder's home.

A jukebox, black-and-white tile floors, chrome tables with red vinyl tablecloths, red-padded chairs, and a soda-fountain bar took her back to the fifties, reminding her of *Happy Days* reruns. Three white-haired ladies were seated at a round table with their Bibles open.

"Why do you have Isabella Snyder?" one of the women said with a lift of a painted brow.

April walked to them. "I'm FBI Special Agent April Ramos, and I'm looking for Vicki and Ted Snyder. This little girl needs her grandparents. Can you help me?"

The woman tickled Isabella's chin but frowned at April. "You know our Jason is innocent. Willis's report is hogwash. He never killed Russell. Why, they were best friends."

Another woman, wearing a wide-brimmed, robin's-egg-blue hat matching her cardigan, squinted. "Where's your ID? After all, a woman kidnapped Isabella."

April shifted Isabella to her hip and fished through her purse. How did mothers get anything done? She produced the ID.

The woman examined it for several seconds. "This looks legit. Of course, you could have gotten it at one of those fancy party stores." She handed April's ID back. "That boy was raised right. In church. Brings Isabella too."

"Yes, ma'am. We're working on learning the truth."

The blue-hatted woman shook her finger at her. "I've known Jason since the day Vicki birthed him. Went to his and Lily's wedding and to the dear girl's funeral. He doesn't have a bad bone in his body. Do you understand?"

April got the picture. "Yes, ma'am."

"Folks call me Miss Ella." She ripped out a piece of paper from a spiral-bound journal and with arthritic fingers wrote, *Ted and Vicki Snyder* and an address. "My guess is you have an app on your phone for directions." She jotted down a phone number. "You call me if you need anything, you hear?" She reached out with the slip of paper.

"Thank you. I will." April grasped it, stuffing the paper into her purse with her ID, and turned to leave.

"Wait a minute, missy. I'm not done yet. You're handing Isabella over to Vicki and Ted now?"

"I am if they're willing to accept custody." If not, April planned to drive back to Houston with the baby—legal implications notwithstanding.

"If you're here on Sunday, I expect to see you in church. Let's all pray before you leave. See if we can speed up God taking care of this."

Miss Ella seemed to be straight out of another era, like the restaurant. But Jason needed all the help he could get.

"Lord, we have a mess here. We're begging

You to right a terrible wrong. A good man has been killed, leaving a sweet widow and two darlin' little boys, and another good man has been falsely charged. But You know all our troubles." Miss Ella prayed until April's arms ached from holding Isabella. How did one person think of so many things to say to God? The woman concluded the prayer for Jason and Russell's widow, Carrie Edwards.

"Thanks for the address and phone number." April's feet were itching, wanting to take flight.

Miss Ella studied April. "You believe in Jesus?"

"I'm a Christian."

"That ain't what I asked."

How could April appease the woman about a subject she rarely visited? On cue, Isabella fussed. "I suppose we should go. Isabella's hungry."

"Mark my word, girl. Before this is over, you're gonna see the power of Jesus."

Bewildered and so far from her comfort zone, April expressed her appreciation to all the ladies. At the counter, she ordered a large coffee and a bottle of lukewarm water. She balanced them away from Isabella on the way to the car. After opening the rear door and placing Isabella in the car seat, she mixed a bottle, half-expecting Miss Ella to see the delay as ample time to come out and talk about Jason or Jesus or both.

None of her life experiences had prepared her for Jason Snyder and these ladies.

Within eight minutes, she found the Snyders' two-story home. Two oak rocking chairs with burnt-orange pillows sat empty on the front porch with a "Welcome to fall" appeal. Green plants dotted the white porch. Simply cozy, and she hoped the subtle invitation was an indication of the type of people living inside.

"Isabella, your grandparents live in an adorable home, almost as adorable as you." She exited the car and adjusted her purse and diaper bag onto her shoulder. No extra hands to take her coffee, so she set it on the roof of the car. Oh, well. With a click of the harness to release Isabella, April drew the baby into her arms. After not being around babies, her heart had been . . . handcuffed, and she wasn't ready to drop Isabella off and head back to Houston. The other problem centered on Willis threatening Jason's family and her persuading the couple to leave the area.

The front door opened, and an older couple rushed toward them.

"You have Isabella." The woman's voice resounded with a mix of joy and a sob. Tall and slender, with shoulder-length blonde hair, Jason's mother wasn't at all like April pictured. April had stereotyped her as short, round, and wearing an apron.

"Yes, and she's just fine. I'm FBI Agent April Ramos. Jason asked me to deliver her and explain the events of the past several hours."

"I'm Vicki Snyder and this is my husband, Ted." She took Isabella, leaving April with feelings of relief and jealousy. Vicki bit her lip, no doubt to conceal emotion. "We were afraid we might never see her again."

"I'm so sorry for your heartache."

Ted Snyder stuck out his hand, and she grasped it. Medium height and full head of dark-brown hair. Same color of eyes as Jason.

"Thanks for returning our baby girl, Agent Ramos," he said.

"You're welcome. And please call me April."

He grabbed her coffee and closed the car door. "We have much to discuss."

"I agree. Miss Isabella just finished a bottle, but she's still hungry."

Vicki snuggled her granddaughter. "I have plenty of baby food. Jason keeps me stocked."

Isabella reached for April. Should she take the baby from her grandmother? Vicki smiled and relinquished her to April. "You have a friend . . . and she's particular."

The moment April stepped into the Snyder home, any apprehensions flittered away. Absent of clutter and decorated in blue and white, the home felt like a retreat. In a large, updated farmhouse-style kitchen, Vicki encouraged her to place Isabella in the high chair. Soon the baby had green beans and banana slices to eat with her fingers. April had a notepad and pen at her fingertips.

Vicki and Ted scooted their chairs close to the kitchen table. He started the conversation. "Two FBI agents have already been here asking a truckload of questions, sometimes rephrased two and three times. They thought we could lead them to you and Jason. Left a business card and said they'd be in touch." He reached into his pocket, pulled a card from his wallet, and read a special agent's name. After she verified knowing the agent, he replaced the card. "Have you contacted your office?"

She nodded. "They're aware of the situation and my plans to bring Isabella here."

"Are you and Jason friends? The missus and I are confused about how you got involved. Did he phone the FBI and request assistance, like a help desk?"

"Not exactly. I'm a hostage negotiator when needed. Otherwise I work public corruption." April described how an unknown woman had shoved Isabella into her arms in a donut shop. "Isabella was shivering, so I wrapped her in my FBI jacket. While I waited, not sure what to do, a man comes up to me and says he's the baby's father." She glossed over the details of the encounter, wanting to spare Jason's parents from any more angst. "I accompanied him outside to get the diaper bag. We drove to my home to talk."

"Hold on." Ted waved his hand. "You're soft-pedaling here. You're an FBI agent. I'm thinking Jason forced you to go with him."

The truth? "He didn't give me a choice, and he explained how he'd tracked Isabella. He also gave me an accounting of what happened leading up to Russell Edwards's death."

Ted frowned, resembling Jason.

Vicki spoke up. "Maybe Jason's decision to force April to go with him was God's way of ensuring she learned the truth."

"Don't think so." Ted's voice lowered. "Jason may have been frantic, but taking April without her consent is downright wrong."

At least Ted hadn't asked her if she was held at gunpoint, but he probably figured it out. "Jason apologized, and the situation is behind us. When Sheriff Lennox called, Jason placed the phone on speaker. The sheriff's comments were not what I expected from a law enforcement official." April added that Jason had come down with a migraine and decided to stop for some needed rest at a motel, where Sheriff Lennox unexpectedly showed up. "For the second time, Sheriff Lennox demonstrated inappropriate behavior. Jason overpowered him and asked me to take Isabella to you. He used the sheriff's handcuffs to restrain him. I stopped at a restaurant downtown, and a lady by the name of Miss Ella gave me your address."

"This is a complicated situation," Ted said.

"Jason made Willis mad, but he neglected to tell me how. Then Russell's killed, and our boy is slammed with false murder charges."

The Snyders weren't the only ones grappling for intel. "Vicki and Ted, I believe Jason is innocent of murder. I'll do all I can to help exonerate him and find who killed Russell Edwards."

14

April inhaled the calm wafting through the Snyder home. She'd instantly liked Jason's parents, and if her instincts were accurate, they were fine people.

"Thanks for believing in our son," Vicki said with a quivering smile. "You are an answer to prayer. How can we help him?"

April turned to smile at Isabella. Such a beautiful baby, one who'd stolen her heart. "The three of you are in danger. Willis threatened Isabella, and we both know that could involve you."

"Wouldn't be the first time Willis knocked down someone who got in his way," Ted said.

He might be referring to Russell. Were there others? "Who?"

"Plenty of folks."

"You?"

"I've crossed his path a couple of times." Ted stared at Vicki. "Willis came by here after the so-called jailbreak and wanted to know where to find Jason. I had no idea. Wouldn't have told him anyway. He said he'd given orders not to kill our son 'cause he wanted him to stand trial for Russell's murder."

"How'd you respond?"

"Not a word. No point in arguing with him. He left wearing his trademark smirk."

"I've seen it," she said. "Have you been approached by his deputies since then?"

"A deputy's parked down the street," Ted said. "Saw his truck earlier." Anger creased his features. "I walked right up to him and asked him why he was wasting taxpayers' money watching the comings and goings of law-abiding citizens. He used to be our paperboy. Never had a lick of common sense. Some days we got our paper, and some days he didn't feel like delivering it. But he was always there to pick up his money."

She grabbed the pen. "Name?"

"Cal Bunion, just like on your big toe."

"His response?" April jotted down the deputy's name.

"Cal told me Jason was a killer, and he had orders to shoot him on sight. So Willis wasn't blowing smoke earlier."

"How many terms has he served as county sheriff?"

"Two. Deputy before that," Ted said. "We heard he either paid or threatened voters. Not us, though."

"Can you verify the rumor?" April said.

"No one crosses Willis," Ted said. "If he's arrested with charges that will banish him from the county permanently, maybe folks will come forward."

April made a note to research Willis's campaigns as a sheriff.

"To the best of your knowledge, are any of his deputies guilty of committing crimes?"

Ted appeared to ponder the question. "Hard to say. I know all but one of them. In my opinion, the more deputies on Willis's side, the more he'd have to pay off or get rid of."

Smart man. "Is there one person you suspect?"

He shook his head. "But there's one man I trust. Kevin Viner. He grew up with Jason. Goes to our church."

The deputy she'd met this afternoon. She'd refrain from mentioning her experience until she received a background on the man. "Since we aren't assured of who is and isn't working under Willis's directives, I suggest you, Vicki, and Isabella leave Sweet Briar until this is over. I'm concerned about Isabella's safety and yours. What's to stop the kidnapper from striking again?"

"My handgun and rifle." Ted sighed, much like she'd seen and heard Jason do.

April hadn't prayed in years. She'd stuffed her rosary into a dresser drawer when she took on her FBI role as negotiator. But still she offered a prayer for guidance. "Jason's insistent you and Mrs. Snyder take Isabella out of town until this is straightened out."

"I'm staying right here. Now's the time to stand up to Willis," Ted said. "I suppose you'll try to persuade us to see matters your way, but I'm going to help my son win this war." He leaned forward. "I have a place where Vicki and Isabella can hide out."

"Why not stay at a safe house in Houston?"

"Is that necessary?" Vicki said. "We have a cabin about fifty miles from here. It's secluded and difficult to get in or out."

Oh, they were a stubborn pair and passed it down in their genes. "What if you're followed? Run off the road? You'd be safer in Houston under FBI protection."

"Really?" Vicki said. "Aren't those the same people who believe Willis's report, that our son is a killer and kidnapped his daughter and you? You mean well, and I'm grateful, but the FBI's credibility lies at the bottom of a catfish pond until they acknowledge Jason's innocence. When they admit Willis is responsible, I'll take our granddaughter wherever you want."

How did she get herself into this mess? But she'd not abandon Isabella to their ludicrous solution.

"Could your cabin become a trap if you were found by the wrong people?"

Vicki paled. "That could be said of any safe house."

"Except trained agents would have your back. I understand your feelings, but will you promise me you'll think about an FBI solution?"

"We will think and pray on it," Ted said. "In the meantime, tomorrow I'll take Vicki and Isabella to our cabin."

Clearly she was being pacified. "Is there any documented evidence of Willis's involvement in illegal activities?"

"Possibly. A couple of weeks ago, Jason gave me a flash drive and asked me to keep it in a safe place. I have no idea of the contents."

"That's not entirely true," Vicki said.

"Well . . . this probably isn't admissible in a court of law, but Jason added it to the flash drive. Just documentation of something I observed. It means nothing in itself. I was in line at the bank behind Willis. He had $10,000 in cash and deposited it in four separate accounts. Wondered how a county sheriff came into that much cash and why he spread it out. So I took note of the date, time, and the teller."

Ted rubbed his chin. "I wouldn't have thought much of it, except it happened downwind of another incident. I head up a ministry designed to help those with addictions. One of the men, Buddy, who comes on occasion, usually when his girl-friend kicks him out, told me a story. Said Willis detained him for dealing, but Willis claimed he could avoid arrest and make the charges go away for $10,000. His girlfriend paid it. Buddy's run-in with Willis happened two days before the peculiar deposit. Too coincidental for me." He sat back.

"Ted, if you don't tell her the rest, I will," Vicki said.

"All right. But none of this can be proven unless

Buddy stays clean long enough to tell his story. Even then, Willis's lawyer would probably find a way to toss it out." He moistened his lips. "The next time I talked to Buddy, I asked if he'd been behaving himself. He'd been arrested for drunken driving and spent a week in jail. Willis offered to make it go away for $3,000. Buddy told him to forget it because he was breakin' the law too. When Willis laughed and locked him up, Buddy told him I knew about the bribe. The following Sunday, Willis stopped me after church and told me not to believe anything Buddy said. I asked him if he was talking about the $10,000 bribe. He sneered and started to walk away. I called after him, 'Willis, if nothing happened, why are you bothering me with it?' Made him mad. Told me to mind my own business or I'd be sorry. I said, 'One of these days, your mischief will come to light.'"

April nodded. The Snyders had their stories about Willis. But could any of them be proven? "Is the flash drive here?"

"It's in my safe-deposit box at the bank. I have it in an envelope labeled *Willis and Buddy*."

"Can I talk to Buddy?" she said.

"He left town with his girlfriend. His landlord said the two moved to Florida. No forwarding address."

She wanted to see the contents of the flash drive for no other reason than to dig deeper into Willis's activities. "Is the bank open?"

"Until five," Ted said. "I have extra flash drives if you want to copy it. Bet we can make it happen at the bank."

"I'd like for Vicki and Isabella to ride along."

"I know where Ted keeps his gun," Vicki said. "No reason to babysit me."

"I'd rather you didn't have to use it and put Isabella in the path of a bullet." Why couldn't the Snyders see the foolishness of their decisions? She wanted to snatch Isabella from the high chair and speed back to Houston.

Vicki wiped green bean slobber from Isabella's mouth. "All right. We'll go with you."

Once April had the flash drive, she'd read the documentation and make a judgment call before copying it and forwarding to Simon. No way would she send information without being apprised herself. It might be a source for further investigation of the county sheriff.

"I'd like to make a phone call before we leave," April said.

He stood. "You can use our bedroom for privacy, and we'll load up Isabella."

She followed Ted to a small bedroom decorated with multicolored quilts. He excused himself and closed the door behind him. She pressed in Simon's number, wanting to see if he'd uncovered anything about Willis.

"April, what's up?" he said.

"I'm with Ted and Vicki Snyder. Isabella is

with them." She relayed the conversation she'd had with them. "Once I read what's there and confirm it's of value to an investigation, I'll put it in your Dropbox." A laptop was perched on top of a dresser. She'd ask to borrow it later.

"Do your best to persuade the Snyders to seek protection," Simon said.

"You must have additional information or you'd not make that recommendation."

"Nothing I can pass on yet. I have a meeting in fifteen minutes with the SAC and two agents who are familiar with an ongoing case regarding Sheriff Lennox."

She startled. "What kind of case? Who are the agents?"

"I can't share that yet, April. I don't have clearance."

"Okay." She didn't like it, but she understood procedure. "Call me when it's over."

"I'd feel better if you'd drive back to Houston."

"Not until I'm assured Isabella is safe. Would you have an agent keep an eye on the Snyders?"

"I'll try. I'm already in hot water from making your other requests without the supervisor's approval. When Sheriff Lennox reported Jason Snyder kidnapped his daughter and a federal agent, he drew in the FBI. He tried to boot us off the case, but it didn't work."

"What's Willis's attitude now?"

"He's cooperating. Offered to come to Houston

111

on Monday and straighten out what he refers to as a civil dispute."

April blew out her exasperation.

"After what you've experienced, I'd like to cuff the sheriff too."

She inhaled. "So far, Willis has covered his rear. But there must be more to Russell Edwards's murder than we're aware. Willis has slipped up somewhere. He has a weak link, and I intend to find it."

"This is not your case, your mission, or your responsibility."

How could she explain her reasoning when she hadn't processed it all herself? Isabella was an innocent victim, and Willis had used her as a pawn for his own arrogance and greed. He'd threatened a child's life. For that alone, she wanted to see him stand before a judge. Willis had admitted to breaking the law to find his wife and son. Make murder charges go away? She believed in Jason's innocence.

"April, why?"

"Willis made it personal."

"Not good enough. Send me everything you find today, then drive back to Houston first thing in the morning. Jason Snyder doesn't need a negotiator."

She swallowed a sharp retort. If she wasn't going to be allowed to work his case in an official capacity . . . "I'm requesting leave."

Simon huffed and was silent for a long moment. "And you're taking a wrecking ball to your career."

"I'll chance it. I'm not leaving an innocent man to face false charges. Neither am I walking away from a county sheriff who threatened a baby and me."

"Think about what you're saying. You've never taken a position like this before."

"I've thought it through." She forced herself to relax.

"Promise me you'll wait for me to handle intel from this end before applying for leave."

"I'll delay until tomorrow." She imagined Simon's response to her next requests. He'd probably quote the page and line of the law. "I want subpoenas to access all of Willis's financials. He offered $15,000 to Jason in exchange for information about Billie and Zack. Said he had the money in the trunk of his cruiser. I'm not saying the money was there, but . . ." She paced the floor. Since he had his money tied up locally, the bank might try to ignore the subpoena or draw a motion for a protective order.

"Doubt your request will be approved. You're not assigned to this case. Neither am I. Interfering in an investigation without clearance can get you in a lot of trouble."

"I prefer the term *undercover*."

"Sounds more like insubordination to me. I'll

do what I can to keep you in the loop. But I'm not doing a thing without approval. You can destroy your career, but I'm keeping mine intact." Simon sighed. "I assume you'll be using this new number until you return to Houston."

"Yes."

"Does Snyder think he can avoid us by using a burner?"

"He understands phones can be traced."

With the conversation over, she dropped her phone into her purse. She shuddered at the thought of what it would take to have the Snyders agree to FBI protection.

She drove the Snyders to Farmers' Bank in Sweet Briar since the car seat was in the Camry. Vicki rode in the rear with Isabella. April took in the surroundings, looking for the unusual or sinister.

"It's broad daylight," Ted said. "Do you really think Willis might pull something stupid in the middle of town?"

"I think you know the answer," she said.

They wordlessly entered the bank. Ted made his request to a customer service representative, and he and April were escorted to the safe-deposit box area. Ted used a bio-scan of his hand, entered a PIN, and inserted his key into the box. He opened a legal-size gray metal container. Sorting through envelopes and papers, he shook his head and repeated the process.

"The flash drive's gone," he said.

15

April saw staggering defeat on Ted's face. He gripped the edge of the table.

"Ted, who else has access to your safe-deposit box?" April said.

He swallowed hard. "Just me and Vicki."

Her mind spun with questions. Could someone have stolen it? Had she been deceived by all the Snyders? She chose her words carefully. "It's difficult but not impossible for a person to gain access to a safe-deposit box, anyone's safe-deposit box. If that person is determined, he'll find a way."

He dragged his hand over his face. "The PIN is kept in a file on my computer. A person could hack into our system and find it. But what about the key and our handprints?"

"Where's the key kept?"

"In a lockbox in my closet," Ted said.

"When was the last time either of you checked your safe-deposit box?"

"When I put the flash drive there. Two weeks ago."

"Do you have a list of everything kept in the box?" April said.

"At home."

"Okay. Good. Right now I suggest reporting the missing item to the bank manager."

Before she could say more, Ted appeared to have regained his composure. "I'll look at our list when we get home and compare it to what's here."

"Do you want to snap a few pictures of the contents?" April said.

He pulled out his phone. "The bank will have record of when the box's been opened, right? Their info could help us figure out who is responsible."

"Others could have missing items too. We could ask to see the security footage." The bank requesting a subpoena crossed her mind.

"Good idea. I've done business with this bank all my life and never had a problem."

In the bank's lobby, Ted told Vicki what he'd discovered.

She clung to Isabella as if for support. "This scares me, Ted."

"I'm not leaving until I have answers." He squared his shoulders and approached a teller and asked to see the bank manager. The four of them were ushered into a small, airy office where a young man who looked fresh out of college introduced himself as Vic Henley, the assistant bank manager. He invited them to sit. April stood while Vicki and Isabella took one seat and Ted eased onto another. The young man closed the door, and Ted outlined the situation.

"Sir, are you sure the flash drive was in the

box? Possibly you removed it and the matter slipped your mind." The young man tapped his fingers on the desk. A nervous habit?

Ted braced his hands on the arms of his chair. "I'm not senile or afflicted with dementia, sonny. I suggest you offer your assistance in getting to the bottom of my problem, or the bank and your insolence will be plastered across the media."

April held her breath to keep from laughing. *You go, Ted.*

"I apologize for sounding insensitive." Henley folded trembling hands. "No one could have gained access to your safe-deposit box without the three items you already mentioned."

"Then you won't have any problem showing me the records for my account."

Henley blinked. "I can look them up, and we can determine the last time you accessed the box."

"Here's my info." Ted gave him his financial information and driver's license for ID.

Henley typed into his desktop. Sweat beaded on his forehead in a room that registered sixty-four degrees. "A week ago, you were—"

"Not me," Ted said. "Now would be a good time to show me the camera footage."

"We can't do that, sir."

"This young woman here is FBI Special Agent April Ramos. I need her counsel." Ted peered up at her. "How should I proceed?"

She pulled her wallet from her shoulder bag and presented her FBI ID. "I can order a subpoena, or you can cooperate. Since it looks like the bank faulted on their commitment to security, it may be in your best interest to show us the footage."

"I need to check with my manager."

"By all means." She gave Henley a smile. After all, he was only doing his job.

The young man made the call, and at 5:15 p.m., after the bank doors were locked, he received permission. A few keystrokes, and he studied the screen before turning it for them to view. "This shows the entrance to the bank five minutes before the timestamp on your box's last access log. The man you're about to see signed in as Ted Snyder."

Ted and April gathered around the screen. Isabella fussed and Vicki tended to her. A man approached the scan. Slender build. Glasses. Heavy beard. Jeans. Boots. Baseball cap.

"Do you know him?" April said.

Ted shook his head. "Never seen him before." He bored a sharp gaze in Vic Henley's face. "Who's the employee who helped the imposter?"

Henley rubbed the back of his neck. "Mr. Snyder, I appreciate your concern. If you could give me until tomorrow noon to rectify this, I'm sure you'll have a full explanation of the issue."

Ted glanced up at April. "What do you think?"

"I suggest taking screenshots of the online records in case they're accidentally deleted."

Henley shook his head. "These belong to the bank."

Ted snorted and pulled out his phone. "Then close your eyes. Looks like you're good at it."

16

As April drove back to the Snyder home, she processed Vic Henley's body language and verbal responses as well as the missing flash drive. Someone broke the law to access Ted's safe-deposit box, and Henley's nervousness indicated he might know about it. Willis? According to Ted, the information on the flash drive was circumstantial . . . unless Willis feared other things were on it too. But how did someone even have an inkling to check the safe-deposit box?

"April," Ted said from the passenger side of the car, "when I first made note of Willis depositing $10,000 in four accounts, Vic Henley was the one who handled the transaction. He seems real shady to me."

"I'll look into it." April would have a private conversation with Mr. Henley in the morning. She formed a mental list of how to move forward. The who on the footage puzzled her because the man shared no resemblance to Willis Lennox or Vic Henley. How many players were involved in the murder and all that followed? Jason's false charges, Isabella's kidnapping, Ted's stolen flash drive?

Was all of this because Jason refused to tell Willis where his wife and son had fled to? Or was this just one more item on a list of other crimes?

After Ted took several screenshots of the freeze-frame showing the unidentified man, she'd sent the data to Simon. Her next and most difficult step was finding patience until the facial recognition software supplied answers. Ted and Vicki must have been reflecting on what they'd learned too because both were quiet.

Or too upset to speak.

At the Snyder home, Vicki baked potatoes and chicken breasts for dinner. April offered to help.

Vicki tossed a gentle smile over her shoulder. "When I'm facing a mental meltdown, I have to keep busy. Cooking allows me to think and pray. Takes my mind off myself. Since food's in the oven, I'm going to ready our baby girl for bed. You go ahead with whatever you need to do." Vicki faced her. "You're welcome to stay tonight, tomorrow night, until this is over. Ted and I want you here."

The invitation touched her. "Thank you. I'm not sure how long the investigation will last. It's not my call or my case. I asked for a few days off to rest up here in Sweet Briar, but I have to be mindful of creating a conflict of interest. In the meantime, show me the door when you're ready."

"Are you kidding? We'll drive you crazy first."

April requested a computer, and Ted brought the laptop from the bedroom to where she sat in the living room. He watched while she pulled up a browser, but she didn't mind. In his position, she'd do the same. Ted wanted to trust her as much as she wanted to believe him and Vicki.

"I'm going to check social media for a few of the people who are a part of this case. Posts, comments, and photos can provide insight."

"I saw a program on TV about how you folks figure out where to locate people and observe behavioral patterns by what people post on social media."

"Right. The FBI will comb through every inch of social media of those involved to look for potential leads, but I want to see a few things for myself."

"You're independent. Small but powerful, like dynamite." He pushed himself up to stand, but she stopped him.

"Sit with me. I don't mind, and I'm sure you can help." She logged onto Facebook to see if Jason had a profile for himself or Snyder Construction. Nothing. She navigated to Lily Snyder's page. A lovely blonde met her. Blue eyes, oval face. Isabella more resembled her father. The account had been inactive for over a year. No photos of the baby, only Lily and Jason. She wanted to see if Jason kept up the page, who'd commented, what was said negative or otherwise, and photos of friends for insight into the man accused of murder.

"We sure do miss our daughter-in-law," Ted

said. "She had a kind word for everyone she met. And when she laughed, the sound rang like a song." He sighed. "Vicki's on Facebook. You won't find any photos of Isabella. Jason won't allow it."

"I don't blame him. Too many predators out there."

"We faced one firsthand."

"I'm really sorry for all you've been through." April clicked to Vicki's Facebook page. Nothing there pointed to a problem. "Do Lily's parents live in the area?"

"They passed years ago."

April paused to think about others who might offer answers either directly or indirectly. She typed.

"Who are you searching for?"

"Willis Lennox, and as expected, he doesn't have an online presence. There's a website for the county sheriff's department. Nothing else. No links to any social media platforms." Later she'd check to see if Billie Lennox had an active online presence.

She pulled up Russell Edwards. "I can't remember his wife's name."

"Carrie."

April wanted a face-to-face with the woman who said Jason had threatened her husband. Willis's sister. Were they alike in temperament?

April's fingers flew across the keyboard. "I

can't find a thing with her name. I'm checking Deputy Kevin Viner, the first responder to Jason's 911 call."

"Fine man. He's the one who needs to be on the next ballot for sheriff."

April found little on Kevin, but his wife kept her Facebook page active. Lots of family photos and posts. None with Kevin in uniform. "She doesn't mention he's in law enforcement. A wise decision since they have children." April concentrated on the woman's other social media favorites.

Vicki announced dinner was ready, and April admitted the smells were more tantalizing than searching another online dead-end road. Later she'd work more on research. The day had thrown one surprise punch after another at her. And it wasn't over yet.

17

Jason stayed off the grid until darkness concealed him. He hid his truck in the woods two miles off a dirt road east of Sweet Briar and walked another half mile to Kevin Viner's home. The deputy's car and motorcycle were parked on the gravel driveway, and the family car was in the garage. Jason stood beside the barn, away from the pole light, and phoned him.

"This is Jason," he said when Kevin answered.

"Where are you?"

"Staying low. I need your help. You and Griff are the only ones who know the truth about Russell's death."

"Willis claims you assaulted him. Said you went crazy."

"And you believe him? You know I had nothing to do with Russell's murder. You were there."

"Doesn't mean you didn't go after Willis."

"Were there marks on him?" Jason remembered nearly strangling him earlier today.

"Jase, I didn't see a thing. Turn yourself in, and we'll get this straightened out."

"Don't play law enforcement on me. I need your crime report in my hands."

"Look, we're friends, but my first obligation is to the law and protecting others. For me to help,

I have to know what went down at the sheriff's office."

Jason explained Willis's accusation, arrest, and the release. "Willis set me up. The proof is in your report. Send me your and Griff's findings."

"Can't."

Jason had counted on Kevin's evidence. He watched the house. "Would you prefer a face-to-face?"

"Thinking about it."

"I'm out by your barn."

Jason ended the call and waited, hoping he hadn't set himself up for a trap. Kevin could be calling Willis now, bringing deputies in for backup. The front door slammed, and his old friend walked his way. Jason willed his nerves to settle, and when Kevin arrived, he emerged from the shadows.

"You're going to get us both killed." Kevin leaned against the side of the barn. "I could be arrested as an accomplice."

"Not unless Willis has sights on your place."

"Wouldn't put it past him."

The slip of doubt in Kevin's voice pushed Jason forward. "Where's the crime report?"

"Gave it to Willis."

"Complete?"

"Of course. Why ask such a ridiculous question?"

"He called me earlier. Told me the report didn't mention a broken window."

Kevin looked back at his house. Jason followed Kevin's gaze to where his wife sat at the table with their two young boys. "I have no idea if he tampered with my report and pics. Never thought he'd falsify a murder report."

"Have you been back to the construction office?"

He shook his head. "Willis said he'd handle the investigation."

Go figure. "I need the truth about Russell's death and why Willis lied."

Kevin wrapped his arms over his chest. "As much as I'd like to rid this county of Willis Lennox, I can't help you."

"Can't or won't?"

"And who will protect my family? You? A fugitive wanted by every law enforcement agency in the county?" Kevin stuffed his thumbs into his jean pockets. "Earlier this evenin' at my son's soccer practice, Willis showed up. He said, 'Pretty wife and two fine boys. A man has to protect what he loves, right, Kevin? Sometimes things happen, and a smart man will just ignore it.'"

Not a surprise, just regrettable. Jason had no means to protect Kevin's family when he doubted he could protect Isabella and his parents. The only possible help came from April and the FBI. He believed she cared for Isabella, but how far would she go to help him? "I get it, man. My daughter was kidnapped."

"And the same thing could happen to any of my family."

In the dim light, Jason bored his gaze into Kevin, taking note of the sweat on the man's forehead, wanting to read his heart and mind.

"I no longer have the crime scene pics. Willis asked for my phone when I turned in the report. Handed me a new one, said I deserved an upgrade."

"Did you send your report to anyone else?"

"Saw no reason to."

No evidence anywhere, except in Willis's possession. "The longer we allow him to break the law, the worse it gets."

"What have you done to Willis? What does he want?"

Jason attempted a casual shrug. "Who knows."

Kevin shook his head. "Run, Jason. Take your daughter and your folks and leave the area. He has your ranch covered on all sides. No one here in the Sweet Briar area has the guts to come forward, me included."

"Run? Put my family through living a fugitive's life? That's not me."

"If I could find the evidence to free you, I'd turn it over to the FBI. But I'm sure it's been destroyed."

"What happens the next time he pulls a stunt like this? Have you forgotten the missing charity money from the chamber of commerce? One of

128

my crewmen said Willis arrested him for fighting. Came back to the jail a couple of hours later and said he'd arranged bail. My crewman raised the money. Oddly enough, there wasn't a court date scheduled."

Kevin walked away, then swung around and took steps back to him. "I'll tell you this much. Our families' lives aren't worth trying to right a wrong. Get out of Tyler County before it's too late."

18

Jason walked toward the rear of Kevin's property, to where he'd left his truck. In the outlying area, absent of light or voices to call attention to him, he allowed his instincts to guide his path. Didn't mean Willis wasn't there too. Jason felt like a lone wolf surrounded by hunters.

Years ago when he and Willis were in high school, Willis wanted to go hunting at night. Jason agreed. Deer season kept every hunter itching for bragging rights. They camped at a deer stand on Willis's parents' ranch with food, two six-packs—courtesy of Willis—and more ammo than two kids really needed. They waited until a buck came into their sights.

"I got this," Willis had said.

"Your mom will have venison for a long time. Look at the rack on him. You can mount it over your bed."

Willis took aim, fired into the buck's head. Not once but repeatedly, until nothing remained of the animal but blood and body parts. Cruel and inhumane, a vile assault against an animal. Jason couldn't watch. The two beers he'd downed earlier soured his stomach.

"Why'd you blow him apart?" Jason said. "You had him on the first shot."

Willis laughed, a morbid sound that caused fear to ripple through Jason and made him cautious.

"I like watching the blood and guts fly everywhere," Willis said. "If I had a grenade, I'd have used it." He walked to the gory remains, kicking at what was left of the buck. "You gonna see this? It's incredible."

"No thanks." Jason packed up his stuff.

"Where you going?"

"Headin' home."

"Coward," Willis said.

Willis's morbid sense of pleasure confirmed why Billie must be protected. Jason returned to his truck and drove toward a place where he could rest and think. He rolled his windows down to better listen for the hum of an engine, telling himself Willis wanted him alive. But the reminder of how he'd killed the buck provided little comfort.

Although Kevin refused to help, he'd confirmed a few things, one being that only Willis had possession of the crime scene report. The other dealt with threatening Kevin's family, just like he'd done to Russell with the same persuasion techniques. But a motive escaped him. If Willis planned to pin a murder on Jason, why not choose someone who wasn't his brother-in-law?

Willis claimed he was covered during the shooting. Did he mean he'd paid an assassin?

Fear for Isabella rose. He needed her safely

out of the picture. As he tapped in April's phone number, his focus stayed glued on the dark ahead of him.

"This is April."

"Checking in," he said.

"I'm at your parents'. Are you okay?"

Was the concern in her voice genuine? "For the moment. How's Isabella?"

"She's asleep, and her bedroom window is locked."

"I'm worried about her. All of you."

"I can take care of myself."

His apprehension eased slightly. "Thanks. What's going on?"

"Your parents and I have been talking."

"Anything I should know?"

"Jason, I'm convinced of your innocence. But I disagree with how you're approaching things. Please, let the FBI handle the investigation."

The one question bombarding his mind sped ahead. "Have you been given an ultimatum to back off?"

Silence told him what he wanted to know.

"So—"

"Simon knows I'm not leaving this alone. I'm taking a few days off. Staying here in Sweet Briar tonight. I can't drive back to Houston and leave this dangling."

"Your confidence means a lot." He thought of saying more, but the FBI agent had touched his

132

bruised heart with the way she'd taken care of Isabella and seemingly believed in his innocence. "The law says I need evidence. When I find it, I'll comply with the FBI's wishes."

"You're not thinking rationally. You were nearly killed today. I heard Willis's threat. Look, I'm vested in this, and I'm sticking with it because of your daughter."

"Isabella is my priority, and I want her under federal protection."

"Let me get this straight. You want to find Russell's killer your own way without involving the FBI, except you'd like my help. Oh, and you're requesting the FBI to keep your daughter safe?"

Her words dripped with sarcasm, and he couldn't blame her, considering all he'd put her through. She believed in him, but she valued the law more. He respected that. "April, I can't find Russell's killer from the inside of a cell. Willis is behind this, and my daughter and my parents aren't safe. What would you do in my situation?"

"I don't know," she whispered. "I want answers like you do." She sighed. "Your dad plans to hide Isabella and Vicki in a secluded cabin."

"I'll talk to him again. My parents are a bit old-school and can be stubborn."

"It runs in the family."

He smiled despite the dire circumstances. "Can

you put my dad on the line?" A few moments later, Dad picked up the phone. "I want Isabella in a safe house as soon as possible. You and Mom, too."

"Your mom, yes. Me, no."

Jason wasn't in the mood to argue. "I've lost Lily, Russell, and almost Isabella. I'm not going to lose you, too."

"I know how to take care of myself."

"Dad, please—"

"Settled. Conversation ended."

Jason knew that tone, but this wasn't the last conversation they'd have about Dad leaving town. "All right. Put April back on." When she responded, he explained the conversation.

"I'm sorry. You can rest assured Isabella and your mother will be safe. I'll make the arrangements," she said.

"Is there anything else going on?"

She told him about the missing flash drive along with the unidentified man on the bank's security camera footage.

He wouldn't tell her right now that the original flash drive came from Billie, and he'd copied it but not seen its contents. "So Willis arranged to get his hands on the flash drive. I assume the FBI is working on facial recognition?"

"They are. You must watch a lot of TV."

"Guilty. Isabella goes to bed early, and I need to unwind."

"Can you and I meet to strategize our next move and plan how to keep your family protected?"

Cicada sounds filled the night. "I'll need to walk into town to avoid those watching the house."

"I have an idea," she said.

"You're the pro. Spell it out for me."

19

Through the shadowed living room window of the Snyder home, April spied a car pulling into the driveway. Sure enough, the woman who emerged from the driver's side was true to her word.

Vicki spread the drapes from one end of the massive window to the other. She snapped on two lamps. "We have nothing to hide. Let all of Willis's hired guns watch."

The doorbell rang and Ted answered. "Come on in, Miss Ella." His voice boomed like a Southern preacher's. "Always a treat to see you."

"With all the sad goings-on and the devil neck-deep in going after ones I love, I wanted to stop by and pray with you and Vicki."

He motioned for her to enter. "We could use it. Vicki's upset about the false charges filed against Jason."

He closed the door. The two had memorized April's script. She joined them in the foyer and greeted the older woman she'd met at the restaurant earlier today.

"Miss Ella, it's a pleasure to see you again." April reached out her hand, but the woman drew her into a hug. They were the same height.

"Glad to help. Praise God, He's using me to put Willis in his place. Jail. Maybe there he'll find Jesus and have eternity with Him instead of pleading for ice cubes in the other place."

April stifled a giggle. Miss Ella had determination etched into her lined face.

"What can this old woman do to help? I can pray about anything if God's in it. Had my own war room long before the movie."

"We can certainly use all the God help," April said. "What I'm wondering is if you'd change clothes with me, including your hat. And let me borrow your car."

Miss Ella clapped her hands. "Um. Um. You're one brave girl. 'Course we can do that. Makes me feel a bit like Rahab, helping out the spies for God, without the job description." She held up her finger. "First we pray. On your knees, little girl. You need divine help."

Awkward. Yet April knelt on the wood floor and folded her hands. How long had it been since she talked seriously to God other than a brief *thank You* or *help*?

"Dear Jesus, we're so glad You're with us. We can feel Your presence, and it's mighty powerful. We thank You for all the things You bring our way, the good and the downright ugly, so we can glorify Your name. You've given us a purpose, and we're saying yes to whatever You ask." Miss Ella continued for what seemed like thirty minutes. Finally an *amen* came from her lips.

Ted helped Miss Ella and his wife to their feet.

"Y'all can change in our bedroom," Vicki said. "Isabella's asleep in the guest room upstairs. Miss Ella, why don't you stay the night? Who knows when April will get back."

"No thanks. I need to get back home to my cat. She misses me when I'm gone."

It was nearly 11:55 when April emerged dressed like Miss Ella. The older woman refused to wear April's jeans and chose Vicki's floor-length bathrobe. The three planned to study the Bible together while April met with Jason. When given the opportunity, April intended to research Rahab and why he or she was important to Miss Ella.

"Without full light, you'll pass just fine for me," Miss Ella said. "Nothing you can do about your pale skin and skinny body."

Miss Ella gave April the keys to her 2011 Buick Regal. "It's a standard." She lifted a brow. "I assume you can drive it?"

"Yes, ma'am." April texted Jason to let him know everything was unfolding according to plan.

The car swung into action like a well-oiled trail bike, but a little smoother. She drove past the truck housing the deputy watching the house. He didn't even flash his lights, confirming he must trust Miss Ella to stay out of Willis's affairs.

Sweet Briar Community Church was nestled in the pine trees off Main Street. April parked in a specific spot, one Miss Ella had indicated. She shrugged Miss Ella's deep purse onto her shoulder and locked the Buick. She feigned an aching back and slowly made her way to the front door of the church. The night air blew chilly around her, and she held tight to Miss Ella's hat. The quiet disturbed her, like the calm in a horror movie just before the killer overpowered the victim. City noises were more familiar, but not the chorus of insects. Miss Ella's sensible shoes tapped on the five concrete steps leading to the double doors. The older woman had insisted April wear them for the complete costume. Using Miss Ella's key, April let herself inside the dark building and locked the door behind her. After several blinks, she gave up on adjusting to God's house of light.

"You could use a little help seeing in the dark," Jason whispered to the right of her. "Might want to consider training at Quantico. Heard they graduate some fine FBI agents."

The sound of his voice lightened her mood. Strange for her to admit or feel. "Be glad I knew you were here, or I'd have opened fire."

"Miss Ella is a crack shot."

"Are you serious?"

"She's walked away with first prize in the shooting competition for the past fifteen or so years. Donates her winnings to the church."

"No wonder I like her." She scanned the dark sanctuary. "By the way, who is Rahab? It was Miss Ella's analogy to helping us."

Jason laughed. "She was an Old Testament

prostitute who helped the Israelites. Those were God's chosen people."

"Oh, my."

"She ended up being in Jesus' lineage."

"Good to know. Is there a place we can talk and possibly have light?"

"In the back of the pastor's office. We'll take refuge in a closet."

"Your idea sounds rather covert. Except we have much to discuss, and I don't want a bullet sailing through a window." She thought about how Jason's friend had died. "I'm sorry I said that."

"It's okay. Both of us want to stay alive. Willis is a deacon and has a key. He'd have no problem shooting us at the altar." He took her arm. "You trust me, right? I grew up in this church. Know the creaks in the floor and how many pews until we take a right. I won't steer you wrong."

She hoped not. Or her career was dead for believing a fugitive, and she'd be spending the next three decades behind bars.

She took one blind step after another and noted the creaks in the floor, more like groans and complaints. They turned right, just as he'd said, and then left. Trust was a big thing. As much as she valued using logic, sometimes she reached conclusions that she simply couldn't back up with facts. Worse, she'd failed to think through where her fragile feelings for Jason and Isabella might lead.

"Hold on and I'll find the closet door."

"What if it's too small?"

"We'll snuggle."

This went beyond awkward. "Seriously?"

"Relax, Agent Ramos. It's a walk-in storage closet."

A click, and she knew he'd located it.

"Take three steps to the left, and you're in."

She obeyed like a submissive child.

Her psychology books held little info about hostage negotiators who swallowed a fugitive's story. She needed to proceed with caution and focus on her training. The guidelines expected a negotiator to use sound reasoning. Feelings never outweighed logic.

Within the closet's confines, light now flooded the area. Both side walls contained metal shelving with papers, books, and boxes upon boxes. All neat and labeled. Most had the letters *VBS* and a date.

April and Jason camped out on the carpeted floor. His nearness left the boundaries of awkward and transported her to uncomfortable. He was attractive, caring, and independent, but not her type. She preferred men who wore suits to work—business professionals—not a man who got his hands dirty for a living.

She pulled the laptop from Miss Ella's purse. She'd compiled a file there containing her notes and observations since taking on the case. She retrieved the report and typed in the date of her and Jason's closet meeting.

"First, the truck parked near your parents' home didn't follow me."

"You're brilliant. You must have taken strategy in college."

She shook her head, unable to conceal a smile. "Miss Ella is a keeper. Second, I have misgivings about Kevin Viner. Whose side is he on?"

Jason's light demeanor changed. "Tough call. Can't fault him for protecting his wife and kids. He's afraid for his family."

She replayed the motel scene with Kevin and his concern for Isabella. "Are you convinced he's *not* siding with Willis?"

"I'd like to be. With the way the past few days have gone, it's hard to sense the truth."

"Willis made a mistake by reporting you'd kidnapped Isabella and a federal agent. That brought in the FBI. My guess is Willis isn't happy the Feds are on this case. He did agree to meet with them on Monday."

"Is it a plus or a minus for my side?"

"Hard to say." She poised her fingers over the keyboard. "A few things more. Did Kevin make a copy of the original crime scene report before handing over his phone to Willis?"

"He didn't see a need. Remember, this is a small town."

April scrutinized him, a man risking his life

to right a series of wrongs. She went over what she'd documented. "Have you told me everything about you and Willis?"

"Actually, I don't know."

Honest but of no help. "Where's the note threatening Isabella?"

"Tossed it."

She frowned. "Promise me if you receive anything else, you'll give it to me."

"Will do my best."

"I'm going to type and talk. Correct me if I make a mistake. These are the CliffsNotes." She paused. "Russell requests a meeting with you. You meet with him, and he's killed before he gives you information about why Willis threatened his family. You're arrested for murder. Willis then releases you, and you learn your daughter was kidnapped. Willis tells law enforcement you escaped jail and are armed. He adds kidnapping charges to the mix. I come into the picture with Isabella. We're on the road together. At the motel, Willis claims he'll make the charges disappear and offers cash if you tell him where to find Billie and Zack. What's the story behind his wife and son? You indicated there'd been some abuse, but what are the specifics?"

He ran his fingers through his hair. "How much do you want to know in one sitting?"

20

April wanted to know every detail about Willis, Billie, and Zack, but not at midnight. Although she craved all the information to help end a crime, only a fool attempted to deny rest.

"Short version," she said. "She's left him, taken their son, Zack, and since you helped them escape, Willis believes you know where they are—his contention with you."

"Right. Vengeance is mine, says Willis."

"Are they alive?"

Silence invaded their space.

"I haven't seen them since I drove her and Zack to Dallas, where they boarded a plane for Chicago."

"When?"

"Six weeks ago."

"Were you two having an affair?"

His jaw clenched, and he stared into her face. "Not hardly. We were friends from before she and Willis got together. Billie came by the construction office with Zack. He'd blacked her eye and broken Zack's arm in a series of abuse incidents. Hurting her son was the breaking point. I followed them to Tyler County Hospital."

The more April learned about Willis, the more she wanted him put away. "What happened then?"

"At the hospital, she claimed her and Zack's injuries were due to a bicycle accident." His features clouded. "The hospital would have the records. A nurse questioned her. I gathered she'd been there for treatment a few times because the woman knew her by name. Billie stuck to her story."

"I'll subpoena those records and request an interview with the nurse and doctor who treated her. So no charges were filed?"

"With Willis as county sheriff? The next time he'd kill her. I'm sure the medical staff realized the circumstances."

April tamped down the anger surging through her veins. "She asked you to drive them to the airport?"

"We drove partway in separate cars. She left her car on a back road and called me to pick them up. On the way to Dallas, we stopped at Walmart and bought a change of clothes and a few other things. She also bought a burner phone." He thought for a moment. "From her actions, she'd been working on a plan for a while. She smashed her original phone and made flight reservations to Chicago on mine. I let her use my credit card, and she paid me in cash. Guess Willis could have accessed my cell phone records to learn that information. I promised to keep her secret." He hesitated.

"What are you not telling me?"

"Billie is the one who gave me the flash drive. Told me to keep it safe and take a look only if Willis was ever arrested for something serious or she ended up dead. I have the original, and Dad had the copy."

"Why didn't you see what was on it?"

"I assumed the contents were photos or documentation of Willis's beatings. She voiced repeatedly her fear of him. Now I see I was really stupid."

April put the pieces together. "The same missing flash drive from your parents' safe-deposit box." When he nodded, she continued. "But we're trying to bring justice to Sweet Briar so she doesn't have to hide."

"Still seems like I betrayed her confidence."

"Does she have family or friends in Chicago?"

"Not to my knowledge." He brushed his hand over his face. "She wanted no means for Willis to trace her. I remember she was amazingly calm."

April understood, a part of fight or flee for victims. "What about her family?"

"Her parents and Willis's retired to Florida together. Longtime friends. Billie has a sister my age who left Sweet Briar years ago and teaches school in North Carolina."

"Name?"

"Gwen Scottard, married to a guy she met in college. Went to Rice University in Houston. And before you ask, Billie called Gwen on the way to

146

the airport on my phone. Must have gotten voice mail. Told her she'd left Willis."

"Who told Willis you'd helped her?" April said.

"No idea. Could have been someone on the construction crew, in the hospital, or even at Walmart. A few guys were in the warehouse when she arrived."

"Russell?"

"He was on a job. Russell and Willis weren't exactly friends."

"Willis might have viewed the security cam footage at the hospital or talked to staff there, who could have given your description."

"True. When I think about it, Chicago might not have been her final destination. This whole mess is tangled, complicated."

"But we're determined to unravel it."

"I wish I had solid answers for you." He snorted. "I'd like to have the truth about all this myself."

"It will come, Jason. When you and Willis were alone at the motel, did he say anything specific?"

"Nothing we can use or haven't already heard."

"Does he have any close friends, someone who might have insight?" If only she could talk to Billie . . .

"He has a lady friend. Her name's Brenda Krew, owns Krew Real Estate. Could be something there."

She typed the info into her document. "I'll

handle an interview with her tomorrow. What's she like? Are she and Willis involved?"

"Friends only. She's older. All business. Hard to read."

She tapped her chin with her finger. "You said he's a deacon. He does the charitable community thing too?"

"You're a fast learner for a city girl. Brenda and Willis are on the same community and church committees. Do the orphan and widow care ministry."

"How spiritual." Those who professed to be Christian while living hypocritical lives cemented her dissatisfaction with faith. "Looks like a solid front to the citizens."

"Some know better, and others need what he and Brenda offer. Neither of the two have many friends, except for each other. She doesn't care for me, and I assume Willis has filled her head with lies. You'll have an opportunity to use your negotiation skills with her."

"I welcome a challenge." She told him about requesting information regarding Willis's political life. "Not so sure I'll get it. Your dad believes Willis buys or threatens voters. Can't you oust him? Not everyone in this county could be afraid of him or need a handout."

He grimaced. "I'm a coward for not doing something about him until now. I thought as long as he ignored me and my family, I'd go about my life."

"Has he always been this way?"

"Yep. But his actions escalated while serving as sheriff. Power does that to a man."

Maybe in Jason's shoes she'd have done the same thing. Newly married. Then a year of raising Isabella alone and mourning the loss of his wife—it would take a chunk out of anyone's priorities. A question burned into her mind. "What can you tell me about Vic Henley?"

"Works at the bank?" When she nodded, he continued. "Why?"

"Curious. Seemed very nervous today and then I learned he handled Willis's deposit, the one your dad witnessed." She didn't want to discuss the matter any more until she talked to Henley in the morning. "Hey, another task for tomorrow is I'm taking a look at your office."

"I'm heading there tonight."

"Have you lost your mind? You know Willis has your office staked."

"Beats walking in at daylight. I have night-vision goggles. Use them for night hunting."

She tilted her head. "You shouldn't go alone." She looked at her blue cardigan, pearls, and black dress. "I guess I have no choice but to go dressed like this."

"Looks cute on you. Ever work undercover?"

"Not until I met you. Look, I've gone along with your antics until now. My instincts are shouting 'no' at a late-night visit to the scene of the crime."

"I'm still checking it out. Besides, if you're caught snooping around a crime scene with a fugitive, you could lose your job and do jail time."

Alone, he could walk into a trap. But her accompanying him had stupidity stamped on it. "Postpone the walk-through until tomorrow. We're both exhausted. Things could change, and don't forget your family's safety."

"My family's safety is exactly why I need to see things for myself."

"If you'll wait until the FBI arrives on the scene, and they will, I'll see about meeting them there. Just tell me what to look for."

"Look, I'm going. Willis claimed the window wasn't broken. I have to see for myself. The stop won't take thirty minutes. I want to see if anything's missing and check my safe."

Arguing with Jason Snyder was pointless. He'd venture into the firing range with or without her. Where had her sound judgment escaped to? With a phone call, she reached out to Ted and asked to speak to Miss Ella. Once permission had been granted to keep the Buick a little longer, she slipped her phone into Miss Ella's purse.

Jason switched off the closet light, and the tension between them knocked at her logic. "When this is over, I'd like to take you to—"

"Don't say it," she said.

He chuckled.

She shivered. He sensed the same attraction.

21

Jason lifted a rear window from the pastor's office that faced the graveyard. His gun was in his waistband behind his back, and he prayed it stayed right there. After his eyes adjusted to the darkness, he climbed out and crept to the east side of the church, where April had Miss Ella's car idling. He gently opened the front passenger door of the car and crouched low.

"Head to Main Street and turn right out of town."

"Where is your truck?" she said.

"Five miles beyond the city limits, not too far from my construction office."

"Nice long walk. How's the migraine? Forgot to ask earlier."

"Imitrex nailed it." A nagging throb persisted at the base of his skull, but he wouldn't mention it. He'd take more meds when they finished tonight's errands.

"Neither of us can continue at this pace without sleep."

"We've become nocturnal. Bats, owls, coons, coyotes, possums. There's a lot of us."

"And bad guys, give or take a few."

His thoughts about Russell's murder, Isabella's kidnapping, and the charges against him screamed unfair, as though God were against him. He dug his fingers into his fists and prayed that his desire for vengeance against Willis would dissipate. "Thanks for talking me down with Willis. If not for you, I'd have killed him."

"It's part of my job as a negotiator, remember?"

"To have such a rough beginning, we get along most of the time."

"About 30 percent. You can crawl up from the floorboard. Nothing but black countryside out here."

He gave her directions to the dirt road where his truck was nestled deep in thick brush.

"Jason, have you told me everything about the night Russell was killed?"

"Think so. But I must have forgotten something," he said. "Willis threatened Russell, and while I don't know for sure, it has to be about finding Billie and Zack. Have you run backgrounds on all the deputies?"

"I sent the request to Simon. But since I'm not working in an official capacity, I may be delayed in receiving the info or anything at all. The FBI has a resource called the FIG—Field Intelligence Group. The techs have access to security intel. If there's anything out there on Willis or his deputies, they'll find it. The problem is if I'm able to access it."

"By now, I'm sure my name is deep in their trenches as a suspect in a murder case and nabbing a federal agent." Jason thought through the years of small-town living with Willis. "How about later I write down what I can remember about Willis over the past few years. You can send it to Simon. Have him analyze it."

"I like you." She flashed a smile his way. "I mean the way you process things."

He chuckled. "I'm trying to shove emotion out of the way and look at Willis like he's a house to build with far too many structural demands. His support beams are his weak spots."

"You majored in architecture and what else?"

"Ready for this?"

"Sure. I asked, didn't I?"

"Greek, Hebrew, and Arabic. Thought I might be an interpreter or translator, but I sensed God wanting me to build homes and shape character through day-to-day living." He shrugged. "So here I am in Sweet Briar."

"The FBI could use your skills."

"Fugitive turned agent?" He laughed, and it momentarily released the tension.

"Does anyone really know you?"

A hint of sadness settled. "Lily."

"I bet you'll find a woman to love again."

"Maybe if I'm not scared off." He instructed her to take a series of turns. "Take this tractor path on the right. Watch, there's a ditch. No headlights." When she'd driven the short distance, he asked her to stop. "I'm going to retrieve the night-vision goggles from my truck. Will take about ten minutes."

"I'll contact Simon while you're gone."

"For updates?" He hesitated. Hostage negotiators performed their jobs well because they knew how to gain the fugitive's confidence. She disagreed with him on not allowing the FBI to handle the investigation. Her words of belief could be a ploy. "What if I asked for your phone? Would you argue?"

April dug into Miss Ella's purse for the burner phone. She held it out to him. "I've already bent the law for you. If I haven't arranged for the FBI to pick you up by now, don't you think I can be trusted?"

He swallowed hard. Was he being smart or alienating his best ally? "Keep it. I'll call or text if there's a problem."

"I'd rather go with you."

"Sorry. If both of us are shot, who's going to get the truth out?" He left the car and jogged across the fall grasses leading into a pine grove where he'd hidden his truck. His body protested the hour after hour of stress. How long did he expect the adrenaline to flow? Without rest soon, the migraine had reason to stop him cold again.

Using the flashlight app on his phone, he explored the surroundings and wove his way to his truck. After retrieving the goggles, he shut down the light and walked back to April. This time he took over driving to the construction office. "What did Simon say?"

"He didn't pick up. I checked Google Earth while you were gone. The ground around your office is open, flat," she said. "There are no woods either. Where do we hide the car?"

"I'm having you park about a mile down from the office to wait for me."

"Jason, I'm a trained agent." Her tone piled on a ton of irritation. "What makes you think you have expertise to handle an ambush?"

"It's enough to say I grew up hunting and tracking. Avoiding being detected by an animal is no different from outsmarting Willis."

"I've seen where that's gotten you." She punched each word.

"April, I'm through putting your life in danger."

"You need backup. Any other move is ludicrous. I've been in these kinds of situations before."

"Don't pull the investigator card. Won't work."

"I came to help, and you deceived me."

"You figured out my plan when you saw the terrain. I'm going alone."

She lifted her chin, and he'd have laughed if the circumstances had been different.

"All right. I'll make a concession," he said. "Give me ten minutes to get there and about fifteen to look around. I want to check my office floor and outside for glass. Also see if the office's been compromised. Then I'll text you."

"That means in twelve minutes I'm walking your way."

"Twenty-five, and I'll text."

"Twelve minutes."

He gave up and drove past the office. It looked deserted. Nearly a mile down, he turned left and parked the car on a grass and dirt road. He switched off the lights. "Keep an eye out."

She flashed him her disapproval. He ignored her and climbed a fence to a pasture bordering one side of his warehouse. The fence also housed the orneriest bull this side of Texas. He wanted neither the bull's horns nor a bullet in his backside.

He needed to hurry before April decided to follow him sooner than his instructions. The only way to get past the guilt of blaming himself for Russell's death was to dig up the evidence Willis thought he'd buried. The Beretta tucked into the back of his jeans waistband felt foreign. Would he use it if necessary? A decision he didn't want to make.

Jason jumped the fence beside his construction warehouse. The building and surrounding area still appeared deserted. If anyone lay in wait, they were invisible in his night-vision goggles.

Dread hit him—Willis might have changed the locks on his office. Or reset the alarm.

He no longer had his original phone with the alarm company's app. But he had a master pass-word memorized. Thank goodness he had connectivity. He downloaded the app on the burner phone and logged into the alarm system. Sure enough, Willis or someone had changed some settings. How had Willis obtained access . . . unless Russell had given it to him?

Jason pushed the goggles back on his head and made modifications to remove all codes except his foreman's. The FBI already had this number, so what did it matter to download the app? Too late to rethink his actions. He'd toss this phone for the third burner later. Entering his own business could backfire. He stole around his warehouse to the rear door of his office. After inserting the key into the lock, he turned the knob.

Quiet greeted him, confirming he'd successfully disabled the alarm via the app.

Using a flashlight from his office drawer, he checked the broken window. Repaired, as he expected. How had someone located a piece of glass this size and replaced it late at night? Another critical piece of the crime. He checked his desk drawer and found it a disorganized mess. Shining the light onto the concrete floor, he saw it had been swept clean. He brushed his fingers near the floor and the wall. No glass slivers. Jason turned to where Russell had fallen. His breath caught. The dark stains on the floor brought it all back, a hideous reminder of blood first spewing from Russell's arm and the second bullet exploding into his chest.

He shone the flashlight on the wall where the first

bullet had entered and ran his fingers over the area. A slight indentation revealed the hole had been patched and painted. Moving to the office closet, he found the patching compound and paint can were not sitting on the storage shelf but on the floor.

Willis or whoever had killed Russell might think he could walk free with a flawless plan, but arrogance paved the way for mistakes.

Jason stood from the cold floor. For a moment yesterday afternoon, he'd doubted his faith. Why would God take Lily and Russell and endanger Isabella? So many things he didn't understand. For certain, God had used April to stop him from destroying not only Willis's life but his own. Never again.

Help me to honor You. And make decisions so no one else is hurt.

An empty space beside his file cabinet indicated his safe was missing. Whoever swiped it would only find his business licenses and five hundred dollars in ten- and twenty-dollar bills, used to help out some of his crew when the stretch between paychecks and poor money management left their families without necessities.

He'd text April to join him once he double-checked no one had walked up while he was inside. Leaving the office through the rear, he remotely set the alarm and stayed in the shadows. Eeriness nipped at his heels.

"Jason. Put your hands up."

22

Jason planted his feet on the sidewalk leading to the driveway and raised his hands. "Kevin, are you sure you want to fall into the same sty as Willis?"

"Listen, you fool. I'm trying to keep you alive. Figured if I stuck around here long enough, you'd be stupid enough to show up. So I waited. You just had to see for yourself the evidence's gone."

Jason heard the wariness in Kevin's voice. "Can I turn around? Or are you here to take me in?"

"Haven't decided. Put that gun on the ground. Then keep your hands above your head."

"We're friends. We share the same faith." He lowered his hands to his thighs and slowly faced Kevin. "Or you'd have shot me when I jumped the fence."

"Your stubbornness is going to get you killed."

"Is this how you want to pave the future for your sons? Have them afraid of the law? Worse yet, pick up Willis's torch and follow in his footsteps? 'Cause it won't get any better."

"My family means everything to me." Kevin's voice dropped a notch. Fear crusted his words.

"Send them away. Tell Willis I threatened them."

Kevin clenched his fists. "I've already stepped over the line. He has eyes everywhere. Ordered your place searched, though I know he didn't find a thing."

"Where is he now?"

"Drove to Woodville. Said he had a meeting with his attorney before giving additional testimony to the FBI in Houston."

The gnawing problem persisted. Kevin showed up at too many scenes . . . always urging Jason to turn himself in. The suspicion cut raw into his heart and mind. "Does Willis have other men on his payroll?"

"Who knows."

"Remember our senior year when we played Woodville for district? Willis got vertigo. Couldn't stand up. We thought we'd lost the title, but we played and won the championship. Without him."

"You made your point. My family is my life. I'm not doing a thing that might get one of them hurt."

"How about talking to the FBI?"

"Willis has a way of eliminating trouble-makers—and keeping his hands clean in the process. Enough of this. Find anything in your office?"

"New window. Swept floors. Patched wall. Missing safe."

"I have no idea who cleaned up the crime scene."

"You were there!" Jason tried to shove the exhaustion mixed with bitterness into some place manageable. Instead he mushroomed with the injustice sprouting up like weeds. Jason breathed in and out. "You told me to take Isabella and hide. Are you going to look the other way again when he intimidates or kills the next person?"

"What's he want from you?"

"I'm not giving that up."

"Must be about Billie and Zack. Do you know where they are?"

Was Kevin attempting to be one step ahead of Willis or betraying Jason? "No clue. Are you going to help me put Willis behind bars?"

Kevin gestured to the once-broken window. "Show me how when everything I have is at risk."

"Isn't God bigger than Willis?"

"I can't stretch myself any more than I already have."

"At least talk to an FBI agent who can bring justice to our families and those we care about."

"Justice doesn't mean a thing if my family's dead."

☆ ☆ ☆

Something had gone wrong with Jason's plan. She'd decided to wait eight minutes, but the time had passed on to ten. He said it would take him ten minutes to walk to his office. April texted

161

him, and when he didn't respond, she drove Miss Ella's Buick past the construction office. A light mounted on a tall pole outside a warehouse revealed only buildings. She drove back to the original spot, pushed the clutch, downshifted, and parked.

Leaving the wide-brimmed hat resting on the seat, she grabbed her Glock and hurried to the pasture. If Jason found it necessary to move along the inside of the fence, she'd do the same. The lack of stars and a cloud-hidden moon concealed any animals, though she assumed there were none. Tugging up on the barbed wire while bending to crawl through it in Miss Ella's dress and SAS shoes, stuffed with Charmin, brought back memories of physical challenges at Quantico. A fence in East Texas should be a piece of cake. As long as she didn't rip any of Miss Ella's clothing.

She managed a brisk pace, listening for ominous sounds, like a stirring of activity at the construction office and warehouse ahead. At the first sign of a headlight, she'd drop to the ground. Her phone vibrated, and she stopped to check it. A report from Simon about Willis Lennox. Good, she must have received clearance. She would read it once she confirmed Jason hadn't gotten into trouble.

A rustling and a snort caused her to whirl around. What in the world? Her fingers found the light on her phone. A bull with horns a yard wide snorted behind her and was gaining speed.

April stifled a scream and raced to the fence. She stumbled, the shoes hindering every step. Kicking them off, she kept her momentum. Needlelike brush pierced her feet and caused her to wince. Something squishy eased up between her toes. The bull heaved closer, his hooves pounding into the ground. The dratted dress tangled between her legs. If given the opportunity, she'd jerk it over her head and hurl it at the bull. She spotted the outline of the fence.

Just a few more feet.

No way would her obituary read she'd died of a bull attack while aiding a fugitive in East Texas.

She reached for the fence post. The barbed wire tore at her hands and legs. Miss Ella's dress ripped. Still she scaled the fence much faster than she'd slithered through it. The bull stopped short of the fence, his hooves grinding his agitation and his massive body pushing against the structure intended to keep him in and idiots out. For a moment, she feared he might topple the fence and continue his pursuit.

She left him to his distress, but her flesh stung. A horrid smell met her nose, and she realized what she'd stepped in. After cleaning her feet on the rough grasses, she picked up her original pace to find Jason—outside the fence.

What a story—full of bull.

Clearing her mind and willing her pulse to

decelerate, she focused on taking her stance beside the warehouse. Stones dug into the bottoms of her feet and slowed her progress. She crept along the side of the building, to the corner at the rear. Silhouettes showed two men. Once closer, she recognized Jason's build. He stood with his back to her and faced a second man, Kevin Viner. They appeared to be alone. Drawing her weapon, April bent and crept closer behind Jason.

"I understand what you're saying," Kevin said with his gun holstered. "If it were only me involved, I'd be helping you hide and searching for the evidence you need."

"Kevin, you've made three commitments in your life—to Jesus, to your wife, and to uphold the law. Which of these dictate blindly following Willis's lead?"

April questioned if Jason should be a politician or a preacher.

"I need a favor," Jason said.

"Better be an easy one."

Jason shifted to one leg. "Find out who replaced the window."

"Are you deaf? Haven't you heard a single thing I've said?"

April chose to speak up. "Deputy Viner, stand down."

"Who's out there?" Kevin pulled his gun.

"Drop it nice and easy," she said. "We've met."

164

She took cautious steps with her gun on target. When Kevin obliged, she walked toward him. "What side of the law do you walk on, Deputy?"

"I'm wearing a badge."

"Your allegiance to the laws governing this land are in question."

Kevin blew out an exasperated breath. "I could say the same to you."

"Is there any doubt how many FBI agents are actively working to unlock this case?" April said. "Now, are you on the side of right or a greedy sheriff?"

"Great question considering you're taking the side of a fugitive."

"Really? You're not concerned your original crime scene investigation report has essentially disappeared and could have been tampered with?"

"My family's lives swing in the balance."

"We can arrange a safe house for them."

Kevin stared at her, motionless. "If you can assure me my wife and sons will be out of the line of fire until this is over, I'll help. I saw the broken window and did my part in recording evidence."

23

The smell of a cow patty squashed between April's toes rose in the confines of Miss Ella's car. So out of her element. Jason drove and had the heat on, which made the odor permeate the Buick.

"Jason, you reek of manure," Kevin said.

"It's not him, but me." April so appreciated the darkness. "I'm barefoot and stepped in it."

"Where are your shoes?" Kevin said from the backseat. "Should you go back for them?"

Jason swung to her. "And why are you barefoot when you were wearing Miss Ella's shoes?"

Embarrassment at the memory of what happened in the pasture swept through her. ". . . After I stepped in the manure, I vaulted the fence and ripped the side of Miss Ella's skirt. For sure, we need the bull on our side."

Laughter broke the wall of stress, and she felt it.

"You met Romeo," Jason said. "He's the construction crew's mascot."

"Just don't get in his way," Kevin added. "Better get rid of the smell before you return the car. Miss Ella treasures this Buick."

Jason drove Kevin to his motorcycle parked about three quarters of a mile in the opposite direction of where he and April had left the car. In the darkness, the three discussed the transition of securing Kevin's family in Houston. April had contacted Simon and arranged for a safe house. Thankfully he'd agreed without hesitation. An SUV was en route to Woodville, where agents would provide an armed escort to an undisclosed location.

She questioned why Kevin's family were immediately whisked away while Jason hadn't received a time for Isabella and his mother to be escorted to a safe house.

"I'm feeling better about the arrangement," Kevin said after ending a call to his wife. "She's packing and telling the boys they're going on a little vacation with no school." He paused, possibly thinking about the separation. Or perhaps his commitment to bring down Willis. At least April hoped those were his thoughts.

"She'll leave a note stating she's leaving and taking the boys. She'll say something about finding out I was having an affair. I'll keep the note in my wallet in case Willis wants to see it."

April formed her words carefully. "I know his wife left him and took their son. If needed, use it as a conversation topic."

Kevin breathed in and out. "He's been a worse pain ever since."

"You've made the right decision," she continued. "I can't imagine the worry you have for your family."

"Their safety has been a huge burden on my

shoulders, especially after Isabella's kidnapping." Kevin's higher-pitched voice revealed his anxiety. "This whole thing makes me wonder if I've lost my senses. Willis never backs down."

"Your family will be okay," April said. "You heard me give the FBI your wife's cell phone number. You simply stay out of sight until she leaves."

April deliberated Kevin's every word. Jason valued his friendship, but the skepticism of his friend's loyalty weighed heavily. She would need to be wise in her discernment. "How many do you think are on Willis's payroll?"

"I can only speculate. Possibly the deputy you met outside the hotel, Griff Wilcombe. Arrived in Sweet Briar about a year and a half ago. Lives in a duplex. No family. Sticks to himself."

"Cal Bunion is parked near my parents'," Jason said. "He could just be doing his job, following orders, though. Never saw anything out of him that pointed to breaking the law. Any others?"

Kevin shook his head. "This hasn't exactly been a topic of deputy conversations." He took a quick look at his watch. "Are Ted and Vicki taking Isabella to Woodville? Thought they could keep my wife and boys company."

"We've made different plans," Jason said.

"Moving Isabella the same night your family disappears would give Willis reason to enlist damage control on you," she said.

"You're right. Maybe they can catch up in Houston later on."

Not until she and Jason knew without a doubt Kevin spoke the truth.

Kevin lifted the handle on the rear passenger side of the car with a click. "Thanks to both of you for persuading me to see things your way. I'm not ashamed to say I'm scared. Been used to Willis calling the plays for as long as I can remember."

"Think district championship," Jason said, and April wondered what he meant.

"How do we stay connected?"

"Pick up a burner." She hoped her advice didn't backfire.

"Probably more than one. If Willis suspects me, he'll find a way to trace what I'm doing." Kevin exited the car, and Jason turned on the engine and drove away, the sound of gravel kicking up under the tires.

She watched Kevin disappear in the darkness. "Do you trust him?"

"I want to. I'd like for him to think we have no reservations. You heard some of the conversation with Kevin at the construction office. Guess we'll know soon." He turned onto a tractor path.

"There's a No Trespassing sign."

"No worries."

Miss Ella's Buick bounced along the bumpy trail. "I'll request Kevin's cell phone records and

169

hope I get them." She yawned. "We can't function well until we get some sleep." She arched her shoulders to stay awake.

"I'll sleep in my truck."

"Is it well hidden?"

"Yes, and the property owner's in a nursing home."

The headlights illuminated a path through the woods. Creepy. "Don't get Miss Ella's car stuck."

He chuckled. "Last words of advice?"

"Call me when you wake up."

"I have spotty connectivity out here, so keep trying if I don't answer. Texting may be best."

"I should have additional intel to review by morning. Simon sent something to me when I was outrunning Romeo." She faced reality. *This could go south if I'm refused. Always been a rules girl* . . . In the darkness she smiled into his face. "Don't do anything stupid until we talk."

"You sure are bossy."

"I haven't even gotten started. Be careful," she said.

"Me? You're the one who lost Miss Ella's shoes and tore her dress."

She covered her mouth, but a giggle slipped through her lips. Whether it be hysteria or sleep deprivation taking its toll, she laughed.

"Whoa," he said. "Let me see your hands." He flipped on the dome light. She reluctantly showed the scrapes she received climbing over the barbed wire. "You're bleeding. Make sure Mom cleans you up."

She jerked back her hand. His touch had been a little unsettling. "I'm a big girl, and I know how to use hydrogen peroxide and Band-Aids."

"Right. Be careful driving back to Sweet Briar. If the FBI orders you to return to Houston, don't argue." He looked away, then back to her. "We've barely met, but I know enough to say I don't want you hurt."

April chose not to respond.

24

When April wakened on Saturday, the shades in Isabella's room were pulled tight, giving no indication of the time. April had slept on a twin bed in the guest room wearing a borrowed gown from Vicki. Her attention whipped to the empty crib. She'd heard neither Isabella stir nor Vicki enter the room to get her. Blinking away the fog in her head, she rose to open the bedroom door and discerned Vicki talking to Isabella downstairs.

She breathed relief.

April crawled back into bed and reached for her phone on the carpeted floor beside her: 10 a.m. Exhaustion had sealed her off from the rest of the world. A quarter of the day wasted. Her phone contained no new texts from Jason or Simon.

She remembered Simon had sent a report about Willis last night. Leaning back on the pillow, she opened the document and scanned it for the most critical information. She'd prefer a jolt of caffeine before studying it, but not this morning.

Willis Lennox had been elected for two consecutive terms as sheriff of Sweet Briar, taking office at twenty-eight years old. Young for a sheriff. Three reports of misconduct during his tenure as deputy and then sheriff with charges dismissed. Wife and son at unknown address. The report read like an employer background check. She could have obtained this with a Google search. What elements in Houston were keeping the brakes on?

Blowing out her irritation, she moved on to what Simon had sent regarding Jason. If her involvement had been approved, she was sure she'd have received clarification and in-depth information. She enlisted patience when working hostage negotiation, but she had little of it when needing critical data. She read on.

Jason Snyder's ranch held no mortgage. He'd lived in Sweet Briar since birth. Widower. One child. No military service. No arrests. The background lined up with what he'd told her and she'd found out on her own.

What Simon hadn't said about the case spoke louder than his instructions to send all her findings to him. He wanted her in Houston. She pressed in Simon's number.

"Mornin', April. Are you on the road?"

"Still in bed. What's the verdict? I saw the sparse report on Willis and Jason."

"You walked into a hornet's nest. There's more to this case than what you've uncovered. At this point, I'm obtaining intel about what's going on with Sheriff Lennox. As of right now, you haven't received clearance. But as a favor, I'm working on it. The SAC headed to DC last night with our supervisor. Said they'd get back with me on Monday. Sit tight."

"Monday?" What was going on? "Are you confirming this is about Willis's illegal activities and Jason is innocent?"

"The matter is under investigation. We've learned Sheriff Lennox neglected to file Snyder's release from jail. It's the sheriff's word against Snyder's. Give me time to talk to the agents working the case. See if I can expedite clearance. Stay safe and watch your back. Take a walk. Rest. Go fishing. Agents will be in contact to take the Snyders into protective custody early afternoon. Probably around 2 p.m."

"Thanks for arranging it. Talk to you soon." She definitely planned to go fishing, but not with a pole.

The call ended, and she received a text with additional info on the crime scene investigation report, which had come from Willis's office. Two bullets were fired. One hit Russell Edwards's shoulder. The bullet killing Edwards was fired into his chest. Ballistics indicated it was most likely fired from a Smith & Wesson 640, but not at close range, and the weapon hadn't been located. According to Jason, the two men were standing together when the shooting occurred.

She read further. No claims of a broken window. Signed by Sheriff Willis Lennox and Deputy Kevin Viner. She wanted a signature comparison for Kevin. What happened to the original report? Obviously destroyed, but who'd gotten rid of it? Willis? Kevin? Or another person?

She'd risk a "no" from Simon and request a list of those who'd run against Willis in the elections. Even if she had to wait until Monday for the results. She typed swiftly, asking for the details about the charges filed against him and dropped—looking for insight into his intimidation methods. Her need for info kept her fingers flying. Now to find the time to research it all and hope her leave in Sweet Briar became a sanctioned investigation.

She called Jason. He answered, groggy. "This is crazy. It's after ten," he said.

"I'm behind too," she said. "How'd you sleep?"

"Like a man who'd been up for too many hours."

She smiled. "I learned a few things." She told him about some of her conversation with Simon.

"Kevin said when he asked to see the report, Willis denied him. But you said two signatures were on it." He paused. "Have you received backgrounds on every deputy?"

"Nothing yet. Griff Wilcombe is a mystery man here."

"I'd never met him until Russell's murder, when he showed up with Kevin. I have lots of work to do."

"You aren't stepping foot from your hideout

without me." She shook her head at his assuming power over the investigation. As soon as she could shower and track down something clean to wear . . . "I'll let your parents know about the protective custody arrangements. What can I bring you?"

"Clean jeans and a shirt—Dad's will do. I'd appreciate coffee and something Mom's made to eat."

"Easy enough." Her stomach rumbled, reminding her of the same need. "Anything else?"

"Call or text first in case I'm carrying out my own search for evidence."

"You listen to me. I'm the agent here, and neither Simon nor Willis is happy with us. If you're no longer in the picture, Isabella doesn't have a daddy, and I'm in this alone. Let me remind you I'm risking my career. While the word is I'm taking a few days' leave, that could change to rogue agent."

"April—" his tone measured calm—"I promise you I'll be careful. I have more at stake here than you do."

"Just sit tight. I won't be long."

"My priority is finding out who replaced the glass at my office. I use two vendors for glass installation. I doubt Willis would use either of them. Too easy for me to follow up. But I'm contacting them first to see if they can offer any insight."

"If Willis paid an installer—and I assume well—would they be forthright?"

"Not everyone is motivated by money. The two vendors are friends."

"You must spend every idle moment thinking about how to stop him. You, O country boy who speaks Greek, Hebrew, and Arabic, have an investigator's mind."

"Everything important to me is riding on this case. I'll do whatever it takes. If you think I'm thinking like an investigator, you're way off. I'm attempting to think like Willis."

"First requirement of an FBI agent—empathize with the bad guy. We're hitting one roadblock after another. Why not join your mom and daughter and let the FBI finish this?"

"I wouldn't be able to live with myself."

"Problem is, will you live through it?"

He huffed. "I'm doing my best." He ended the call.

25

April stood from the bed, and a flash of the previous night after her arrival at the Snyders' home swept across her mind. Miss Ella didn't appear to be concerned about her shoes left in the cow pasture or her torn dress. Fortunately, her hat and car were in good shape or the woman might have rolled up her sleeves for a fight. The barbed wire had taken a toll on April's hands, which didn't escape Vicki's or Miss Ella's scrutiny. They cleaned the wounds, and April fell asleep before Miss Ella left the Snyder home.

April groaned. She'd forgotten to check the floorboard mats for manure.

She peered out into a sun-filled day. A car drove past and she recognized the Ford—belonged to a Houston FBI agent. Must have been assigned to watch the Snyder home. April hadn't been abandoned, merely uninformed. But why? What was the security level on this case? Monday seemed a long way off.

She opened the bedroom door and made her way down the hallway and stairs to the kitchen. Isabella was playing on the floor, while Vicki flipped through a *Southern Living* magazine.

"Feeling better?" Vicki had the same dimpled grin as Jason. She laid the magazine down, open to a pic of Thanksgiving table decorations.

"Oh yes." April greeted Isabella and kissed her irresistible cheek. The baby babbled on.

"Starved? Coffee?" Vicki said.

"Both."

"I have some breakfast casserole from this morning."

"Perfect."

Vicki stood from the table and gestured to April. "Have a seat. I'll get you a pod of coffee now, and you can be drinking it while I grind beans and brew a fresh pot." She pointed to a small machine. "Ted bought us a Nespresso for those times when we want just a single cup. It's a spoiler."

"No need to wait on me. Just point me in the right direction."

"My kitchen. My rules. Once you get to know me, you'll learn I'm fierce about my kitchen. Sit down and I'll get your tummy filled and caffeine flowing through your veins. Ted's working in the yard and is available if you need him. By the way, the car you drove here has been replaced with a Chevy Malibu."

"Good." She'd given her word to the desk clerk, and Simon had kept his.

Soon the humming sound of the Nespresso coffee machine and the intoxicating smell of coffee swirled around the kitchen. Vicki handed her a cup. "Cream or sugar?"

"Just black."

"Like Jason. He says he likes his coffee the color of oil."

April breathed in the first cup of the day and took a sip. Exactly as she imagined. "This is heavenly."

Isabella crawled to April. Definitely a positive sign. She pushed her hot cup beyond reach and lifted Isabella into her lap.

Vicki reached into a cabinet and pulled out an orange Fiesta dinnerware plate. "I'm amazed at how fast she took to you. As I said yesterday, she's very particular."

April felt the same way, although she'd tried to guard her heart. "Thanks for all you've done for me."

"Nonsense. We owe you." Vicki opened the microwave door and set the plate of food inside.

April kissed the top of Isabella's nose. "What's your opinion of Willis?"

"Pardon my words, but the man has a bowling ball for a head and brains to match."

April burst out laughing. The imagery fit him. "Good call."

"His folks spoiled him rotten, and it stuck. The older he gets, the worse his actions. I understand why he doesn't care for Ted, but why is he after Jason?"

"Difficult to pinpoint."

Vicki smiled. "Which means you can't tell me."

"Best talk to Jason. What can you tell me about Carrie Edwards?"

The woman's shoulders rose and fell. "Sad situation. The elder Lennox ruled the house and abused his wife and children. I never understood why his wife stayed. Anyway, Willis naturally became a bully like his father . . . except when it came to Carrie. For some reason, he took overprotectiveness to extremes." She paused as though thinking. "Could be the only way Willis could control the dysfunction in the home was to shield her from what he saw as a threat. Honestly, April, I don't know. I'm not a psychologist. He ran off every friend she ever had except Lily. Our Lily told him to take his tough-guy act somewhere else."

April formed a mental picture of Carrie's and Willis's lives. The abuse he experienced spilled over into how he treated his wife and son.

"Russell tried to make up for what Carrie missed in her childhood. He arranged for her to see a psychiatrist and made sure she took her medication. As long as she stayed on the meds, she was an amazing wife and mother. Without it, she sank into severe depression. Our Lily loved her, became Carrie's 2 a.m. friend."

Now she better understood the complicated situation. "Russell's death must be hitting her hard."

"I pray she has the strength to bear it all for the

181

boys' sake. I tried calling yesterday, but it went to voice mail. We're organizing meals at church, and that will carry over until after the funeral."

The microwave beeped with the completion of its warming cycle. April relinquished Isabella to Vicki. The home-cooked eggs, sausage, jalapeños, onions, bell pepper, and fresh biscuit with soft butter and local honey came straight out of a fill-my-belly-with-comfort-food recipe book. She finished the breakfast and downed another cup of coffee.

"Big favor here. Can I shower?" April said. "Do you have anything I can wear? My weekender is in Jason's truck. I forgot to retrieve it."

"Got you covered, so to speak. Last night when you changed into Miss Ella's things, I noted your sizes. Isabella and I did a Walmart run early this morning." Vicki balanced Isabella on her hip and picked up a huge store bag sitting on a kitchen chair and handed it to her. "Two pairs of jeans, a sweatshirt, sweater, undies, socks, tennis shoes, and toiletries."

Bewildered best described April. "Wow. I never expected this. You went to more trouble than my own mother. How much do I owe you?"

"Nothing. I'd be insulted. I enjoyed shopping for your size and style. I'm stuck in the seasoned women's clothes."

"I can't take these without reimbursing you. It could be interpreted as a bribe."

"Mercy. FBI guidelines are ridiculous. Take a look inside. I had no idea of your tastes. If something is dreadful, I'll return it. Won't hurt my feelings a bit."

April pictured elastic-waist pants in denim blue and a sweatshirt with a deer on the front. Feigning a smile, she pulled out a pair of faded blue jeans. Great choice. Next came a pale-blue sweater. Perfect color. The socks and tennis shoes were basic, and she sighed with relief at the second pair of jeans. "You can shop for me anytime."

"I'm so pleased." The welcome in her soft drawl brought a longing in April's spirit, one she'd never experienced before. Her encounters with civilians usually involved emotionally distraught people or those thankful a loved one had been talked down from doing something harmful. But she rarely ever saw them again other than at a court hearing. Neighbors spoke and she responded, but she kept to herself except for other agents and an occasional social meetup with Simon and his wife. The Snyders made her feel like family, though she hoped it wasn't just a grand show for her to help their son.

"Ted and I are so glad you're on Jason's side." Vicki changed her tone. "The trumped-up charges on the heels of the anniversary of Lily's death have the potential to cause his migraines to flare up. He's an incredible father and a talented builder, but Willis is up to no good. Just wish we knew why."

"I'm not giving up until we have answers. I promise you. Thank you for agreeing to go to a safe house with Isabella. Maybe Ted will be on board before the afternoon exchange. I'd wanted the escort earlier, and I'm sorry it's taken a little longer than anticipated." The car she'd seen this morning meant they'd been in place last night. Normal protocol would have the Snyders protected until they left Sweet Briar.

"No problem. I'm nearly done packing. Ted, on the other hand, has closed the door on the matter."

Like father, like son.

April refilled her coffee cup. "Vicki, before I forget it, I need to give you a number to reach Jason." Once the woman jotted down the digits, April hurried to the shower. In less than thirty minutes, she emerged from the bathroom ready to take on Willis and his goons single-handedly. She grabbed her purse and made her way to the kitchen, where Vicki and Ted awaited her.

Dressed in jeans, he gave her a hug. "I put cold water and food in the truck parked in the garage. It's an old '63 Ford but drives like a charm. Two containers of coffee are in the front. I don't like the looks of the tires on your car. Some of the country roads aren't paved, and my truck has good tires." He held up his hand. "No argument."

Oh, the Snyder men with their demands. "The deputy will still see me leave."

"I'm walking down there now to distract Cal. Vicki will join me to the end of the driveway, then return inside. I'm hoping the deputy will think she's backing out of the driveway and not you. Should work, and the plan gives this old man something to do."

April saw where Jason had inherited his ingenuity. "You're far from an old man. Might need you in law enforcement."

"I'm a chiropractor," he said. "I make adjustments to people's bodies, not their attitudes."

She laughed lightly. A sense of humor always helped in tense situations.

"The important thing to remember is this family believes in sticking together."

26

April walked into Farmers' Bank in Sweet Briar with one item to cross off her list. She requested a meeting with Vic Henley to ask a couple of questions.

In his office, Henley sat behind his desk and steepled his fingers. "The man who posed as Ted Snyder hasn't been identified or your superiors would have notified you. Our agreement was for me to have information by noon."

"Have you talked to the employee who permitted the breach?"

"We haven't had time. I assure you we're doing everything possible." Henley spread a professional smile over his face like a thick layer of mayonnaise.

"Mr. Henley, I need to speak to the person who approved Ted Snyder's signature when the theft occurred." She allowed silence to punctuate her words. "Unless *you* arranged for the thief to gain access to the safe-deposit box?"

A muscle below his left eye twitched. "There's no way I'd jeopardize the reputation of this bank."

"Were you working that day?"

"Excuse me?"

"I'm sure you wouldn't mind pulling up the video footage from the date in question. I'd like to see it again."

He typed into his computer and swung the screen her way.

"Please zoom in on the far left-hand corner," she said.

"It's empty space," Henley said.

"Then you should have no problem complying with a federal agent's request."

He zoomed in. A man's shoes could be seen.

"See those shoes?" April said. "Those are Tod's, a brown leather loafer called a driving shoe. When I researched them, I saw a $640 price tag. A bit much for a small-town bank employee, but I see you're wearing them today."

A momentary startle met her. "Are you suggesting I had something to do with the theft?"

She plastered on professionalism. "Mr. Henley, how did Willis Lennox persuade you to allow the person in the footage to bypass security protocol?"

Henley swallowed. "Your accusation is ridiculous."

"You can make this easy by telling the truth, or I can place you under arrest and charge you with bank fraud and possibly as an accomplice to murder."

Henley's ashen face revealed his guilt. "Willis made it impossible for me not to follow his orders."

April lowered her voice. "How?"

"Doubt you could use it in court. He said he

needed a favor and explained the particulars. He told me where my girlfriend lived and worked. Said the road she lived on had been the site of bad accidents. Be a shame if she was the next victim."

"Are you willing to swear to Mr. Lennox's words and testify in court?"

"Yes, ma'am. Will it reduce my sentence for what I've done?"

"The judge will view your cooperation favorably."

"Am I being arrested?"

"The FBI may choose to take you into custody."

"I understand."

"Do you know the identity of the man who posed as Ted Snyder?"

"No, ma'am. Never saw him before."

"Thank you," April said. "The man's facial features aren't clear. It appears he knew the camera's location and avoided it. Can you describe his voice?"

He shrugged. "Average. Didn't say much."

"All right, Mr. Henley. You've been a tremendous help, and I will attest to your cooperation." She shook his hand. "I still like your shoes."

On the way out of the bank, her phone alerted her to a call from Simon.

"April, can you talk?" he said.

"Yes. What's going on?"

"Sheriff Lennox has made serious allegations against you."

"What's he claiming?"

"You're aiding a criminal, threatening a bank employee to lie about a bank transaction, and living with Jason's parents."

"Really? I am staying at the Snyders' while on vacation." She struggled to contain her irritation. "Have you seen any evidence that I've conducted myself in something other than a professional manner?"

"He's assembling it for Monday."

She tapped her foot on the sidewalk. "Probably witnesses to go with it. Where's the additional info I requested? Has the FIG been taken hostage?"

"How many times do I need to say this? As soon as I receive your clearance, you'll have it. I let others know you're taking a few days off. We'd like for you to keep Jason in line. Do your job. Taking the law into his own hands sets him up for a jail sentence and means your career will take a nosedive. This allows the agents there to continue. When and if I can, I'll update you."

She inhaled relief. "Great. Thanks."

"Document all findings on your end, and we'll follow up by filing charges on all those involved in the crimes."

She recounted her conversation with Vic Henley. "No identity on who gained access to the safe-deposit box. Did Willis make any other statements?"

"He says the circumstances surrounding the

death of Lily Snyder sent Jason into a period of depression and violent behavior. In our opinion, the sheriff is trying to establish a valid reason to shoot Jason and claim self-defense. We have eyes on the situation."

"I'm in this for the long haul. I see an innocent man charged with an unspeakable crime. There are no gray areas in my record. No reason for the FBI not to trust me with the truth."

"I'm on your side, Jason's too. We all are. It's simply a matter of confidentiality in some of the details."

She'd not argue at this point. "How many other agents are in the area?"

"Four. And that's private knowledge for you only. You're to work through me until further notice. Trust my lead on this, okay?"

"I don't think I have a choice."

"Right now we have a new problem requiring your assistance."

"What?"

"An eyewitness just phoned the FBI and stated Jason Snyder assisted in his wife's death. The woman said she couldn't keep it a secret any longer with the Russell Edwards murder charges. Gave her name as Vicki Snyder."

27

Jason eased onto a felled log in the woods near his truck. It had been a long time since he'd roughed it. No running water, a fall chill, and his stomach rumbling like a storm rolling in. He'd wakened sporadically last night but always gone back to sleep. Dreams were like demons stalking him, and they all looked like Willis marching after him with a thousand deputies.

A new obstacle had taken root. His truck needed gas, and he couldn't afford to make the trip in broad daylight. Tonight he'd devise a plan to buy fuel and avoid ending up in handcuffs.

This morning, or rather near noon, his list of places to scout out information grew. Where was April?

A gnawing matter pounded at his brain. Should he let the FBI handle the investigation? They were trained and had the technology to get the job done. But even if they were successful in clearing his name, would they find the evidence to shove Willis into a cell? Arrest Russell's killer? Jason needed answers. For now, he'd stick to running down evidence on his own.

His phone rang: Dad. Jason greeted him.

"Everything okay?" Dad said.

"So far. Did April give you this number?"

"She had Vicki write it down. Son, I canceled my patients today, and I'm staying home with my rifle loaded until we have instructions on how and where Vicki and Isabella are to meet the FBI."

"And you?"

"Running's not my game."

"As a favor to me?"

"Conversation over. April asked me to give you a call. She's behind schedule. She needed to stop at the bank and then Brenda Krew's office. Shouldn't take too long."

"All right."

"Kevin called me. Wanted to know how to contact you. I'm not cooperating with anyone associated with Willis."

And the deputy might be playing them. "Did you recognize the number he called from?"

"He's not phoned me before. Can't help you there. Got a pen for the number?"

Jason wrote it on the palm of his hand. "Thanks."

"Be careful, Son. I'm praying for the truth to surface soon."

"Constantly." Jason pressed End. Kevin could have critical information, something to bring justice to the forefront. Maybe he should have April contact him. No, Jason didn't like that idea either. Willis wouldn't find it odd that Jason contacted Kevin, since he was at the scene of the shooting, but April was officially taking time off. Might not be a good idea to connect her and

Kevin. Only one way to find out what Kevin wanted and possibly expose his allegiance.

Jason pressed in the number. "I hear you want to talk to me."

"My family's safe. Wanted you to know I'm grateful. Willis isn't around, which gives me time to think about my story. I'll do my best to play the deputy role while searching for what we need to put Willis away."

"All of us working together will get the job done." Jason wanted to trust Kevin, see his face.

"Is April sticking around until this is over?" Kevin said.

Caution nipped at him. "I can't speak for her. I suggest you ask."

"All right. I'm at the sheriff's office. Just finished going through paper files and now I'm working online. Finding Willis's password was a booger. Took me forever to discover it's n2Billie1Zack2."

Strange, since he treated them so badly. "What have you learned?"

"The original investigation report from Russell's death isn't listed, so Willis must have destroyed it, and the one filed reads the same as the one given to the FBI. My signature is forged."

"Not a surprise. Did you see anything unusual after I left that night and Griff followed me to the sheriff's office?"

"Nothing."

"Did Griff mention my arrest when he returned?"

"In detail. He acted upset. Said he'd never seen Willis so mad. Anyway, we finished the report and drove back to the office. I asked to see you, and Willis said you were asleep. He reached into his desk and gave me a new phone. Asked for my old one and told me to go on home."

"Anything in your files about Griff?"

"Nothing incriminating."

"Is his previous employment listed?"

"US Army, honorable discharge. April could verify his military service."

"What's his work ethic?"

"He's friendly, does a fine job, but keeps his distance from the rest of us. Haven't seen anything to label him one of Willis's men, but he wouldn't advertise it either."

Jason walked to his truck and grabbed a small notebook and pen. "April has requested backgrounds from the FBI, but I'll ask her to check into him further. What's his Social Security number?"

Kevin gave him the number. "Hey, gotta go. A patrol car is here, and I need to shut this computer down."

As Jason's phone went silent, he heard a car slow and stop on the main road. A man got out. He stared into the woods where Jason was hiding, then walked his way.

Jason remained in the shadows and waited for the man to approach. Leaving his truck behind and venturing deeper into the woods made little sense until he discovered what the stranger wanted.

After living his whole life in this area and doing business for the last ten years, he knew at least 90 percent of Sweet Briar's population. Which meant this man was either trespassing or working for Willis, or a card-carrying FBI agent. Jason gambled on the man not having intentions to blow him away. In the meantime, he'd make observations.

He texted April. Stay clear until I give the ok.

The man, in his early fifties and wearing casual slacks, moved closer. Not quite six feet tall and thick snow-white hair. Guys around here wore Wranglers and Levi's, not golfing pants. Jason reached behind him for his gun and felt the hard, cold metal.

The man walked into the treed area and pulled a semiautomatic. He raised it to firing position and approached Jason's truck. He peered into the trees. Then moved stealthily toward the cab. Once he confirmed no one was inside, he bent to study footprints. After a few moments, he laid his gun on the ground, stood, and raised his hands.

"Snyder, I know you're watching me. Smart man to see who's tailing you. I'm Special Agent Simon Neilson. Just want to talk."

Jason listened. Did April know Simon was paying him a visit?

"Okay, I'd be leery too. I'm reaching inside my jacket for my business card. Going to stick it under your windshield wiper blade."

Jason had no inclination to open a conversation. Yet.

"I'm leaving now. I understand you don't want to expose yourself and may not find credibility in my words. Do this for yourself and your daughter. Let us take you into protective custody with your family. Or at the very least stay in hiding until this is over. Move to another secure spot today."

"Give your gun a kick," Jason said. Simon sent it whirling about twenty feet. Jason stepped from the shadows, just enough for Simon to see him. "When are the agents transporting my daughter and mother today?"

"I told April around 2 p.m." He started to lower his hands.

"Keep them up. How about publicly exonerating me?"

"I agree the announcement would handicap Willis."

"You wouldn't be going to this much trouble if you weren't sure of my innocence. Did Willis kill Russell?"

"I have no idea."

"So why are you here? Apparently I wasn't that hard to find."

"The FBI has ways. I'll give you credit for swiping license plates and not using a credit card in any transactions."

Jason sighed. "I just want this straightened out."

"I understand. We're investigating Willis's probable mishandling of the case."

"What do you want from me?"

"What does Willis Lennox have against you?"

"It's personal."

"Must be for him to frame you for murder."

"I plan to keep searching on my end."

"No, leave this alone. The investigation is for trained law enforcement. I'd hate to see your independence get you killed. Worse yet, find your and April's bodies dumped on the side of one of these roads. I get your stake in Russell Edwards's death. But dead heroes can't raise their daughters."

Unfortunately, Simon made sense, but Jason had made his choice. His concern did center on Isabella and his family. "How will the transfer happen?" he said. "Unless you say it's too dangerous, I'd like to tell my family good-bye."

"I anticipated you'd want to see them off. Here's the deal. I'm suggesting a Woodville location, the parking lot nearest to the restaurant at Heritage Village."

"I know the spot."

"The busy locale is the best solution for everyone's safety. I've told April your family needs to leave their home at precisely 1:40. Agents will follow them from there to the transfer spot."

He'd prefer to have the FBI drive into Sweet Briar and escort them to Houston in an armed tank. "And the Viners won't be told? Kevin had suggested his family and mine keep company together. Not smart until we're assured of his allegiance."

"This isn't a 'we' operation. You are a civilian, and if you step out of line or interfere in a federal investigation, I'm tossing your rear in jail. Listen to April. She has questions that need answers. Now, if you don't mind, I'll collect my gun. Call me if you come to your senses."

28

April drove curvy country roads to where Jason kept a low profile. He'd texted her to stay clear until he gave her the word. Now she was on her way, navigating a dirt-and-gravel road, and curious as to what he'd encountered.

Sunshine bathed the quiet countryside. Pretty autumn drive if not for her attention swirling in every direction. Patches of sparse brown grass hinted at fall and the few months of winter to come. Most of the trees were dressed in vibrant gold and scarlet, but the pines retained their year-round color.

Without responses and solutions from Simon, she vowed to stay on the investigation. The crime had the FBI's attention, and she believed in the mission statement—even if she didn't have all the facts.

Still, the missing details left her frustrated.

Ted reminded her of a hero from the Battle of the Alamo. He refused to desert his home. But the Alamo ended badly, and the old story needled her.

She couldn't help but think about Carrie Edwards's sorrow. Had emotional instability caused Carrie to lie when she said Russell and Jason argued before their meeting? What about

Willis's claim that Russell contacted him for help? Could Willis be afraid Carrie might present new information? April craved an interview alone with the widow. Questions tumbled over into questions.

The newest maze of confusion had her mind on overload. She couldn't continue one step farther on Jason's behalf until she learned the truth behind Lily Snyder's death. Simon's startling piece of information regarding an alleged call from Vicki Snyder tied her in knots. And as much as she believed Willis had arranged the accusatory call to the FBI, she feared he could have evidence, something April missed in her conversations and analysis of Jason. She groaned. A good lawyer would kick her testimony against Willis out of court—a hostage negotiator who supported a fugitive.

Why identify the woman as Vicki Snyder? What if Vicki's voice matched the woman who'd made the call? April had to process the possibility Jason could be innocent of one murder and guilty of another. Doubts always had a way of surfacing until the true picture came into focus.

Every phrase entering her mind began with a "why."

The turnoff ahead captured her attention, and she followed the narrow tractor path leading into the woods, squeezing Ted's truck between towering pine trees.

When she pulled next to his vehicle, he emerged from behind a tree. His lips framed a slight smile, but the lines fanning from the sides of his eyes indicated far too much stress. Had the migraine attacked him again?

Jason cleaned debris off his truck bed with his hand and grabbed a can of bug spray. "Sitting inside my truck gives me claustrophobia, like being locked up for a murder I didn't commit." He pointed to the tailgate. "Air-conditioned," he said. "Mosquitoes aren't quite as bad as in the summer. Use this spray and keep your sweatshirt tight around you."

While she updated him on Isabella and his parents, he drank coffee and ate his mother's breakfast casserole. She moved on to what she'd learned from Vic Henley.

"I'm not surprised," Jason said. "Another reason why Willis has to be stopped."

"Brenda Krew wasn't at her office, so I left a message." She hesitated a moment before continuing. "Simon called me."

Jason stopped chewing and stared into her face. She could feel his scrutiny. "He paid me a visit."

She blinked. Why hadn't her partner said anything about it? "Here? What did he say?" This revelation added a little crust to her and Simon's friendship. Maybe he hadn't told her his intentions because . . . She'd ask him.

Jason relayed the conversation. "He knows I'm

not leaving the area. He advised me to listen to you."

"Based on the timing, he must have called me from his car," she said. "And never said a word about his attempt at a face-to-face with you." Denying her growing annoyance with Simon, she moved forward. "His appearance is a positive sign."

"Is it?" He shook his head. "There's so many things about how the FBI uses technology to track down people, but do they have my best interests? I try to pacify myself by thinking the bullet that killed Russell must have been meant for me. Except then I'd go to my grave with Billie's secret, and Willis wouldn't have the info he wants."

"Unless they're already dead."

"The thought's crossed my mind."

She pointed to his breakfast. "You need your energy."

"The look on your face says bad news is coming."

"I have to ask you a couple of hard questions."

"Okay. Bring it on."

"Where were you when Lily died?"

"Unusual question." Jason set his half-eaten casserole on the truck bed. "In the hospital room. What's this got to do with Willis?"

"Were you alone?"

He frowned. "Isabella was with me. Why?"

"The FBI received a call from a woman who claimed you assisted in Lily's death."

Color mounted in his face. The memory of him losing his temper yesterday with Willis when he threatened Isabella and April at the motel put her on alert. Jason might have killed Willis if she hadn't talked him down.

"I have to run down every piece of evidence and hearsay that comes my direction," she said.

"The accusation is a lie." He blew out what she figured was a string of his internal expletives. "You know Willis is behind this. He's using both barrels to try to show I'm a killer."

"I agree the move fits his MO. But I have to hear from you what happened." His answer would determine if she'd made an erroneous judgment call with him.

Jason looked away and rubbed his face before speaking. "Lily was my reason to climb out of bed every morning."

"You loved her. I see it in your face. Hear it in your voice." She offered silence for her words to register before posing the critical question. "Did you love her enough to end her pain?"

"No. A mercy killing is murder. I'll say this once, then you choose who you want to believe. As much as I hated Lily's suffering, God held the keys to her life and death." He dug his fingers into both palms.

"A woman made the call." April poured

sympathy into her tone. "She gave her name as Vicki Snyder. Said she couldn't keep it a secret any longer since you'd been charged with Russell Edwards's murder."

He left the truck bed and took several steps. When he lifted his face to the sky, she longed to read his thoughts.

"I'm glad Willis isn't here. My vow to keep my anger under control would be tested. April, give me a moment to calm down."

She kept her composure and waited, part of her training.

"Have you already interrogated my mother?" Irritation laced his tone. Before April could form a response, he shook his head. "Sorry. I'm way off base here. I understand this is part of your job."

"I've only talked to you. No point in upsetting your parents. But I need to know where Vicki was during Lily's passing."

He rejoined her and began again. "Mom and Dad were in the waiting area with Russell and Carrie. We knew Lily's end had come, and they wanted to give us her last few minutes. I remember Carrie cried to be with Lily, but Russell insisted she wait with him and my parents. Lily's vitals were monitored at the nurses' desk, and as soon as she passed, two nurses were immediately in the room. I was holding Isabella . . . not trying to find a way to end Lily's life."

"I asked Simon to retrieve those records and send them to me. The security cameras with a time stamp will show Vicki couldn't have been in two places at the same time."

"Can you use voice recognition software to show Mom didn't make the call?"

"We'll ask for a recording from your mom for comparison."

"Could the findings be used against Willis?" he said.

"A gray area at the moment. If we are able to identify the caller, and the woman could be persuaded to testify that Willis put her up to the call, she could be an integral part of your defense."

"Giving her a plea bargain? Don't ask me how I feel about a criminal walking the streets," he said. "Especially if she's the same woman who kidnapped Isabella."

"She'd still face punishment."

"The jury is filled with humans who allow sympathetic testimony to sway their opinion."

"Justice is not supposed to work that way, but I see your point."

Anguish etched his features, and she longed to reach out to him. Her phone alerted her to a text.

Jason absolved of guilt in murder of Russell Edwards.

She handed him the phone, and he read the message.

"Willis will come after me like a rabid dog,"

he said. "Sic all his buds and their friends on me. You too. But I welcome the risk to expose him. Anytime you want to head back to Houston, I'm okay with your decision. You've done far too much now. Trust me, you don't deserve Willis's vengeance. No one does."

"I took this case seriously after experiencing him firsthand."

"Thanks, April. You're amazing."

His gaze into her eyes caused her to momentarily lose herself in the depths of his brown eyes. An uncomfortable silence lingered, and her heart soared into double time.

Jason yanked his phone from his pocket. "I'd better call Mom. Let her know the latest."

He'd felt the awkward moment too.

"Can you put it on speaker so I can record it?"

"Sure."

Jason phoned his mom, verified Isabella was fine, and reiterated the FBI's directives about the transfer. "Yes, I've been exonerated. Everything else is the same, unfortunately. Has Dad changed his mind? The danger of him getting hurt is not worth the risk—"

"He's already told me not to bring it up again."

Jason shook his head. "Tell Dad stubbornness is for mules, not men." He glanced at April. "Mom, there's more I need to tell you. A woman using your name phoned the FBI. She said I assisted in Lily's death."

"What?" Vicki's voice shrilled.

"It's all right. April's recording this. The FBI will compare the woman's voice and yours to confirm they aren't a match."

"Good. And tell her to check my cell phone records for such an outrageous call. Ted's too. Mercy, what's next?"

"I'd like to think we're on the downhill side of things." Jason's attempt at optimism sounded flat. "Stay put until it's time to leave. See you soon. Love you."

He ended the call, and April sent the recording to Simon before reverting her attention to Jason.

"I'm looking for more info about Brenda Krew's relationship with Willis."

"As in she could be the mystery woman?" He shrugged. "I'm at the point of believing anything."

"I'll talk to her before the day's over. Avoiding the FBI never pans out."

"Unfortunately, true."

She caught his gaze. The stress in his eyes overwhelmed her. "Shake off the unfairness, Jason. Think like Willis and use logic and not emotions. If you can't wrap your brain around how he operates, the anger will destroy all we're trying to accomplish."

"Willis has always been a bully and self-centered. I went off to college, and he qualified as deputy sheriff. Took the training. When I graduated, I built a construction business, but Willis's activities seeped deeper into muck. Rumors mostly, and nothing I can swear to. Willis and Billie dated for years. They married when Billie got pregnant with Zack. She told me he'd roughed her up a few times when they were dating, but he always apologized, and she took him back. Most people thought Willis's new responsibility of husband and father might instill good stuff."

"But it continued?"

"Yep. His tough-guy attitude grew worse. A womanizer. Willis ran for county sheriff and won. More abusive to Billie. She filed assault charges twice that I remember but later dropped them. Been downhill ever since. The rest you know about—Billie asking me to help her and Zack leave him."

"He has over two thousand acres. How does a man acquire so much land on a sheriff's salary?"

"Inherited from his grandparents and parents. I'm sure he's dabbled in things illegally, but I don't have proof."

She sighed. "About time we took the offensive. After ensuring your family's safe, what's your number one priority?"

"Same as earlier. Finding out who replaced the glass in my office window. Before Simon arrived, I made calls to the commercial and independent installers in the area. Nothing yet."

"Could Kevin have replaced it?"

He grinned. "Last summer, one of his boys broke a window in his living room. I tried to tell him how to do it, but he had me call an installer. Besides, the office window was a custom size."

"Any of your crew able to replace it?"

"Where would they have gotten the glass? I have another idea."

29

Jason stretched his shoulders. The stakes weighed heavily on his heart, as though a bulldozer sat on his chest. A part of him wanted to walk away from this. He had no investigative skills and a flimsy plan. "There's another company east of Woodville. I've met the owners a few times and worked on a community project with them. Might as well check there." He pressed in the number.

A woman answered the phone. "City and Country Glass, Tessa Barker."

"Afternoon, Tessa, this is Jason Snyder of Snyder Construction."

"Yes, sir, what can I do for you?"

April heard a perky lilt in the woman's voice. Jason gave her the memorized spiel.

"I really doubt any of our installers handled the job, but hold on while I pull up the logs." A moment later she confirmed nothing in her files corresponding to the night of the crime. "We have three installers, all our sons. Let me talk to them. If they did the job, the work order could be still in their trucks. We're a family business, and sometimes paperwork doesn't arrive in the office in a timely manner."

"Do you have security measures after hours?"

"We sure do. It's not monitored by the police

department, just a camera mounted on a pole. The device sends footage to our computer. Anyway, I'll check with the boys and get back to you."

"Thanks."

"You doin' okay? Just heard your name's been cleared in that horrible shooting. The news has to be a blessing."

Simon had kept his word. "Without a doubt. The FBI's helping Willis with the investigation. I'm just snooping on my end. Appreciate your looking into this."

"Good luck. If I learn anything, I'll call you back."

Another call completed. Jason's determination climbed the ladder of hope, one rung at a time. "Tessa is organization on steroids," he said. "Nothing gets by her."

"Better yet if she has a name to give us."

"I'm not holding my breath. Willis thinks he's developed a foolproof plan, so it'll likely take time to unravel it."

"He'll slip. There's too many working to stop him. We're gaining information. You and I know he's breaking one law after another, but that means nothing without evidence."

Jason made two more calls to glass companies, but no one could help him.

The isolation, the sounds of birds, and the growing awareness of the beautiful woman beside him stirred feelings he thought were long gone.

He took a glimpse at his watch. "Thirty minutes before leaving for Woodville."

April touched his arm. "Your mom and Isabella will be protected until this is over. It may be only a couple of days. In the meantime, we can keep digging without worrying about them."

"Would you rather I go to Woodville alone?" he said.

"No, sir. Which vehicle do we take?"

"If Willis stops us in Dad's truck, my parents will be charged as accomplices." He stuffed his hands into his jean pockets. "As much as I don't like driving his, we have no choice unless we hoof it. My truck needs gas." He retrieved his gun from the truck and placed it in Dad's glove box.

"I have a weapon," she said.

"We're in this together."

Predators were everywhere.

On the way to Woodville, April listened to Jason hum and recognized the tune. "Do I hear 'Small Town Boy' by Dustin Lynch?"

"Didn't take you for a country-western fan." He arched his shoulders. "Not sure where the song came from since my life's in swampville."

"We're working on clean water." She smiled, but not at him. Jason Snyder affected her in ways that were . . . scary.

"Russell knew every song and artist on the charts. Sang all the time. Used to drive me crazy, but now I'd do about anything to hear his sour notes. Makes me feel badly for Carrie, too. Lily and me, Russell and Carrie. We spent lots of good times together."

She listened to him reminisce. He needed to verbalize the grief before it ate him alive. She thought of her failure with Benson . . . She'd do anything to keep Jason from taking the same fall.

She thought about the nobility of Jason's actions with Billie. He'd proved repeatedly that he was a man of solid character. She valued his stand, even though it could get both of them killed.

They approached the welcome sign to Woodville. "Wish your dad was joining Vicki and Isabella."

"I'd like to shake him."

"I'm sorry it has come to this with your family."

"But I made the right decision. Anything else is selfish. Should have insisted on a safe house yesterday morning. My hesitancy shows a lack of good judgment." His voice grew scratchy.

"Hard to think about leaving Isabella?" April said.

"I've never spent so much time away from my little girl. But I know Mom will take great care of her." He took a glimpse in the side mirror. "Haven't seen any vehicles following us."

"A skilled tail keeps a safe and effective distance behind whoever they're following."

He chuckled. "Thanks. You're full of optimism. This trip is risky, but telling my daughter goodbye is important."

April intended for him to survive whatever lay ahead to fulfill his need to father Isabella.

She mentally scheduled a long conversation with Simon later tonight, the magnet type designed to draw out game-changing details.

At Heritage Village, she parked in the restaurant area beside a white Lincoln Town Car with tinted glass, the vehicle Simon had described that matched the license plate number she'd been given. The moment she turned off the truck's rumbling engine, two agents emerged—a man and woman, both of whom April recognized. Relief calmed her scattered nerves. She introduced Jason, and within five minutes, Ted joined them with Vicki and Isabella. The three emerged from Vicki's car. A second car pulled in behind Ted, and two male agents exited their vehicle.

Jason took Isabella into his arms. "Daddy's girl looks pretty today. Grandma put a pink headband in your hair." He kissed her, and she wrapped her little arms around his neck. "Can I have a few minutes with my daughter alone?" he said to one of the male agents. When Jason received permission, he carried Isabella several feet away. The agents, including April, circled the area at a respectful distance while keeping an eye on those around them.

Vicki made her way to April's side. They both watched a touching scene between father and daughter. "I have to talk to him," Vicki said. "I know my son, and this separation is tearing him up. Isabella is the reason he takes one breath after another. If you come along, it will be easier for him."

April let the lead agent know the plan and silently walked with Vicki, not sure what was about to transpire.

Vicki laid her hand on her son's back. "Jason, I'll be the only one who cares for her. She'll never be out of my sight."

"I know, Mom. It's just hard. Isabella senses something's wrong."

"Remember how you felt when Lily left us? You said Band-Aids and casts fixed broken parts of people, but Lily's leaving shattered your heart. Then you realized God had given you Isabella, and He used her to put you back together. Now He's asking you to trust Him again."

Jason planted a kiss on his mother's forehead, and April wanted to melt into the background. No one knew the future, and if this case blew up in their faces and not everyone survived, these tender moments needed to be private.

Before she could move away, Vicki took her hand. "In the short time I've come to know April,

I believe she's a friend, a woman you can work alongside to prove your innocence. We all want Russell's killer to be arrested and the woman who kidnapped our little girl to be found."

Jason gave a slight smile to his mother, and although it looked forced, the conviction in his eyes showed his strength. He walked with them back to the Lincoln, all the while whispering to Isabella. "You and Grandma are taking a little vacation. I love you, and I'll see you in a few days." He placed her in the car seat and stepped back.

"Perhaps you or April can call?" Vicki said.

"I can't risk it, Mom. If the wrong person traced my phone, a safe house wouldn't do you or Isabella any good." He paused. "Isabella's tracker needs to come off."

"I'd forgotten about it." April spoke with tenderness in her words. Isabella had become an important part of her heart too.

He took a tiny gold key from his wallet and unlocked Isabella's anklet. He gently removed it and placed both in his pocket. Isabella reached up from the car seat, and he hugged her one more time. "You've got to go with Grandma, sweetheart." Isabella clung to him, sobbing. "Mom, help me with her."

Vicki peeled Isabella's fingers from around Jason's neck. This had to be nearly as heartwrenching as telling Lily good-bye. Both farewells heralded an uncertain future.

He closed the door of the car and hurried to the passenger side of his dad's truck. April couldn't bear to see his face because she knew his tears were there. Hers were on the verge of flooding her eyes.

30

Jason rode in his dad's truck while April drove, leaving Woodville behind. He should make conversation, but the words refused to come. While his eyes watched the miles evaporate, he gulped for air as though drowning. With a slick hand, he rubbed his pant leg.

Concentrate on what needs to happen.

Get the work done.

Live again with his daughter.

Build and remodel homes.

Laugh until his sides ached.

Watch Isabella take her first step.

He could do this, see it to the end. He was doing the right thing, putting Isabella and his mother under FBI protection. For his family's well-being, communication had to slide to a halt until Willis wore cuffs. Perhaps Isabella would never remember the time her daddy left her.

As for April . . . he liked her. Maybe too much for a man widowed just a little over a year.

Since Thursday night, he'd lost sight of his normal mode of operation, the habits that kept him rooted to life.

Why couldn't the FBI get Willis off his rear? With all the dirt dug up on Willis, why hadn't he been relieved of his position?

Trust God. To another desperate person, the words tumbled out easily, but not for Jason, when his personality wore control like a pair of work gloves. He'd gotten past the anger with God taking Lily. She'd suffered nonstop for months and deserved peace and healing. And he'd been given a beautiful daughter to love.

Trust God. Sure. Threadlike faith was all he had left.

Another accusation seared through him—the murder-assist for Lily. One lie after another. How long before Jason shifted from broken to shattered?

He moistened his lips and reached for his bottle of water. The high probability of meeting a bullet with his name on it made him tremble. But how could he live with himself if he didn't throw his whole being into proving his innocence and getting Willis behind bars?

"You're hurting. I can see it, feel it," April said. "How can I help?"

He forced himself to look at her. "Missing my baby girl already."

"Allow yourself to grieve."

"Have you grieved since that man committed suicide?"

"Not yet." She touched his arm. "You're always thinking about others. I admire that trait."

Focus on the now. "The most important part of building a house is the foundation. No point adding walls until the foundation's laid. And I sure want to build a case against Willis. Assign me a task, because I've hit flat bottom. I'm no closer to finding out who killed Russell and kidnapped Isabella than yesterday. My plans are matchstick brittle."

"I need to talk to Brenda Krew. But she's still not answering my phone messages." April stared at her watch. "What time does her real estate business close?"

"Sunday mornings."

"Married to her career. I get it. Maybe I should camp out at her office and wait for her to appear."

"She and Willis are friends, and I don't want you caught in cross fire." He infused his tone with sincerity, couldn't help himself. Her tiny frame and huge brown eyes made her appear fragile. And while he knew her training made her tougher than first impressions might suggest, his tender heart had a hard time believing it.

"I'm all right." She bit her lip.

Did she feel the same attraction, the one that had slammed into his heart when they were talking earlier?

His phone rang, and a "saved by the bell" thought coursed through him. "Hey, Dad. You doing okay?"

"I will be. Son, two things here. There's a situation with your company. Edwardo called, and four of the crew walked off the construction site.

They're worried about job security. Willis told them you couldn't make payroll if you were in jail."

Jason blew out a sigh. "I can't fault any of them with families to feed. Did he mention who'd quit?"

"No. Edwardo said the others offered to pitch in until this is settled."

Jason nodded. "Tell him thanks. I'll be back to work as soon as I can. You mentioned two things."

"Billie Lennox just called me. She's been trying to reach you. Gave me her number."

He inwardly startled. She was alive. "Hold on. I want April to hear this." He tapped Speaker. "Are you sure it was Billie?"

"She identified herself, and I recognized her voice."

"Good. Text me her number. Did she sound okay?"

April slid him a sideways glance.

"Hard to tell. Seemed anxious to talk to you."

"Upset?"

"Very much."

"I'll get on it."

"Son, on the way back from Woodville, I had me some think time. I'm pretty sure you helped Billie and Zack get away from Willis, and that's why he's after you now."

Jason let silence be his answer.

221

"You should have known Willis wouldn't take this sitting down. He's gonna keep firing from both barrels until he's stopped. Does the FBI think he killed Russell and set you up because of Billie and Zack? Did he hire the woman to kidnap Isabella?"

"Maybe on all counts. I refused to tell him where they are, and the truth is I have no clue. Please keep this to yourself."

"I will. But Willis is a strong enemy."

"So let April make arrangements for you to join Mom and Isabella."

"What about you?"

"I'm not a coward."

"Neither am I. Willis needs a permanent adjustment, because his head isn't aligned with the law." Dad humphed. "Nothing more to report. Be safe. I'll text you Billie's number."

"Lock your doors." Jason ended the call and turned to April. "Now we know she and Zack are alive." His phone sounded with Dad's text. "I'm not putting this on speaker. Might scare her."

"You're right." Her eyes widened. "Is she in the area?"

"One way to find out."

Billie answered on the third ring.

"This is Jason."

"I was afraid to answer, but I'd just talked to your dad. Thank God you're all right." She sounded weak, tired. "When I couldn't reach you on your phone, I was afraid something had happened to you. I decided to contact your parents. I'm really sorry about Russell." Her voice cracked, and he pictured the blonde with a battered face holding on to her son with a broken arm.

"Precautions have been taken."

"I can only imagine how Carrie feels, but I can't call her."

"Are you and Zack safe?"

"Yes. New names. New life. We'll be fine. But Willis can't get away with this."

"The FBI's on it."

"I may be able to help you."

Jason's senses charged. "How?"

"I think Willis killed someone and buried him on the ranch." She sobbed. "What I'm about to say is on the flash drive. This is the first time I've told anyone what I saw."

"It's okay. You can tell me."

"About seven months ago, Willis said he was meeting Kevin Viner for coffee on a Wednesday night in Woodville. He seemed on edge, like trouble was brewing. Questioning Willis meant facing a beating, so I didn't probe him. Maybe he and Kevin were working on a case, but Kevin rarely missed Wednesday night church. Willis told me to stay home, said I looked tired. You know how I feel about church, so I protested. Received a smack in the face for it. When he left,

I grabbed Zack and followed him with my lights off. Willis hadn't slept at home for two nights, and I suspected another affair. Even hoped he might leave me. He drove the narrow dirt road along the east side of the ranch and parked. I ordered Zack to stay in the car. Told him if I didn't return in thirty minutes, he was to walk back to the house and call you. I took off on foot after Willis." She paused. "He opened the trunk of his cruiser, and in the dim light, I saw him pull out a man's body. The man may have been wearing a red jacket. I couldn't tell for sure. Willis carried him into the woods. I hurried back to Zack and drove off. That's when I started making plans to leave him."

Jason tuned out everything but Billie's words. "Are you sure you weren't mistaken?"

"Positive."

"Do you remember the exact location?"

"The footpath midway down the road next to your place."

Jason knew where she meant. "Thanks for reaching out to me, for putting yourself at risk. I have friends at Houston's FBI, and I'll make sure they're aware of this."

"If he did bury a body and shoot Russell, he's guilty of two murders. I went back the next day and took a few pictures of footprints and over-turned dirt. Those are on the flash drive I gave you with a few other things. But no one is to see them unless Willis is arrested, and his attorney can't bail him out. Or I end up dead. Promise, Jason."

"I give you my word." Willis now had the proof, but he probably didn't count on Jason having the images too. One more reason for Willis to find Billie and Zack.

"I'm sorry for involving you in this mess." Billie's voice broke. "I told myself I wouldn't fall apart."

"It's okay. You've gone through enough. I'm praying for you and Zack. You know you can trust me." When the call ended, Jason set his phone in the console. "Billie risked a lot by contacting me." He relayed the conversation.

"The flash drive is in a safe place?" He nodded and she continued. "Are you calling Simon?"

"Not yet. I want to look for evidence myself first."

She tucked black hair behind her ear. "You're making a mistake. Willis will shoot you for trespassing."

"If I call Simon, he won't let me within a hundred yards of the site. Drop me off, and I'll call you later."

"No way. We're taking a look together."

"I know the location Billie's referring to. We'll enter Willis's ranch through a remote side bordering my land. I'm guessing if the FBI is involved, they'll need a search warrant."

"The law states the issuing magistrate must have probable cause. Billie's statement may get us the warrant, but if something is found, we'll need her to testify."

"I refuse to drag Billie into it."

"A search warrant won't mention her name. It gives the FBI authority to search, and if necessary, seize things and people. Without one, we are violating Willis's rights, and he knows how far to push."

"Are you sure you want to risk getting shot on Willis's land?"

"No. But I'm in."

31

The idyllic setting of the Big Thicket had an antagonistic streak. April weighed Billie's story. If what the woman saw was accurate . . . "Anyone turn up missing seven months ago?" April said.

"Not to my knowledge." Jason had taken over the driving, and he inched toward a road she hadn't seen before. He pointed to binoculars on the console. "On your right is my land. Scan the area and make sure no one has us in his rifle sights."

"I can see the headlines—'Former Fugitive and Federal Agent Shot for Trespassing.'" She peered through the binoculars, but nothing caught her eye. Three buzzards hovered over a thick wooded section. "I think we're okay. Unless they're camouflaged."

"Camouflage is what the good old boys wear to church."

She welcomed the lightness.

Jason turned right onto a gravel road and followed it about a half mile to a thick line of trees. A rickety barn leaned on the outskirts.

"You could sell the siding and replace it," she said. "That look is very popular at the moment."

"And lose the barn's character?"

She smiled. How unusual to enjoy a man's company in the middle of a case.

The truck bumped in and out of ruts until it reached the partially standing barn. Weeds grew two feet tall between the gaps in the siding.

She eyed the rotted wood piecing together the barn. "We're parking in there?" she said. "I don't want to be inside when a gust of wind blows it over."

"If you're worried about the truck, I have canvas to protect it. You're the one who ruined Miss Ella's dress and lost her shoes. I'm going to be careful with Dad's vintage truck."

Jason parked the truck in the middle of the barn and reached inside the glove box for his Beretta. She pulled her gun from her shoulder bag and slipped it into her back waistband.

"Ready for a hike?" He glanced toward the sun dipping farther west. "We have enough daylight to scout a little."

Although the woods looked foreboding, she took comfort in his familiarity with them. Jason took the lead, and she trailed behind into the thickest part of the pines.

The earthy smells beneath the canopy of treetops enveloped her, foreign from the city but not unpleasant. The sun trickled through like fingers of light with rare glimpses of the blue sky. Jason found his way through the undergrowth and around the trees. Stray, frail branches from brush flew back and whipped across her chest. The next time she shielded her body and caught it.

He turned to her. "Sorry. Are you okay?"

She nodded.

He continued to lead, walking close enough for them to have a quiet conversation.

"What have you done in your previous life that you know the creepiest and most secluded areas?" she said. "Or do the people here grow up with an instinctive means of survival?"

"When I was fourteen or so, I'd come out here alone and camp overnight. Thought it was cool to be by myself. Envisioned myself as a forest ranger. I'd build a fire, explore, and set traps for rabbits. Made me feel like a real hunter. I'd dream about hunting bear in Alaska and lions in Africa. Never did either one."

"And your parents approved?"

"Dad did. He could have found me if he wanted to. The first couple of times I couldn't sleep for fright. Every sound jolted me straight up from my sleeping bag. But I refused to let it intimidate me."

"Like now."

"You're beginning to understand my drive," he said. "Let me warn you, the population of snakes outnumber people in these parts."

She cringed, and her gaze darted around her feet. "Thanks for the tip. I'm not a freak when it comes to snakes, but I'm not stupid either."

"I'm watching out for you. The cooler temps keep them away, but be careful."

"Count on it."

He stopped and held up a hand. "We're nearing the fence bordering Willis's property line. Sound carries."

She hoped there wasn't any barbed wire or a bull roaming on the other side. "How many men work Willis's ranch?"

"Three, I think."

They continued in silence and skirted a pasture on Jason's property. Black-and-white cows and horses grazed, obviously uninterested about anything outside the boundaries of the pasture. Not a single bull in sight. Oops. One lifted his head and stared at the tree line. She kept walking. Occasionally her new tennis shoes sank into low-lying holes, covering them in wet mud. Better than what her bare feet sank into last night.

With the pasture behind them, a barbed-wire fence soared five feet high. Her flesh still stung from her last encounter.

"Willis's land?" she whispered and pointed to a sign—*No Trespassing. Violators will be shot.*

Jason lifted the wire for her to crawl through. "Enjoy the tour."

Her knees hit chilly, wet ground. A brown-and-gray snake slithered past, and she held her breath in an effort to figure out if it was a good snake or a bad one.

"It's okay," he whispered. "Just a hognose. Won't bother you."

Once through the fence, he paused and listened, slowly turning in every direction. She heard nothing but birds. When he appeared satisfied, they plodded through thick brush and trees, moving with the sun fading from their view.

Several yards later, Jason stopped. "I'm going to make sure Willis doesn't have any guards posted. I'd feel better if you waited here."

"Who's going to watch your back? Or mine?"

"I can cover ground faster." He stopped and looked straight at her. "There are low areas where you'll sink above your knees and slow me down."

"I'd rather face Willis's men." She yanked out her phone and saw she had no connectivity. "I can't even call you."

"I'll make it fast." He jogged away.

The sounds of the forest could have been intimidating. No reason to fool herself. She'd rather face down a gang of drug dealers. A crow's harsh call ground at her fear button. Wind whistled through nearby trees, giving the site an ominous quality. A rustling in the brush behind her caused her to draw her gun. A squirrel scampered away.

What if Jason met up with Willis's men? What if she did?

⋆ ⋆ ⋆

Jason slipped through the trees and brush, following instincts and years of tromping through the

231

dense woods. He recalled the many times he and Lily had hiked his property and along the border between his and Willis's land, sometimes talking but usually quiet. They both enjoyed the beauty of nature. Even when she wrestled with cancer and carried Isabella, they took weekly hikes through the trees. When Isabella entered the world a week early, a little fighter like her mother was born.

His thoughts took an unbidden swing to April. Graceful. Intelligent. Spunky. Her smile stole his breath. She stood up to him when they differed in opinion and treated him as a peer instead of an East Texas home builder redneck. She'd made a choice to risk her career and life to help him, to prove his innocence, and he wanted to protect her even though she had the skills to defend herself. Her fierce determination resembled Lily's, and that realization moved him closer to what could be more emotionally frightening than losing his weapon.

Jason wondered about a future with the feisty FBI agent, who adored his Isabella. He never thought he'd be attracted to another woman. But a twinge of something had latched on to his heart, and he didn't know how to handle it. Guilt collided with every thought of April, as though he were cheating on Lily. Had it been only twelve months since she left him and Isabella? The grief books advised waiting two years before making any changes. Was he wrong to think about another woman? Did life offer a different guidebook on the proper time to shake off mourning?

Lily, I'm confused. I wish you could tell me what to do about April. About everything.

He hoped God gave messages to those who sat at His feet in heaven. If so, he wanted Lily to know he'd only replace her with a woman who loved Isabella as much as he did.

Drop it, Jason. Trying to figure out why the world spun in a direction contrary to how he thought it should invited a well of depression. He'd better run from April before his heart took another beating.

But if he read her expressions correctly, she felt the same interest.

About a half mile in on Willis's ranch, Jason observed several white-tailed deer. He followed signs of the animals to a winding creek. A deer feeder offered plenty of corn. Willis was building the deer population for hunting season. He spotted a salt lick. Too many hunters thought the salt was only for the bucks to grow large antlers, but the entire herd needed the minerals. A few deer lifted their heads and sniffed the air before dashing off. After using his binoculars to inspect up and down the marshy creek, he trekked farther.

He kept close to the creek and explored the deep, thick wilds. More deer. Another salt lick. Willis planned to hunt in style.

A snap captured his attention. He reached for

his handgun. To his left, a stirring and the distinct snorting of wild hogs. He peered into the brush at several females. The tank-built animals possessed tremendous strength and could easily overpower their prey. Female tusks were smaller than the males', but still sharp and able to kill a man.

Then he saw the piglets. Their mothers were the most dangerous and easily agitated of all. Best make his way around them.

He hadn't detected guards in this section, but any sound of gunfire would likely bring a rifle-totin' man running at top speed. They'd shoot him on sight, ship his head to the local taxidermist, and mount him in Willis's office.

Being eaten wasn't the way he wanted to meet his Maker either.

Dad's words resounded in his head. *"A wild hog is the fourth most intelligent animal in the world."*

Debating the mental capacity of the animal seemed useless. He just needed to get out of there. He quickly took in the terrain and moved quietly with his attention on the herd of hogs.

The extra distance between him and the animals offered safety. He released a smothered breath.

A male wild hog ambled across his path. It caught sight of Jason, and the two had a stare down. Suddenly the animal lowered its helmet head and barreled toward him.

Jason aimed and fired. The beast didn't slow.

He fired two more times.

32

April cringed with each crack of gunfire. Three shots. But the sound of a handgun, not the louder *pop* and reverb of a rifle. Too many scenarios exploded in her mind, and she fought the urge to race after Jason. He'd told her to stay put. She attempted to phone him, although nothing magical had given her connectivity. Her attention leaped from one theory to another. Had he been shot? Had he fired at someone else?

Wrapping her hand around her Glock, she dashed down the narrow trail Jason had taken. Several feet later she met him running toward her.

"We need to get out of here," he said between breaths.

"Is someone shot?"

"Met up with wild hogs."

She'd learn what happened later. Evening had settled as they kept pace to the rickety barn. They tugged back the canvas and climbed inside the truck. Jason wasted no time getting on the road.

She had a feeling his wild pig story might top her escape from Romeo. "I'm ready to hear about your fling."

He palmed the steering wheel. "I nearly became the night's menu special for a bunch of wild hogs." He relayed the story. "Downside is Willis will learn about the gunfire. Deer season isn't open either. Maybe he'll suspect overeager hunters on his property."

"With No Trespassing signs and the barbed wire?" she said. "I'm sure his men can tell the difference between the sound of a handgun and a rifle."

"True. Either way, I'm glad we got out of there. But I never got to the point where Billie indicated Willis might have covered up a crime. To pull what looked like a body from the trunk of his cruiser doesn't sound like law-abiding to me." He reached for a bottle of water on the seat. "Have you noticed my attempts at rectifying this keep slamming into my face?"

"The FBI wouldn't need to sneak around."

"Not yet, April."

She fumed. "You realize I have to tell Simon about Billie's accusation."

He took a sip of water. "How long does it take to get a search warrant?"

"Depends on the judge. It can be fast."

"Involving Billie concerns me. We've all experienced how Willis seeks revenge."

"We can protect her." Why did these people shy away from federal protection? "If the worst scenario occurred and her life was in danger, FBI protection has to be a better option than hiding herself."

"Billie is a great gal. If she has a fault, she's too trusting, naive. Always wants to believe the best about people. I'm sure she's rethought those traits after living with Willis."

She held up her phone, the only way she could think of to bring peace to all of Willis's victims. "Which one of us is calling Simon?"

"We do it together. Use the speaker."

She glanced at her phone and confirmed connectivity. She laid it on the seat between them and tapped in Simon's number. "Jason and I have an update."

"We need a good one."

Jason took over. "I talked to Billie Lennox, and she claims . . ." He briefed Simon on his conversation with Billie.

"Is she in Sweet Briar?" Simon said.

"Doubt it. I understand you need probable cause to search his land."

"We may have it. But talking to Billie is imperative."

Jason glanced at April. "I'll encourage her to contact you."

"We might have to—"

"I'm not exposing her after giving my word." Jason's shoulders stiffened.

"If a body is found, she'll have to testify. Tell her if she cooperates, we can protect her," Simon said.

"From whom?" Jason continued, his tone even. "Willis or one of his paid men?"

"Anyone."

April focused on what Billie saw. "Simon, is

there a missing person in the Sweet Briar file?"

"Give me a little time and I'll get back to you." He clicked off.

"Is he always this helpful?" Jason said.

"Okay, you're frustrated." Never mind how she'd like a face-to-face with Simon. "I am too. Willis has rights. Even if a judge sees probable cause, issues a search warrant, and the FBI finds a body, without Billie's testimony, the investigation will be drawn out and much harder."

"Simon hinted at a missing person."

"And the next one could be you or Billie and Zack."

He clenched his jaw. "Or you."

☆ ☆ ☆

With the dark night closing in around them like Jason's infuriation with Willis and Simon, he drove into the woods of his temporary residence. Once he parked his dad's truck, he snatched his phone and rolled down the window. A blast of cold air rolled in.

"I know you're worried about Billie's and Zack's safety." April placed her hand on his shoulder. "Billie may surprise you."

Jason considered what the FBI requested juxtaposed with Billie's fear. "I'll try." He pressed in her number. She answered on the first ring. "This is Jason. I relayed what you told me to the FBI. The law requires a search warrant to investigate

Willis's potential crime. If a judge signs it, the FBI can look for a grave. But they'd like to talk to you."

"He'll find us," she whispered as though Willis were listening to the conversation.

"All I'm asking is for you to make a phone call to an FBI agent and tell him the same thing you told me. It will get the legal ball rolling."

"Would I have to testify in court?"

"If a body's found, probably so."

"Willis threatened to kill me if I ever tried to leave him. And if I testify against him, Zack and I have no future."

"The right thing to do is seldom easy. They can protect you."

"For how long? Even I know Willis can reach out to me from prison."

His head hammered as though the migraine had broken through the wall of resistance. "You could ask for witness protection."

"How is this connected to Russell's death?" she said.

"Anything I say is speculation."

"Are you asking me to call the Houston FBI office?"

"Yes, or I can give you a number for an agent working the area."

"I prefer a man," she said. "I don't trust a woman. Willis is the master of manipulating women to see things his way."

"All right. His name is Simon Neilson, and here's his number." Jason rattled off the digits. "Billie, I know this is hard."

"I'm not sure I can go through with what you're asking. Before I go . . . the envelope I gave you?"

"Yes. I have it." She'd requested he keep it and the flash drive safe, to talk to law enforcement outside of Tyler County if she turned up dead.

"Read it. You'll understand why no one can find out where I am."

After she told him good-bye, Jason deposited his phone in his jacket pocket and leaned his head back on the seat. "If doing the right thing gets her and Zack killed, I won't be able to live with myself."

"Willis is not infallible. But he's smart, so bringing him down means having patience and following protocol," she said. "I have a question about him. You told me he acquired his land from his grandparents and parents. What did Carrie receive?"

"Russell told me they deeded their Florida condo to her. It's in the will."

"Not exactly a fair inheritance," April said.

"Nothing about the Lennox family works on fair or Christian values. Why Mrs. Lennox stayed married to Mr. Lennox and allowed her kids to be abused is beyond me." He shook his head. "I'm rambling like an old woman."

"And I need to get back to town. Can't forget that I want to get an audience with Brenda."

"In the meantime, I'm going to make a list of all those considered to be Willis's victims. Dad can help me with details. He and Mom haven't been separated in years, and I'm sure he's down." The two men needed each other for support.

Jason's phone rang: Tessa.

33

Jason tapped Speaker on the call from Tessa Barker. April had a way of seeing things differently than he did.

"Jason, this is Tessa. I found interesting footage on our security camera. Can you meet with me and my husband at our office?"

They needed a break. "Sure. I have an FBI agent friend with me. Mind if she comes along?"

"Sounds like a good idea. We're here now. We'll see you in a little while."

The call ended, and he turned to April. "This could give us the answers we need to find out who killed Russell and maybe even kidnapped Isabella."

"I hope so," she said. "The people of Sweet Briar need peace . . . especially you."

Jason drove toward City and Country Glass Company, near Woodville.

Nate and Tessa Barker met them outside their office and showroom. Jason had talked to the middle-aged couple at chamber of commerce events. Good people, but when he requested a bid for a building project, their prices were higher than his current vendors. Nate had recently recovered from a massive heart attack, and his weight loss had taken ten years off his appearance.

Tessa, thin as a fence post, still looked the same.

After shaking hands and sharing a few pleasantries, Nate invited them inside and locked the door.

Nate ushered April to a desktop computer. Once she was seated, he gave her the credentials to access the security footage.

"A few hours ago, I found this," Nate said. "Our security system is closed-circuit, not monitored or anything. Scroll to the 10:05 p.m. time stamp. It's after the crime took place, and we were closed."

When April found the footage, Jason watched the video with her. A man in a black hoodie appeared at the side entrance of City and Country's warehouse. Average height and build. No visible facial features. He pulled something from his sweatshirt pocket and inserted it in the lock. The door opened.

"I haven't figured out why the alarm didn't signal." Nate wrapped his arms over his chest.

April studied the screen. "The system could have been hacked." The frame ticked by.

Nate typed. "This is thirty minutes later."

April zoomed in.

The man exited the warehouse with a piece of glass. A replacement the night of Russell's death meant the installer already knew the custom size required for the office window. Once there, he'd have cleaned up the broken shards, positioned the push points in the four corners to hold the frame, added putty, and completed the project.

Jason added up two more crimes—theft and breaking and entering.

"I'd like your permission to copy this and send it to the FBI," April said.

"Go ahead." Nate sorted through a desk drawer and produced a flash drive. "When you identify the thief, I'm filing charges."

April jotted Simon's number on the back of her business card. "I suggest contacting Special Agent Neilson and telling him you want to report the crime."

Nate took the information with a promise to contact Simon as soon as they departed. Jason breathed in and slowly let it out. They'd made a little progress.

34

A little before 8 p.m. on Saturday, April drove Ted's truck into Sweet Briar. Jason remained in seclusion with the assignment of making a list of all those in the area who'd experienced Willis's bullying and possible illegal tactics.

Darkness covered most of the sleepy town, but the business area hosted electrical poles to keep the downtown lit. One such stood near a small barn-replica structure with a welcoming porch filled with pots of blooming mums. *Krew Real Estate Office* in slanted country letters hung above the door.

April turned off the ignition and exited the truck.

Before she could reach the door, Willis emerged from the shadows. "Evenin', Agent Ramos. I see you haven't left Sweet Briar."

"It's a nice town to visit. Most of the people are friendly."

"You're out of your element here."

"How? I'm just taking a few days off to rest and relax."

He snorted. "Right. Jason's on the loose, but I hear he's in the vicinity. It's just a matter of time before I find him. The FBI's plumb stupid to free him of murder charges. Be sure to tell him I don't take the same line. He'll make a mistake, and I'll be right there to handle it."

She'd had enough of his threats. Her placating style ended. "Sweet Briar isn't your corner of the universe, Sheriff Lennox. You kill an innocent man, you face murder charges."

"I have many ways of getting what I want." He punched each word.

"Are you threatening me again? I've seen you in action, and I've reported your misconduct."

"You mean my responsibility to take down a fugitive? I've already turned you in to the FBI, told them you tricked me while I was trying to do my duty. Held me at gunpoint. I'm giving a fellow law enforcement official a warning. Accidents can happen to anyone when they're in unfamiliar territory."

"Willis, I'm quite aware of what you can do to those who get in your way. Your lies will soon catch up." She stared into his fleshy face. "Or perhaps they already have."

He tapped the brim of his hat. "Have a fine talk with Brenda. She's expecting you." He disappeared into the darkness.

Shaking off Willis's arrogance, she pasted on a smile and stepped into the real estate office. The antiques and farm decor might make potential clients comfortable, but not an FBI agent on a mission.

"Brenda Krew?"

An expressionless woman in her midforties looked up from typing on a laptop. "You must be Special Agent April Ramos." The woman stood and stuck out her hand, and April reciprocated. Brenda had spiked black hair and wore designer jeans and a white blouse with an abundance of turquoise jewelry. "I've heard a lot about you from Willis. It's a pleasure." Brenda's green eyes lacked luster. "Won't you sit down? Sorry about not returning your call. Saturday is one of my busiest days."

April eased onto a blue chair across from a white sawbuck desk. She reached inside her purse for her phone. "I won't take much of your time. As I said in my messages, I have a few questions about Jason Snyder. Do you mind if I record our conversation?"

"I've been advised to guard what I say and not to have my words end up in an audio file. Unless you want to have this conversation with my attorney present." Brenda pushed a pad of paper and pen with *Krew Real Estate* printed on both toward April. "You can use this."

Her nails were manicured in dark purple, not the chipped red Ted reported the kidnapper wore. But a fresh coat of paint covered a multitude of sins.

April dropped her phone back into her purse. If Brenda had phoned the FBI to accuse Jason of assisting in his wife's death, her voice recording could be used as a comparison. Although the woman didn't have a husky voice like the kidnapper, the tone could be affected.

"I'll get right to the point," April said. "I'm curious about the real Jason Snyder. I'm hoping you can help me sort through some of the statements from local people."

Brenda touched her throat. "Of course. But I have a business to run." She crossed her arms over her chest.

"I'll do my best to expedite my questions." April dated the empty page on the Krew Real Estate pad and printed Brenda's name. "Have you always lived in Sweet Briar?"

"All my life."

"How long have you known Jason Snyder?"

"He and his parents attend my church."

"Is it safe to say you're well acquainted with him?"

"I've sold land to those who wanted Jason to build them a home."

"Can you describe his temperament?"

"Short fuse. No one in Sweet Briar deliberately makes him mad."

April glanced up. "Does he become physical?"

"I'm not aware of physical assaults, but someone murdered Russell." She scratched the side of her neck. "I hear the charges have been dropped. But I'm entitled to my own opinion. It makes sense Jason's guilty since he was with him. According to our sheriff, he's unpredictable, a menace to our town."

"The law demands evidence. To the best of your knowledge, have there been any problems with his construction business?"

She leaned back in her chair. "He's expensive. Shoddy workmanship."

"But you've sold land to those who've engaged Jason to build them a home."

"I tried to talk them out of it and go with a contractor outside of Sweet Briar. Their choice, really. I deal in real estate, not construction."

"He's received several awards for his out-standing building designs."

Brenda stiffened. "If you want facts about Jason and his construction company, I suggest talking to Willis."

She'd signaled with her body language at least three indications of nervousness and possibly lying. "I'd like the names of your clients and those who've experienced problems with Mr. Snyder."

"Your request would take a considerable amount of time, and I'm extremely busy. My notes are scattered in physical and online files. Most are here, but some are at home."

"Do I need to request a search warrant?"

Brenda glared. "I'll add the task to my list."

"I'd like the information by 10 a.m. Monday."

Brenda reddened. "I have appointments—"

"They can be rescheduled." When Brenda opened her mouth again, April gave her no time to interrupt. "What can you tell me about Willis Lennox?"

"He's a very smart man, a voice of authority in the community and church."

"Are you two dating?"

"Seriously? He has a wife and son." Brenda closed her eyes dramatically. "We share an occasional coffee and work together on various committees. Nothing else."

"Where are his wife and son?"

"Good question. Willis is extremely distraught about their absence."

"So he discusses his personal life with you?"

"Are we finished? I haven't had dinner." Brenda began to stack papers on her desk, putting some of them into her briefcase.

"Neither have I. Want to grab a bite together?"

"No thanks."

"I'm buying."

Brenda ignored her. She reached for a small piece of blank paper and knocked it onto the floor. April bent from her chair to retrieve the paper and flipped it over in the process. A photo. Smiling at the camera was a young woman, one April had seen in a Houston donut shop, the same person who'd shoved Isabella Snyder into her arms. "What a beautiful young woman. Your daughter?"

Brenda snatched the photo and slipped it into her briefcase. "Yes."

"What's her name?"

"I keep my daughter out of my affairs. She doesn't live in Sweet Briar."

"Where does she live?"

"None of your business."

"We always want to protect our loved ones. Mr. Snyder is very concerned about the welfare of his daughter, especially since the kidnapping."

"It's a parent's job. Good night, Agent Ramos."

April scooted back her chair. "Thanks for seeing me. Have a great dinner." She left the real estate office and walked to Ted's truck. After getting on the road en route to the elder Snyders' home, she called Simon and rehashed the conversation. "I'd appreciate it if you'd try to match Brenda's voice mail against the woman claiming to be Vicki Snyder."

"If you're lucky and come out of this without destroying your career, you might consider giving up hostage negotiation and public corruption to work homicide."

"We'll see if I survive—professionally. Ted probably knows the daughter's name." April paused and reviewed the conversation. "Brenda said her daughter doesn't live in Sweet Briar, which makes sense because Jason didn't recognize her."

"I'll dig into locating her from my end."

"Seems like Jason and I are caught in the middle of a sewage retention pond. You demonstrated no surprise when Jason indicated Willis might have disposed of a body."

"It's a factor in the investigation."

"Really, Simon? When will those factors be revealed?"

"Soon. Hold on a bit longer, and keep Jason from going all vigilante on me. I wouldn't enjoy tossing him in jail."

April released a pent-up breath. So much for peaceful small-town living. Next on her agenda was a chat with Ted about Brenda Krew.

☆ ☆ ☆

Jason leaned on the hood of his truck and stared into the darkness. A flying squirrel scampered past, a nocturnal creature who'd earned its name not by actually flying but by jumping from one high branch to another. He listened to the night sounds, frogs and insects competing in a chorus to see who could outsing the other. But the choir and occasional swoosh of brush lulled his mind to a place where he could reason and rest.

God had brought him through Lily's death, Billie and Zack's escape, Russell's death, and Isabella's kidnapping. God would take care of the justice part with Willis. His faith . . . such a fragile thread when he needed a lifeline.

After April had driven away, he'd talked to

Dad and compiled a list of actions where Willis had crossed the legal line and gotten away with it. Names, dates, and a brief explanation of each incident had occupied Jason's time.

A few thoughts about the glass installer stayed fixed in his mind. He couldn't do much in the way of private investigation when his gas tank was running on fumes. He needed to drive to a twenty-four-hour convenience store and gas station in Woodville, about fifteen miles away. Would have to take a gamble on Willis or one of his men finding an excuse to stop him.

He'd fill up his tank. Then he had a stop to make.

35

Jason filled up his truck at the twenty-four-hour Check Point in Woodville and attempted to avoid security cameras. But the front license plates were visible, and he paid for the gas with a credit card. Keeping out of the public eye was a myth.

On his way back to Sweet Briar, he phoned Tessa Barker. "You mentioned your sons are the installers. Have you ever used anyone else?"

"About a year ago when Nate had his heart attack, we hired two installers temporarily."

"Would they have been given an access code to the warehouse?"

"No. We handled their comings and goings."

"Can you give me their names?"

"I'll look them up and send you their addresses and phone numbers. Or should I send the info to Agent Ramos?"

"Both." He and April were a team. "Thanks."

Jason drove into Sweet Briar with caution aimed in every direction. This might not be a smart move. Under the guise of using the Internet, Jason wanted to check on his dad and see if he could change his mind about FBI protection. Dad was expecting him, and the garage door was raised so he could pull into the spot where the old truck normally sat.

Expelling a deep breath, he listened for the grounding of the garage door on the cement and switched off the engine. So much had gone wrong in the last forty-eight hours, pelting him from every direction.

Tessa's text landed in his phone with the names of the two men who'd helped out during Nate's recovery. Both were from Woodville. Stepping into the kitchen, he smelled fresh coffee and the tantalizing aroma of chicken potpie, his favorite food. His stomach growled.

Dad sat at the kitchen table with the laptop ready for Jason to use. "You made it in one piece."

Jason plastered on a grin. "Still driving a truck with stolen plates. Need to return them before I'm arrested."

He stood. "Your food's ready. Planning to eat while you do your online research? You mentioned this was about finding who replaced the glass at your office?"

"Yes. April and I talked to Tessa Barker this evening, and the conversations stirred up a few questions."

Dad set a full cup and a sizzling potpie on the table. "I'm going to bed. Long day. Holler if you need me."

"I'd feel a whole lot better if you were with Mom and Isabella."

"Nope."

"Dad, you're walking a dangerous path."

"Not going there."

"What will it take?"

"God telling me I'm an old fool."

"Sleep on it." Jason powered the laptop to life. Might as well get online. Whoever had done the installation had agreed to a late-night replacement, possibly on short notice, which meant he lived in close proximity to Jason's construction office.

The person had probably been paid well.

The person understood the need to keep the job secret and possibly lie about the install.

He googled the men, but nothing hinted at infractions.

Could Jason have been looking in the wrong place? He took a bite of food with a swallow of coffee. The Barkers' three sons were involved in the family business. Andy was in high school—nothing on him except a Snapchat account.

Jason typed in the oldest son, Mark. Active in the community. Led out on the City and Country website and Facebook page, a young man following in his dad's footsteps.

His probing turned to Hunter. Interesting, two sites indicated that for a fee, a background and criminal check was available. While April had the credentials and tools to learn what Hunter might have done, Jason wondered if the presence of the sites were an indication that the young man had a propensity to break the law.

His thoughts tumbled over each other while he

ate. Hunter had an average build and wouldn't have a problem getting into the warehouse. Earning a little extra money might appeal to him.

Jason reined in his musings. He'd been accused wrongly of a crime, and he certainly didn't want to do the same to anyone else. But doubts lingered. Jason dug into his second pie, burning his tongue in the process.

The front door opened, and April entered her home away from home. He walked into the living room to greet her. . . . Her smile lit up his frenzied heart. "Hey, did Brenda give you a lead? Sell you a house?"

She rolled her eyes. "She's a prize, but I got our lead. The short version is her daughter is the young woman who nabbed Isabella. I saw her pic."

He choked and coughed. "I knew Brenda had a daughter, but I haven't seen her since she was a little girl and moved away with her dad. I think her name started with a *J*. . . . Where does she live?"

"I'm hoping Ted can give us insight."

"He's in bed. Attempted to talk him into leaving town, but no go."

She nodded. "I'll talk to him in the morning about Brenda's daughter. You're taking a big chance by being in public."

"I know." He quickly explained his search for info about the Barker boys.

April typed into the laptop. "Hunter does have a record. Been arrested twice for DUI. He also has a charge for assault. Guess who made the last arrest?"

"Willis?"

"None other."

"What do you think?" He studied her. She needed sleep. "Am I way out there?"

"Not sure. But the person videoed going into their warehouse could be the same."

He grabbed his phone and called Tessa.

"Have you identified who broke into our warehouse?" Tessa said.

"I need some help, and I think you, Nate, and the boys could help."

"Andy has an overnight church event. But the rest of us are here. Nate and I want this settled."

"Great. April and I will be there by 10:30." He dropped the phone into his jacket. "I'm driving."

When they arrived at City and Country Glass, a light shone through the window. He hoped his suspicions about Hunter were wrong, but Jason had to follow through and find out if the middle son was the one who installed the custom glass in his office window.

Nate opened the door before Jason and April left the truck. "The four of us are chomping at the bit to see if you've identified the thief." Nate reached out and shook Jason's hand and then April's. "Come on in."

Did Nate suspect anyone or was he simply wanting justice served? Jason greeted the family.

Mark and Hunter appeared open and friendly. Nate pointed to chairs positioned in the office.

April began the conversation. "Thanks for seeing us on such short notice at this hour," she said. "The FBI is diligently working with local law enforcement to untangle the death of Russell Edwards. We've been looking into the workers you hired during Nate's illness." She paused. "Did you have any problems with them?"

Mark answered. "No, not at all. They were hard workers. I wished we'd had more jobs to keep them on. I have a hard time believing either of them would have broken into the warehouse."

Hunter took over. "Their wives took turns sending cookies and stuff with them." He ran his hand over his mouth. "But do we ever know folks and what they're capable of? Mr. Snyder, I'm sorry for what's happened to you."

"Thanks." Jason eyed him. Hunter could have taken a step in the right direction. Maybe his wild ways were behind him.

"You said neither of the workers were given an access code to the warehouse," April said. "Is it possible they obtained one of your keys or figured out the code?"

"I have mine," Tessa said.

Mark and Hunter responded by pulling out their keys.

"What about Andy? Does he have a key?" Jason said.

"Oh, he's in school and only helps out on the weekends," Nate said. "I'll tell him about y'all's questions, but I doubt he has anything to offer."

April thanked the family. "We appreciate your being here late."

"We're sorry this has been a waste of time for the FBI." Nate crossed his arms over his chest. "I don't care about the missing glass, but I know you folks are looking for a killer. Let's call it a night and talk tomorrow. We're all tired."

"Of course," April said.

Jason and Nate shook hands. Again on the road, Jason turned into a farmer's lane, switched off his truck lights, and put his vehicle in park. "Could Simon request search warrants for cell phone records from the sons?" he said.

"I'll do my best."

"Now we wait to follow Hunter."

"What if you're wrong?"

Jason reached across the seat and took her hand. "I have nothing to lose and everything to gain." He unbuckled his seat belt. "We can pretend we're sixteen and enjoy the quiet."

"I don't think so." She laughed. "We have a job to do."

Jason grabbed his night-vision goggles and pointed to City and Country Glass. "Nate's truck is pulling out." Five minutes later, another vehicle left. "It's Hunter in his truck."

36

April kept her eyes on Hunter's truck. Jason kept his distance behind him with his lights off.

"He's not heading in the direction of his parents' home but into Woodville," Jason said.

"So is he meeting buds, a girl, Willis, or a person who works for Willis? The million-dollar question." She recalled how Nate had crossed his arms over his chest. "When I talk to Simon, I'll add Nate to the search warrants. A father would protect his son."

"Nate vowed to find out who entered the warehouse. Do you think he might suspect one of his sons was the culprit?"

"The short answer? Yes."

Upon entering Woodville city limits, Jason turned on his lights. Hunter drove to Whataburger, still open. The clock ticked toward 11:15. Jason passed by the fast-food restaurant, and the two watched from farther down the street.

"If he's hungry, he'd have used the drive-through, right?" April said. "But he hasn't gotten out of his truck."

"Must be waiting on someone. The question is who."

In less than five minutes, Nate's truck pulled in beside Hunter and parked. Nate and Hunter emerged from their trucks and walked to the Whataburger entrance.

"I thought they were tired," April said.

The Barker men talked outside the restaurant door. Hunter ran his hand over his face, and Nate wrapped his arm around Hunter's shoulders as they walked in.

"Hungry?" Jason said. "That doesn't look like father and son bonding to me—more like desperation."

"We should scope it out."

Once inside, Jason and April ignored Nate and Hunter and moved straight to the counter. Jason put in an order for burger and fries, and she requested a grilled chicken melt. After filling their drinks, they looked for a place to sit and appeared to notice father and son seated in a booth.

"Hey," Jason said. "Mind if we join you?"

Nate paled but quickly recovered, reinforcing the theory that Hunter could be in some kind of trouble. Perhaps this was unrelated to the glass replacement. "Sure." He pointed to a table for two beside him and Hunter. Nate's hands trembled.

"Strange to see you two here," Jason said.

"We're talking business," Hunter said. "Hope we don't bore you."

Jason sat at the table and faced Hunter. "If you're doing an estimate for me, make it low."

April eased onto a chair across from Jason. Nate offered a slight smile. She unwrapped her sandwich and ate slowly while observing father and son from the corner of her eye.

"What's it like being an FBI agent?" Hunter dipped fries into a mound of mustard and ketchup.

"Interesting. You learn the best and the worst about people," she said.

"Do you always work murder cases?" Hunter said.

"No. I work hostage negotiation when needed and public corruption in between."

"Interesting."

April took a drink of her Diet Coke. "Have you met Sheriff Willis Lennox?"

"No, ma'am."

"Son, the agent here needs to eat." Nate looked at his watch. "Are you about ready? Your mama wants to talk to us, and we don't want to keep her waiting."

"Gotta keep Mom happy." Hunter gathered up an uneaten sandwich and wrapped it in a napkin. He shoved his food toward his dad. "You can have this. Good talking to you," he said to Jason and April.

Nate and Hunter exited.

April turned to Jason. "Don't look, but I think Hunter drove off but not Nate. I need to talk to him."

"Okay for me to tag along or does it look like we're ganging up on him?"

"Not a good idea. If we're right, Nate's emotions may be off the charts."

"I understand being overprotective about kids."

They ignored their food and walked outside.

April knocked on the passenger side of Nate's truck. She didn't wait for his approval but opened the door and seated herself. Jason waited by his vehicle. In the faint light, lines dug into the outer corners of Nate's eyes. April worried about his failing health. Permanent heart damage had a way of slowing a man down.

"Are you all right?" she said.

He stared straight ahead. "What do you think?"

"Stress can do us in."

Nate breathed in sharply. "When did you figure out Hunter was the man in the security video?"

"Jason had a hunch this afternoon. I checked his background. When he said he'd never met Willis, I knew he'd lied because Willis has arrested him in the past."

"Once you and Jason left, I told him we had to figure this out. He agreed, said he wanted to do the right thing, a step up for my son."

"I hear your love for him."

"I sent him home. Told him I'd talk to you."

"Nate, he hasn't broken the law if all he's done is replace a window and used glass from your warehouse."

"I told him the same thing, but he's scared about his past record. Sheriff Lennox paid him $500 to install the window and keep his mouth shut."

37

"Hunter, to the best of your knowledge, have you broken the law regarding the murder of Russell Edwards?" April's soft voice wafted about the room.

Jason recalled the first time he'd heard her gentle tone. Although she had an objective—to find out about the glass install—he recognized her compassion.

The twenty-one-year-old sat at the kitchen table with his family, Jason, and April. "I kept quiet about replacing the window. But there was blood on the office floor of Mr. Snyder's construction office."

"Start at the beginning," she said. "I'd like to record our interview if it's okay."

Hunter stared at his parents. "What do you think?"

"I prefer not," Nate said. "When we hear the whole story, we'll decide together."

Sweat beaded on Hunter's forehead. "Sheriff Lennox called me around 8:15 last Thursday evening. Told me he needed a glass replacement for a friend done that night. I asked if it could wait until the morning, and he offered me $500. All I had to do was keep quiet. The installation was a surprise for a friend. He mentioned not arresting me the last time he picked me up for a DUI. In my opinion, he didn't offer much choice. I've been trying to behave myself. Sheriff Lennox gave me the window's measurements. I saw right away it was a custom size, and I'd have to cut it in the warehouse. I assumed he'd have replaced it himself if it had been a regular size."

"Son," Tessa began, "would some water help?"

"No thanks, Mom. My stomach's queasy. Feel awful."

Hunter was showing the classic signs of alcohol withdrawal. Poor kid.

April touched the knuckles of Hunter's clasped hands. "Do you feel well enough to finish?"

"Yes, ma'am. Have to. I couldn't figure out if I should turn the security camera off." He shrugged. "I decided if a problem ever surfaced, I'd rather it look like a break-in. So I got the glass, cut it, and met Sheriff Lennox at Mr. Snyder's office around 10:30. He stood around while I installed the glass and cleaned up. He insisted the inside and outside of the office were spotless."

"What did the broken window look like? Did it show any holes that could have been bullet holes?"

"When I arrived, the whole thing was busted out."

"What else did you see?"

"The blood on the floor bothered me big-time. Found the guts to ask about it, and he told me it was wine. Told me I was being paid for replacing glass, not asking questions."

Willis hadn't been sitting in the sheriff's office during Jason's hours in jail but standing over Hunter while he replaced the glass.

"Was there a hole in the wall opposite the window?"

"No, sir."

"Did you hear anything we can use?" April said.

"He texted a lot. I could tell by the sound of the messages going out and others coming in. Someone called him. I heard, 'Finish what you were paid to do and disappear.' I thought the call had something to do with the blood on the floor."

"How were you paid?"

"Cash."

"When this case goes to trial, we'll require you to testify."

"Yes, ma'am. My plans are to straighten up my life before it all goes down the toilet. I haven't spent the money either. It's in my bedroom closet."

"Hunter," Jason said, "since I learned the window in my office was replaced, I've wondered how this could have been handled so quickly. You've provided answers, and I'll never forget it." He reached across the table and shook Hunter's hand. "Thank you for your courage to stand up for truth."

"We have a witness," April said on the way back to the Sweet Briar area. "Hunter's statement shows Willis is in clear violation of the law."

"How soon before Simon can act on it?"

She'd sent a text from Nate and Tessa's home, but he hadn't responded.

Her phone rang, and she recognized Kevin's number.

"April, we have a problem," Kevin said. "Willis had Ted brought in as a person of interest and accomplice in Russell's murder. I'm at the Snyder house with two other deputies, looking for a weapon—the murder weapon—to keep him behind bars."

"Willis is an idiot. Does he think conjuring up evidence exonerates his actions?" April chewed on her fury. "Tell me what you know."

"Hold on." Kevin muffled his conversation. She counted to five before he returned to the line. "They've found an S&W. It fires the same caliber as the bullet used to kill Russell."

She glanced at Jason. His presence at the sheriff's office could erupt more than false charges against Ted. "I'm on my way. Stall the others until I get there."

38

Jason listened to April explain Kevin's call. His heart thumped like a racehorse's.

"I'll handle getting your dad out of jail," she said.

"I'm going with you." Anger topped his words. He heard it. He owned it. "Willis has stabbed my family for the last time."

"Let me handle this. The anger only works against you. Plus, you're exhausted. It's nearly 2 a.m."

"You have no clue what I'm feeling."

"I see a man who lost his temper yesterday and nearly killed Willis. You're heading in the same direction tonight."

Willis hadn't given up pushing him into a corner. Left to Jason, he'd give Willis a dose of his own trash.

"I have no idea what this is like for you. I'm on your side. The FBI is too. But if you lose your temper, Willis gains it all."

When had he allowed anger to take over his life? Since the note left in his mailbox about keeping an eye on Isabella, he'd breathed fury and fear. No, before that . . . since Lily's death.

"Jason?"

He let out a slow breath before speaking. "I

don't recognize myself. For the past year, I've pushed myself to keep the business running and be a good dad. I thought the anger came from the grieving process, and maybe some of it does. I have to harness it instead of stuffing it until I explode. Put the slow burning of my soul where I can deal with it logically."

She touched his arm. "You're a man of faith. Use it."

"God hasn't sheltered me from life's ugliness," he said. "I've always heard adversity causes spiritual growth. But I'm not growing closer to God. Just the opposite."

"If Lily were here, what would she say?"

He stared out into the black countryside. She'd tell him to pray. Revenge against Willis wasn't his call. Not now. Not ever. "Get my dad out of jail." He heard the frustration in his own voice. *God, help me rely on Your wisdom, not mine.* "Slap your cuffs on him and drive him to a safe house."

"I'll do my best."

The tenderness in her voice didn't go unnoticed. He clasped his hand over hers, still touching his arm. "I'm not always a self-centered, desperate man. When this is over, I'd like to show you the better man."

"You already have."

Words of gratitude burned in his throat, and he smiled despite the disconcerting circumstances. "Maybe so."

"Do you mind hiding out one more night? I'll contact you as soon as I have your dad's arrest resolved."

"No problem."

★ ★ ★

April's doubts about Kevin swung like a pendulum. Granted, he'd taken a few risks to protect Jason. Claimed to be on their side and requested the FBI tuck his family away. Informed her about Ted's arrest. Told her about finding the gun. She wanted to trust him, but he always seemed to be at the right place at the right time. Or the wrong place at the wrong time. Coincidence?

She feared Willis might rough Ted up and claim he resisted questioning, similar to what he'd stated about Jason. She notified Simon and asked for guidance in how to proceed.

"Willis will use him like a magnet to draw Jason out of hiding. I have an idea . . . ," Simon said.

She drove into the parking area of the county sheriff's office in Sweet Briar and turned off the engine. Exasperation swirled like a swarm of bees. Hard to negotiate when she wanted to twist the head off Sheriff Willis Lennox and toss his remains to the wild pigs who'd been after Jason.

Locking the truck, she strode inside the office. Kevin, Griff, and Willis stood with Ted. Kevin ignored her.

Willis smirked and gloated, reminding her of Romeo the bull. "Agent Ramos—" Willis opened his palms—"the murder case implicating Jason Snyder is about to be tied up with a big red bow."

"By picking up a man who happens to have a registered gun that uses the same caliber of bullet as the murder weapon?"

"No need to get your feathers all ruffled up. I had a tip and did my civil duty."

If she tore into Willis, she'd be pushed off the case for misconduct. "Where's your search warrant?"

"Protecting innocent people comes before procedure."

"Are you saying you violated Ted's rights?"

"We'll see how the judge views it."

She started to ask if the judge was on his payroll but bit her tongue. "Is he a friend of yours?"

"He's an elected officer of the law. Ted's taking up residence here until we have the ballistics report on the gun found in his possession." Willis lifted a bag of peanuts from his shirt pocket and downed a few. "Same type of gun adds to him being a person of interest and my suspicions of him knowing details about Russell's murder. Deputy Griff Wilcombe says the chamber's dirty, so it's been recently fired—"

"Sheriff, I said I'd have to check the weapon," Griff said.

Willis ignored him. "We'll have the report

tomorrow. Funny thing about bullets—they always match up to a gun somewhere." He tapped papers on the desk.

"As I said before April arrived, I demand a lawyer." Ted's calm voice was a refreshing counterpoint to the high-voltage tension.

"I've got this." April plastered on a pleasant demeanor. "I'll have you out of here shortly. Don't say a word to any of these men."

"Really?" Willis snorted, reminding her again of Romeo. "You'll have to contact a fancy criminal attorney from Houston or Dallas. Those around here don't take felony cases." He anchored his hand on his hip. "Same advice I gave Jason when I arrested him for murder. For now, Ted's booked as an accomplice in the murder of Russell Edwards."

April had never heard such a violation of a citizen's rights. She paused for a moment of power-thinking before turning to Willis. "You won't like the way this ends."

"By the way, Agent Ramos, in your background search for all those involved in Russell's murder, I'm sure you saw Ted here spent two years in Huntsville prison for aggravated assault with a deadly weapon."

Poker face time.

"It's true," Ted said.

"That has nothing to do with now," she said.

"It's a game changer." Willis leaned on one foot.

He was acting in such a stereotypical fashion, no one at the Houston office would believe her reporting of him.

"When did this happen?" she said.

Willis grinned. "Ted here was jailed about thirty-five years ago. Should have been in for life."

"Do you have documentation of the prior charges?"

"The victim happened to be my uncle," Willis said. "Do your research and you'll discover I'm a man who knows the law."

"I'll check into it."

"With my blessings, Agent Ramos. Make sure Jason is aware of his dad's arrest. We can work this out."

"I'm taking Ted into FBI custody. You invited us into this case with the report of Jason Snyder on the loose for murder and kidnapping his daughter. As you've been previously reminded by the FBI, we have jurisdiction here. You are ordered to release Ted Snyder to me."

"I'll release him to FBI agents who are not harboring a fugitive. They should be taking both of you to jail."

"Your phone will be ringing anytime now, Sheriff," April said. As if on cue, Willis's cell phone chimed. "Might want to take that."

Willis swore and snatched the phone. "Sheriff Willis Lennox." The room quieted. Red crept up his neck and face. After a booming "Yes, sir," he squinted at Kevin. "Release Ted into the custody of Special Agent Ramos."

April spoke up. "Return his personal belongings and all the items confiscated from his home."

Willis's jaw tightened like a permanent case of TMJ. He glared at her, no doubt planning her demise.

Kevin produced a small box of papers and Ted's wallet, an S&W, and keys. Not a word to Ted or eye contact.

Ted took the box. "Willis, keep my gun. I got nothing to hide."

"No way," April said. "Not without a search warrant." If the weapon had been recently discharged, fingerprints or trace DNA might be on it. She wanted to see for herself.

Brenda's daughter could have planted the gun while the Snyders were locked inside their garage.

They left the sheriff's office. She gave Ted the keys to his truck so he could drive while she explored his box of personal items.

"April—"

"Wait until we're on the road."

The investigation hadn't indicated anything incriminating about Ted, but the focus had been on Jason. Aggravated assault? Willis's uncle? Sounded like she'd be up all night piecing this together. The case had one gray twist after another. The rift between Willis and Jason went back generations, before either one of them was born.

Once Ted drove out of the sheriff's parking area, she grabbed her phone and texted Jason.

Ur Dad & I r heading back 2 the house.

On the way to the Snyders', she brought up online county records for Ted's arrest and conviction. With an inward groan, she studied the trial and case.

County deputies were sent to the Lennox residence, located outside of Sweet Briar, after receiving a call about an assault. At the residence, deputies found John Lennox with noticeable injuries. He told deputies he'd been assaulted by Ted Snyder. Theodore Andrew Snyder was immediately arrested and transported to the Sweet Briar jail, charged with multiple counts of injury with a deadly weapon.

An ambulance took Lennox to Beaumont Hospital with head trauma, a busted rib, and a broken arm. Lennox testified Snyder threatened to kill him over a dispute regarding a woman. Snyder claimed Lennox displayed a knife and threatened him. Snyder went after him, broke Lennox's right arm, and proceeded to slash him with the knife. Snyder was tried and convicted of aggravated assault with a deadly weapon and sentenced to two years in Huntsville prison.

April lifted her gaze from the report. "Okay, what's the story about your arrest?"

He blew out a sigh. Father and son shared the same method of venting frustration. "Nothing I'm proud of, but good came from it. I was twenty-three at the time and dating Vicki. John spread some nasty rumors about her, basically us, and I went after him at his parents', the same place Willis lives now. When John pulled out a knife, I took it away from him. In the process, I cut him bad. My fault, and I own it." He turned in to his driveway and raised the garage door. The light overhead came to life. The Chevy rental was parked in front of Vicki's car, and now she was gone. She'd ask Ted to move it tomorrow.

"Does Jason know what happened?"

"Yes. When he and Willis were little boys, Willis brought up how Jason's daddy was a jailbird. I'd planned to tell him but not at eight years old. I explained it to him as best I could." Ted cut the engine and lowered the garage door.

"You said good came from it."

"Right. Vicki came to see me soon after I started my time in Huntsville. She refused to put up with my bitterness and told me to get right with God or rot there." He chuckled. "We were both young. I told her never to come back. She mailed me a Bible. I had a lot of extra time in a cell, hours to read Vicki's Bible, as I called it. I became a Christian six months before my release.

Wrote her a letter and told her so. We married less than a year later."

"Pretty amazing story," she said.

"But the best part belongs to John. He couldn't believe the change in me and got real curious. Asked me about it. I told him about Jesus. He started going to church, and not long afterward, he stepped into the family of God. We were best friends for a lot of years, still are. John's in a nursing home now. Dementia took over his mind. Every Tuesday, I go see him. For some reason, he still remembers me. His property is where Jason's been hiding."

Despite the comfortable temps inside the truck, a chill swept up April's arm. Where did she fit with God? Being with the Snyders and experiencing their faith seemed to restore hers.

39

April shivered to dissipate the strange sensation of God listening, being there in the truck.

"Do you mind if I look at your S&W?" she said.

"Go ahead. You'll find it clean."

She examined the chamber. "It is. Griff spoke up on your behalf."

"Don't know him very well, but I appreciated him stepping in tonight." His shoulders slumped. "This is a nightmare."

"I'm really sorry. I'd like to tell you this won't get worse before it's resolved. But I can't."

"The difference is we have truth on our side. Truth reigns. Always."

"Jason says much of the same."

"You aren't a believer?"

"I was brought up in the Catholic church. Every Sunday as a girl."

"Doesn't matter to me what denomination or church. Do you have a relationship with Jesus?"

April recalled a statue of the suffering Jesus in church, how His passion moved her to be a better person. "Yes." But it wasn't the same as his. "Why don't we pick up our conversation inside? Can I get you anything?"

"No thanks."

"Tell me everything about tonight's arrest in detail."

"It's been a long time since this old man pulled an all-nighter." He exited the truck and walked through the kitchen to the living area, where he turned on a lamp and gestured for her to sit. The time registered 3:05. He eased into a recliner, his drawn features indicating he needed rest. "Bring on the questions, April."

"When was the last time you fired your gun?"

"It's been at least two months. Not sure what Willis meant about the chamber being dirty. Number one, I clean my gun after it's used. Number two, I haven't fired it." He paused. "Do you suppose there's a way to make it look like it was recently fired and date it to the night Russell was killed?"

"Money and technology can take care of just about anything. Your gun's always kept in the same place?"

"In my nightstand."

"Tell me exactly how this went down tonight."

Ted folded his hands in his lap. "I was asleep when I heard a banging at the door. When I saw two patrol cars with their lights flashing in the driveway, I was afraid something had happened to you and Jason. I opened the door. Kevin Viner led the way with Griff Wilcombe and Cal Bunion. Told me they were there to search my house for proof I'd hidden evidence regarding Russell's murder. I asked for a search warrant. Kevin claimed Willis had handled it. I told him to show me the document, then he could look through my house."

"And?"

"He pushed me aside."

She wanted answers to the questions banging against the side of her mind. Was Kevin playing her and Jason and working for Willis? "How long were they here?"

"About twenty minutes. Griff found my gun in the nightstand. If he'd asked, I'd have told him where I kept it. Kevin was on the phone."

"That must have been when he called me."

"He arrested and cuffed me. But they left my rifles and two shotguns in the locked gun cabinet. Never asked for the key to see them."

"They were on a mission."

"Apparently so." Ted stretched his neck. Deep lines furrowed into his forehead.

"Did they rough you up?" she said.

"At the sheriff's office, Willis shoved me around, but Griff stopped him. Told him a good attorney would nail him for mistreating a man in his custody. I'll take care of Willis when arrests are made. Speaking of, did you and Jason make any progress on the lead Tessa Barker gave you?"

She sketched their meeting with the Barkers. "The huge step forward is finding out who replaced the window in Jason's office."

"Wonderful news. Makes sitting here early in the morning worth it."

"If you don't mind, tell me about Brenda Krew."

"A piece of work. She was born and raised here. In and out of trouble in high school. Parents deceased. Married a guy from Colorado. They lived in Sweet Briar and had a child together. Brenda had a bad drinking problem. Her husband filed for divorce and used the drinking to gain custody of their daughter and move to Colorado. Brenda cleaned up after that and started the real estate business. Got active in church. She and Willis are friends—both alike. Appear all community-interested, especially when it benefits them. Neither of them have friends, so they fit. She can be kind of standoffish."

April gave him additional insight into her conversation with Brenda. ". . . I turned the photo over and recognized the young woman who'd handed me Isabella in Houston."

Ted gripped the side of the chair. "So now it appears Brenda and her daughter have joined forces with Willis."

"Shouldn't you or Jason have recognized the young woman?"

"Doubtful. She left with her dad as a child. I suppose she was six or seven." He cocked his head. "Her name's Joey. She's about twenty-three now."

"Joey Krew?"

"No. Brenda took her maiden name back after the divorce. Joey Frederickson."

"Her dad's name?"

"Karl Frederickson."

April typed the info for Simon. "She's back in her mother's life and facing kidnapping charges. Serious stuff."

"She was a sweet little girl."

April had more questions, especially about Brenda, who appeared to have unresolved issues. But Ted's eyes were bloodshot and rimmed with dark circles. "You need your rest."

"Not until we finish talking this through. How else can I help?"

"Willis is risking everything to find out where his wife and son are. Something has him scared into making reckless decisions, and any of them could give him lengthy jail time. No one in their right mind takes the law into his own hands unless the stakes are so high he feels he has no choice."

40

By the time Jason realized his phone battery had died and connected it to his truck's charger, he saw he had a missed text from April. She and Dad were home. Too late for him to contact either of them. He should be asleep, but it was hard to settle down with so much happening.

His phone rang . . . April.

"Everything's quiet," she said. "Your dad's in bed again."

"You should be headed there too."

"Nearly there." She gave him an overview of the evening.

"My guess is Willis has gotten rid of the real murder weapon—tossed it to the bottom of a swamp. But we've still found two huge pieces tonight with Hunter's admission and the identity of the woman who kidnapped Isabella."

"Simon's working on a BOLO so we can question her. That's a be-on-the-lookout."

"Does she have a record? Hard to believe she began a life of crime by nabbing my daughter."

"Her criminal history reads like a who's who. First arrested at eighteen in Colorado Springs for shoplifting. Went downhill from there. Arrested and charged for selling cocaine. Moved to

Houston, where she spent a court-mandated term in drug rehab. Three stints in jail. At age twenty-three, she's behaved herself for seven months."

"Either Willis reached out to Joey or Brenda enlisted her, but we probably won't know until she's picked up. I'd like to see her locked away until she's ninety."

"A judge will decide her fate. I have to wonder if she had previously arranged to pass off Isabella to another person, or did she panic and then take frantic measures? My FBI status might have alarmed her. And Isabella was very upset. Joey might have been hit with a dose of reality for what she'd done."

"Willis's plan backfired because he had no clue about the tracker. He was betting on me giving him Billie's whereabouts in exchange for Isabella." How many times had he gone over this? "But when will it all end?"

"Jason, we won't know all the details and motivation factors until Joey's brought in. Maybe not then. Don't torture yourself with what didn't happen to your daughter. Take comfort she's in the best hands possible."

"You do a good job of talking people down off the ledge."

April was quiet for a long moment. He wanted to slap himself upside the head. When she finally spoke, her voice was soft. "Sometimes. Are you okay? Do you want me to drive out there?

Keep you company? I seem to have a new zip of energy."

"Stay put," he said.

"The connection isn't staticky. Have you left the woods?"

"I have an errand."

"Where are you?"

"Parked near my ranch."

Her voice rose. "What part of 'stay low' do you not understand?"

"Willis has zero patience, which means his tactics for finding Billie and Zack will grow worse."

"But why are you at your ranch?"

"A shower for starters."

"You could get one in a swamp."

He chuckled. "I need to see if anything's missing from my house."

"I understand, but you scare me. Text me when you're back in hiding."

The phone clicked off, and Jason switched to vibrate. Fifty percent charged, so he placed it in his pocket to charge the battery once at home. He had about two and a half hours until sunup. After parking on the west side of his land, he grabbed his gun and jogged to his house. All those years of camping had provided him with reliable instincts. So long as he didn't stir up any wild hogs or Willis Lennox.

He hadn't been home since the evening of

Russell's death. According to Kevin, law enforcement had conducted a thorough search and his place came up clean. That surprised Jason since Willis had doggedly gone after him. Maybe there hadn't been time to plant evidence. How much could Willis accomplish in one night?

Fluffy had a bark that woke the dead unless he smelled Jason first. The dog came bounding toward him, and Jason gave him the attention he deserved. After ensuring no one kept watch, he entered the rear of his two-story home, which he and Lily had designed. She'd wanted a farmhouse with an L-shaped porch, rocking chairs, and hanging plants in "strategic spots." She adored landscaping, and together they'd laid out flower beds for year-round color. He smiled in the darkness, remembering how Lily called him the Fixer-Upper of East Texas.

Lily never met a recipe she didn't like, and her kitchen contained everything she dreamed of—a farmhouse sink, concrete countertops, plenty of her favorite distressed white cabinets, and hardwoods. Together they'd overseen every inch of the four-thousand-square-foot home. They talked about having four children. Now he and Isabella had more room than they'd ever need.

Jason leaned against the doorway to the dark kitchen, allowing a few memories of those final days with Lily to wash over him. He'd watched her endure one stab of pain after another. Death had been a blessing no matter how much he missed her. The reminders were no longer as haunting but left a bittersweet feel.

He took a moment to relish a what-if. He'd snap on the kitchen light and see Lily smiling at him with those ocean-blue eyes. She'd ask about his day or tell him about one of her second graders. And she wouldn't have a trace of cancer or pain. Her blonde hair would lie on her shoulders, and her pallor wouldn't be the gray so characteristic of chemo and radiation treatments.

They'd planned a wonderful future together . . . taking Isabella camping . . . teaching her how to ride, hunt, and fish. For a moment, he thought he heard Lily's laugh. When this nightmare ended, he'd never take family and friends for granted again.

April slid into his thoughts, and he pushed her away. This house, these memories, were his and Lily's. Spending time contemplating April, especially here, in this place, seemed wrong.

With a deep breath, Jason locked the door behind him and, leaving the room dark, walked through the kitchen and on to the living room. A light from a pole mounted outside shone through the living area. Furniture cushions lay on the floor, desk drawers were pulled out and dumped, a lamp was shattered, and a closet door stood agape. The FBI didn't destroy people's belongings when they conducted a search. This was Willis's trademark.

He stole looks through the windows to verify no one was lurking outside and hoped Willis had grown lax in watching his house—Jason needed a break. Mounting the stairs, he listened for indications of a trap. Using his flashlight, he searched each room and respective closets, finding his upstairs in the same disarray as the first floor. He showered and changed clothes.

The test to see if Willis or anyone else had found important papers or the flash drive was hidden downstairs. One of the extras he and Lily had incorporated into their home, but not in the original design, was a fireproof safe recessed in the pantry wall. Jason made his way to the kitchen, stepped inside the pantry large enough to be a small bedroom, closed the door, and snapped on the light. Pulling on a bulletin board revealed a small safe.

After entering the code, he reached inside. At first glance, everything looked to be in order. Lily wanted personal documents and some keepsakes within reach and not locked inside a bank. Jason believed banks were the safest, but she'd been right considering the invasion of his parents' safe-deposit box.

He took out the deed to his ranch, his and Lily's marriage license, birth certificates for the three of them, Lily's death certificate, life insurance policies, his and Lily's wedding rings, and a copy of his will giving Isabella his estate and making his parents guardians. A stack of twenty-dollar bills rested in the bottom. He stuffed ten of them into his jacket pocket and reached for a sealed, business-size envelope on the very bottom. Billie had asked him to keep it as well as the flash drive, and now he would read the contents. She must have suspected Willis would not give up until he found her and Zack.

He held the envelope in his hand. A photo was stuck to it, one of Isabella with chocolate smeared all over her face. Oh, to see her. Hold her. Inhale the sweetness of her.

Unwanted tears burned raw. Helplessness had him chained. The closer he attempted to grow to God, the more life tossed him explosives. He hated the deficiency in his character, the resorting to tears. Some said they cleansed a person's soul, but Jason's experience claimed otherwise. Being a man meant walking through trials and facing problems head-on, not this loathsome display of weakness.

The tears and agony refused to let him go. Each time he tried to stop, a new wave overcame him. Finally, wrung out like an old mop, he wiped his face.

Fluffy barked. His doggy alarm repeated.

Jason switched off the pantry light and opened

the door. His eyes adjusted to the dark kitchen, quickly finding the window facing the side yard. Nothing stirred. Yet Fluffy's bark persisted.

At the back door, Jason peered into the dark surroundings. He reached for the gun in his waistband and opened the door. Fluffy kept a loud vigil, facing the detached triple garage to the right.

"Jason."

The familiar voice called his name again. April stepped from behind the garage, her small frame visible.

Jason quieted Fluffy.

"Thanks." She walked his way.

"What are you doing here?" Agitation ground at his nerves. He tucked his gun away. "I could have shot you."

"I'm sorry. I thought you might need my help if Willis or one of his men showed up."

"You could have texted me."

"I did."

He groaned. "I put my phone on vibrate. Where's your car?"

"I have your dad's truck. The Chevy's blocked in by your mom's car." She joined him on the porch. "I'd appreciate an introduction to Fluffy. He has a vicious bark."

He shook his head in the darkness and encouraged Fluffy to his side. "Fluffy, this is April. She's an FBI agent who shows up at unexpected times. Be nice to her because she carries a Glock."

"Was that necessary?" she said.

"Let him sniff your hand."

She obliged. "Pleased to meet you, Fluffy."

"Was anyone watching the house?" he said.

"No. I simply wanted to offer my help. You're a man who was caught off guard by a well-thought-out scheme. For the past year, you've been forced to stand strong during one tragedy after another." She took his hand.

In the darkness, his eyes moistened. The warmth of her hand soothed the ache in his soul.

"You're not alone, Jason."

41

Inside, Jason lit up the kitchen breakfast area. If anyone approached the side of the house, he'd deal with them. He retrieved Billie's note from the pantry and gestured for April to have a seat at the table.

April had been right, and the reminder was perfect timing. He wasn't alone.

"I came for this envelope." He held it up. "Billie asked me to read it. Whatever's inside, she trusted me with the contents." He lifted the seal with his finger and eased out a single sheet of paper. A report from a medical clinic in Woodville.

Life had just gotten more complicated for all of them. He wiped his palms on his jeans.

"Is it serious?"

"Potentially. Billie's pregnant with twins."

April blinked. "She has three children to protect."

"Now I understand another reason Billie chose to run. It's the mothering instinct. When Lily learned we were pregnant, she'd already been diagnosed with cancer. Her ob-gyn suggested aborting the baby, but she refused. She wouldn't choose her own life over her baby's."

"I understand Lily's and Billie's viewpoints."

April stared out the window to the darkness. "If in the same circumstances, I'd feel the same way."

"You put Isabella above your own needs."

She swung him a smile, a sad one, and he wondered where her thoughts had taken her. He glanced at his watch. "It's late—or rather, early—but I want to talk to Simon."

"We both have things to discuss with him." She pulled her phone from beneath her sweatshirt. "But I want to make a list first."

Jason stretched his back. "Let's match yours to mine." He grabbed his legal pad from the table and started writing:

1. I think Simon should know about Billie's pregnancy. I just hope she's not upset with my decision.
2. Where's Joey Frederickson?
3. What's Joey's relationship with Willis?
4. Where does Brenda fit in all of this?
5. Who else is working with Willis?
6. Who killed Russell?

He shared his list. "What have I missed?"

"Who else Willis might have coerced?"

"If I try to put myself into Willis's head, I'd have to ask, What matters the most? What sacrifice means spending the rest of his life in prison? For me it's Isabella and my family. Willis is fueled by power and control, and the one thing he desperately craves is Billie and Zack. He's angry, driven, and will do anything to have them under his roof again. If he had any idea about her pregnancy, he'd stop at nothing to find her."

"When he's already committed murder, what remains?"

He shook his head. "Burn down my house? That seems trivial after what he's already done. For certain if he finds Billie and Zack, he'll put me facedown in a pool of blood."

☆ ☆ ☆

At Jason's kitchen table, April initiated a call to Simon.

Simon released a string of words that belonged in Romeo's pasture. "It's after five in the morning. Can't a man have a few hours' sleep? Unless you have a signed confession, this can wait until daylight."

"We have critical information, Simon," she said. "Turn on the light and listen." She laid her phone between her and Jason, then pressed Speaker before continuing. "Has Billie Lennox phoned you?"

"Not yet."

"Billie's struggling with a decision to help us. Jason has a report from a clinic in Woodville indicating she's pregnant with twins."

"An abused wife on hormone overload?" Simon said. "Give me a sec. I'm bringing my laptop to life. The FIG has been working to track her down via the national database, so I'll check the progress." The clicking suggested he was typing. "Looks like I would have received this update in the morning. Billie's living in Seattle and working as a receptionist for an accounting firm. We have her address. I'll notify agents there to initiate an interview immediately. In the meantime, we should all try to get rest."

"A little hard to rest when a man wants me dead," Jason said, his voice void of emotion. "Before you head back to bed, I have questions. You just demonstrated how easy it is to find people. With all the FBI's technology, why haven't you found evidence to arrest Willis for suspected crimes?"

"We need solid proof that's tied to a federal statute being violated in order for the FBI to charge him—proof admissible in a federal court."

"As if April and I haven't sent documentation? The whole Houston FBI should be camped here."

"For every suspicious activity incriminating Willis, we have one against you or April."

"I'm not a fool, Simon. He's an elected public official responsible for upholding the law—and none of you have acted to remove him even temporarily from office while the investigation takes place," Jason said. "What's really going on? Are you thinking if he kills me, you have the evidence to put him away for good?"

"Simon, he deserves to know the truth." April took Jason's hand.

He jerked it back. "Have you been using me right from the start? Am I the bait to trap Willis? There's nothing to lose since I was charged with murder." His voice rattled around the room.

"You're wrong." April watched her credibility disappear before her. She hadn't been briefed until driving there, and she feared losing his trust . . . and where her heart had taken her. "I'd never betray you. Neither would the FBI."

"What's the truth? Are either of you going to tell me?"

"Jason," Simon began, "we need time to work out details so we can address your questions."

"Maybe from where you sit."

"You decided you were above the law and took an FBI agent hostage. After your fiasco, we saw you were in danger and requested a safe house. While you took advantage of protection for your daughter and mother, it appears you have little to no respect for law enforcement."

Jason frowned. "You want to go fishing? Find someone else to be your lure." He grabbed her phone and ended the call with Simon. "I'm done here."

April gasped. "I just learned about—"

He stood and faced her. "Leave my home. Now."

42

April drove dark, tree-lined back roads from Jason's ranch toward Sweet Briar. The narrow gravel road forced her to stay under forty miles per hour, typical of the area. Jason had told her about snakes and wild animals that dwelled in marshes along those trees. She shivered and blinked back the moistness gathering in her eyes. The comforts of her own home drew her toward Houston.

Or were her tears for Jason? Her heart had taken a dive for him and Isabella. But friendship, affection, and potential love had no future when the beginnings were steeped in deception.

Anger burned inside her for not being told all the facts about Sheriff Willis Lennox. She'd been thrust into this situation and tried to peacefully bring Jason into custody without knowledge of the background. When Jason had flung his anger about being used, she'd attempted to shove aside the nasty attack on her self-confidence. Hadn't worked. Once again she'd failed in her career, a pattern of late. Heeding her parents' demands to teach political science on a university level swirled through her mind.

Breathe in and out. Dig deep for self-talk.

She squeezed her fingers around the steering wheel of Ted's vintage truck. A week ago, she'd been cycling in a spin class. Obviously going nowhere. Life for certain had spun out of control.

She had to find the right words to tell Ted about the argument. Or should she say nothing? Concealing the emotional upheaval chipped at her upbringing of respecting her elders. Plus, the dear man was allowing her to stay in his home. She counted on him being asleep, and yet when he wakened, she'd feel compelled to reveal what little the investigation permitted. Ironic when she still didn't have all the details herself.

Her career was the one aspect of her life that she depended on for security and significance. But since meeting Jason, she'd tossed all the rules out the window. She wasn't sure she'd ever find herself on solid ground again.

She pressed in Simon's number. When he answered, she placed herself in negotiation mode. "Tonight's surprise could have been avoided."

"Do you have any idea how I've fought to give you answers? I called you as soon as I received authorization."

"We're partners, Simon. You could have trusted me with the truth instead of being all clandestine. Especially when I've been threatened and so have other innocent people." She shoved calmness into every word in an effort not to unleash vile words she'd regret later.

Simon groaned. "We'll talk more when we have a face-to-face."

"I'm furious over how this has been handled."

"April, you were the one who sided with Jason and took off on a course to prove his innocence. You should have brought him in. Period. We could protect him from Willis and those who are in his camp. But he refused and you supported him."

"Are you suggesting the delayed arrests are my fault?"

She heard him blow out his angst. "Your work is commendable. Your record outstanding. But you made decisions without considering my recommendations."

"Because I don't understand the whole picture. All you've said is I don't have clearance and the investigation with Willis remains ongoing."

The silence fueled the heat rising up her neck and face.

"All right. I'll give you more. Willis has been under surveillance for several months."

How generous. "The fact that you kept me in the dark is a tough pill to swallow."

"April, I don't want predetermined protocol above my pay grade to cut a hole in our friendship."

It already had. "What do you expect me to say?"

"Verbally punch me. Say what you're feeling, anything but using psychology to beat me up."

Simon really had no choice, and it was her pride

that hurt. She wanted to forgive, but the case, her friendship with Simon—all looked murky.

Headlights in her rearview mirror caught her attention. They moved closer at incredible speed. She crushed the gas pedal. "I'm being tailed."

Dropping the phone onto her lap, she took another look in the mirror. An SUV rode her bumper. She raced toward the highway three miles ahead. How fast could this truck go?

The SUV swerved into the oncoming lane and collided with the driver's side of the truck. The sound of metal grinding against metal launched her into action mode. Adrenaline kicked into gear. She wrestled to keep the truck on the road.

Again the SUV smashed into her side. The second impact caught her off guard. She veered dangerously near a waterlogged ditch.

She whipped the truck to the left and smacked the SUV. But the driver retaliated with a massive strike into the engine. She stomped on the gas and turned in front of the SUV. Speeding around it, she had an edge.

A quick glance in the rearview mirror gave her no indication of the license plate numbers.

A bullet sailed through the rear window and whistled past her head and on through the windshield, creating a spiderweb crack. She drove straight down the middle of the gravel road. Let the jerk try to get past her.

God, if You're there, I need help.

The SUV crashed into the truck bed and pushed her hard.

April lost control. The truck leaned to the right and rolled. She remembered screaming before her mind numbed.

43

Jason paced his kitchen. He couldn't believe he'd been deceived. With shaking fingers, he slipped the personal documents back into the safe. Even if Willis set his house on fire, the documents would remain intact.

How many more crimes would Willis commit before the FBI made an arrest? Jason despised the fear coursing through his veins. It felt like he was alone in a battle against a man who wanted him destroyed.

Each moment that ticked by served as a reminder of how low April and Simon had stooped to hide the truth from him. Stupidity marched through his brain. Had the tender looks from April been a ploy to gain his confidence?

Calm down. Give yourself a little time to push aside the anger. Think. Reason. His rage drove him like a madman, but he needed to get his priorities straight—protect Isabella and his parents, figure out who'd killed Russell, and stop Willis from abusing or killing those who got in his way.

He hurried upstairs for another change of clothes when his phone rang. Simon. Jason refused to take the call. Let him find another worm for his fishing line.

In the kitchen, he put together a few things to eat and packed them in an ice chest.

Simon called again.

Forget it, buddy.

He opened the pantry for a few bottles of water.

Simon called a third time.

Jason hesitated. If he didn't answer, when would Simon give up? Jason's emotions teetered near eruption, and who better to hear his fury than the man who appeared to be leading the operation?

Jason answered. "You have my attention. Am I supposed to thank you for putting my family in danger and a price on my head?"

"Look, you're angry. April's not at fault. She wasn't given clearance until five minutes before I called her this morning. Right now we have a situation on our hands requiring your help."

"Not interested." Jason clicked off. Three seconds later, Simon buzzed him again. No thanks. Not until his head moved into a sensible position.

He closed his eyes, convicted of behaving like a child. He returned Simon's call. "What's going on?"

"I'm afraid April's in trouble. She phoned me after leaving your place. Said someone was following her. We lost contact, and she's not picking up. The FBI is currently out of the area, and it may take a while before an agent can get there."

His fingers wrapped around his keys on the kitchen counter. "On my way." The keys slipped from his fingers onto the floor. Bending to snatch them, he sensed panic threatening to take over his senses.

What if Willis had sent one of his men after April? How far would he go to get her off the case? His gut burned. He refused to think about finding her hurt or dead. Not after losing Lily. Not after losing Russell.

He rushed out the door to his truck, taking two steps at a time from the porch. Fluffy raced with him and barked, as though he knew the turmoil inside Jason's head. His parting words to April had been vicious.

That's when his heart registered with his mind. April had become more than a friend, and no matter what she'd done, he couldn't refuse her help or deny his feelings.

Slamming the truck door, he gunned the engine and spun it around to the road leading to Sweet Briar. His left foot tapped the floorboard. She had to be all right. The words he'd spit at her in anger needed to be reset. Talked out.

God, are You listening? Seems like You haven't been paying attention to me. And I don't care if I'm being self-centered in this.

In the distance, swords of fire pierced the near-dawn sky.

He floored the gas pedal. Stones crunched beneath the tires. Faster. Hurry. No other vehicles in sight. Slamming on the brake, he cut the engine several feet behind the inferno of Dad's truck. Jason bolted toward the hot flames.

"April!" Another whoosh, and metal shot in every direction. He shielded his face as the force tossed his body onto the road. Crawling away from the blaze, he shouted her name again.

"Jason . . ."

Her weak voice sounded like angel music, and he managed to get to his knees, open his eyes. His whole body stung from the tumble onto gravel. She stumbled his way.

"Are you okay?" he said.

"I think so."

He reached for her, drawing her into his arms and holding her tight. She trembled, and he probably did too. He didn't want to let go. "I'm sorry," he whispered.

"So am I for not pressing Simon and our supervisor."

He put her at arm's length. In the firelight, blood and bruises stained her face. Dirt and more blood streaked her sweatshirt, and both hands were scraped raw. The legs of her jeans matched but no signs of gushing blood. "I don't see anything requiring stitches yet," he said. "I've got a first aid kit in the truck."

"You're the one who needs a doctor. There's a nasty gash on your forehead." She raised a bloody hand to indicate where. "I . . . I saw you fly across the road when the truck exploded."

"I've had worse." He peered up and down the road. Desolate. The heat from the fire grew hotter, and they stepped back. "You were run off the road?"

"An SUV. I couldn't get the license plate. Possibly a Toyota. Dark blue or black."

"Willis drives a silver Land Cruiser."

"We have a new suspect, and the vehicle now has dents on the passenger side."

"We'll talk about it later. I'm letting Simon know I found you."

The agent answered before the first ring ceased. "April's okay. I'll take her by the ER in Woodville to make sure."

"No," she said. "Willis will have his men everywhere. Let's get out of here. Don't report this either to—"

"Jason," Simon said. "I have agents close by. Drop her off at the hospital, and get back into hiding."

"I don't need a hospital," she said. "It's just dirt."

"We'll get back to you when we're at Dad's. If he says she needs the hospital, I'll carry her there myself." Jason slipped the phone into his jean pocket and took another look at her battle scars. "Your eye's swelling."

"I need an ice pack, not an ER visit. You look worse." She peered into the fiery remains. "I hate to tell your dad his truck's destroyed."

"His insurance will cover the replacement." He

wrapped his arm around her waist, and together they walked to his truck.

"Ted and Miss Ella can swap stories of what I do to things I borrow," she said.

He wanted to add humor but nothing surfaced. "Both of us tend to destroy what matters."

She inhaled sharply, and he didn't know if her reaction came from what he'd said or the pain of her injuries. "I want this over," she said. "Willis in jail. You and Isabella together with your life back."

The unspoken longing between them shouted louder than their words. What he realized earlier surfaced, and he turned to her. "I was afraid I'd lost you."

"Jason, what is happening between us?"

He lifted her chin, and his lips slowly met hers. She returned his kiss with the same newness, a sweet hint of the future. When they parted, she laid her head against his chest. Holding her felt like coming home.

"I feel your heart," she whispered. "Steady and strong like you."

"Only when I'm with you. You've seen me at my worst, and you're still here."

"Yes, I am."

☆ ☆ ☆

At the Snyder home, April stood in the kitchen and attempted to wash off the blood and grime, but her lack of energy won.

"Let me help," Jason said.

"I'm not an invalid. It's only a few scrapes."

"Sit, missy." Ted walked into the kitchen with an armload of first aid supplies.

"I suggest you listen," Jason said.

"What are you going to do?" April watched Ted set the supplies on the counter, but when he raised a brow with a look that must have sent Jason running in his younger days, she slid onto a kitchen chair.

Jason dabbed at the open gashes with hydrogen peroxide while Ted used tweezers to rid her flesh of gravel. Most of the time she held her breath and counted until they moved to another spot that hurt worse than the previous one.

"Is this my punishment for totaling your truck?" she said to Ted.

He laughed, but she recognized forced humor. "Nope. This is a labor of love."

"The way I see it—" she gasped as he yanked out another piece of stone or debris—"not much difference."

"You two sure aren't warrior material."

"Thanks," she managed. "I do have my finer moments, but this isn't one of them." She peered into Jason's face, the man who had touched her with his honesty and caring. "I didn't know the plan in Houston. Still don't entirely know what's going on."

"Simon said the same thing. We're good."

She smiled and her mouth stung. When Jason kissed her, she'd only felt his lips on hers.

Afterward, she and Ted disinfected Jason's head wound. He too had gravel embedded in his flesh, especially in the palm of his right hand and shoulder.

Simon called repeatedly, supposedly checking in and updating her on the agents at the crime scene. They'd found the remains of Ted's truck.

Poor Simon. He'd coated himself in guilt, as though keeping her out of the loop had caused the accident. Maybe so, but regret left a bitter taste, and right now she needed to give him grace. His parting words were *Willis had an alibi for tonight*.

Crawling into bed hurt like she'd been whipped with a strap. Whoever had smacked into her had better be wearing armor when she found him. Just before falling asleep, she relived Jason's kiss, a gentle reminder of something scary and beautiful.

44

April woke from a deep sleep in the guest room of Vicki and Ted Snyder's home—the same room containing Isabella's crib, minus the baby girl who'd stolen her heart. Shadows played across the room, indicating an early hour.

She opened one eye to check the time and moaned. Every muscle ached, and the wounds on her arms and legs stung.

The clock registered 9:20. She'd slept a whopping two hours and ten minutes.

When the truck flipped, she'd cried out for God's help. Church had been a part of her childhood with first Communion and catechism. She grasped rules like essential vitamins, but those things never satisfied the deep yearning of her soul. Once she left home, God showed up only on holidays and some saints' days. Her prayer was likely born of instinct and desperation, yet she'd experienced deliverance and a miracle.

Jason and his family talked about God as though He were real, as though He stood invisibly beside them. She'd heard the "saved" and "accepted Jesus" lingo before. She had a vague idea of what the words referred to, but after being saved from death last night and accepting God had been the one who managed the feat, she wanted to explore the whole relationship thing.

If she were to trust Him beyond this world, she needed to begin now. From the way she was seemingly walking a tightrope between life and death, she needed to begin marching with God this very minute. The rules that governed her life—work extra hours, give it your best, fill your résumé with awards and commendations—didn't give her lasting satisfaction. The performance trap to show her parents she'd chosen the right career only left her empty and tired. She needed a Savior.

Closing her eyes, she prayed and closed the gap between her and God—no negotiator was needed.

The dilemma of how to proceed stretched across April's mind. Time to climb out of bed, no matter how comforting it was to lie there. Releasing an anguish-filled sigh, she dug her hands into the mattress and made herself stand. Dizziness threatened to overcome her battered body, and she blinked several times until her head cleared. She crept across the small room to peek behind the blinds. Her right eye must have been swollen because her vision was limited. A streak of clear blue crossed the morning sky. Wonderfully strange how a new day offered promise and hope.

Jason craved his life back, and Isabella surely missed her daddy.

Ted needed a truck.

The FBI was searching for evidence of who'd run her off the road.

Despite these things and how she ached, her heart overflowed with newfound peace.

She made her way into an adjoining bathroom. The mirror confirmed her earlier thoughts. Her swollen right eye left only a narrow slit for her to see out of. A black-and-blue bruise had spread across her right cheek, and dried blood around her mouth gave her a vampire look. Unfortunately Halloween had already passed. She suffered through a lukewarm shower when the hot water stung her wounds and noted the pink-tinted water flowing into the drain.

She dried herself lightly and wrapped herself in a warm robe belonging to Vicki. No sounds of Ted stirring met her ears as she tiptoed downstairs to the living room.

She moved slowly into the kitchen, ground coffee beans, and eased onto a chair while the coffee brewed. With a grimace she predicted a nap in her future. Her gaze fell on Ted's worn Bible, and she leafed through it. Passages were highlighted and underlined, the ragged pages filled with handwritten notes. Curious, she read a few notations, but they were personal. She abruptly closed it, her heart rending as though she'd been caught looking through a diary.

"Something in my Bible disturb you?" Ted said from the doorway.

She swung a smile his way. "I felt like I was snooping."

He grinned, and she saw Jason's smile. "God wants us to be snooping in His Word. The answers to life are there. He doesn't hide them."

She understood and told him so. "Your family has shown me what I've been missing in my faith. Thank you."

"You'll do the same thing for someone else. You have a kind heart, April." He moved toward the table. "How are you feeling?"

"Like a truck ran me over. Twice." She pointed to the cuts on her wrist and hand. "Not far from reality."

"Glad you still have your sense of humor." He nodded toward the coffeemaker. "Smells like the perfect conversation starter. Can I get you a cup?"

She clamped her palms on the table to stand, but he gestured for her to sit. "You made the coffee. I'll pour it. Nothing personal, sweetheart, but have you checked the mirror?"

"Yeah. Makeup will have a rough time covering up my face."

He poured her a steaming cup with little bubbles and joined her with his own. "Really glad Isabella and Vicki are safe. I'm heading to church. There's an 11:30 service. Want to join me?"

"Yes, I think I will and surprise Miss Ella. I'm waiting on several requests from—"

The doorbell rang.

Ted turned toward the living area and foyer. "I wonder who's come callin' on a Sunday morning." He scooted back his chair.

"Want me to go with you?"

"No, ma'am."

As long as the person at the door wasn't Willis. But she wouldn't say it. Her Glock was upstairs in the bedroom, and in her physical condition, she couldn't take on anyone in hand-to-hand combat. The muffled voices—her ears were probably still recovering from the explosion last night—offered no clue to the person's identity.

"Come on in. Been wanting to meet you," Ted said from the living area. "She's in the kitchen."

April didn't trust the lilt in Ted's voice.

"Good morning." Simon entered the kitchen. "I could use a cup of your wonderful-smelling coffee." He stared at her. "April, are you sure you shouldn't be in the hospital?"

She managed to stand and give him a hug. "I've been better. Nothing's broken but Ted's truck."

"I heard, a '63 Ford." Apologetic sentiment spread all over his face. "I'm here to answer a few questions. April, I—"

"Hush, we're friends."

"Makes me feel slightly better."

Ted reached inside a cabinet for a cup. "Have a seat. Coffee's on the way."

April never fared well with surprises, even on

a Sunday morning after putting God front and center. "Should I tighten my seat belt?"

Weary lines fanned from Simon's eyes. "Jason will meet us at his place."

"Simon, are you sure it's wise to expose Jason at his home? Willis may have his men watching."

"Agents are posted."

"The same agents who are surveilling Willis? They're not doing their jobs very well."

"There's more going on here than you're currently aware."

"When will I find out?"

"This morning."

April could nudge him to tell her now, but no doubt he had an agenda. She took a sip of coffee while Simon added a heaping spoonful of honey to his. "Have you talked to Billie?"

"No. I'm hoping to persuade Jason to give us her number. Her sister claims she hasn't heard from her. We'll see what her cell phone records show."

She thought back over the other times they'd worked together. He took more chances than she did. "I don't understand why you scheduled a meeting with Jason."

"I need a favor."

"I'm ready to leave when you are."

45

Through binoculars inside his house, Jason observed a car parked on the eastern side of his property. Two men were positioned outside the vehicle. He moved to a southwest window and saw another car. A man and woman were stationed outside nearby. All four were dressed in jeans and hiking boots, with rifles slung over their backs and Glocks attached to their waists. Simon had called him at 8:30 this morning and requested he return home. The FBI had arranged to keep him safe, but Jason felt better confirming it.

He'd been misled too many times lately, and for him to survive, he needed to work smarter.

Before he judged Simon or the FBI for keeping April out of the loop, Jason's growing list of questions demanded answers.

So he'd hear Simon out. Control his temper.

From what he'd learned about the five stages of grief, anger took the number two spot. After a year, shouldn't he be past it? Step four was depression, and he'd spent far too long in that hole too. Every time he believed he'd surrendered the claws of grief to God, something caused him to draw it all back. Perhaps healing came in daily relinquishing the power and control to God. Perhaps he still needed a moment-by-moment reminder that God had a better purpose in taking Lily, and her healing belonged in heaven. Some people had shown Jason how to live an exemplary Christian life, and others, like his Lily, demonstrated how to pass on to Jesus' arms.

April texted him of her and Simon's arrival within ten minutes. He checked on one of the vehicles and noted the man must have received an alert on his phone. But cynicism kept Jason cautious.

The people waiting at both entrances looked like agents. But uncertainty of Willis's whereabouts prompted Jason to tuck his weapon into the back of his jeans waistband, under a flannel shirt.

He ground beans for coffee and brewed a huge pot. If he were a drinking man, he'd've added a shot of brandy. Snatching four cups from above the coffee bar, he readied himself. His dad's presence would help him keep his head focused on listening.

The low hum of a car engine and Fluffy's resounding bark validated they'd arrived. Two doors slammed. The back doorbell rang.

Time to make progress.

He unlocked the back door and gestured them inside. April met him with a bruised smile and a swollen face. She limped inside.

Simon stuck out his hand. "We meet again. Good to see you."

Jason grasped the hand with a firm grip. He gave a slight nod. "I haven't decided yet."

"I deserve that." Simon lifted his nose. "Fresh coffee? Never met a cup I didn't like."

His friendly tone eased Jason a bit, but he'd not relinquish his guard. "Just finished brewing. Where's my dad?"

"I persuaded him to join his wife and granddaughter. Showed him a pic of his truck after the explosion. Told him about our concern for Billie and Zack. If Willis believed he could get to you through Ted, then he's in as much danger as your daughter and mother."

"Glad you were able to pull it off." One more worry gone from Jason's mind. "FBI escort?"

"Yes. An agent will call me when they reach the safe house. Your dad regretted not telling you good-bye before connecting with your family."

"I want to talk to all of them," Jason said.

"Of course. I'll arrange it later on my phone."

He studied April. "Are you sure you're up to this? Maybe you should run by the ER."

"I'm fine." She walked to the coffee bar. "I'll pour." She obviously had a heads-up on the reason Simon requested the meeting.

"Truth serum is in the sugar," Jason said.

April laughed lightly. "He likes honey."

"It's there too. Local and good for allergies."

"Ouch." Simon wrapped his arms across his chest. "Seriously, we need to establish trust."

Jason studied him. "Until I see proof of your sincerity, those words are empty."

"I'll make sure you see it."

Jason couldn't read a thing from Simon's facial expressions. "Have you heard from Kevin Viner?"

"Why?"

"I've known him since we were boys." Jason's mind swept back to the years of growing up together. "I have doubts. He shows up at suspicious times."

"He doesn't know I'm here."

"Should he?" Jason said.

April set cups of coffee before them.

"Thanks," Simon said. "We're going to bring Willis and his buddies down."

"Today would be good. You sidestepped my question about Kevin."

Simon took a drink of coffee. "He's not on my list of concerns."

"What about Griff Wilcombe?"

"At this point, he checks out." Simon scrolled through his phone. "Griffin H. Wilcombe served in the US Army from 2011 through 2015, the last two years in Afghanistan. Decorated for bravery."

"He proved helpful when Willis took Ted into custody," April said.

Simon laid his phone on the table. "Are you ready to discuss what's been going on?"

Jason chose to listen. See if he could draw out the truth. "Yeah, what *is* going on?"

Simon continued with a stoic look. "Some things are confidential. Some things I couldn't tell April until now. And there are some things I can't tell you."

Jason digested Simon's words. "I'm not risking my life to add a notch to your career. My words to you still stand from last night. I'm not going to be your bait for Willis. And—"

April touched his arm. "I agree you deserve answers."

Simon stared into his cup. "We have a search warrant for Willis's home and land. But he's disappeared."

46

Jason stared into the white-haired agent's face and stuffed the irritation of not knowing critical information about Willis into a place where nothing was gained with demands. He resolved to see the FBI's perspective.

"You're telling me with all of the FBI's surveillance efforts, Willis can't be found?" Jason said.

"For the moment," Simon said. "Agents called him last night after the accident, and he claimed to have been with Deputy Cal Bunion at his home. We made contact, and Bunion confirmed Willis's statement. Agents drove to the Lennox place. No one home. His cruiser and truck were parked in the garage."

"Kevin and Griff?" Jason said.

"Neither man is responding to our calls."

Jason reached to the far end of the table for his legal-size pad of paper. "Are you thinking he's taken off in another vehicle or on foot?"

"Both are viable options."

"Do you think Griff and Kevin might be with him?"

"Again, viable options."

"And this is for additional questioning regarding April's hit-and-run?"

"We have cause to question Willis since he threatened her on multiple occasions."

"What else?" Jason kept his tone low.

Simon seemed to toy with the decision to say more.

April slowly eased onto a chair. "Simon, I understand confidentiality, but you can provide a few answers."

"Willis may be running scared from the FBI. We've been investigating him for over a year."

"Russell's death expedited things?"

"Yes."

"I'd like to know when the investigation began and what initiated it."

"About fourteen months ago, we received a call from the area that Willis was involved with illegal activities."

"From whom?" Jason tried to form a mental picture. But no one seemed a likely candidate.

"If I could, I'd tell you."

"Over a year is a long time not to have something."

Simon took a drink of coffee. "Funds appropriated for the county went missing. The act had Willis's fingerprints on it. Also suspicions of pocketing bail money and taking bribes. As a result, we sent in an agent undercover, posing as a software developer who wanted to live in a rural area where he could hunt and enjoy nature. All he needed was connectivity. He hung out at

Willis's bar, established a friendship, and went hunting."

"What's his name?"

"Eric Deckett."

"Where is he now?" During hunting season, people drifted into the area and left again. Between his job, Isabella, his family, and church, he didn't explore much else.

"He disappeared. I'm not telling you anything you couldn't find out on your own. Look in the county records, and there's a discrepancy in the figures. If you google the FBI site, you'll see a report about the missing agent."

Comprehension slammed into his brain. "And Billie might have seen Willis haul Deckett's body into the woods?"

"Yes."

The series of incidents fell into place. "Here's what we've learned. Willis thinks I know the whereabouts of his wife and son. I imagine he has a flash drive that has photos she took the day after the killing. Dad has added things too, but I have no clue if they'd be tossed out in court." Jason paused. "He, or someone he paid, murdered Russell, and I was framed for it. For added punch, he has Isabella nabbed. Then he released me and claimed I'd escaped jail and kidnapped my daughter. But that was his mistake. That and me taking April hostage brought in the FBI, which allowed you to probe deeper into his activities and move closer to learning what happened to your missing agent."

Simon sighed, a sign Jason was on the right track.

"Billie contacted me and explained what she'd seen, which gives you a solid lead to finding your man. All roads point to Willis heading up a little empire with a strong possibility of two murders to his credit. But he's gone."

"Sums it up," Simon said. "The fact that Willis is missing says he's attempted to cover his tracks one too many times."

"Or someone has put him out of his misery."

"Did you?"

Jason huffed. "No. But I've thought about it." He thought through what he knew. "Doesn't public corruption fall under April's division?"

"Other agents were working the critical case. There was no need for April or me to have the details."

April swung a quick look at Simon. "I complicated things. When I'm back in the office, I'll ask for a full explanation. But what's more important than my ruffled feelings is securing evidence to arrest Willis."

"How long since your agent disappeared?"

"Seven months," Simon said. "Deckett was last seen at a bar in Sweet Briar with Willis. One other bit of info here. Billie and Zack left their apartment sometime yesterday afternoon, and she ditched her car at a park-and-ride at the Seattle airport. We lost track of her."

April spoke up. "What about the security cams at Sea-Tac?"

"Nothing there. We're investigating public transportation and the airport."

Jason couldn't bring himself to write Billie's and Zack's names on the notepad. "She has resources to stay hidden. When I saw her last, she had determination stamped on her face. But Willis doesn't give up either." The thought of another tragedy sailed into his mind. "Simon, do you have reason to believe Willis has found her and that's where he's at?"

"He didn't have time to fly to Seattle, but he could have hired someone and had them delivered here. We're working hard to locate Billie and Zack. Right now, I want to make sure Willis isn't hiding out in these woods. We know what he's capable of doing." He turned to Jason. "I know you looked for a possible grave yesterday, and I appreciate it. But the FBI is going to take over."

Jason swallowed his ineptness and hoped Billie and Zack were safe and not in the hands of death.

"We can arrange for dogs or heat-sensing technology to track him down, but there is a concern that he's holding hostages."

Jason guessed where Simon was heading with this. "You need a man who knows this part of the country to find him. And this on the heels of using me as bait to corner Willis."

Simon tapped his fingers on the mug of coffee. "The FBI is not in the business of putting innocent people in danger. If you're willing to lead agents across your land and his, we'd be grateful."

Jason eyed him. "With the suspicion Kevin Viner and Griff Wilcombe could be with him? All three men would be armed."

"We have agents to assist."

"This is crazy." He shook his head. "I forgot it was Sunday. I know where Kevin is." Jason pressed in Kevin's burner number.

"Jason, what's going on?"

He nodded at Simon. "Wondered if you'd seen Willis."

"Not since yesterday."

"Griff?"

"He's helping me set up for the high school youth group."

"Why aren't you two answering your phones?"

"Why all the questions? Neither of us are on duty, and my phone's on vibrate. Look, these kids are piling in, and the sound system isn't cooperating with the computer."

"I'll talk to you later. If you hear from Willis, let April know." Jason breathed relief and gave Simon and April the basics of the conversation. "The teens use the elementary school on Sunday mornings. It means setting up the equipment, then taking it down once things are wrapped up." He waved away his unimportant explanation. "If I help you, I have a few requests."

"I already have your list." Simon hesitated as though he wasn't sure what to relay. "Your best friend is dead. Your daughter's kidnapper—the daughter of Brenda Krew—is on the loose. Billie and Zack could be in danger. Someone attempted to kill a federal agent last night. We are on those aspects. There's an issue at your parents' bank with a missing flash drive from their safe-deposit box, containing information we need, specifically the photos the sheriff's wife took. Although we know who allowed the theft to happen, we have no idea who has it. We'll get all those answers."

"I have a duplicate of the missing flash drive."

"Here?"

Jason nodded. "I'll make a copy before you leave. I haven't looked at it myself." He stared out through his kitchen window to the horses and cattle grazing together. Fluffy lay in the side yard watching the animals. Normal. He was ready to see these tragic crimes solved and get his life with Isabella back.

He stuck out his hand to Simon. "Let's start tracking."

"Your handgun stays here."

47

April studied the thick trees and brush on the eastern section of the Lennox property, the area where Billie had seen her husband unload from the trunk of his cruiser what she feared was a body and carry it into the woods. Simon claimed they were after Willis, but she'd worked with him long enough to recognize another purpose—find an unmarked grave.

The four agents who'd been on protective duty at Jason's home joined them in the search for Willis. The three men were familiar agents from Houston, but the young woman, who had hunting skills, came from the Dallas office. She'd lead one effort with another agent. The other two agents took a second trail that Jason mapped out, and Jason and April took the third.

"We want to find Willis Lennox ASAP," Simon said. "With his wife and son missing, we're concerned he has them. Joey Frederickson is also missing, and these woods would be a good hiding place."

"Here are a few guidelines," Jason said. "Don't wander off. These woods are filled with wildlife, and some of them aren't friendly. Although the weather is cool, this is home to water moccasins and other poisonous snakes. If you can't identify a deadly snake, leave them all alone. The low-lying areas are perfect for gators, although they tend to prefer the warmer weather too. So stay out of the marshes. Wild hogs will kill you. Period. Avoid approaching piglets 'cause Mama is bound to be close by. Camouflaged deer stands are prime spots for a shooter, or should I say a sniper. No Trespassing signs are posted, and Willis's men will pull the trigger first and ask for your search warrant later. Be on the lookout. Wear bug spray. Got it? This could take a lot of hours. Stay hydrated."

A huge dose of satisfaction laced with pride filled April. Jason's leadership surpassed most agents she knew.

Simon took over the briefing. "Keep in contact. I've summoned the Woodville Police Department, and they're en route to help with the manhunt. If Willis is here, we'll track him down."

Jason signaled for Simon's attention and held up a map for the others to see. "Your phones will have spotty connectivity, and as we go deeper into the woods, those radios and mics might not work. April and I will move southwest while group two tracks northwest and group three moves centrally."

While Simon waited on the dirt road for the Woodville police officers, April followed Jason into a thicket. For the next forty minutes, they tramped deeper into the woods.

He shoved aside brush and often bent to study the ground. The sounds of birds amid the cool quiet should have been soothing. But mosquitoes swarmed like flies on rancid garbage. The insect repellent did little to keep them at bay.

"Tell me what you see," she said.

He stood from examining the ground. "Deer tracks. We're circling a marsh. You can probably smell it. If anyone's been here, their footprints will be easily detected."

A snake slithered past on their right side.

"Water moccasin," he said. "Be careful."

"How many are around in hot weather?"

"Lots."

They trekked for the next several minutes through the woods not far from Jason's land. Their phones remained silent.

"If we suspect trouble, you stay out of the way and call for help," he said.

She considered smacking him. "Right. I'm the trained agent here."

He stopped and swung to her. "April, have you checked the mirror?"

"Doesn't mean I can't shoot. You kissed the road too, remember?"

He grinned. "You're adorable with a black eye."

"Are you flirting with me out here in the middle of mosquitoes, snakes, wild pigs, and animals that want us for lunch?"

He stopped and held up his hand. She immediately hushed. He turned and mouthed the words, "Get down."

She obeyed and strained to hear. Nothing but the rustle of nature. She prayed the snakes were busy elsewhere.

He peered through his binoculars for a moment. Wordlessly, he handed them to her. Opposite them about 150 feet, on a moss-covered bank, a huge, jean-clad man with his back to them stood as though listening. The man did a 180 and stared straight into the brush where she and Jason were crouching.

Willis.

April lowered the binoculars. "We need to let Simon know we've found Willis," she whispered.

"I will," he mouthed. "And give him the coordinates." He checked his phone and frowned. Undoubtedly no connectivity. While she continued to observe Willis through the binoculars, Jason composed a text and tried to send it. He pocketed his phone and shook his head, followed up by an attempt on the radio. "Must be too far from the vehicle's repeater."

"Can't let him escape," she said.

Jason bent low and moved effortlessly around the marshy terrain in Willis's direction. She crept after him. A snake uncoiled on her left—short . . . black, yellow, red . . . a venomous coral snake. She couldn't move.

"Jason," she uttered barely above a whisper.

As if he could smell danger, he yanked a pocket-knife from his pant pocket, released the blade, and sank it into the snake's head. Took him three seconds to save her life.

April clutched her chest and inhaled as though her life depended on it. She'd take bad guys over snakes any day. Never would she walk these woods in the summer without her gun in hand. Jason touched her arm, and she expressed her okay.

She pulled her weapon. "Let's go make an arrest."

"I want answers, not a dead body," he said.

April took the lead, and Jason stayed at her heels. Stooping in a low position compounded with the beating her body took last night and made her back ache.

They pressed in closer until they were about twenty-five feet from Willis. She slowly stood and aimed her Glock. "Willis, stop. Raise your hands. You are under arrest."

The big man froze, but his right hand crept toward his holstered firearm.

"You know the drill. I pull the trigger. You're a dead man." She feared if he chose a firefight, they'd never get their answers. "Now."

"You two just made a terrible mistake. Add trespassing to that." When he raised his right hand, she moved closer.

"With your left hand, remove your firearm and place it gently on the ground."

Still Willis hesitated.

"Willis, don't be a fool. No one else has to get hurt." April poured softness into her tone in an effort to mollify him.

He dropped his weapon and raised his hands. "Your and Jason's playtime isn't a secret," he said. "Deputy Wilcombe and Deputy Viner witnessed your behavior. They're prepared to testify."

The tide was turning against the two deputies. She hated it for Kevin . . . a friend to Jason.

Regroup.

April approached Willis and Jason joined her. "Do you have Billie and Zack out here?" she said.

"Have no idea where they are."

"Then what are you doing in these woods?"

"Enjoyin' a stroll across my own property."

"Where can I find Brenda Krew's daughter, Joey Frederickson?"

"I'm not her daddy."

"Help me, and I'll tell the judge you assisted in solving a series of crimes. She's wanted for assault and kidnapping."

Willis shook his head.

"Did you arrange for her to kidnap Isabella Snyder and force Ted and Vicki at gun—?"

Willis lowered his arms.

Jason moved forward. He reached for Willis's hand, but the big man grabbed Jason's right thumb, twisting it under and out, rendering Jason helpless with his arm flipped to his back.

"As I said, you two just made a terrible mistake. You aren't going to pull the trigger and hit Jason."

"Let him go."

Willis laughed. "Couldn't leave it alone, could you? But we can talk about this. Make it easy for the three of us." He wore a familiar sneer. "Put down your gun and I'll release lover boy."

"Don't do it, April." Jason's face was distorted in pain.

"Tell me where I can find Billie and Zack."

"Why?" she said.

"My wife has something that belongs to me."

"Your son?" Jason said.

"This is worth a whole lot more than a sniveling kid who's just like his mother. The original flash drive. I have the one she gave you."

"What if she made more than one copy?"

"My wife isn't that smart." Willis's lip curled. "Here's the deal. Tell me where they are, and I'll tell the FBI who killed Russell."

"You can't bargain with the FBI." Jason's words rose through the obvious pain of Willis twisting his arm.

"Willis, you're in enough trouble without facing additional murder charges," April said. "If you didn't kill Russell, who did?"

"You think because you're a hostage negotiator, I'll talk to you?" Willis said.

"No. But you need to consider helping yourself, because this will get ugly real fast."

"Gotta violin and I'll wail you a tune. I'm the one in control here." He jerked Jason's arm, and he winced. "Put down your gun, Agent Ramos. Or I break his arm."

She couldn't bear to lose Jason, not when life seemed to be making sense.

"I warned you."

She heard the bone snap. Jason cried out, and she slowly lowered her gun.

"Kick it my way," Willis said. When she obeyed, he dragged Jason several feet into the dense woods. "Don't try following us."

48

Jason struggled to his feet, the agony in his arm radiating throughout his body. Willis had laid a punch along the side of his face. Tossed him into a pile of brush. Then disappeared into thick underbrush. Another mistake on his part—underestimating Willis's wit and strength. He drew in his right arm and made his way back to April. He despised defeat.

She stood in the same path as when he'd left her. Only this time, she held her gun. Blinking back the tears, she hurried to his side. "I'm so sorry. I heard your arm snap."

He wanted to sound all brave, but he felt like a fool in pain. "By the time we get back to the others, Willis will be in the next county."

She wrapped her arm around his waist, like he'd done for her when she'd been run off the road. Such a little battered thing to try to support a grown man. "Let's get you to the ER."

The walk to meet Simon and the female agent at a designated spot took far too long, each step reminding Jason of his disastrous attempt to bring Willis in. The only thing he'd accomplished successfully was finding his daughter. That counted for something.

"Whoa. What happened?" Simon said.

"Willis got the best of us," April said. She relayed the story, and her tone sounded as though she was experiencing the same frustration as Jason.

Simon squinted at Jason. "He got away this time but not the next. I'm ordering a chopper, but it may be too late." Simon instructed the other team to see about picking up Willis's trail. "Woodville officers found what appears to be a grave, matches the one in Billie's photo. I've requested a dig to exhume a body, if one is found."

"Do you need a court order?" Jason said.

"Not with what Billie Lennox reported. Thanks for your help. I'm staying in the area through tomorrow. Can you drive yourself to the hospital?"

"I'll take him," April said.

"Okay." He bored his gaze into Jason. "I'm grateful for your help, but this is where it ends. Do not interfere in a federal investigation."

"Do you have Russell's killer? Joey Frederickson? Willis in jail?"

"You heard me."

Late that afternoon, with his arm casted, Jason walked out of Tyler County Hospital into a chilly fall breeze from the north. The doctor had taken one look at April's bruised face and examined her, too.

"We're pathetic," she said.

"My dad would say we looked like we got beat by the end of an ugly stick. But you're still cute."

She feigned a glare at him, then smiled. The tense muscles in her bruised face said volumes about the unsolved crimes. "Willis is in huge trouble."

"So we lost the battle but the war's not over?" His idiocy still frosted him.

"Optimism."

He caught her gaze. "Hungry? I can make a mean grilled cheese. Even have a jar of Mom's homemade tomato soup."

"Perfect. I'm starved. How are you at left-handed cooking?"

"A pro. I whipped up plenty of them while holding Isabella."

Jason drove with April beside him. He breathed in, letting the air fill his lungs. "Don't suppose Simon will allow me to watch the dig, see who or what's buried there?"

"You already know the answer."

"Were he and the agent friends?"

"No. Just from the same family of risk-takers."

Jason had never viewed himself as much of a risk-taker until his loved ones were facing down the barrel of a gun. "Simon isn't thinking straight if he believes I'm going back to pounding nails."

"I assumed nothing had changed."

"You know me well."

"I learn more every time we're together."

He peered her way, but her focus was occupied by a squirrel scampering across the road. "Professionally or personally?"

"Both, I suppose."

He stared at the gravel driveway leading to his farmhouse. Coming to a halt in front of the porch, he uttered the words pelting his mind. "I like you, April . . . more than I thought possible."

She slowly faced him. "Friendship is easy, comfortable. What we're feeling, thinking, is scary, for me anyway." She glanced out the passenger-side window, then back to him. "It's only been a little over a year since Lily passed. What would she say about us?"

He'd wondered the same thing. "She'd like you, who you are, and what you stand for. I think she'd be happy for us." He leaned across the seat. "I sure want to kiss you, but it looks painful."

She closed the gap between them and touched her lips to his. "This is healing."

"In more ways than you can imagine."

Fluffy bounded up to the truck door and greeted him.

Her phone alerted her to a text. "It's Simon. He wants to talk privately." She left the truck and walked onto the front porch.

49

As April and Jason sat at his kitchen table and munched on grilled cheese sandwiches with Mom's homemade soup, he wanted to ask about Simon's conversation with her. Maybe it had nothing to do with the case. Maybe she'd made arrangements to drive back to Houston.

"What kind of cheese did you use?" she said. "I taste provolone and cheddar."

"You're right, and two kinds of cheddar, sharp and mild."

She laid the half-eaten sandwich on her plate. "Simon wants to talk to me face-to-face at your parents' home," she said. "About 6 p.m. He'd like to add you to the conversation at 6:30."

"What about?"

"The obvious."

"And keeping me in line." He sighed. "I understand his position and yours. We all have stakes. Mine are personal. I'm worried about Billie. Too many reasons for why she might have disappeared, and most are not good." He finished his soup, flipped to a new page on his legal pad, and grasped his pen.

April took another bite of her sandwich and studied him. She'd probably guessed his thoughts. "You're blaming yourself for Billie's disappearance."

"You've taken up mind reading?"

She pushed back her plate and bowl. "Regrets keep us chained to guilt." She'd experienced her share. "There's nothing you could have done to prevent this."

"My head says you're right, but it will take time to get past it. She trusted me, and I betrayed her."

"You are looking out for her safety. Jason, you have an integrity this world craves. You're honorable and filled with caring for others. Those traits are why Billie came to you for help."

Simple words of encouragement and support— those used to come from Lily. "I should be this pillar of strength without flaws."

"Perfection isn't in the human DNA."

"We strive for it."

"I was told with God's help we do our best to model Jesus. When we slip, we ask for forgiveness and God is merciful."

"I thought your views on Christianity weren't solid."

"After the accident this morning and seeing the miracle God performed, I gave Him control. Biblical principles were in my head, and now they're in my heart. The things I learned as a child—from nuns in school, from those who are believers, and on to you and your family—keep pouring into my mind. Thanks to what I've seen in the people around me. Including you. Don't discount your positive impact on others."

Her words should have inspired him, but instead they hit him hard. "Right. Sure."

"Can the darkness be replaced with treasured memories?"

He grimaced. "Isabella deserves laughter."

"So do you. When the ugliness of Willis's attempts drags you to the bottom, think about your precious daughter. Plan a vacation with her."

Would April be a part of the future? Did he dare even consider it?

Taking notes was no longer important. He wanted to kiss her, and he fought a losing battle with the emotions surging inside him.

He lightly stroked her cheek and leaned toward her. Their lips met. He tasted the soft sweetness that he remembered from the early hours when he feared she was dead. The soft glow in her eyes told him what her words failed to convey. When he felt an urge to deepen the kiss, he pulled back instead. "Should I apologize?" Hoarseness wove through his words.

"I'd rather we talk about it."

Jason grinned. That sounded like a line from the hostage negotiation handbook.

"Never mind," she said, growing flustered. "I take it back. I don't want to discuss us."

He took their bowls and plates to the sink to give her a little time. He leaned back against the counter and faced her at the table. "Okay, we won't. For now. But when life around here calms down, can we explore the next step after friend-ship?"

"Okay."

"I'll put you and me on a to-tackle list for later."

"Like football?" She smiled.

"You—" he paused to form his words—"are not a sport or a game."

"Thank you." Taking a deep breath, she moistened her lips. "What's up next?"

"Lots of unfinished business. I'm making a list of people to visit."

"Can you hold off contacting them until I'm finished with Simon? We're still partners."

"April, we're a team too. Our skills complement each other. Well, mostly yours."

"Promise me you won't break the law or undermine the FBI's work. If you do, I can't protect you."

"I understand. But I know the people of Sweet Briar, and while they might hold back talking to a stranger, they'll open up to me, especially with Willis on the run. People in the community loved Russell, and they want justice served. I have a license to carry a handgun, but no technology, no fancy connections or resources for information. But I can't let this go."

April wished she could relieve Simon's stress, evi-dent in his pinched features. Shortly after 6 p.m., he sat upright in Ted's brown leather recliner while she eased onto the sofa across from him. These last few years before Simon retired at fifty-seven were shadowing him.

"So Kevin Viner is the deputy who contacted the FBI."

Simon dragged a hand over his face. "Yes. He's kept us informed while looking for evidence to prosecute Willis. If the body is Eric Deckett, and we're able to find Billie Lennox, we can put Willis away for a long time."

"I imagine Billie, like others in this community, has more than one tale. Any clues to her where-abouts?"

"A few but nothing definite yet."

He looked so tired, her friend and partner. "Want me to brew a pot of coffee?"

"No thanks. I'm on a caffeine high, and my stomach's raw." He pressed his lips before speaking, obviously choosing his words with care. "I asked the SAC why you weren't the one working the public corruption case against Willis since it is your area of expertise."

She gazed out the huge window facing the quaint property across the street, an image of small-town peaceful living. "Honestly, being out of the loop bothers me tremendously."

"Remember the case in south Houston where a dozen young women were being held hostage by their pimp?"

"Took me days to interview each one. They were malnourished, abused, and required medical care." The case unfolded in her mind. She had helped the girls obtain counseling and reconnect with their families. Some she still visited on a regular basis.

"You were involved for nearly three weeks, then you took a week off."

"That's when Willis's case came in?"

"Right."

"I was consumed by every woman's situation." She breathed in. "I understand."

"Okay, back to Sweet Briar and the criminal activities here. Quantico is backlogged, so the behavior analysis will take more time. We have the typical motivation of power and control, but the underlying factors require intensive psychological research." Simon clamped his palms on the arms of the recliner. "You've managed to turn up evidence which we were unable to find. Good job."

And she intended to work every angle. "Does Willis have a lawyer? I'm thinking he's aware of at least some of Willis's illegal activities."

"We've learned his name is David Canfield. Lives and works in Woodville. Has his own one-man office and specializes in business law. Willis is his main client. He also has a PI license."

"So he might be involved in hunting down Billie and Zack?"

Simon nodded. "Accessing Canfield's financials and phone records will take a subpoena. We know he's flown in and out of IAH twice since Billie left the area. The first trip was to Chicago. The second to Asheville, North Carolina, where Billie's sister, Gwen Scottard, lives."

"Have you talked to her?"

"Claims she has no idea where her sister is. Jason went to school with her. She might open up to him." He tapped the chair arm. "I hate to involve him further, though."

"He's wanting to stay involved, no matter what you or I mandate. Contacting Billie's sister is a way for him to help."

"Thanks," he said. "Keep me in the loop."

She lifted her chin. "I'm in this for the duration. This case has a weak spot, and I'm going to find it."

50

At 6:28, Jason parked in his parents' driveway behind April's rental. Simon's SUV was lined up with the curb, the same spot where Joey Frederickson parked when she held his parents at gunpoint and nabbed Isabella. Right behind Simon's vehicle, Kevin pulled in.

Exiting his car, Jason waited for him. "What's this about?"

"Laying the cards on the table," Kevin said.

"I want to believe you." Did Jason really know Kevin? "Strange, though, the obscurity is getting to me. Too many crimes have you benefiting from Willis's payoffs."

Kevin glanced over his shoulder. "Trust me. I'm your friend. I have a role to play, one that's been in place for almost a year. Every minute I spend with you puts me in a bad position. Willis thinks I'm covering him."

"Griff too?" Jason said.

"Hard to say. No one in the department is aware of what I've been doing. I'm working on finding answers. If I had insight into Griff, I'd tell you. It's a little lonely at the house without my family. So in case you doubted whose side I'm on, I want my wife and kids back but not until Willis is in prison." He touched his sidearm. "We're going to stage an argument and Simon's going to stop us," he said barely above a whisper.

"Are you being watched?"

"Strong possibility. Have no idea where Griff and Cal are right now, and I'm not taking any chances."

"For me to oblige, I need answers to what's going on."

"You'll get them. Look, I don't like this any more than you do."

That was the Kevin who'd been his friend since they were boys. "I'll play."

"I'm ready to cuff you until this is over." Lines plowed across his forehead. "Willis is missing, and you have reason to make sure he never surfaces again."

Jason stepped into Kevin's personal space. "Willis killed Russell, a man who was like a brother to me. He arranged for Joey Frederickson to kidnap my daughter. I have no idea where Willis is hiding out."

"You're a liar."

"Here's a question for you, Deputy Viner." Jason spit each word. "Where is Joey Frederickson? I'm sure you know. Tell me now before I beat it out of you."

"Just try and I'll throw your rear in jail."

April exited the front door and raced toward them. "What's going on?"

Jason raised a fist. "Last chance. I want to know how to find Joey Frederickson."

April tugged on Jason's fisted hand. "Leave him alone. This doesn't solve a thing."

The door slammed, and Simon hurried toward them. "Stop now. Inside, you two."

Jason shook off April's hold. Simon took a stance between him and Kevin. "I said inside."

Jason glared at Kevin. "All right."

"Cool off, Snyder," Simon said. "This isn't your town any more than it belongs to Sheriff Lennox."

April led the way, and the men trailed her through the front door of the home, which had become a temporary FBI office and April's hotel.

Once the door closed, Simon nodded. "You two staged a good one."

"A little too real for me," Kevin said.

"We're all tired and want answers." Jason rubbed his face. "I'm just glad you're not on Willis's payroll."

Kevin reached out to shake his hand. "I wanted to tell you in a bad way that I was working with Houston's FBI, especially the night of Russell's murder. But I couldn't trust Griff. And then Isabella was kidnapped and I wasn't sure if both incidents were connected."

Jason breathed in. "Were you aware of the possibility of a grave on Willis's land?"

"No," Kevin said. "If Billie had come forward,

we could've arrested Willis a long time ago." He paused. "Can't blame her, considering the times he used her and Zack as a punching bag."

Simon suggested they sit at the kitchen table. He bored an in-charge stare into Jason. "I wanted you here because you suspected Kevin might be working with Willis. This is by no means a go-ahead for you to investigate on your own terms."

Jason would need a hydraulic press to flatten the tension. "So why am I here then?"

"We've gotten nowhere with Gwen Scottard. We'd appreciate it if you'd give her a call. Finding Billie is critical, especially with Willis dodging us."

"If anyone can reason with those sisters, it's you," Kevin said.

"I grew up with Gwen." Jason recalled a few high school memories. "It's hard for me to swallow she wouldn't know where Billie's hiding."

"Go for it," Simon said. "I can give you the number."

Jason pressed in Gwen's number but hesitated before pushing Send. He hadn't seen her in years. "I'm not using Speaker in case she's nervous and hangs up. She may not pick up on an unfamiliar call anyway." The phone rang four times before rolling to voice mail. "Gwen, this is Jason Snyder. Billie contacted me, and now she's missing. Willis is missing too. Can you ask her to contact me? I'm concerned she and Zack are in danger. Please call me."

He ended the call, and an idea washed over him. "Russell's funeral is tomorrow. How about I fly out to Asheville and talk to her face-to-face on the next flight after the services?"

Simon appeared to think about the request. "You doubt she'll return the call?"

"Probably not. If she does, then I'll do my best to locate Billie. Understand Gwen would do anything to protect her sister." How much should he tell? "Gwen and I have history."

"The kind of history that builds trust?"

They'd dated two years in high school then went separate ways as friends. "Yes."

April narrowed her eyes. Nice to think she might be jealous. "I'm going too. You might need a negotiator. In my experience, sisters are fiercely loyal."

Jason held more confidence in the case moving forward. He'd made mistakes, but he refused to sit by and allow the FBI to finish the case without him.

Simon took over the discussion. "Here are the priorities on the FBI's list: Number one—find Willis. Number two—safeguard Billie and Zack. Number three—figure out who, if anyone, is buried on Willis's property. Number four—locate Joey Frederickson. Number five—discern if Brenda Krew is withholding information on outstanding cases."

Simon turned to Kevin and Jason. "Have either of you ever dealt with David Canfield, Willis's lawyer?"

Kevin denied any knowledge of the man.

"Do you have a pic?" Jason said. "Maybe I've seen him before."

Simon handed him his phone. "Anything?"

Jason returned the phone. "Saw him last Memorial Day. I stopped at the restaurant for lunch. Willis and Brenda were sitting with him at a corner table. He caught my attention because he drove a silver Corvette."

Simon made a note before pocketing his phone. "I'm staying until Tuesday. Got a room booked in Woodville. The arrangement allows me to keep my eye on things."

Jason nearly laughed. "Simon, I'm not a martyr or a lawbreaker, but a man who needs answers. I owe Billie and her boy an opportunity to live their lives in peace. Plus, Joey Frederickson is still out there." Jason drove his focus into Simon's face. "The personal stakes are too high for me to walk away. What happens the next time a crime spills into our town, friends, and family? How would I face parents whose child had fallen into the hands of a kidnapper? I understand if I break the law, you, Kevin, or April will toss me in jail."

"And I'll snap the cuffs on good and tight," Simon said. "That's a promise."

"I'd like to talk to my family," Jason said. "Is it possible?"

"Only from my phone, and I'm late as it is. We'll do it tomorrow."

Kevin rose when Simon got up, and Jason followed the guys to the front door. Simon stopped there, waving Kevin off. "April is like a daughter to me."

"She's important to me, too."

"Take some advice," Simon said, lowering his voice. "No relationship lasts when it begins with danger and supercharged emotions."

When Jason returned to the kitchen with his legal pad, April was on the phone leaving a message for Brenda to call her. She tilted her head at him. "Something wrong?"

"Nothing but what we're facing." He wouldn't repeat Simon's words until he'd thought them through.

"I hope Brenda hasn't left town and taken Joey with her."

"Hard to sneak out when the FBI has agents watching the roads. She could be showing property and just not picking up."

"Thanks for the optimism. I know you'd like to face off with her about Joey," she said, "but I need to do this without you. If you're there, she could become hostile."

"You're right. This is about getting the job done."

She smiled, a gesture he could get used to. "I'd like to check a couple of websites before tracking her down."

He retrieved his dad's laptop. At the table, they sat side by side. A few keystrokes, and she sat back in the chair. "Ready for this? According to FBI records, Brenda visited her daughter in jail and bailed her out three times, all within an eighteen-month period. Brenda also financed an upscale drug rehab on two occasions. Remember when I stopped at her office, and she had Joey's pic half-hidden on her desk? With Joey's rap sheet, I think she suspected her involvement." She nodded. "I'll ask her."

April appeared to have newfound energy, and her go-getter attitude invigorated him. She brought up Brenda's website. "She's done a few Facebook Live videos showcasing property. Twitter posts and Instagram are business related." April's fingers flew across the keyboard. She studied the screen. "Take a look at this. Brenda's Facebook friend's photos."

Jason viewed the photos. Brenda and Joey smiled back at him. "Weird to see Joey in these pics knowing she took Isabella."

"And your wanting to wring her neck." She hesitated. "By the way, you'd be a great agent."

"Bad fit. I'm approaching this mess the same way I'd build a house. Lay the foundation, and work up. Besides, I'm too old to go to the academy."

"No, you're not. I already checked. You're almost thirty-five, and the age limit is thirty-seven."

"Have you checked me out?"

"And if I have?"

He rose from the chair, her nearness distracting him. He towered over her tiny frame and looked into her sweet and battered face. "You scare me to death."

51

At 7:45 p.m., April called Brenda Krew for the fifth time, and this time the woman answered. She reluctantly agreed to meet at her real estate office.

"Is this about Willis?" Brenda said. "If so, your questions can wait until tomorrow. I'll have my attorney present then."

"David Canfield?"

Brenda hesitated, and April had her answer. "My concerns aren't about Willis."

"Jason Snyder? I've already told you all I know about him and his construction company."

"Indirectly. I'll be there in about ten minutes." April ended the call before Brenda could object further.

"Good luck," Jason said. "But my guess is Brenda will shut you down the moment you mention Joey."

April opened the door of Krew Real Estate Office. Brenda stood in front of a map of Tyler County using pushpins to designate specific areas. She met April slowly with a lift of her chin and lines Botox could never hide.

"Good evening, Brenda." April was carrying two cups of coffee. "The restaurant was still open due to a Bible study. The waitress prepared your coffee exactly the way you like it." She set the cups on the desk, glad to release her fingers from the heat radiating through the cup sleeves.

Brenda peered at her and cringed. "I heard you were in an accident."

April smiled. "Yes, I took a beating. I look worse than I feel."

"I'm sorry. Are you sure our discussion is necessary? I'm really tired, and you look—"

"Awful. But the caffeine will perk us up. This won't take long. I've been researching, and I found a few things I'd like to talk about."

"Regarding?"

"Joey."

Brenda bounced a green pushpin in the palm of her hand. "I've changed my mind."

"Why not take a seat?" April said. "Perhaps you can help me understand a few things about your daughter."

Brenda's stilettos appeared to be cemented to the floor. "My daughter is none of your business."

"Unfortunately, Joey is in a lot of trouble. More than ever before. And I'd like to help."

"Why would you want to help my daughter?"

"She's young. Impressionable."

"Just like I told the other FBI agents, my daughter had nothing to do with Russell's murder. Nor do I know where she is."

Brenda had been made aware of her daughter's crimes from the agents' interview. But the woman continued to claim ignorance of Joey's activities.

"We have evidence and security camera footage in Houston at the donut shop where she handed Isabella Snyder off to me, implicating her in the kidnapping and making her a person of interest in an assault case."

"You're telling me there's no doubt she kidnapped Jason's baby?"

"Right." April had learned a lot about parents being protective of their children in the last few days. "Brenda, I see the pain in your eyes, the kind of pain that comes from love. The kind of pain that fears what the next minute will bring."

Red crested Brenda's face. "Get out." She reached down and tossed her cup of coffee at April.

April stepped back a half second before the scalding brew flew her way. It splashed the front of her sweatshirt. She gasped at the feel of the hot liquid.

"Don't ever bother me again."

April pulled her emotions into focus. "I hope you change your mind before Joey's arrested or worse."

She counted the seconds to the front door, hoping Brenda would replace her worn mothering emotions with a sacrifice of love.

Outside, the temperatures had dropped, and the coffee-soaked sweatshirt did little to keep her warm, but it had stopped a serious burn. She shivered, prompting her to stick her hands into the pockets of her jeans.

Home in Houston sounded better than dry clothes.

The Chevy rental unlocked with a chirp, and she slid inside. Dreading the finality of starting the engine, she rested her head on the steering wheel. Failure inched over her. She never took defeat well. Did anyone? Her thoughts drifted back to her and Simon's discussion in the wee hours of Friday morning about choices and her compassion for others. Caring about others didn't seem like a character flaw. While she despised the way crimes affected victims, sometimes the bad guys were as much victims as the innocent.

Her thoughts returned to Brenda. She'd lived a troubled past, wrestled with alcohol abuse, and lost her daughter. Could she really be in denial, or was she covering up her daughter's serious offenses? Brenda wasn't doing her daughter any favors by hiding or protecting her. Quite the opposite, especially if Willis viewed Joey as expendable.

April swung her attention back inside the real estate office. Brenda sat at her desk, her face buried in her hands. Her outward anger of tossing coffee at April was Brenda's symbolic display of her own guilt, regret, and frustration. Did the woman even recognize that?

God, I need help. Why is life harder since I gave You control?

52

April's car fumes still lingered in the air when Jason left the driveway of his parents' home. He had no intentions of kicking back and watching TV on a Sunday night or catching up on sleep when the need to see Carrie, to talk to her before the funeral and try to clear the air, was growing.

Carrie claimed Lily and Jason weren't friends but family. When Willis objected to her friendship with him and Lily, she told him to mind his own business.

Lily had chosen Carrie as maid of honor at their wedding. She'd held Lily's flowers and his wedding ring. Russell had supported him as best man and held on to Lily's ring. What a happy day.

Until death parts.

Carrie surprised Lily with a baby shower after they learned they were expecting a girl. Everything in pink, reminding Jason of Pepto-Bismol, but Lily loved it.

Carrie promised to be a godmother to Isabella—forever.

Carrie accompanied him and Lily to every chemo treatment.

Carrie cried with Lily when the doctor announced hospice needed to take over her care until it was time for the baby to arrive.

Carrie and Russell comforted him and Isabella at the hospital when Isabella was born and Lily slipped into eternity.

While Jason understood, even shared, Carrie's grief over Russell's death, he expected Willis to taint his image. In Carrie's shoes, he'd have a problem deciphering whom to believe: her brother, Willis, or her brother-in-law Jason.

Tonight, if she refused to open the door, he'd resort to asking April to arrange a meeting. Carrie had emotional problems, and if she still thought he'd killed Russell, she might unload her gun on him. But he'd take the chance. He wanted five minutes to grieve together with her.

Russell's funeral was scheduled for 10 a.m. Jason planned to be there and hoped Carrie didn't deny him the opportunity to celebrate Russell's life. He regretted Mom and Dad wouldn't be at the services, but their condolences could be shared later.

He entered Carrie's long lane and inched along the quarter mile to the restored farmhouse. He and Russell with Carrie and Lily had spent hours fixing, replacing, and adding to the charm of the century-old home. Memories cut into his heart.

Jason parked and waited for Carrie to check her driveway. When he saw a slight fluttering of the kitchen blinds, he left his truck, squeezing his keys into his palm before dropping them into his pocket.

The porch light came to life as he mounted the wooden steps leading to the door. He held his breath and knocked.

The door opened. Carrie wore a heavy robe wrapped tightly around her. Her dark-brown hair and pale face gave her an eerie look. She had to wade through this swamp for the welfare of her sons.

"Jason, why are you here?" Her voice trembled.

"Because Russell was Lily's brother, and we're family. We look out for each other. Grief is to be shared, not spent alone."

Her lips quivered. "My sons are in bed. Pastor and his wife left about thirty minutes ago." Her shoulders slumped.

"Can we talk out here?" He pointed to the swing where she'd rocked Isabella after Lily's funeral and wept kisses on his daughter's face.

In the porch light, she shook. He smelled alcohol, and the realization of where she was trying to find peace brought a lump in his throat.

"Please," he said. "Imagine Lily is with me."

"I miss her so. She was the best sister-friend I ever had. Why did you let her die? You could have done more."

This wasn't the time for Jason to address Carrie's imbalanced emotions. "I'm sorry. I really believe the doctors did all they could."

"But now she's gone." Despite her words, Carrie stepped over the threshold in a point of reconciliation. She positioned herself at the far end of the swing and gripped the chain that secured it to the porch ceiling as though it were a lifeline.

He sat at the other end. "Tell me what you're thinking."

"Russell's gone, and I don't know how to go on. I felt the same when Lily died. But now I don't want to face another day."

April had shown him how listening to people who were hurting demonstrated compassion, a trait he desperately needed. He needed to let Carrie toss all the verbal daggers. "What else, Carrie?"

"My sons will forget their daddy's face, forget the things he did for them, how much he loved them. I hurt so badly I wish I'd died with Russell." She pulled the rope of her belt tighter as though to hold in the pain. "The ironic truth is no matter how much I want to despise you for being alive, only you know how I feel."

"I do," he said. "Some days are better than others. Some days I'm angry at God and then glad He freed Lily from the pain. Such a dichotomy."

"And what about Willis? How am I supposed to find peace with him missing and a person of interest?" She shook her head. "Those three words tear me apart. My brother a person of interest in my husband's death." She slowly faced him. "The FBI has to be wrong. They think my brother arranged the murder of my husband and set you up? Never. The thought is like someone stabbed my heart." She sighed. "Willis stretches my patience, but murder? And why?"

Jason stared up at the night filled with stars, looking for clarity, a word or phrase to ease her. Mom would see Carrie as a soul in distress. Her soft weeping broke nature's night songs.

"We'll soon have answers."

"I wonder if Billie has someone telling her what's happening."

Was that a ploy? "I have no idea. She hasn't contacted you?"

She shook her head.

Jason stifled a sigh. "Carrie, who is driving you to the funeral tomorrow?"

"Kevin offered since Willis is gone. I'd hoped Mom and Dad would come. But Willis said Dad's struggling with dementia, and Mom won't leave him. She hasn't even called, and Willis asked me not to bother her. Said it would be too devastating for her to leave Dad." Carrie touched a tissue to her nose. "She'll find out eventually. Seeing life through my brother's eyes is hard. But he is the favored son, so I'll do as he says."

"I'm sorry." The lack of caring didn't sound like the older Lennox woman. Suspicion nipped at his mind. Were the older couple even aware of Russell's death?

"Dad's physical health is deteriorating, so I understand Mom's reluctance. Please tell me you'll be there."

"Of course."

She retrieved a tissue from her pocket. "How he loved you and Lily." Carrie sniffed.

"Do you mind if I bring FBI Agent April Ramos?"

"Does she think Willis murdered Russell?"

"She only wants the truth, like me."

"I think that would be fine. I'd like to meet her." She closed her eyes. "Russell didn't have a malicious bone in his body. He loved and cared for us, even Willis. Said Willis had a good spot somewhere, and he'd find it." Her voice broke, and she paused as though to gain control. "For my sons' sake, I want to get past tomorrow and go on with our lives."

"Law enforcement won't stop until Russell's killer is found, I'm certain. I'll keep looking too."

"Good." She sighed. "I'm tired, and tomorrow's a long day."

His signal to leave. "Thanks for talking to me." He headed toward the porch steps, relieved he'd followed his instincts to talk to her.

"Jason," Carrie said.

"Yes." He turned.

"Russell didn't tell me you two had quarreled. Willis told me about the argument, said Russell didn't want to worry me with it. Does this mean my brother knows who shot my husband?"

53

As the hour moved toward 9:30 p.m., April sat in the dark of Vicki and Ted's living room. Her coffee-soaked sweatshirt was spinning in the washing machine, and she wore a sweater Vicki had purchased for her. Occasionally a car drove by, headlights spilling into the room like the sun shining through an eastern window and revealing tabletop decor and lamps. Then the light would vanish, hiding all traces of the life inside.

Four days ago, she'd never heard of Jason Snyder, Isabella, Vicki and Ted, Miss Ella, or any of the fine people she'd met in Sweet Briar. Now Jason's existence was entwined with hers in a peculiar way. She craved and feared what his presence meant in her life. She drew in a weary breath. *Jason Snyder, what have you done to me?*

How had her ordered life taken such a detour in less than a week? Prior to this weekend, she depended on established habits and her career to stay in balance. But now she had a new priority—God.

Would Jason be part of her new life? And Isabella? Were their sweet conversations about new fragile feelings and kisses merely a way to relieve tension? She hoped not.

She closed her eyes and inhaled the scent of a

home not her own, a lingering of cinnamon and apples tossed with a measure of love. Inside her cottage, sage and lavender welcomed her. She treasured both scents.

Headlights targeted the driveway, and she opened her eyes. The vehicle stopped on the driveway. The wandering Jason had arrived. As much as she questioned where he'd been, she hadn't felt a need to text him. She'd learn soon enough. She flipped on a lamp and met him at the door.

"Am I past my curfew?" He grinned.

"Not at 9:45."

He closed the door and enveloped her in his arms, a warm surprise. "I paid Carrie a visit."

"How is she?"

"In shock. Confused."

An awareness of being in his arms soothed her longing to be home. "Were you able to talk?"

He nodded. "Carrie told me a couple of things." His voice held a wisp of sadness.

"We can sit and chat."

They sat together on the sofa, and he took her hand. "First I want to hear what went on with Brenda."

She gave a quick rundown. "Brenda's protecting Joey like a she-bear. But I feel sorry for her. Anyway, I requested a subpoena for her cell phone records and financials and learned Simon was one step ahead of me. Hope to have the info tomorrow." She held up her hand. "I want to hear about your evening."

"Willis invented an argument to discredit me in Carrie's eyes." Jason outlined his conversation with Carrie, mentioning that the senior Lennoxes wouldn't be at the funeral. "Willis is one selfish man, and Carrie is no stranger to his low-crawling attitude. But why keep a mother and daughter apart?"

"People aren't born thieves, killers, or any other base behavior. Surely there is an ounce of decency in him. If we could tap into it, the case might unravel."

"If only he'd changed with Billie and Zack. Become a new man." He paused. "Carrie wants to meet you at the funeral."

"I'd like that." April wanted an opportunity to speak to Carrie too. But her husband's funeral wasn't the appropriate place to ask questions. Still it bothered April that Carrie had lied about Russell and Jason's supposed argument, even though she suffered from emotional issues.

Jason stared out the window facing the street. "We have company." A set of headlights moved behind his truck.

April's apprehension sailed with the lengthy list of those who might have arrived at the Snyder home.

"Expecting anyone?" Jason said.

"Not unless you ordered pizza." She shook her

head. "Bad joke." She pulled her Glock from her shoulder bag.

The doorbell rang. "I've got this," he said.

At the sound of a woman's voice, April approached the front door.

"Hi, Brenda," he said. "Come on in."

Brenda was the last person April expected tonight.

"Evening, Jason. Is April available?" Her voice quavered.

"I am." April faced the woman who'd thrown coffee on her earlier.

Brenda reached out her hand, and she took it. "An apology is in order, and I'm sorry. Really sorry. Are you burned? Because—"

"No worries," April said. "I'm fine. Can I get you something?"

"I had a great cup of coffee before I threw it." Her lips trembled. "I've done a few miserable things in my life. Tonight is near the top. I was so angry but not at you."

April's interpretation of what happened had been right. "All is forgiven. Want to sit here or in the kitchen?"

"Here's fine." Brenda slid into a chair.

"I'll leave you two ladies to talk." Jason retreated to the kitchen. Out of sight yet he could hear every word.

"Thank you for seeing me," Brenda began. "I've spent a little time tonight soul-searching

371

about what is best for Joey. I'm sure you've done your research and discovered her dad raised her. When she arrived on my doorstep less than two years ago, I thought I'd been given a second chance at motherhood." Brenda paused and moistened her lips. "Could I have a glass of water?"

April patted Brenda's hand and rose to retrieve it. When she presented the water, the woman struggled with her emotions. She took a sip and nodded, as though the extra few seconds had calmed her.

April tried to focus on what it might be like to have a wayward child who'd committed serious offenses. She leaned closer. "I'm sorry. It's impossible for me to understand because I'm not a mother. What I know is disappointments are difficult to bear, but when they are inflicted by those we love, the pain is tremendous."

"At first, I believed she simply needed a mother in her life. But it wasn't too long before I detected the signs of drug abuse. Money disappeared from my wallet. I confronted her and offered to pay for rehab. She agreed. Twice. Both times she reverted to drugs. No idea where she got the cocaine. And like a fool, I repeatedly gave her money. Occasionally she opened up to me, and we experienced wonderful moments together." Brenda shrugged. "Now I wonder if she was high then. I caught her stealing money again. She pawned my grandmother's jewelry. Two weeks ago, I attempted to talk to her about rehab, but she blew her top and left."

"I'm really sorry for what you're going through."

"I'm afraid for Joey. She's been accused of terrible crimes, and I'm at a loss as to how I can help her. For her to hold Ted and Vicki at gunpoint, kidnap Jason's baby, is deplorable. Perhaps Joey justified it since I abandoned her for a bottle of liquor." Brenda's hands shook, and she placed them in her lap. "I've been a fool thinking I could change her."

Brenda abruptly stood and walked into the kitchen. April followed her. "Jason, I was the one who alerted Willis to you and April being at the motel. I was showing property nearby and saw your truck. Much of this is my fault. Please forgive me."

Learning one more person was guilty of working for Willis had to try Jason's patience.

"Brenda, I'm not saying this isn't hard. But I forgive you if you can forgive me for not trying harder to be friends. Let's hope we can move forward."

"I want that. I'm done covering for Willis and pushing others away." She stopped. "Admitting I'm wrong goes against my normal method of dealing with people. I've said incriminating things to the FBI about you, but there's no substantiation in them at all. I'm sorry for that, too."

"The question is why," he said. "Did Willis prompt you?"

"He claimed you had vowed to destroy his credibility as county sheriff, and you were having an affair with Billie."

He frowned. "That's absolutely untrue."

April gently brought the conversation back to Brenda's daughter. "We need to find Joey. The address we have in northwest Houston isn't valid."

"She kept two addresses—mine and her Houston apartment. Joey values her privacy." Brenda touched her fingertips to her lips. "Probably used the Houston address to get high."

"Have you called her?"

"I tried, although she doesn't like me contacting her. Says it's disturbing."

"May I have her number?"

Brenda produced a pen and pad of paper from her purse but stopped before writing anything. "Tomorrow is her twenty-third birthday."

The same day as Russell's funeral. Joey was wanted for assault, kidnapping, and theft. Drug abuse. Certainly not a birthday celebration for either mother or daughter.

"She'll cast me out of her life for giving you her number."

"What is the alternative?"

"She might change. I did." Brenda's hand with the pen hovered over the paper. "I feel like I'm betraying my own daughter, and yet she can't go on this way. Why did she commit such horrid crimes? Is it money? Does every action of a lawbreaker trickle back to what money can buy?"

Was Brenda referring to her own past actions?

"Please, Brenda. I need to contact Joey. Perhaps I can reason with her."

Brenda blinked and jotted down the number. She tore off the piece of paper and handed it to April. It was the same cell number the FBI had on file, which had been disconnected.

"Will you call me if you hear from her?" April said.

She hesitated. "I should, and I want to. When depressed, she threatens to take her life. When she's stressed, she panics and reacts in outlandish behavior."

April remembered Joey shoving Isabella into her arms. "The charges against your daughter are serious. If I can talk to her, persuade her to turn herself in, I can arrange care and counseling."

"I'll do my best. She disappears when she's using."

"What is her relationship with Willis?"

"She's had dinner with him and me twice. Sulked the whole meal. Claimed to dislike him."

Could have been part of a charade. "Who are her friends?"

"I've never heard her mention anyone. I've asked, but she said friends were personal, and I wouldn't like them."

"Does she have a job?"

"Off and on. No idea where she's working, if at all."

"Tell me about the last time you spoke with her."

"Joey called to tell me she had a new job. From the high pitch of her voice and how fast she was talking, I assumed she was high. She said she'd call later when she got home. But she must have forgotten."

"Do you have a recording of Joey's voice?"

"Why?"

"It will help the investigation."

"With her erratic behavior, I never know when will be the last time I see her." Brenda wrung her hands. "If I refuse, I know you'll get the recordings legally."

"Are they on your phone?"

Brenda gave her device to April. "Check voice mail."

April recorded two separate calls with Joey's voice and sent them to Simon. "Thank you. Does she have a car?"

"I bought her a truck, but she sold it for an old, dented Honda."

That car matched the description of the one Joey drove to Houston with Isabella.

"April, has Willis drawn her into his scheme? I mean, he asked me to cover for him last night." She touched her stomach.

"Are you okay?" April said softly.

"I think so. Seeing what Willis might have done to you last night makes me sick, physically. I'm sorry. Really sorry." She took a deep breath. "He said if the FBI asked too many questions, to use his lawyer, David Canfield."

April wondered how much Canfield was earning from all this. "You've taken a brave step in coming here tonight."

"I wish I had the answers you need."

"Have you told me everything about Joey and Willis?"

"I think so."

"Do you suspect they're involved?"

"Not to my knowledge." Brenda lifted her shoulders. "I might have to kill him myself if that's the situation. My relationship with Willis has been strictly business and community involvement."

"We believe he abused Billie and Zack." April would let Brenda fill in the blanks.

"I asked him about Billie's bruises, and he said she was clumsy and fell a lot. I should have done something about it. If she's smart, she'll never show up here again."

Brenda's demeanor suggested she was telling the truth, but the woman also feared for her daughter and possibly herself. Many times people in desperate situations refused to be transparent, much to April's regret, and the need to dig deeper and count on physical evidence came into play.

The doorbell rang, and April stood from the table. "Jason, do we know who's out there?"

"I'll take a look," he said. "Busy place tonight."

Until April learned the reason for the near 11 p.m. house call, she was keeping her gun close.

54

Jason pulled back the drapes and recognized a deputy's car in the driveway. What now? "Two deputies are paying us a visit," he said. "Brenda, is this your doing?"

"No one knows I'm here," she said.

He refused to call her a liar when she appeared sincere, but she could have been followed. Kevin and Griff wound around the sidewalk to the front door. April kept her Glock tucked inside the back waistband of her jeans.

He responded to the doorbell. "Evenin', Kevin, Griff. What brings you here?" His thoughts darted toward a potential trap.

Kevin gave a thin-lipped smile. "Cal Bunion got a text from Brenda Krew, said you two had her trapped here."

"Brenda—" Jason kept his eyes on the deputies and his hands at his sides—"do we have a problem?"

"Of course not. I didn't send Cal a text. Check my phone. I'm a guest in this home, not a prisoner." Brenda moved beside him. "I came to see Jason about a boundary question on a tract of land."

Kevin shifted. "It's late to be doing business on a Sunday night. Dangerous too. Might be best to head home."

Silence swirled around the room. Kevin played

his part well. "April and I will make sure she has an escort," Jason said.

Kevin waved his hand. "No need. We'll handle it." He peered at Brenda. "Ready?"

"I'm not quite finished here." That was the Brenda Krew he knew, the one who could shut down a growling wildcat or tromp through a gator-infested pond.

"Tomorrow's another day," Kevin said. "I'd feel better if you'd let me escort you home. You might have company."

"I've been at the office," Brenda said.

"A light was on when I drove by. I'd have stopped if not for following up on Cal's text."

"Why isn't he here?" she said.

"Not his shift. He asked Griff and me to handle it."

"Are you thinking Joey's at my home?" Brenda said with a slight gasp.

"If she is, we need to take her in." Kevin paused as though thinking through his words. "Sure would be easier if you could talk to her. Having Joey give herself up sounds better than an arrest or resisting arrest."

"Griff, did you see lights on at Brenda's place?" Jason had no clue about Griff's allegiance. The man never said much—but when he did, it meant something.

"Nah. Kevin took a run by the house and called me."

"Are you questioning my word?" Kevin's eyes narrowed at Jason. "Told you what I saw."

"It's late," Brenda said. "If Joey is home, I want to talk to her." She turned to Jason. "Thanks for seeing me tonight."

"No problem. Call when you get there."

"I will."

Kevin turned to Jason. "We'll take a walk through Brenda's house to make sure everything's fine. If Joey's there, we'll handle the arrest."

Brenda left with Kevin and Griff close behind.

"Why do I think this isn't going to end well?" he said.

☆ ☆ ☆

Jason paced the kitchen. Brenda had left thirty minutes ago, plenty of time for her to get home. She could be talking to Kevin and Griff or Joey.

He pressed in Kevin's burner number, and his old friend picked up. "Jason, we just left Brenda's house. No one was there or any signs of anyone. Brenda must have left a light on and forgot. See you in the morning."

"All right. Thanks." He stared at the phone. "Ten more minutes and I'm calling Brenda."

April massaged her neck muscles, then glanced at her watch. "Call her now. Use your parents' landline."

Jason waited while Brenda's cell phone rang four times, then switched to a perky outgoing voice mail message about the housing market. He asked her to call, stating he had a question about his property. Dropping the phone back in the charger, he studied April, who looked like she needed to be in a hospital bed.

Thirty more minutes ticked by. He called again with no answer.

"I'd feel better if we checked on her," he said. "I'll drive. My left arm works just fine."

He alarmed the house and locked up behind them. April struggled to keep pace with him to the truck. She no sooner slipped onto the seat than he sped in reverse to the street. The streetlights of Sweet Briar faded in the rearview mirror as his mind told him Brenda could be in trouble.

"Jason, you're doing seventy-five." She patted his cast. "Remember Kevin and Griff were with her an hour ago."

Her actions were like a soothing balm. He lifted his foot from the gas and apologized. "About another mile."

"Did you build her house?"

"Yep. Her design."

"A two-story?"

"One. Twenty-eight hundred square feet of open living space. Commercial-type kitchen. Impressive."

"She likes to cook?"

"Went to chef's school before obtaining her real estate license. She has a cookbook at the Sweet

382

Briar restaurant. Not fancy food. Down-to-earth home cooking. Sometimes she cooks for church dinners."

"You don't really despise her."

"Only the greed and her relationship with Willis."

He slowed and parked in her driveway. A motion-activated light illuminated the manicured grounds, but the house stood dark. He turned off the truck and stepped out. Brenda's German shepherd barked from inside the house. Jason's gaze traveled up the sidewalk to the arched stone front. The door stood open.

"Not a good sign." Jason swung his words over his shoulder. "Watch out. Her dog's aggressive. Check to see if her Mercedes is in the garage." He hurried to the open door. "Brenda? Are you okay?"

The dog growled. Jason flipped on a light in the foyer, hoping the dog didn't jump at him. He'd faced run-ins with the animal during construction when Brenda brought her dog for a visit.

The home's alarm wasn't set.

"Her car's here." April's footsteps rushed closer.

The dog snarled behind a long, five-foot-tall gate, keeping the animal inside the breakfast area.

"He's bigger than I am," she said.

"We're okay as long as he doesn't knock down

his barrier." Jason snapped on lights while calling for Brenda. He knew this house. He tromped down the hallway to her office on the left, opposite the utility room and garage entrance.

Brenda was slumped over her glass-topped chrome desk facing the window. Blood coated her short, dark hair.

"I'm calling 911." April requested an ambulance and the sheriff's department.

Jason touched the left side of Brenda's neck for a pulse. "She's alive."

"Good." She looked at the source of blood from the back of her head. "I think someone hit her with a blunt object. She might not have seen him." April studied the wound. "The cut doesn't appear deep. But I can't tell for sure." She bent to Brenda's ear. "This is April. Hang on. Jason's here with me, and help is on the way."

April's compassion never ceased to amaze him. "I'm thinking we shouldn't try to deal with the cut or move her."

"Right. We could injure her further."

His mind's time machine returned to last week when Russell didn't survive. Now Brenda was clinging to life. He took her hand, praying for her to pull through this.

"Don't touch anything else," April said. Papers littered the floor. "Whoever has done this wanted something bad enough to risk killing her." She snapped pics with her phone. She aimed at the open closet, where the drawers of Brenda's file cabinet had been yanked off their tracks, and files were tossed as though a twister had passed through.

"Where's her computer?" he said. "She has a laptop. It's like an appendage."

She studied the home office. "Nothing here."

Had it been taken because Brenda had incriminating evidence stored on it? He examined the area beneath Brenda's desk and around her chair. A burnished metal candlestick with droplets of blood lay between the right desk leg and built-in bookshelves. "Looks like we have the weapon."

She joined him. "Rather stupid to leave it behind."

"Maybe we surprised him or her."

"I'll put it in your truck for analysis."

"Isn't that illegal?" he said.

"Russell's murder scene was tampered with. I intend to preserve this. We need a break, and I'm ready to ID someone." She stepped into the bathroom and returned with a towel to pick up the candlestick. She left the house with the evidence. A siren in the distance brought help for Brenda— medical assistance and law enforcement.

Would Kevin and Griff respond to the call? His thoughts soared into overdrive, and he raced to the alarm system. Using his jacket to cover his finger, he accessed the activity log. Not exactly legal either, but he wanted the information.

The sirens grew closer.

He snapped a pic of the data. Someone had entered Brenda's home while she had been with him and April. He checked the camera programmed to image her office, the one area where she felt most vulnerable.

The device had been disabled.

55

The paramedics stabilized Brenda and carried her on a stretcher to the ambulance. Destination: Tyler County Hospital. April saw a range of emotions on Jason's face—from despair to regret.

"She's a fighter," April said.

"I hate what's going on in our town. Too many tragedies." Jason walked to where Brenda's dog was growling and jerking against his leash. "The dog senses his master's been hurt."

"Is there anyone who can take care of the animal?"

"I'll do it."

Such a complex man—chivalrous, caring, and confounding in a six-foot frame. Before she could say a word, a deputy's patrol car arrived with flashing lights and sirens. Two doors slammed, and Kevin and Griff approached as the ambulance driver roared the vehicle to life.

"You two sure have a way of attracting trouble." Kevin strolled up to them, wearing a snarky attitude, one she'd seen in Willis. "Why are you here? More unfinished business with Brenda?"

"I tried to call her, and when she didn't pick up, April and I drove out."

"You didn't see anyone?" Kevin took out a pad of paper and a pen. "We hadn't left Brenda very long before this happened."

"Strange," Jason said. "Every time there's a serious crime, you two are the first on the scene. Your timely attention to crime hasn't gone unnoticed."

Kevin's face reddened. "You're at the scene of crimes before Griff and I get there. Maybe you need to spend a night in jail."

Griff stepped between the two. "The last few days have all of us on edge. Jason, why don't you just tell us what happened."

After Jason finished explaining what they'd found, April added the possibility of a missing laptop.

"Griff and I will take pics and sweep the crime scene," Kevin said.

"Seems to be your specialty," Jason said.

"I'm trained, and my record shows it."

Jason's jaw tightened. "Like the last time?"

April touched his casted arm. "Let's go. I'll notify the FBI of the assault."

"Appreciate your attention to detail." Griff had said more tonight than she'd heard since arriving in Sweet Briar.

"We'll be in touch."

She and Jason left the house for his truck. They were no sooner on the road than he told her about the disabled alarm system. "Brenda insisted upon installing a security camera in her office. Whoever awaited her knew the code and the camera location."

"Joey would have the access codes to get inside."

"Right. Or she could have given them to Willis."

★ ★ ★

Jason despised hospitals. Being greeted by familiar faces when he was here to set his broken arm had been bad enough. The chill and antiseptic smell brought back memories of Lily's many emergency trips. But Brenda's condition came before his emotions, and he'd not let selfishness take over. Tyler County Hospital was a level IV trauma center, and they'd take excellent care of Brenda.

April introduced herself and flashed her ID to the ER receptionist. "I'm investigating Brenda Krew's assault. Can you tell me how she's doing?"

"Yes, ma'am. A doctor is with her now. I'll check." The round-faced nurse disappeared.

April placed her hand on his arm. "I'm sure Brenda's in the best possible hands right now."

The nurse returned. "The doctor reports Ms. Krew is in critical condition. He's requested a Life Flight to Memorial Hermann Hospital at the Texas Medical Center in Houston."

"Is she conscious?" Jason said.

"No, sir."

The urgency to find Joey or Willis hit another level.

56

Monday morning arrived, and efforts to find Willis or Joey had been unsuccessful. While law enforcement continued to comb the area, the lack of viable leads left April and Jason free to attend Russell's funeral. Maybe Willis would show up.

Jason gazed into the mass of familiar faces at Russell's funeral service. Definitely a man well-loved and long remembered in the community. Residents of Sweet Briar young and old paid their respects to Carrie. Some bent to talk eye to eye with her sons—Russell's sons—who were left without a father. Jason intended to be Uncle Jason for the years ahead, showing his honor for their father by remaining in their lives.

Before leaving in the caravan to the cemetery, Carrie stopped to talk to Jason. He hugged her and introduced her to April. While he drew the boys into his arms, April spoke her condolences.

Carrie's tone to April hit him hard. "I don't mind your being here as a representative of the FBI, but Lily's barely been gone a year," Carrie said. "Anything else, even friendship, is inappropriate. Please tell me you haven't spent time with Isabella."

He stood, not that April needed defending.

"Carrie," April said, "Isabella was forced into my arms by the kidnapper. I'd have shown the same care and concern for any child."

"All the same, I'm Isabella's godmother."

Jason steered April away from Carrie. "I'm sorry," he whispered. "She's grieving."

"I'm a big girl. I know Carrie is grieving, and I'm sure she can't bear losing one more person in her life."

Was April just making excuses for Carrie's behavior?

April hooked her arm through his. He'd come to recognize her caring touch not only with him but with others. His thoughts moved from grief over losing his best friend to Willis, who'd tried to saddle Jason with the blame. Yet Willis and Joey escaped authorities, and Brenda's assailant walked free.

The graveside service caused folks to huddle together beneath a tent in a spit of rain and chilling winds. Not the way Jason wanted to celebrate Russell's life. Maybe he'd feel better when justice brought the killer to light. But nothing would bring Russell back.

Afterward, Simon met Jason and April at his parents' home. He shook Jason's hand. "We have an update, a little good news."

"You've arrested Willis?"

"I wish. April sent a recording of Joey Frederickson's voice, and it matches the caller who claimed to be your mother and implicated you in your wife's death."

Jason breathed his thanks. "Will you let my folks know?"

"You can do it. Is this a good time to talk to your family?"

"Perfect time."

They sat in the living room, and Simon pressed in numbers. He handed Jason his phone. "It's your mom."

At the sound of her voice, he relaxed. "How are you doing?"

Jason listened to Mom talk about Isabella's antics. "She misses her daddy."

He physically ached, he missed his daughter so much. "I'm nuts without her. Any new words?"

"*Cup* and *book*. I've told her she can't take a step until she's with you."

"Right. Take lots of pics for me."

"Any word on when we can come home?"

"No."

"The news said Willis is wanted by the FBI for questioning."

"True." Giving additional information about Willis destroyed his chances of another call. He told her about Joey being identified as the woman who called the FBI and claimed to be Vicki Snyder.

"Wonderful news, Jason. I'm thanking God."

"Me too. Dad doing all right?"

"He's antsy. Having Isabella to care for helps us both. I'll give her the phone."

Jason closed his eyes and envisioned his daughter. "Hey, sweet girl. This is Daddy." A string of unintelligible sounds met his ears. Solid reasons for him to see this nightmare through to the end. "Be good for Grandma and Grandpa. I'll see you soon. Love you, Isabella."

He returned the phone to Simon. "Thank you. Hearing my daughter's babble is just what I needed today." The tightness eased in his shoulders. "What else is new?"

Simon smiled. "Technically nothing. But Tyler County Hospital has released medical records showing Billie's and Zack's treatment for so-called accidents. Willis's attorney could have the hospital records tossed out in court. It will take her testimony to nail a conviction. I'm assuming she'll want a divorce and custody of their son."

Jason checked his phone to be sure Billie hadn't texted or left a message. "She hasn't gotten back with me."

"At this point," Simon said, "confirmation she's alive would suit me."

Simon's phone vibrated with a text. "I can give you this update. The media is getting word now. This morning a body was exhumed on Willis Lennox's property. He's been identified as Eric Deckett, the missing FBI agent. Shot in the head with a bullet matching one of Willis's handguns that was confiscated at his home. Billie is a witness to a murder cover-up. Assuming Billie and Zack are safe, they won't have to worry about Willis ever bothering them again."

57

Late Tuesday afternoon, April and Jason left the small Asheville airport in a rental car with the destination of the Scottard residence. Gwen should be home from teaching at a local elementary school. April took a moment to breathe in and hope some semblance of rest magically entered her system and healed her battered body.

Jason parked at the curb in front of a light-gray, two-story traditional home trimmed in black shutters. He and April exited the car and made their way to the front door. He pushed the doorbell, and a dog barked inside.

The door swung open, and a striking red-haired woman shook her head. "Jason Snyder, why am I not surprised? I should have realized you'd show up when I didn't return your call."

"Good to see you, Gwen."

The two definitely had history.

Jason continued. "This is FBI Special Agent April Ramos."

Gwen frowned. "Have you two been in a fight?"

"Several," Jason said. "We could use your help in finding Billie."

Gwen leaned against the doorjamb. "Come in.

I should have replied to your message. Just couldn't decide what to say." She stepped aside for them to enter and grabbed Jason for a hug. "Jase, I'm really worried about my sister."

"Me too."

"Do you know why she ran?"

"Yes, and I understand her need to stay in hiding. I had to tell two FBI agents, April and her partner. I apologize if I betrayed her confidence, but we need to find her."

"I agree," Gwen said. "Willis is a jerk. Always has been. Hate my sister had to find out the hard way."

Jason and April followed her into a traditional living area, decorated with kids' books and toys. Gwen cleared two Barbie dolls and a dump truck from a leather sofa.

"Excuse the clutter. The kids are in the back-yard and might barge in at any minute. So please don't say anything to alarm them. Can I get you something to drink?"

"No thanks," Jason said. "Unless April wants something."

"I'm fine." Once seated with the pleasantries out of the way, including information about Gwen and her husband's two children, ages five and six, April deferred to Jason. Their link to Billie was encouraging.

"Here's the deal. The FBI has evidence connecting Willis to a murder of one of their own.

In fact, the body was buried on his property. The search began due to a comment Billie made about seeing Willis possibly taking a body into the woods. The FBI needs her testimony to cement Willis's charges."

"If he's serving a life sentence for murder, Billie would be free to raise her children." Gwen closed her eyes. "She told me about talking to you. When you asked her to talk to the FBI, she got scared. She tossed that phone and bought another one."

"Will you give us the number?" he said.

"Jase, that's a tough call. She's over five months pregnant with the twins and sick every morning. Zack is being a little man, and yet he needs his mommy."

Time to get woman to woman. "Is Billie under a doctor's care?" April said.

Gwen dabbed beneath her eyes. "Not since she and Zack escaped Willis. He threatened to kill her if she left him." She stared at her hands. "I can't imagine what she's going through."

"This is not a time for her to be alone." April spoke genuine caring into her words.

"Do you think Willis killed Russell Edwards?" Gwen said. "I've been following the news online."

"We're not certain. But all of this is tied together somehow."

"Poor Carrie—she never handled life well." She trembled. "What happened to small-town living?

I'm going to call Billie now. See if she'll listen to reason." Gwen excused herself from the room.

"You made the right decision in seeking out Billie's sister," April said. "She cares about her sister and is concerned on many levels."

"They were always close, and being the older sister gives Gwen influence." He sighed.

When Gwen returned, her eyes were rimmed in red. "She consented if FBI agents escort her from a hotel in Phoenix to the airport, and Houston agents meet her at the airport and drive her to a hotel. She doesn't want to return to Sweet Briar until everything is settled. Maybe never." She inhaled in an obvious attempt to contain ragged emotions. "Billie will tell the authorities all she knows about Willis's activities."

April leaned back against the sofa. "Thank you. I can make the arrangements now."

Gwen gave Jason a slip of paper. "This is her number. She wants to talk to you."

★ ★ ★

In the rental car outside of Gwen's home, Jason spoke to Billie. "I'm proud of you for protecting your children and your willingness to testify against Willis."

"I'm afraid. I won't deny it. But my children have given me strength to fight for them. A part of me would like to return home, and another part of me is fine with starting all over."

"It will work out. How quickly can you be ready to leave?"

"There's a 4 p.m. flight tomorrow. Zack and I can be on it. We aren't exactly at the hotel in Phoenix yet."

Another protective measure. "Agent April Ramos is with me, and she'll ensure travel and lodging arrangements are taken care of."

"Jason, I'm frightened. Willis is out there somewhere."

"You'll be protected all the way. I imagine Willis is more afraid for his own hide right now."

Billie sniffed. "Thanks. Are you flying home soon?"

"We each have rooms for tonight, then we'll head back to Houston on a 6 a.m. flight. Call or text me when you arrive or if you need to talk." He thought about his parents and Isabella. "On second thought, don't contact me until the FBI says it's safe to do so."

The call over, he started the rental car's engine. "Whether Willis killed Russell or knows who did, I'm satisfied we're helping Billie. Spending hours on this may seem foolish when we haven't found Russell's killer, Joey Frederickson, and whoever attacked Brenda. But it was the right thing to do." He drove toward the hotel.

"I'd like to check on Brenda."

"You read my mind."

April contacted the hospital in Houston. "She's

conscious. Do you want to stop there in the morning after we land?"

"Yes, let's do that. But right now I'm dead tired and hungry. What about an early dinner?"

She slid him a sideways glance. "I'd settle for a cold burger and sleep."

58

The morning drive from IAH to Memorial Hermann Hospital in Houston smacked into traffic, temper to temper, lurching ahead, swinging and jerking from one lane to another. Making minuscule progress. One more reason why Jason didn't live in the city.

"It's 10:15, and look at this mess," he said. "I refuse to let this get under my skin, but it's tempting."

"I haven't missed this part of living in Houston," April said.

He laughed. "I'd never get used to it."

In the parking garage at the medical plaza, Jason turned off the truck engine. Memorial Hermann was an easy walk, and after being stuck in the truck and battling traffic, he wanted to sprint to Brenda's room.

The lobby hit him with the same foreboding smells as the night Brenda had been taken to Tyler County Hospital. The assault of sterile, antiseptic reminders could take him years to get over. What would he do if Isabella ever needed to be hospitalized?

Hold on to God—which made more sense than losing sleep and having fear as a constant companion. For the past few weeks, he'd allowed emotions to rule his actions and allowed his faith to become a thin thread.

But the odds no longer rolled like weighted dice. Evidence, like opposite poles of a magnet, rushed together, implicating those who'd been forced or willingly took orders from Willis.

April approached a young man at the information desk and gave him Brenda's name. "Just a moment," the man said. "I have a note here to check with the nurses' station before allowing visitors in." He made the call and listened, then faced April. "Ms. Krew is conscious but unable to speak."

"Is the damage temporary?" April said.

"You'd need to speak to the doctor."

April thanked him, and the two walked to the elevator. Even if he didn't agree with some of her actions, he hated the thought that Brenda's vibrant personality might be drastically changed.

Jason took April's hand. "Is every case this complicated?"

She frowned. "Some are much worse. Imagine how we'd be feeling if Brenda's attacker had succeeded."

The elevator door opened, and they stepped inside. "Communicating with Brenda will be a challenge," she said. "I should have checked with Simon or the hospital before we drove in."

"I'd still want to see her."

She whirled to him. "You've done all you

could. You're stressed, and I get it, but it could be worse."

"Yes, she could have died."

Outside Brenda's room, an HPD officer stood guard. After presenting their IDs, April and Jason entered the private room.

He sucked in a breath. Her pallor and the cavernous pits below her eyes added years to her face. "Brenda," he said, "it's Jason. April and I are here to see you."

Her eyelids fluttered and opened.

He took her hand into his. "I realize you can't speak." He smiled. "Can't imagine Brenda Krew not having a sales pitch or putting me in my place."

Her eyes watered.

"Don't you get all emotional on me. The woman I know would give me a piece of her mind. We're here because we care about you. Whoever hurt you won't get away with this. I promise."

Brenda attempted to lift her arm with the IV. The strain must have been too much. She nodded. Good, she could answer yes and no questions.

"I assume the police and FBI have been here." When she affirmed it, he asked if she could identify who'd struck her. Her positive response joined forces with drawn features. "I'm sorry you're going through this, but lots of folks at home are praying for you."

A slight smile met him.

"I have an idea." April whirled around. "Be right back."

Jason watched her small frame disappear. "Know what, Brenda? She's special, and I think Lily would have liked her too."

April returned with a notepad. "The nurse said Brenda's head injury affected the Broca's area of the brain, controlling her speech, and while she hasn't been able to write anything, we're welcome to try." She handed the notepad and pen to Brenda. "Can you tell us who hurt you?"

Confusion shadowed the woman's eyes.

"It's okay." April smiled. "Just a thought."

After promising to return in a few days, Jason and April left the hospital, taking a quick jaunt to her home in the Heights so she could grab a few outfits.

"I requested the protection for Brenda," she said. "Although she isn't able to clearly communicate, I believe she does know who attacked her."

"I agree she's in danger," he said. "We have our work cut out for us since Joey is on the loose."

"Word is out on the streets, including informants in the drug world. The problem is she could be anywhere, dead or alive."

He had questions upon questions to ask Joey. Number one being why she nabbed his daughter. "Willis eliminates those in his way. Like you, I hope Joey isn't one of them. We've been working this together for a week now. Progress isn't fast enough."

She looked up from watering an ivy plant in her kitchen. "It hasn't been all bad. We've made arrests, and your family's tucked away."

He acknowledged the truth of what they'd uncovered. "Are you a better person for it?"

She moved on to another plant. "We both are." She set the small sprinkling can on the kitchen counter. "Stronger. Wiser. We're survivors."

"And this thing between us? Where are you with that?"

"Nothing's changed." Brown eyes caught his attention. "Mr. Snyder, have you changed your mind?"

"Not by a long shot, but something Simon said won't leave me alone."

She stepped in front of him, and he wrapped his arms around her. His chin fit on the top of her head. "Tell me what he said."

" 'No relationship lasts when it begins with danger and supercharged emotions.' "

"Sounds like Simon. He's the big-brother type. Told me to be careful with you. I told him not to worry."

"I understand how he'd want to protect you from getting hurt. Considering how we started with me nabbing you, this relationship gives 'love your enemies' a different slant."

"Simon will be all right. He and his wife have

taken over the duties of family since mine aren't happy about my career."

"Are they afraid for you?"

"They expected me to use my doctorate in political science to teach at a university or dive into politics. I pursued the degree to please them, but neither of those two careers appealed to me. Serving the FBI fills me with satisfaction. It's where I'm supposed to be."

"Have you told them how you feel?"

"Our relationship is more surface than what I see with you and your parents."

"How would they react to you seeing me?"

She pulled back from him. "Ecstatically. Don't ask why." She patted his arm. "I'm good to go."

Oh, the master of changing the subject. "Not yet." He drew her back into his arms and kissed her.

The moment gave him a much-needed break from overthinking, overworking, and over-stressing about Isabella and even where this crazy friendship with April was going. But lingering questions demanded answers, and the unsolved aspects of the case slammed back to the forefront.

"Ready to get back on the road?" he said.

She put the watering can away under the sink and hoisted her shoulder bag. "When all the arrests are made, you'll discover none of these horrific crimes were your fault."

59

While Jason drove back to Sweet Briar, April watched the landscape zip by, seeing little but a blur. Joey Frederickson took precedence in her thoughts as a critical component of wrapping up this crime. April didn't want to think about what Joey had planned to do with Isabella after kidnapping her. And she could have attacked her own mother. Drug users often partnered with desperation, which made Joey extremely dangerous.

"What have we missed?" Her words echoed her thoughts. "Could Willis have schemed his own vengeance and used only Joey Frederickson, Vic Henley, and Hunter Barker to accomplish it? Neither man resembles the one who walked into the bank and gained access to your parents' safe-deposit box. He didn't even look like your dad."

"But you have a theory," Jason said.

"Speculating here. The one characteristic the video footage couldn't hide was the man's slender build. Joey has the height, and the rest of the disguise is easy."

"We won't know until she's found. That girl has lots of information." He parked the car outside an antique shop, closed for the day.

"Hungry?"

"Grilled cheese and Vicki's tomato soup?"

"Not exactly. The restaurant down the street is open late on Wednesday nights. Helps people get to church on time. Tonight's special is liver and onions and greens."

She scrunched her nose. "Anything else on the menu?"

He laughed. "Lots of down-home eating choices."

"Sure, Mr. Liver and Onions. Guess I can deal with the smell."

In the distance, the cadence of the high school band's fight song broke out. The football team had scored the winning touchdown last week and was heading to district. Home. He loved it.

Out of the truck, he took April's hand, not caring who saw or what rumors might start simmering about them. Inside the restaurant, Miss Ella, dressed in orange from a wide-brimmed hat to orange shoes, approached them. In the midst of the other diners' talking and a crying baby, she poked her finger at Jason's chest.

"You weren't at church on Sunday." Miss Ella slid April a sideways look. "Neither were you. Tell me, were you two working on bringing justice to Sweet Briar or off doing something you shouldn't have been?"

"Working," Jason said, "and making headway."

"New information is keeping us busy," April said.

Miss Ella lifted her chin. "Good. I'll get back to praying and enjoying my liver and onions. The greens are a little tough tonight. But you can't find fresh ones this time of year."

"You have a good evening, Miss Ella." He bit back a grin April would have termed insolent.

"I think she'll have a special place in heaven," April whispered as she studied the evening specials. "But remind me to never cross her."

"Aw, she likes you. Did you figure out what you want?"

"The harvest salad."

She'd passed on the chicken potpie and smothered pork chops and fried apples. "A biscuit?"

"Corn bread. With honey."

He'd found her Southern spot.

The normalcy of having a meal among the people he loved relaxed him, but an empty high chair along the side wall momentarily set him back. He shoved aside the depression and raised his determination. People stopped by the table and shook his hand and encouraged him. They greeted April, too.

The calendar was moving toward Thanksgiving, and he wanted all this behind them before smelling the turkey. Before the evening was over, he'd ask April to join him and his family for the holiday dinner. He wanted to know if what they felt for each other was linked to the danger they'd experienced together, like Simon had claimed, or if there could be something more between them. Nearly a week with this woman, and he wanted more time with her. Sure, she exasperated him at times, but differences of opinion made life . . . challenging in a good way.

Lily, is this okay with you?

After dinner, they strolled back to his truck. He took her cold hand into his, marveling at how small it was.

"People will talk," she said.

"My self-worth is not based on what others think of me."

"But you haven't forgotten what Carrie said at the funeral."

He shook his head. Guilt had a way of eating into his soul, regardless of being unfounded. He changed the subject. "Anything else for us tonight?"

"Nothing on my end. I'd like you to drop me off at your parents' home. I'm reading emails, then going to bed. My whole body is feeling the short nights."

"Great idea." Tonight he'd retire to his own bed, rest up. Maybe he could sleep instead of allowing his whirling thoughts to seize control.

"You look exhausted." Her voice sounded sweeter tonight. "We need your brain in full gear."

"Yes, ma'am."

The fall chill settled in his bones. This time of year brought short days, making him more tired when the sun went down. He preferred light and lots of it.

"Talk to me a moment," she said. "Brenda said Joey had stolen money from her and pawned an heirloom. She could have money at her office. What if Joey ransacks the real estate office?" April waved away her ramblings. "Never mind. I'm fishing for answers."

"We can walk over there. Not sure we can get inside, though."

She lifted a brow.

"Okay, let's do it."

"This is a whim, but it will drive me nuts until I check it out."

His phone rang. "It's Edwardo." He tapped his phone to answer his foreman. "April, wait on me."

She shook her head and mouthed, "See you there."

60

April picked up her pace toward Krew Real Estate. She preferred being stupid by herself. The farther she walked, the more she questioned if her hunch came from a divine nudge, a professional evaluation, or simply a lack of sleep. Had she officially headed into the why-isn't-this-case-resolved zone?

The dark real estate office was nestled beneath a canopied oak tree that still held tightly to its leaves. The blinds were closed. April tiptoed up the three steps to the small porch and twisted the doorknob. Locked, as it should be. With the stealth of her training, she descended the steps and crept around the small building to the rear door. She inwardly moaned. She'd walked straight into a rosebush with thorns, adding a few more open sores to the top of her hand.

The back door refused to budge. The rear window was locked. She'd hold off using her own methods of gaining entrance until Jason joined her.

She walked toward the front and took in her surroundings. Splotchy areas of light danced shadows on the street. Rustling behind her caused her to whirl around.

Someone rushed toward her. Too late in reacting, she felt a knife scrape down her left shoulder and arm.

April grabbed the attacker's wrist and twisted until the woman screamed. The knife fell to the ground. April pinned the woman's arms around her back. "Start walking." She pushed the assailant.

The woman struggled against April's hold. She yanked up on the woman's arm, and she cried out again.

An image of Willis breaking Jason's bone flashed. "If you don't want a broken arm, I suggest putting one foot in front of the other," April said. "I'm not in the mood to play around." She shoved the woman ahead.

"You'll regret this."

The voice sounded husky. "Who are you?"

"None of your business. Does your shoulder hurt?"

It stung, but she wouldn't admit it. Half a block down, April spotted Jason heading her way. She welcomed the sight of him. Blood dripped down her arm. She probably needed stitches.

"Who do you have here?" he said when they met up. He startled. "Joey Frederickson."

April released a breath, a mix of relief and pain. "I haven't seen her face. Would you take over for me?"

Jason turned the woman to face April.

"Joey Frederickson, you are under arrest . . ."

She grabbed cuffs inside her shoulder bag and secured Joey while her left arm throbbed. A text sailed into her phone. Simon.

Billie & Zack arrived in Houston. She signed a statement about what she saw the night the agent disappeared. Asked her not 2 contact anyone until assured all arrests have been made.

✯ ✯ ✯

Maybe Jason should consider law enforcement because helping April apprehend Joey Frederickson, the woman who'd kidnapped his daughter, gave him a jolt of adrenaline. He grabbed Joey's arm and noted blood on the sleeve of April's sweatshirt.

He tightened his grip on Joey. "She did this?"

"Surprised me with a knife from behind."

Joey huffed. "Too bad I missed her."

"You need to get something to slow the bleeding." He eyed Joey. "Did you sneak up on your mother? Slam a candlestick onto her head?"

"You won't find my fingerprints."

The fall temps cooled the heat in his face. "You answered my question. You've been one busy gal."

April got Simon on the phone. "I've arrested Joey Frederickson. Could use a little help. We're at Brenda Krew's real estate office on Oake Drive."

She closed her eyes and wished she could take comfort in Jason's arms.

"You don't have Willis," Joey said. "He's smarter than all of you combined."

61

April wished Jason could be privy to Joey's interview, but regulations prohibited it. He could jeopardize any confession with an outburst. They stood outside the real estate office with Joey in cuffs.

"You need medical attention," Simon said. "I'll handle the questioning."

"This interview needs two agents," she said. "A few more minutes without doctoring won't matter."

Simon swung to Jason. "Can you persuade her to listen to reason?"

"Forget it."

To their advantage, Joey hadn't requested an attorney. The four of them drove to the sheriff's office. Once situated in a small interview room, April attempted to shove away the pain battling against her entire body. She removed Joey's handcuffs in hopes of garnering her trust. Jason waited in the front office with Kevin and Griff.

"Joey, you've been charged with several serious crimes," April began, mustering up her negotiating skills. "Assault with a deadly weapon, kidnapping, and an accomplice to a murder. I'd like to help you secure a lesser sentence by enlisting your cooperation."

The same green eyes as Brenda's, except Joey's eyes were hollow and dilated. Dry, brittle hair hung loosely around her shoulders. She sniffed continuously. How sad so many people fell to addictions.

"I'm innocent of anything illegal," Joey said. "You came after me, and I defended myself."

It wasn't worth arguing this point when they needed Joey to confess to bigger crimes. April tilted her head. "Joey, you held a gun on Vicki and Ted Snyder and kidnapped their granddaughter. You shoved Isabella into my arms in Houston."

"I won't be charged with kidnapping when Jason Snyder is a fugitive for murder."

Distorted thinking. "The FBI exonerated him. Are you ready to help us bring justice to the community?"

Joey licked her lips. "What kind of cooperation?"

"I need you to answer a few questions for us. If you give us appropriate answers, we can talk to the judge on your behalf."

"Is Mom okay?"

She studied the young woman. Was she expressing any remorse?

"Your mother nearly died," April said. "The doctors aren't sure if there's permanent brain damage. She's regained consciousness, but she's unable to speak or write. Are you responsible for her injuries?"

Joey jerked. "She planned to call the cops. Tell

416

them I was in Sweet Briar. Said she had proof I'd been involved in crimes that would give me prison time. How could she have her own daughter arrested?" Her eyes blazed. "I guess it was no big surprise since she abandoned me to my dad."

"I'm sorry you've had a rough life."

Joey stiffened. "Dad tried really hard. Can't blame him for my problems. Brenda Krew gave me up so she wouldn't have to pay child support."

"I'm glad your father was there for you."

"I should have listened to him when Mom asked me to come back to this—" Joey swore in her description of Sweet Briar. "Dad said if I left, not to come back. But Mom offered a car and to pay my fines. Even paid the rent on my apartment in Houston. At the time it seemed like only a fool would refuse."

"Why were you at your mother's home the night she was hurt?"

She cursed. "Money. The witch refused to give me what I deserved. All those years Dad raised me alone. She owed me. Still does."

"My mother makes me furious," April said. "Tries to boss me around."

"Yeah, you got it." She tapped chipped red nails on the table.

"When your mother made you angry, did you hit her in the back of the head?"

She frowned. "I don't remember."

"Did you find what you were looking for?"

"Not exactly."

"So you lost control and hit her?"

She nodded. "It was her fault, though. She kept telling me I could get help."

"Joey, what were you going to do with Isabella in Houston?"

"Raise her myself. Be a better mother than Brenda." She narrowed her gaze at April. "She cried until I thought I'd lose my mind."

"You did the right thing by giving her to me." April kept her voice devoid of feelings. Isabella wasn't a pet but a child. "Why was Isabella important to you?"

"A man promised me a lot of money."

"Willis Lennox?"

"He said he'd kill me if I ever used his name, but I'm already in so much trouble."

"Willis paid you to kidnap Isabella Snyder?"

Joey seemed to crumple under the pressure. "Yes. Paid me three grand."

"Where's the money?"

Joey shook her head. "Gone."

Like water when buying drugs. "Where is the gun you used to kidnap Isabella Snyder?"

"Gave it back to Willis."

"What kind of make?"

"A .22."

That matched the description Ted noted, but it wasn't the same gun used to kill Russell.

"Okay." April nodded. "Why did Willis pay you to kidnap Isabella?"

"He told me Jason Snyder had taken his wife and son from him. Maybe even killed them. Snyder's daughter deserved a good mother. He said I'd be perfect." She faced April with an air of arrogance.

"Did you enter the bank and impersonate Ted Snyder to gain access to his safe-deposit box?"

Joey snorted. "Whatever."

"Is it true?" When Joey confirmed, April pushed forward. "Where is the flash drive you found inside?"

"Gave it to Willis."

"Did you view the contents?"

"No reason to."

"I have another question about the night of Russell Edwards's murder."

Joey waved her hand in front of her face. "I have no idea who killed the man. All I know about is what Willis paid me to do."

"Have you heard from him?"

"No." Joey swiped at her nose. "In the beginning, I thought Willis was a friend, but later he threatened me. When I drove to Houston with Isabella and called to check in, he told me Jason had shot Russell Edwards, and he'd pay with his own life. If I ever surfaced again, he'd tell the Feds what I'd done."

"Mr. Snyder is an honorable man who loves

his daughter. Mr. Edwards was his best friend."

"Are you saying Willis is the killer?"

"This is a fact-finding mission. And the sheriff has been charged with other crimes. Your testimony will assist the FBI's case against Willis."

"My mom said he was a nice man." Her shoulders slumped. "I thought so too."

"Do you know of any others who took orders from Willis to conduct illegal activities?"

"No. Just me."

"Is there anything you'd like to say?"

"Tell Mom I'm . . . No, nothing else."

How sad for mother and daughter.

Unless Willis confessed to pulling the trigger on Russell or definitive proof could be uncovered, the FBI had no case on that matter.

☆ ☆ ☆

Jason listened to April report what she could about Joey's interview. Justice had surfaced like rich cream. While the results of the interrogation might not have been exactly what Jason wanted, he valued the confession.

While April and Simon finished the questioning and placed Joey in protective custody, Jason took a walk outside to clear his head.

An insistence to forgive Joey refused to leave him alone.

It felt impossible. The woman had taken his

child, frightened his parents, stolen evidence, attacked her own mother, and that didn't even take into consideration any drugs she'd done.

Yet the nudging persisted no matter how much he fought it.

All right, God. I see where You're taking me.

Willis's actions rose in his thoughts as well as Hunter Barker and Vic Henley. All had broken the law. All would be facing a judge. If Jason chose not to forgive, he'd be a prisoner in his own cell. Vengeance had destroyed too many lives. With a prayer for strength, Jason silently forgave them.

Another poke at his heart prompted him to forgive himself for those moments with Lily when he could've done more, said more.

He'd heard adversities were classrooms for spiritual growth and positive change—a purpose and a plan beyond the current situation. Didn't make this any easier to bear. For certain, he'd never look at life quite the same.

Next stop—the hospital. April's arm still needed medical attention.

62

Once again April found herself in Tyler County Hospital's ER. "I'm thinking of taking up residence here," she said to the same doctor who'd examined her when Jason broke his arm.

She gritted her teeth during the six stitches, the numbing shot having failed to meet expectations. Or maybe her body was tired of fighting cuts and bruises.

Simon and Jason watched like helpless little boys.

"Can't you do more for her pain?" Jason practically growled.

"I'll prescribe a pain reliever." The doctor peered into her face. "Do you have plenty from the other prescription?"

"I haven't filled it."

"Figures." Simon paced the room.

The doctor glanced at them. "I'll give you an injection until a pharmacy opens tomorrow."

Simon crossed his arms over his chest. "April, in the morning, you're driving home. I've had enough."

"No way, big brother," she said. "I'm not finished here."

"You're a candidate for a convalescence center." Jason's words brought a smile to her lips.

Afterward, Simon drove them back to Sweet Briar to drop her off at the elder Snyders' home and then to retrieve Jason's truck.

Jason walked her to the door and unlocked it. "I'll be right back."

"I can put myself to bed."

"I'd feel better sleeping on the couch."

"Sweet, but not necessary."

"This country boy understands the meaning of chivalry."

April sensed the effects of the doctor's injection for pain and sleep. She wouldn't know what Jason chose to do until morning.

☆ ☆ ☆

April woke to the smell of coffee and the distinct aroma of frying bacon—validation Jason was busying himself in the kitchen. With both vehicles in the driveway, neighbors would believe the worst . . . and Miss Ella. Then again, if the people of Sweet Briar followed the news, they'd been gossiping before last night.

She turned and moaned aloud. Every inch of her ached in protest to her BBB—bruised, battered body.

Ten minutes later, she finally succeeded in rolling out of bed, literally, and hoped the crash didn't send Jason racing up the stairs. Which he did. Flinging open the door, he knelt at her side.

"I'm fine. This was the easiest way for me to get out of bed. I just missed putting my feet there first." She closed her eyes. "Jason, out of here. I'm wearing pajamas."

"My mother's, and I've seen them plenty of times."

"Not me in them. Go on downstairs. Breakfast smells lovely. I'll dress and join you."

"Why don't I believe you?"

" 'Cause you're as stubborn as I am. Okay, wait for me at the stairs."

"I have your prescription. The pharmacist advises you eat first."

Nearly fifteen minutes later, she emerged from the bedroom dressed for the day. She linked her arm with his. "Thanks for being my knight in shining armor."

"Since my problem caused the multiple cuts and bruises, it's the least I can do. If Simon were here, he'd cuff you and drive back to Houston."

She tried to cover a wince at the first step down. "Don't call him."

After the best coffee she'd ever drunk and a feast of bacon and eggs, she swallowed the pain med, realizing it could put her to sleep. Before that happened, she reached for her phone to read the latest and pass on to Jason what she could.

"The FBI has contacted the people you and Ted listed as victims of Willis's potential crimes. The family of the ninety-five-year-old woman who insisted Willis coerced their mother into selling her land at a quarter of its worth said their attorney claimed the transaction was legal. They live in Austin, and my guess is they don't want to deal with it. The other three on the list who were injured while Willis interrogated them refused to comment."

"People are afraid and skeptical, especially when Willis hasn't been arrested. We need hard facts to get any of them to budge. Any word on Brenda?"

"Nothing's changed."

He frowned and took her hand. "Do you feel up to a couple of hours at my place?"

"Of course. I'm sore, not sick."

Jason drove out of town until they met with woods on both sides of the road. An SUV whizzed by, causing Jason to veer toward the ditch.

April's attention flew to the dark-blue Toyota. "Follow that vehicle. It looks like the one that ran me off the road. I saw dents on the passenger side."

Jason spun gravel and gassed the truck after the SUV speeding away. It turned right onto a dirt-and-gravel road. "He knows we're tailing him."

"I want to cuff the jerk who nearly killed me."

"Imagine how I feel."

The driver of the SUV used the back roads to his advantage. Had to be the one who caused April's accident. She yanked her phone from her shoulder bag and got Simon on the line. She explained what was happening and gave him their location.

"Keep me on the line," Simon said. "I'm heading your direction."

Jason gained ground and rode the SUV's bumper. A new model with temporary tags. This close she could tell there was a passenger in the front seat.

"Gun. I saw the driver raise it." Calmness wrapped around Jason's words. He lowered the windows on both sides. "Hand me my gun."

"That's ridiculous with your cast."

"I can drive with that arm. My hand works fine."

"Can you shoot with your left hand?"

"I can do damage."

"Don't fire unless he does first." She pulled his gun from the glove box and he grabbed it. She wrapped her fingers around her own weapon.

The driver twisted and fired, but the shot went wild.

"That's Cal Bunion. Recognize the tattooed arm." Jason stomped on the gas and rear-ended the SUV.

The deputy who'd watched Vicki and Ted's home but a different vehicle.

On the passenger side, a gun came into view. "Watch your side," Jason said.

She blinked to fight the medication and nausea, then fired, sending a bullet into the SUV's passenger-side mirror.

Cal turned to fire again and must have lost control. The vehicle swerved, then abruptly rolled, landing upside down in the ditch on the right side of the road.

Jason slammed on his brakes and jumped from the truck. April raced behind him.

The driver's door of the SUV swung open. Cal crawled out, wielding his gun.

"Stop, Cal," Jason shouted.

Cal aimed.

April fired into his wrist when she meant to hit center mass. Cal screamed and dropped his weapon. Blood spurted down his arm.

April kicked Cal's gun out of the way. "Be glad I missed your heart."

Jason hurried around the rear of the SUV. "Come on out of there. Who's on the other side?"

Willis yanked open the passenger door and crawled out, waving a gun. A gash on the side of his head bled down his face. He took off running, jumped a ditch, and headed to the edge of the woods with Jason behind him. For a big man, he moved fast.

Willis turned and aimed at Jason.

April gasped.

Willis fired.

The bullet went wild.

Both men disappeared into a thicket of trees.

April had her hands full with Cal. He held his bleeding wrist and clumsily stood on the road.

"What's this about? Running a deputy off the road and shooting him?"

Adrenaline flowed, overriding her need to sleep. "How about running a federal agent off the road and leaving her for dead?" April said. "And it appears you're harboring a fugitive."

"I should have left tire marks on your body."

April wanted to black his eyes. "Mr. Bunion, you just confessed to a serious crime."

She trained her weapon on him while keeping an eye on the tree line where Jason had disappeared after Willis. "Simon, are you far out? I need backup. Jason is chasing Willis on foot."

"Nearly there. Hold tight."

Cal tried to move. "Stay put or you'll regret it."

How would Jason manage Willis with a broken arm?

63

Jason's years of staying fit helped him stay on Willis's heels. The big man carried the weight of one about to be tackled, and Jason brought him down between two pines. Willis's fist slammed just above Jason's casted arm. Instead of the pain debilitating him, it sent a burst of strength into his body. He grabbed Willis's wrist with his left hand and clamped down hard with his casted arm on Willis's throat until the sheriff released his gun. Jason grabbed the weapon and tossed it several feet away.

Sirens sounded. He took a deep breath and slowly let it out.

✳ ✳ ✳

Jason and April waited in the ER area at Tyler County Hospital with Cal while Simon sat with Willis in the rear of the room.

Cal complained about his wrist wound repeatedly.

Not so long ago, Jason would have experienced anger at learning of another player. Instead of fury at what Willis had orchestrated and Cal had done to April, pity washed over him for the skinny kid who'd never had friends. Both men's futures were likely to include four walls and a cot.

Were Jason's realized feelings a part of the healing? Or did the knowledge that he was moving closer to Isabella's return cause him to see life differently?

"Did you pull the trigger on Russell?" he said to Cal.

He shook his head, his thin face drawn. "No."

April captured Jason's attention, probably concerned he would explode or Cal would ask for a lawyer. He nodded at her. "I have one more question for Cal."

"Simon and I have plenty," April said.

He returned his attention to Cal. "We've known each other since we were boys, but I haven't been a good friend. I apologize. I'm asking you now to help us find who's behind these crimes."

"If I agree, I go to jail with Willis and end up dead."

Jason took the response as a cue for April to use her negotiation skills, and she dove in. "Cal, cooperating with the FBI means you've done the right thing. We've learned people in this case have been threatened to follow Willis's orders. You're not alone. Willis won't have contact with anyone where he's headed."

A nurse called Cal's and Willis's names, and the group accompanied her to an exam room. Jason backed off for now. Simon displayed his ID to the doctor and explained the wounded men were in FBI custody.

After both men underwent X-rays and stitches, the five left the hospital for the drive back to Sweet Briar's jail. Once at the sheriff's office, April and Simon questioned Cal in an interview room while Jason again waited. Unsurprisingly Willis had lawyered up.

"Jason, stop your pacing and take a seat," Griff said from behind the desk. "There's nothing you can do to hurry along the interviews."

This was the perfect time to probe deeper into Griff's loyalty.

✯ ✯ ✯

April handed Cal a tissue from her shoulder bag to wipe the perspiration dripping down his face. This man could expose the whole case. She shoved aside her desire to punch him for nearly killing her.

"Thank you." Cal used the tissue. Wadded it up with his uninjured hand.

Simon motioned for her to continue the interview. "You have a flawless record," she said. "This speaks well for you. I want to help you through this."

He stared at the white bandage on his wrist. A tattoo of a skull in an hourglass was above it. "I didn't kill Russell Edwards."

"Do you know who did?" she said evenly.

He dragged his tongue over his lips. "No, ma'am. Willis said Jason Snyder killed him."

"Why? He must have had evidence to make such a claim."

"Jason helped Billie run off with Zack. He thought those two were messing round."

"That doesn't explain why Jason would kill his business partner."

"No, ma'am, I suppose it doesn't."

"What else did Willis scheme?"

Cal sighed. "I only followed orders from the man who made sure I had a job."

April softened her features. "Did he pay you?"

Cal stared as though not really seeing. "He offered me a new SUV for keeping an eye on Jason. Said he had a few more odd jobs for me to do and would let me know when the time came."

And April had successfully dented his payment. "Did he give a reason why he wanted you to watch Jason?"

"I never asked."

"Why?"

"A sixty-five-thousand-dollar SUV seals my lips."

April hid her irritation. Willis and Cal had sworn to uphold the law, but neither of them had read the handbook.

"I see," Simon said. "April, I'll take over from here. Were Willis and Russell together the day of the shooting?"

"Oh yeah, around noon. I saw them talking in the sheriff's parking lot."

"A pleasant conversation?"

"Nah. Russell was upset."

"And this happened before or after Willis made the SUV offer in exchange to follow Jason?"

"Before. We went to Woodville right after Russell left and bought it."

Simon cocked his head. "So this all transpired in a matter of a few hours?"

Cal exhaled. "I guess."

"Who shot Russell?"

"I already answered the question for the lady. I don't know."

"Willis?"

"Not likely. He and Russell were brothers-in-law."

"Are Deputies Kevin Viner and Griff Wilcombe working with Willis?"

He shrugged. "Doubt it. Both of 'em have talked about applying for Woodville City Police."

"Why did Willis want you to go after Agent Ramos?"

Cal shook his head.

Simon folded his hands on the table. "Deputy Bunion, you have serious charges against you. Why not make things easier and unload what you know?"

"Exactly."

Cal again stared at his bandaged wrist. "All right. Willis told me I had to get rid of her. When I refused, he reminded me about the new ride. I refused again. Then he asked about my grandmother who lives in the Sweet Briar Nursing Home. Asked me how long I wanted her to live."

April inhaled sharply. "I'm so sorry."

"Shouldn't have shocked me. But it did. I thought me and Willis were friends."

Simon picked up the conversation. "So your orders were to eliminate Agent Ramos?"

"Yes."

"Do you know Joey Frederickson, Brenda Krew's daughter?"

"What does she look like?"

Simon pulled up Joey's pic on his phone and showed it to Cal.

"Yeah, I saw her with Willis at the office once. Look, I've answered a lot of questions. What are you going to do for me?"

"Inform the judge of your cooperation and how you were pressured to cause a federal agent's death."

Before April and Simon talked to Willis, she wanted to reassure Jason of a confession. After locking up Cal, the three stepped outside into the afternoon sunshine.

"I'm surprised Cal was willing to talk," Jason said. "Willis uses threats like a dog going at a bone. Vic, Hunter, Joey, Brenda, Cal—who else has he forced to do his dirty work?"

"You," Simon said, "but you stood up to him.

Cal signed a confession. I'll have him transported to Houston in the morning."

April spoke up. "I think Cal's a broken man. Following Jason seemed like an easy swap for his new SUV. But Willis had baited him for the next job, and Cal didn't expect it to be killing me."

"Now he has to pay for his choices," Jason said. "I talked to Griff. He's proud of his military service. Told me he hoped everything worked out in finding who framed me for murder and kidnapped my daughter. I think he's clean."

"Good." She managed a smile for his sake. "As soon as Canfield gets here, we'll interview Willis."

"I doubt you get anything but sarcasm."

64

An hour later, David Canfield arrived. A middle-aged man with a receding hairline and wearing designer jeans and shirt, he strode into the sheriff's office with the ego April expected. Jason busied himself talking to Griff.

Simon introduced himself and April.

Canfield offered a firm grip and penetrating eye contact. "Identifications, please."

April acceded to his request. His smug attitude conformed with his client's. No wonder Willis had him on retainer.

"Once I talk to Willis," Canfield said, "we can proceed with questioning."

April and Simon waited another thirty-five minutes until they were seated in the familiar interview room with Willis and Canfield facing her and Simon. April hid her satisfaction at seeing the sheriff in cuffs.

Simon explained the charges against Willis: murder, public corruption, extortion, bribery, assaulting a federal officer—the list continued.

"This is ludicrous. My client was run off the road by a man accused of murder accompanied by a rogue FBI agent," Canfield said. "This appears to be ineptness on the part of the FBI." He took a breath, no doubt for effect. "I'm filing defamation of character charges against the FBI for slandering my client's name and reputation. Sheriff Lennox is a fine man who is being held on trumped-up charges without due evidence."

April's negotiation skills were about to be tested. With both feet planted on the floor and her hands folded on the table, she took on the challenge. "Mr. Canfield, I work the public corruption division of Houston's FBI. I witnessed Sheriff Lennox's inappropriate behavior. Regarding the murder and extortion charges, we have witnesses."

"All these false accusations happened since you've been in Sweet Briar. Makes me wonder how a court of law will view a female agent taking the side of a fugitive and staying at his parents' home."

Canfield could build his case on his own time. She'd assumed her personal involvement aided Willis's defense, but all the objections in the world had no bearing once the FBI secured court-admissible evidence.

April plastered an impassive look on her face. "Let's get started by going through the charges against your client individually. Willis, where were you the night Russell Edwards was killed?"

Willis gripped his fists and laughed. "For the record, I have an alibi. I was in Woodville at a chamber of commerce meeting."

"Great. I'll have Agent Neilson check it out right now."

"I already have," Canfield said. "He's on a security camera that documents when he arrived and when he left." He wrote a name and phone number on a piece of paper, then pushed it to Simon, who dialed the number. "I suggest a search warrant for the footage."

April waited until Simon finished the call. From the conversation, he was talking to the president of Woodville's Chamber of Commerce. Within two minutes, he set his phone on the table. "Willis checks out, but we will need to validate the security footage."

"I'm not stupid enough to fake footage," Willis said.

"Easy." Canfield touched Willis's arm, and the big man shook it off.

"I have this." Willis glared at Canfield. He turned to April and laughed, a fake sound that ground at her nerves. "What do you think of the new info, April?"

"If you've had an alibi all along, why haven't you come forward and saved us all time?"

"I enjoyed the game, all the who-killed-Russell stuff. Ever hunt, April? The pleasure is in watching the animal squirm."

He'd not get the best of her. "Unfortunately, an alibi doesn't absolve you from other charges."

Willis gave his infamous sneer. "I'm not worried. Want to talk about the weather? Or the advantage of deep-frying a Thanksgivin' turkey?"

She kept her composure. "Agent Neilson, would you like to continue the interview?"

"Willis, we received a tip you buried a man on your land. Because of this report, we found and exhumed the body of FBI Special Agent Eric Deckett, sent here undercover to investigate suspicions of public corruption. A bullet from one of your guns killed him."

"You're crazy. Who made the claim?"

"Does it matter? You resisted a federal officer and threatened her in a previous documented conversation. You offered her a bribe. You tried to pin a murder on Jason Snyder, who has been exonerated. You also violated Ted Snyder's rights. Those charges are only the beginning." Simon paused. "You will be a guest of your own jail until I finalize a transport to Houston."

★ ★ ★

Jason and April looked up at the night sky at his parents' home. All this began when Kevin alerted the FBI of public corruption. It escalated with the murders of two good men.

Willis, Joey, and Cal were en route to Houston with an FBI escort. Hunter had agreed to testify and would stay under the guardianship of his parents until the trial. Jason should have been relieved, but frustration took front and center of his emotions. "It's hard for me to accept Willis has a confirmed alibi. We may never find out who killed Russell."

April took his hand. "The FBI were successful in arresting Willis for his crimes. I believe Russell's killer will surface too."

He glanced into the dark night. "Has Willis confessed to why he murdered Eric Deckett?"

"Won't give up his not-guilty plea. Says the killer framed him and to look into your whereabouts. It appears the owner of the bar where Eric Deckett was last seen originally had a lapse of memory of what happened the night Deckett was killed until he learned of Willis's arrest."

"What's he saying now?"

"Deckett and Willis had an argument. Willis flipped over a barstool and stomped out. Eric waited about fifteen minutes before leaving."

Although innocent until proven guilty, Willis had committed far too many crimes in Sweet Briar, Jason was confident. Just not the one that kept Jason wondering. But he had no intentions of ever giving up on who killed Russell.

Push it aside. Isabella's coming home.

"Tomorrow morning, I'll have my daughter. Thank you for not giving up on me."

"We will find out who killed your best friend."

65

Friday morning, Jason paced his kitchen like a caged animal, and he knew it. Pink balloons dangled from the ceiling. Pink and purple streamers were draped from corner to corner. Isabella would think the celebration was another birthday party.

Having his daughter home brought more joy than all her future milestones. He stopped to stare out at the road, anticipating agents pulling into his driveway with his baby girl.

He shook his head and turned to April. "What if she's upset after the agents dropped Mom and Dad off in town?"

April brushed her hand over his arm, a familiar touch of caring. "The sight of home and her daddy will dry any tears. Besides, your parents wanted the reunion to be the two of you. Why I'm here is a mystery."

"Because you helped make it all possible." He smiled at the tiny woman who'd captured his heart—black eyes, bruises, stitches, and filled with compassion for others. He liked her hair in a ponytail. She looked downright cute. "And you do a great job of blowing up balloons and picking out cupcakes."

"Thanks, I think." She giggled, and he relished the sound.

"When are you driving back to Houston?"

"Trying to get rid of me?"

"I'd rather make plans, concentrate on us. How's that for subtlety?"

She stood on tiptoes and kissed him. "A few more days in Sweet Briar sounds wonderful."

As he drew her to him, Simon's words of *No relationship lasts when it begins with danger and supercharged emotions*" drilled into his brain. He wouldn't bring up the future. She had responsibilities with the FBI, and he built houses. The dilemma would have to wait.

Jason kissed her lightly, pulling away in time to see a white Lincoln Town Car turn in to his driveway from the road. "They're here." Grabbing April's hand with his left, Jason hurried through the kitchen to the back door, across the porch, down the steps, and toward his Isabella. He swallowed the lump thickening his throat. Isabella would always bring tears to his eyes.

The vehicle seemed to approach in slow motion. But it finally stopped where he and April stood. She let go of his hand.

The engine ceased to hum.

The click of the power locks.

A female agent stepped out of the rear passenger side, the woman who'd escorted his daughter to safety. She greeted him and April before moving aside and gesturing for him to release Isabella from a car seat.

Isabella reached for him, and the musical sound of "Da" met his ears.

She wore pink corduroy pants and a pink-and-white sweater. Her blonde curls were swept back with a huge bow. His girl.

"Hey, sweet girl. Welcome home." His fingers fumbled in unlatching the seat belt.

And then Isabella nestled in his arms. Where she belonged.

✳ ✳ ✳

April watched father and daughter catch up from the days apart. Isabella clung to Jason for several minutes, but the familiar sights and sounds won out. Fluffy wagged his tail until she wiggled to be on the floor beside the boxer. Isabella hugged the dog, and Jason grinned. She crawled all over the kitchen, ending her adventure by spotting her high chair and reaching for Jason to place her inside.

He tied a bib around her neck. "Daddy is breaking his rule of healthy snacks. We're having white cupcakes." He kissed the top of her head. "We did the same thing a few weeks ago for your birthday, but who's keeping track?"

A few moments later, with frosting smeared all over her face, she signed, *Done.* He cleaned her face and set her on the floor. "Ball," she said.

"It's a balloon, sweetheart. But they're for you to look at, not play with. They will go straight into your mouth unless I'm with you." Jason turned to April. "Life doesn't get much better than this. Every moment of the nightmare was worth this. And having you to share it with me." He sighed. "I'm pressuring you, being presumptuous. Sorry."

"Don't be," she said. "Our ordeal became a time for me to get right with God and dream about a special man and his daughter."

He ran his fingers through his hair. "Before you leave next week, we'll have to figure out how to—"

She covered his lips. "Commute? Take Isabella to the zoo? Share ice cream? Picnics? Watch baby-friendly TV shows together? Hike through these thick woods?"

He nodded. "All of what you said and more. Will you return for Thanksgiving? I heard Mom and Dad say the guest room has your name on it."

"I'd like to. I have much to be thankful for this year."

"Me too. I just wish we knew who killed Russell." He shook his head. "I'm not going to think about it right now."

She pointed to Isabella speed-crawling across the room to Fluffy. "Look at her go."

He laughed at Isabella's little rear swaying. She pushed on Fluffy and slowly stood. An impish grin met them.

Jason knelt on the floor about six feet from her

and held out his arms. "Walk to Daddy, Isabella," he said. "What are you waiting for?"

April yanked out her phone and slid the camera's setting to Video.

Isabella wobbled as though she'd crawl to him. She caught her balance and righted herself. Jason coaxed her again.

One step.

Two steps.

Isabella reached Jason's arms. Her first steps with Jason coaxing her all the way.

April's mind swept back to when Joey had pushed Isabella into her arms, how she fell in love with the sweet baby, met Jason, realized his innocence in a murder case, and started down the dangerous path to finding evidence to convict a crooked sheriff and those who'd fallen prey to his tactics.

Looking around the country kitchen, a scenic view in every direction, she wanted Jason's life free from the horror that had stalked him. But unanswered questions still dangled like Isabella's balloons.

66

April cleaned up the kitchen while Jason played with Isabella. He'd protested, but she won the round. Daddy and daughter needed special time together. April etched in memory the two building a house with large LEGOs. She wanted the day to go on forever. A dream for the future.

Since Jason and Isabella had walked into her life, she'd found God and made progress in eliminating the guilt over Benson's suicide. She'd done her best in persuading him life had more to offer, but he'd made his decision. More and more, she was pulling away from the guilt.

Soon the three were on the road to see Carrie. Jason had felt guilty that Carrie lost Russell and now Willis, and he hadn't checked in on her. He asked April to accompany him to Carrie's house, where she was expecting them.

"Are you heading back to work tomorrow?" April said.

"Yes. I don't normally work on Saturday, but we've been shorthanded, and a new home is nearly completed. Edwardo deserves a bonus for pulling together the crew."

"Can I keep Isabella some of the time while you're working? I don't officially head back to work until next Thursday. I know you like for her to be with you. But I could come to the house so she'd feel comfortable."

"Absolutely. Great idea. We could do lunch together too."

"Oh, when you see Romeo, tell him I'll never set foot in his domain again."

He laughed. She loved the sound—real and pain-free.

Carrie was sitting on the front porch swing when they arrived. She rose to meet them. She looked a little thin. April knew she'd need counseling and lots of support. Jason hugged her and so did April.

"I apologize for what I said to you at the funeral," Carrie said to April.

"It's fine. I just want us to be friends."

"Thank you for your grace." Carrie touched her mouth at the sight of Isabella. "My sweet baby girl." Jason placed his daughter in Carrie's arms. Tears streamed down her face. "You're home, and I'll always take care of you. No one will separate us again."

April stole a look at Jason. He frowned. What did Carrie mean? Maybe the two had an arrangement about Carrie staying active in Isabella's life.

"Come inside." Carrie clung to Isabella. "I started a scrapbook about Russell, and I wanted your opinion about a few of the photos. I can't figure out who some of the people are."

"We can't stay long," he said. "Where are the boys? I thought they'd be home."

"Kevin picked them up for ice cream with his kids. I probably shouldn't have let them go, but they've been through so much, and they deserve playtime."

"A wise decision," April said. "Let them be children for as long as possible."

Carrie's features softened. "I think we'll be great friends. Lily was my one and only."

The scent of pumpkin bread wafted through the house. "Smells like Thanksgiving came early," April said. "My mouth is watering. Do you share recipes?"

Carrie carried Isabella into the kitchen and pushed the button on the coffeemaker. "Only with very good friends and family." She faced Jason and planted a kiss on Isabella's cheek. "Have you changed your will to give me guardianship of Isabella?"

April drew her brow down at another inappropriate comment. Had Carrie's sorrow made her delusional?

"There's no need," he said.

"Lily wanted me to have her."

"My parents are named as guardians."

"They aren't getting any younger," Carrie said.

"I think we'll take a rain check on the coffee and bread," Jason said. "Isabella's tired. This is her first day home, and she needs to be in her own bed."

As if on cue, his daughter reached for him, but Carrie pulled her back. "I have a crib ready. Please stay. I apologize for my comments."

He hesitated.

April supported Jason either way. This had to be tough.

"I really need your help with Russell's scrapbook. Just a few minutes, please."

He took a deep breath. "All right. I'll take Isabella upstairs." Jason took his daughter.

"Of course. Follow me."

He reached into the diaper bag and retrieved a prepared bottle. Glancing at April, he shook his head. "We won't be here much longer."

Carrie led the way to the second floor to a nursery decorated for a little girl. Pale-pink walls, a pink teddy bear, pink-and-white rabbit, a pink-shaded lamp on a white dresser. How very strange when her youngest was a boy and in kindergarten.

"Carrie, are you pregnant?" Jason said.

"No. I did this for Isabella. I'll keep her while you're working."

"I wish you'd have talked to me about this," Jason said, concern evident in his words. "Isabella is fine in our current arrangement."

"I've made up my mind." Carrie smiled. "She's happier with me."

An alarm triggered in April. Russell's death, along with mental frailties, had left Carrie in a precarious situation.

Jason laid his daughter in the crib and lightly covered her with a pink-and-white quilt. Carrie stepped in front of him and rearranged the quilt.

"Carrie, are you taking your meds?" he said.

She focused on his daughter. "Not anymore. Look at Isabella—her eyes are already closed."

"You need your medication to help you get through the grief," he said.

"I know what's best for me."

April studied Jason. She didn't understand Carrie's unhealthy attitude, but he'd been around her his entire life.

"Are you two ready for conversation?" Carrie said. "I've been planning your visit all day."

Downstairs, the three sat at the kitchen table. Carrie offered coffee and pumpkin bread, but neither Jason nor April had an appetite for them. A framed photo of Russell sat on the counter.

"Have you reached out for grief counseling?" Jason said.

"The pastor is looking into the right fit for me. A doctor in Woodville prescribed antidepressants, but they left my mind foggy, so I tossed them."

"I'm glad you have so many wonderful people in the community to walk through this with you," April said.

"Yes, I'm very fortunate." Carrie rose from her chair.

"You mentioned looking through photos," Jason said.

"Getting those now." Carrie reached inside a drawer and spun toward them with a Smith & Wesson.

"Carrie." He bolted to his feet. "What are you doing?"

"Finishing what I started before Russell stepped into the path of my bullet."

67

Carrie aimed her S&W at April. "Toss your bag this way. I know you have a gun."

April placed her shoulder bag on the floor and used her foot to push it to Carrie. Without hesitation, the distraught woman reached inside with her left hand and pulled out April's Glock. She laid the S&W on the counter and switched the Glock to her right hand.

April sensed Carrie's anguish, the finality of a plan that in her mind would right her world. "I understand you're upset with the loss of your husband." She laced her words with sympathy. "Let me help you find someone who can guide you through the tragedies."

"I hate Jason." Carrie tucked a strand of brown hair behind her ear.

April played along. "He makes me angry too."

"He took Lily away from me and tried to take Russell, too."

"How, Carrie?"

"He could have done more for Lily, found better doctors. I suggested an alternative method of cancer treatment, but Lily refused. Jason must have been against it. Then he offered Russell a partnership in the business. The extra hours would have taken him away from us. I had no one but my husband to help me stand up to my bullying brother, and I hate him, too."

April dug deep for prayer and guidance. "Russell didn't listen to your objections?"

She tightened her jaw. "He claimed it was for our benefit. Said we could save for the boys' education. I asked him why being project manager wasn't enough."

"So you wanted Jason gone?"

"Not then. I wanted another baby, a girl this time, but Russell said we had enough children. Jason put him up to it. I'm sure of it."

Russell must have realized the extent of his wife's mental illness. "Let me help you."

"You can't. Besides, I have this worked out."

April ached at Carrie's pain. "I promise this can be resolved. Just put down the gun."

She shook her head. "I can't." Her eyes flashed a wild gaze. "I learned how to avoid the law from Willis. He thought things through, and he wouldn't be in jail now if Billie hadn't betrayed him. The news has Billie's testimony splattered all over the state. I'm happy, though. All those years he smothered me with his overprotectiveness finally paid off."

"Why don't you and I take a walk, and we'll figure out how to make your life easier?"

"No!" She waved the Glock. "I'm going to shoot you first. Then turn my S&W on Jason."

"Your sons need you." April heard the insanity

in Carrie's voice. "If you don't stop, they not only won't have a dad but your loving care."

"The law will believe I tried to save you, but Jason went crazy. He took your gun and killed you. Then I killed him to protect myself. See how simple that is?" She sneered at him. "Isabella will be mine. Lily would have wanted it this way."

April feared she was running out of time. She and Jason were only twelve or so feet from Carrie. If they attempted to apprehend her, someone would be shot. "You and Lily were close."

"Like sisters. Now she's gone and so is Russell." She swung her aim at Jason. "I despise you."

April spoke compassion into her words. "Tell me about some of the times you shared."

The back door in the utility room squeaked open. "Carrie?"

April recognized Kevin's voice. She hadn't heard a car drive up.

Carrie's brown eyes widened, the same intensity as her brother's. "Are the boys with you?"

"They're still playing. It's just me and Griff. Can we come in? We'd like to talk to you."

"Later sounds better. I had a crying spell, and I don't want you or Griff to see me."

"Jason's truck is outside. Isn't he with you?" Kevin said.

"Yes, we're—" Carrie hesitated.

April leaped across the kitchen, tackling her to the floor. The gun fired toward Jason.

As though in slow motion, she watched the bullet soar across the room . . . past Russell's photo . . . past Jason's head, missing him by mere inches . . . before it lodged in the wall.

"Before this is over, you're gonna see the power of Jesus."

Miss Ella's words when April first arrived in Sweet Briar with Isabella.

April pinned Carrie to the floor. Kevin took over and flipped Carrie onto her stomach, then snapped cuffs into place. Griff grabbed both guns.

Kevin knelt beside Carrie and helped her stand. "Be glad I got here before you committed murder."

Carrie sobbed. "I didn't mean to kill Russell. He moved too close to Jason."

Color vanished from Kevin's face. "What?"

"You killed Russell?" Griff said.

Carrie lifted her chin. "I want a lawyer. Where's Willis? He'll help me."

Kevin and Griff escorted her out the back door. Jason helped April to her feet. Oh, she hurt.

"It's over." He pulled her close. "Finally over."

"Did you see the bullet?" she said.

Confusion settled on his face. "What bullet?"

"The one Carrie fired at you."

"What do you mean?"

April leaned against Jason's chest and basked in the realization of a power greater than any of them. "Just like Miss Ella said, I saw a Jesus miracle."

68

THANKSGIVING

April passed the platter of turkey to Jason. He smiled before forking generous slices onto his plate—white and dark meat.

The day of Carrie's arrest, Griff had come to Kevin with his suspicions. The ex-military man had overheard Willis tell Carrie to stay on her meds and not talk to anyone. He'd take care of everything. The instructions had played in Griff's mind until he took a chance and talked to Kevin.

After a psychiatrist's review, Carrie was deemed incompetent to stand trial. The childhood abuse from her father and Willis's unhealthy big-brother attitude might have contributed to her mental issues. When Carrie called him at the chamber of commerce meeting the night she killed Russell, he promised to make it all go away.

Child protective services had placed Carrie's two sons in a foster home. But promising news came when Kevin and his wife decided to seek custody of the boys.

Brenda was slowly recovering in Houston. It would take months of rehabilitation to bring her back to normal. Joey faced kidnapping and assault charges as well as violation of her parole.

Dessert today would be delayed. Billie and Zack and Kevin and his family planned to join them. Apple, pecan, pumpkin, and chocolate pies, along with a carrot cake, awaited them all in the kitchen. New friends, relationships she'd craved but never allowed herself to embrace until now.

Isabella, who sat between April and Jason, signed, *More* and pointed to the mashed potatoes.

"Say please," Jason said.

"Peaz."

"That works." He scooped more onto her plate.

She reached for a pink sippy cup with both hands. Jason watched and complimented her. April loved being a part of a loving family . . . and hope for the future had her bubbling with excitement.

April had God, and He'd given her a wonderful man in her life and a darling baby girl. Neither she nor Jason expected things to be perfect, but they had the beginnings of a grand life together. It all started when the negotiator became the hostage.

Life doesn't get much better than this.

A Note from the Author

Dear Reader,

Life is unpredictable. We aren't guaranteed tomorrow, and we don't know what sorts of mountains and valleys we'll experience along our journeys. The age-old question of why do bad things happen to good people can become our mantra. Or we can choose to ignore our bruises and travel the road of good and prioritize truth and justice above all things.

April blamed herself for a hostage negotiation that ended in a tragic death. She couldn't seem to get past it. She held tightly to guilt, not realizing that setting it free could bring healing.

Jason ignored the truth about what was going on in his community until the injustices left a staggering blow. He was forced to make a decision to ensure his community was safe for young and old.

April and Jason's story shows how God can work in the unexpected and the tragic for good. Together they learned that, with God, *Life doesn't get much better than this*.

Be blessed, my friends.
DiAnn

Discussion Questions

1. After a negotiation goes wrong, Agent April Ramos struggles to find peace in forced platitudes and rote words. In what ways does her partner's encouragement help or hinder her as she wrestles with guilt? If you were in Simon's shoes, what would you say to April?

2. When Jason Snyder is first introduced, did you believe his claim of innocence? Why or why not? What finally convinces April to trust Jason? At what point did you believe him?

3. As Jason alleges that the county sheriff is involved in corruption, April reminds him, "No one is above the law." How does this play out for the characters, especially when Jason seems bent on taking the law into his own hands? Is he justified in doing so? Why or why not?

4. Before her death, Lily reminded Jason that "the darkest moments of our lives are intended for God to use in a mighty way." Give some examples from the story of ways in which this proves true for Jason and April. Have there been times in your own life when God has shown His mighty power in your darkest moments?

5. According to Jason, Sheriff Lennox is operating a reign of terror in Sweet Briar, Texas. What makes people so reluctant to stand up to him? Consider the story of the fiery furnace in Daniel 3. Under what circumstances is defying authority the right thing to do?

6. After meeting Miss Ella, April wonders, "How did one person think of so many things to say to God?" Do you know a prayer warrior like Miss Ella? Or are you that person? Since 1 Thessalonians 5:17 encourages us to "Never stop praying," what steps can you take to increase your prayer life?

7. Ted Snyder tells April about God's work in his life, a testimony that includes his dementia-stricken friend John still being able to recognize Ted. How does April respond to this story? Were you affected by it? When you encounter things that don't necessarily make sense, what do you attribute that to? A miracle of God? Coincidence?

8. When Jason finds his house torn apart, he releases his anger and prays, Help me to honor You. Does this feel like a genuine prayer to you? Or does it seem like he is merely paying lip service to God while still fighting for control of the situation? What steps should he take to honor God?

9. As April and Jason struggle to uncover the

proof that will put the sheriff behind bars, Jason reminds his friend, "The right thing to do is seldom easy." Think about a time when that was true for you. What happened? Did you do the right thing in the moment or back down?

10. Both April and Jason struggle with the idea that "regrets keep us chained to guilt." What does April regret? What does Jason regret? Do you have regrets that leave you with guilt? Can there be such a thing as "good guilt"?

11. After April gets thrown out of Brenda Krew's office, she feels compassion for the Realtor and thinks, "Sometimes the bad guys were as much victims as the innocent." Do you agree with that statement? Why or why not? How much should a person's circumstances—upbringing, financial status, etc.—be considered a factor in their culpability?

12. Near the end of the story, Jason is prompted to forgive those who conspired against him, his family, and his town. Do you think he could have done so even if justice wasn't served? If you were in that position—waiting for justice—what would it take for you to find true forgiveness?

13. Early in the story, Miss Ella tells April, "Before this is over, you're gonna see the power of Jesus." In what ways does April realize this? What stands out most to you?

14. Simon warns Jason that a relationship born in "danger and supercharged emotions" won't last. How much truth do you give that statement? Where do you think April and Jason will end up?

About the Author

DiAnn Mills is a bestselling author who believes her readers should expect an adventure. She combines unforgettable characters with unpredictable plots to create action-packed romantic suspense novels.

Her titles have appeared on the CBA and ECPA bestseller lists; won two Christy Awards; and been finalists for the RITA, Daphne du Maurier, Inspirational Reader's Choice, and Carol Award contests. *Firewall*, the first book in her Houston: FBI series, was listed by *Library Journal* as one of the best Christian fiction books of 2014.

DiAnn is a founding board member of the American Christian Fiction Writers and a member of Advanced Writers and Speakers Association, Sisters in Crime, and International Thriller Writers. She is codirector of the Blue Ridge Mountain Christian Writers Conference, where she continues her passion of helping other writers be successful. She speaks to various groups and teaches writing workshops around the country.

DiAnn has been termed a coffee snob and roasts her own coffee beans. She's an avid reader, loves to cook, and believes her grandchildren are the smartest kids in the universe. She and her husband live in sunny Houston, Texas.

DiAnn is very active online and would love to connect with readers through her website at www.diannmills.com or on Facebook (www.facebook.com/DiAnnMills), Twitter (@DiAnnMills), Pinterest (www.pinterest.com/DiAnnMills), and Goodreads (www.goodreads.com/DiAnnMills).

Center Point Large Print
600 Brooks Road / PO Box 1
Thorndike, ME 04986-0001 USA

(207) 568-3717

US & Canada:
1 800 929-9108
www.centerpointlargeprint.com